DARK BLOOD
AWAKENS

MICHELLE CORBIER

A Mwindaji urban fantasy
1589 Skeet Club Road Suite 102 Box 146
High Point, NC 27265

For more information:
www.MichelleCorbier.com

Cover and interior design by Karen Phillips at PhillipsCovers.com

Dark Blood Awakens
Copyright © 2023 by Michelle Corbier

978-1-7375252-4-0   Dark Blood Awakens, paperback
978-1-7375252-5-7   Dark Blood Awakens, eBook
978-1-7375252-6-4   Dark Blood Awakens, hardback
978-1-7375252-7-1   Dark Blood Awakens, audiobook

For Jean-Michel, all my love.

ACKNOWLEDGEMENTS

This book came to fruition through the assistance of many people. Special thanks to Dr. Jean-Ronel Corbier for helping create the Baoumali language. His integrative neurology practice can be located at www.brainrestorationclinic.com. Thanks to Dr. Corbier and Jean Richardson for the Haitian Creole translations. Finally, I want to recognize my girlfriends, Maria and Mary, for being my beta readers, listening to my complaints and offering suggestions.

"In traditional West Africa, humans and spirits have always stood side by side occasionally reaching over to tap one another on the shoulder, as if to remind each other of their mutual existence. Whatever tenuous line is drawn between them is porous; humans must hold their ground as spirits—malicious, capricious and sometimes benevolent—wander."

Shhhh! There Are Spirits Lurking... Cultures of West Africa, May 20, 2019

CHAPTER 1

March 2010

FROM THE PARKED RV'S windows, Makeda peeked between the blackout curtains, searching across the grassy expanse. A pale, yellow moon hung high in the Carolina sky.

Headstones winked at her through the darkness, between trees dripping with Spanish moss. Their polished ghost-white surfaces contrasted with the surrounding foliage. Even with binoculars, moonlight proved insufficient for her to decipher their writings. Salty Atlantic wind and water had etched away their epitaphs.

"I'm leaving," Peter said, grabbing a machete and lance.

"Wait for me." Makeda slipped into a light jacket and scrambled to the side door of the RV.

"No, stay and look after Thomas." He gazed down at his brother and grimaced. "His wound looks bad."

"That's simply an excuse to keep me here." Makeda huffed, folding her arms over her chest.

Peter grinned. "You're smarter than you look. Stay put—and make sure Thomas is okay." He hustled out the door before she could reply.

She stared after him until he disappeared between the trees. Time passed as she gazed into the darkness.

Thomas moaned and rolled over on the couch.

Makeda shut and locked the door but peeked outside

around the plastic blinds. If she recalled correctly, the grave-yard was over two hundred years old. In middle school, her class toured the North Carolina lighthouses. Old Baldy, estab-lished in 1794, had been her favorite. Neither the largest or most attractive of the lighthouses, she loved its history and sur-rounding area of Cape Fear—nicknamed the Graveyard of the Atlantic.

Like ancient relatives, the gravestones remained ever pres-ent. Silenced, but vigilant, standing at attention. She imagined they desired to speak, to impart secrets and reveal mysteries regarding the lighthouse. If they could talk, would they guide her to safety or lead her to their inevitable fate? With effort, she pulled herself away from Cape Fear's dead and returned to her patient.

She tried not to grumble about playing nursemaid to her brother. After all, as a registered nurse; it made sense for her to care for Thomas. But the real reason they left her behind was to keep her away from the fighting.

While Thomas slept, Makeda adjusted his bandages. As she bent over his knee, her shoulder twitched. She startled and inadvertently squeezed the dressings. Had she heard a scream?

"Ouch," Thomas said. "Why'd you do that?" He winced and rubbed his knee.

She automatically swatted his hand away from the wound. "Don't mess with the dressing."

Reclined on several pillows, Thomas pushed himself up along the couch. "It's too tight, and it itches."

"That's the stitches. Leave 'em alone." She loosened the dressings and gazed into his groggy face. "Did you hear a scream?"

"No." He yawned and scratched his shaking head.

When he reached for his knee again, she smacked his hand harder. "Stop it, or I'll have to redo the stitches. You sure you didn't hear a scream?"

"What's wrong with you? Why are you being so—"

A loud wail interrupted his question. He jerked upright, gawking at Makeda, who returned his gaze. They stared at each other for a second before she jumped off the couch and ran to the back of the RV.

Careening his head in her direction, Thomas asked, "What're you doing?"

"Peter or another mwindaji might be in trouble. I'm going out there." She packed several weapons inside a backpack, then slung it over her shoulders.

"You're supposed to stay here." Thomas hobbled off the couch. While trying to catch up with her, he knocked a game controller off his lap and onto the floor.

She glanced at him, then the door. "I'm not going to sit here when the team could be in trouble."

As she hurried by, he reached out and grabbed her arm. "Wait. I'll go with you."

Accident-prone—and a little goofy—Thomas would slow her down. Makeda gave his arm a brief squeeze. "I'll be fine. Stay here, and off that knee."

Before dashing out of the RV, she handed him several guns and ammunition. In her left hand, Makeda clutched a gun. In her right hand, she wielded a machete.

Outside, heavy salty air stung her nostrils. On the other side of the grove of trees, she knew, stood Old Baldy. As she approached the woods, headstones loomed large, welcoming her to their hallowed grounds. What secrets did these troubled lands possess?

She raced past grave markers. Like a train whistling through a tunnel, scenery flickered across her mind. She swooned, became disoriented, and paused. For a moment, she leaned against a tree, blinking rapidly, as if to capture the visions swirling around her mind. *Why does this seem familiar?*

There was no time to tarry. She shook off her déjà vu and sought out the origin of the scream. Was Peter in trouble?

As if on cue, another cry echoed around the woods. This time she pinpointed its location. Charging across a grassy expanse, she neared another tree line. Her pace slowed, and she treaded cautiously. Werewolves were in the area.

The mwindaji had tracked a group of six werewolves to Bald Head Island. An anonymous tip led them to a fete where the lycans gathered at an inn beside the harbor. During the ensuing battle, Thomas had been injured, and the hunters split up. She and Thomas had been relegated to the security of the camper while the other mwindaji chased after the fleeing monsters.

Roots and brambles threatened her progress. As she inched through the thicket, she touched a cedar tree. Makeda remembered a story her great-grandmother had told her about how trees could speak—if you listened. Right now, she didn't have time to communicate with the vegetation except to say "hi-bye."

Careful to step over tree stumps, she spied a clearing about two hundred yards away. She spotted Peter engaged in hand-to-hand combat with a towering werewolf. Because her brother stood over six feet tall, Makeda calculated the monster to be about eight feet. Standing on its hind legs, the werewolf gained an advantage.

His shirt sleeve bloodied and frayed, Peter didn't fare well. Makeda couldn't see his gun anywhere, but he swung a machete widely, managing to keep the werewolf at bay. Peter gripped the machete in his left hand, though Makeda knew him to be right-handed. Neither he nor the lycan detected her approach.

At the edge of the clearing, Makeda leveled her gun and aimed. Before she could lob a shot, a movement rustled on her right side. She dropped to a squat as a cool wisp of air eddied above her head. Peripherally, she saw a large, hairy arm swipe past. Werewolf.

Jumping down from a tree branch, the lycan landed not three feet away on all fours. When its feet met the earth, Makeda fired two shots into its hairy torso. After a brief shriek, the werewolf crashed to the ground.

Without glancing upon it for another second, Makeda sprouted to a standing position. Her gaze reverted to the scene of her brother.

In a large arc, Peter swiped repeatedly at the werewolf. None of his strikes met the target. He was drenched in sweat, and his right arm hung limply at his side. Blood soaked his tattered shirt, trickling down his arm from exposed muscle tissues. Moonlight glinted off what she believed to be his humerus bone.

With her weapon leveled at the werewolf, Makeda advanced upon their position. Two shots ripped into the monster, emitting small popping noises. Bullet one struck its left lateral shoulder, and the second shattered its throat. Choking and sputtering, the werewolf grabbed its neck, where those sharp claws added to the trauma around its throat. Blood gurgled, flowing down its hairy chest.

Still holding the machete, Peter stumbled away from the injured beast.

Collapsing to the ground, the werewolf bled out as Makeda embraced Peter. She switched from hunter to nurse and reached into her backpack for supplies.

Peter searched the ground around them as she evaluated his wounds. "What're you doing here?"

"You're welcome," she said. After retrieving gauze, she let her backpack slip to the ground and treated his wound. "What are you looking for?"

"My gun." He must have spotted it because he started to pull away.

"Hold still. Let me finish this tourniquet, and then you can get your gun." Hastily, she tied the cloth around his arm. Once she secured the dressing, she let him retrieve his weapon. "Where are the others?"

Peter angled his head toward the aged lighthouse.

Her left brow arched. "You can't be serious."

He shrugged. "The monsters went in there, so they followed." As he set off toward Old Baldy, she fell in step beside him.

In constant movement, her eyes scanned the area. Whether because of the headstones or the full moon, a shiver thrilled up her spine. Her shoulders tensed. Makeda detected something different but couldn't discern the source.

Her nostrils twitched at an unusual scent. Adjusting to the dark, her pupils dilated like camera lenses. She pushed those sensations aside and concentrated on their present situation.

"Where's—" Before she completed her sentence, three men exited the lighthouse.

With a shotgun looped over his arm, the oldest man carried several weapons across his back, and others in his hands. Two younger men hauled a plastic tarp between them. As the trio approached, a dirt-caked hand fell loose. With a booted foot, one of the young men kicked the hand back onto the drop cloth.

Makeda's lips rose into a smile, but the older man's brows crinkled in return. Watching his stern gaze, Makeda detected a forthcoming argument.

Without removing his eyes from her face, he said, "Take the bodies to the RV."

"Right, chief," her cousin Brian said, adjusting his grip on the tarp.

The old man's attention returned to her. "What are you doing here? You were told to stay in the RV with Thomas. If you're gonna work with us, you have to obey orders."

"Makeda came to help me," Peter said, turning to the side, revealing his injured arm. "She probably saved my life."

Probably. She watched the old man examine Peter's arm. The old man's brows straightened, and in a quick motion he reached out and hugged her. Initially surprised, her body stiffened, but in seconds she relaxed and hugged him back.

After giving her a big kiss on the cheek, he said, "I know you can help, but I worry. If something happened to you, your mama couldn't take it."

He collected Peter's machete and placed his arm around her shoulders. "Let's go."

Their journey to the RV took them near the werewolf she shot in the woods. A quick glance showed it had reverted into a man. As Makeda passed the body, she looked down. A vision of his haunted, pained face followed her back to the camper. Those deep brown eyes, wide nose, and full lips. It seemed incongruous to kill something resembling herself—someone human.

The ongoing battle between the mwindaji and monsters left her conflicted. This war had raged for over a millennium.

Big Mama, her great-grandmother, had explained the history of the mwindaji, and how the conflict began. Makeda wished she could remember more of those childhood stories. Recall the sorcery Big Mama taught her. Now, she couldn't do more than kasi kasi.

Would the war ever end? She shuddered.

Probably assuming she was cold, the old man hugged her tighter. Her tremors came not from the temperature though, but uncertainty. Gritting her teeth, she hid her unease. If their mwindaji leader had any doubts about her commitment, he'd dismiss her from the team.

Breezes along the cape increased in intensity as winds rolled in off the Atlantic. Their steps quickened. Once they reached the RV, he held the door open for her. Warmth greeted them. Her shoulders relaxed as the vision of the werewolf vanished from her mind.

Standing at the opened door, the old man said, "Store the bodies in the RV hidey-hole and then collect the other two. I'll call the other mwindaji and tell them to meet us at the dock. We'll drop the bodies out to sea. Let's go, guys. Time to hustle."

Inside the RV, with Thomas's help, Makeda tended to Peter's injuries. Thomas cleansed the skin while she debrided dead muscle tissue from around the lacerations. As she stitched the wound, Makeda thought back to the initial scream she had heard.

It seemed like a shout came from inside her head. Perhaps the bracing sea air heightened her perceptions. Her hand trembled as she completed a running stitch.

Hold it together, girl. Weakness wouldn't be tolerated in a mwindaji, especially if the hunter was their leader's daughter.

CHAPTER 2

CADMIUM-TIPPED FLAMES DANCED ACROSS the fireplace. Chilly Kentucky spring weather led Korlemo to sit before the hearth. His long legs stretched forward along a Persian rug as he watched blazing embers prance inside the fireplace, throwing fiery colors across the walls of his study. High ceilings drew the heat upward. Ornate furniture gave heady rich detail to the room.

His fingers traced the outline of his decanter, half-full of Kentucky bourbon. It had become his preferred drink since he had settled in the Bluegrass State, replacing the red wines of the Rhône Valley. Though pleasant, bourbon in no way resembled the rich bouquet of the wines he consumed in southern France.

More than fifty years had passed since he made Kentucky his home. He'd learned the importance of adaptation long ago. Over a millennium, he had conformed to different customs, acclimated to the changing mores of the people his tribe called bindimèn, colloquially called humans.

Korlemo snorted. Evolution was the nature of champions. Survival required guile, strength, and cruelty. Traits he mastered, surpassing bindimèn. He stood and brushed up against the side table, causing his goblet to wobble.

Herman rushed up from his seat to steady the vessel—apparently concerned liquor would stain the prized Persian rug. After carefully placing the glass on a sideboard, he returned to his seat. With a smile, he looked up into Korlemo's face.

If he expected a thank-you, he would be disappointed. Uninterested in Herman's domestic concerns, Korlemo paced the room.

"Where's the zauber?"

"I'm not sure," Herman stuttered.

"What time did you tell her to arrive?"

"Eight o'clock. She probably got lost on the back roads. The streets aren't well lit once you leave Ramsey city limits. I'll mention it at the next city council meeting."

Korlemo's narrowed eyes brooded toward Herman. "Someone should have picked her up. I need answers and should not be expected to wait all night. These dreams have disturbed my peace for too long."

"I'm sure she'll be here any moment," Herman said as the left side of his face twitched. "Would you like me to call Dayo? She could—"

"No. This does not concern my wife."

With long strides, Korlemo marched in front of the floor-to-ceiling windows framed by heavy burgundy drapes. Shadows stretched across the manicured lawn. Disregarding the star-laden evening sky, he instead searched the inky black night, peering hungrily into the dense surrounding woods.

He scanned the oak trees lining the edge of the property. Razor-sharp, his acute vision spied an opossum scampering along the forest floor. An owl scavenged among the trees. His mobowou sense detected the odor of rotting flesh. Probably a kill from one of the foxes in the area.

The scenery failed to distract his mind or quiet the unease mushrooming inside him. Over the past month, violent images of his death had impeded sleep. At first, he had attributed the dreams to the current unrest in their community. However, the frequency of the visions had increased. Now, they were more distinct and alarming. He believed the images were an omen. A warning. Of what, he couldn't fathom.

Tormented by the escalating, threatening nature of those dreams, Korlemo had consulted a witch and a diviner, but neither could interpret his dreams. To appease his distress, Herman arranged for a zauber—a sorceress possessing the knowledge of a witch and the vision of a diviner—to come and assure Korlemo all was well. Once he received an interpretation of the dreams, Korlemo knew his mind would be at rest—if the zauber ever arrived.

Whirling around from the window, he stomped over to where Herman sat in a wingback chair drinking wine. He slammed his hand down on the top of the chair and glowered upon his friend. "Where is she? I will not wait any longer. Go find her."

Herman's saucer-shaped eyes gawked. His face twitched, causing his left eye to blink repeatedly. With shaking hands, Herman patted Korlemo's arm. "I'll find out where she is. Don't get upset." He withdrew.

Pieces of the dreams flittered across Korlemo's mind. The more he thought about them, the angrier he became. He stomped around the study, marching before the bookshelves, then hovering over his large wooden desk. Someone was warning him. *But who, and why?*

All mobowou had enemies, especially those as powerful as himself. He struck the desk, creating a dimple in the soft wood. He never left an enemy alive. How could anyone consider threatening him?

Restless, he paraded around the study several more times, opening and closing his large hands while reconsidering his dreams. Before he completed another circuit, Herman reentered the room with a woman. Before the door shut, Herman stuck his head out and addressed someone unseen. While he waited, Korlemo scrutinized the woman.

She stood beside the door, surveying the study. Her thin gray braids curled into a bun centered at the nape of her neck. The impression Korlemo garnered from her appearance was not positive. He scowled.

Herman closed and secured the door. He motioned for the woman to proceed farther into the study, directing her toward couches in the middle of the room.

Square wire-framed glasses perched at the edge of her nose. Despite the lenses, she squinted. Her eyebrows had been plucked to almost nonexistence. Age had gnarled her unadorned fingers.

Korlemo made no attempt to hide the disgust scribbled across his face. If she detected his displeasure, she hid it. Her countenance remained neutral.

With a small grin, Herman escorted the woman up to him. "Mrs. Jackson, this is Dr. Winters."

As the distance between them decreased, so did her squinting. Her gaze widened. Neither he nor Mrs. Jackson attempted to shake hands. They studied each other.

Korlemo wondered if she suffered from poor vision or if she was confused by the surroundings. If the former, he hoped being nearsighted would not impede her abilities as a sorceress.

Herman suggested Mrs. Jackson take a seat on the long honey-brown leather couch.

She thanked him and sat. A long bead and shell necklace encircled her neck. Adjusting it and the multiple sweaters hanging low over her wide-legged slacks, she perched on the edge of the couch, back straight, face flat.

Responding to a knock at the door, Herman retrieved a tray from a servant waiting there. On the table between the couches, he placed a salver containing a carafe and plate of hors d'oeuvres. He poured steamy liquid into a dainty cup and handed it to her.

Though she accepted the beverage, she didn't drink. Instead, she placed it on a table and surveyed the room.

"Thank you for coming, Mrs. Jackson," Herman said. "I hope your trip wasn't too inconvenient."

"I apologize for the delay, but your directions—" She paused. Tilting her head back, she sniffed the air. "It was difficult to see the turnoff in the dark."

"Yes, yes. Completely understandable. We're glad you finally made it."

She gave Herman a lengthy evaluation. After a minute, she shook her head and regarded Korlemo. Fingering her shell necklace, she stared.

On the opposite end of the sofa, Herman sat down. "Well, perhaps we should get started. It's already late, and I'm sure you'd like to be on your way."

Drumming his fingers along the desk, Korlemo watched and assessed her actions.

"This isn't right," she said, peering closer.

The old cow frowned, folding her arms over her large bosom. Korlemo's posture stiffened. He leaned forward, senses heightened.

"What's wrong?" Herman asked.

Creases furrowed her forehead. She didn't answer but again smelled the air.

"You understood what we required before you arrived. Dr. Winters would like his dreams interpreted. You'll be paid well for your work."

From his desk, Korlemo observed and remained silent. If she was a zauber, he would know from her response.

Mrs. Jackson glared at Herman. "You lie."

A twitch wrinkled Herman's face. "What? What do you mean?"

Her pinched nose continued sniffing. Again, her gaze fastened upon Korlemo. Her bent brows rose, and her eyelids peeled back. An arthritic finger pointed at him. "You are not a doctor."

A smirk crossed his mouth. She recognized him. *Good.* She was what he needed. Sauntering over to the couch, he loomed over her. "What *am* I?"

Without hesitation, she stood, mere inches away from him, her face only reaching his chest. Her examination began with his feet. When her perusal arrived at his chest, she trembled. Beginning at the top of her head, tremors consumed her entire body.

"No. It can't be. You—you can't be." She stepped backward, bumped against the couch, and collapsed onto her buttocks.

His lips crept up the sides of his face. "But I can. And I am."

Her head snapped right toward Herman. "You liar. You didn't tell me who this—what he is." Her body shook. She clasped her fingers together and rested them on her lap. Her shoulders slumped.

Herman stammered. "I ... It doesn't matter. We need you to interpret a dream."

"Do not be afraid, old woman," Korlemo said. "If you do as I ask, no harm will come to you."

Avoiding his gaze, Mrs. Jackson stared at her hands as her tremulousness decreased.

Herman scooted along the couch toward her. "Don't worry. Dr. Winters simply wants you to interpret his dream."

Her finger shot out toward Korlemo, but she glared at

Herman. "That is not a doctor."

Korlemo bared his canines. "Who I am is unimportant. You are here to interpret my dreams."

"I will not." She lifted her chin and gazed toward the fireplace.

"Will you not even look at me?" Korlemo asked, leaning toward her. "I will not entrance you."

Though her shaking stopped, she inclined away from him, resting back against the couch cushions.

"Do you refuse?" Korlemo's fingers elongated as he reached forward and grasped her chin. He angled her head upward to face him.

She trembled and shut her eyes.

"Interpret his dreams and you'll get paid more money than you could ever imagine," Herman squeaked.

Korlemo's sharp nails dug into her cheeks. His grip tightened around her chin, leaving impressions on her weathered skin.

"If you refuse, you *will* die."

Her shaking ceased and her countenance cleared. "*Mawu, mbabire*," she whispered in an aside. For a second, she chanced a glance into his face. "I will die either way."

Chuckling, he released her face and sauntered over to the hearth. "Tell me the meaning of my dreams, and I promise you will live."

With a deep sigh, she rose, touching the impressions along her cheeks from his fingernails. "You won't let me live. You're a mobowou, a vampire. An abomination. You'll kill me to keep your secret. I can't leave and your existence remain unknown."

He grinned, ignoring her comment. Firelight cast a shadow across his profile. He fixed her with his gaze, then recounted his most recent dream.

"The visions begin differently each night, but the endings are similar. They start in the center of a luscious garden with a large tree. The tree is old and barren. It displeases me, and I decide to chop it down. As I cut the tree, it weeps. Wherever tears fall, saplings grow—some flower. I reach down to touch a sapling, and a flower cuts my hand. My palm fills with blood. I cannot stop the bleeding. More saplings grow until I am surrounded by flowers. I try to flee, but the stalk of the flower that cut my hand grabs my ankle, yanking me to the ground. I thrash around but cannot break free. Saplings cover me, choking me. Before I awake, a face forms on the tree trunk. It leers at me."

Standing beside the mantel, Korlemo paused, awaiting her response.

For a couple minutes, the only sound came from logs crackling in the fireplace. Korlemo regarded Herman, who seemed to be holding his breath, not moving or twitching.

Instead of responding to the recitation of Korlemo's dream, Mrs. Jackson glanced around the room. Korlemo wondered if she was considering an escape, which he knew would be futile. Fortunately, she seemed to have no intention of going anywhere.

She bolted toward him, clasping his hand with a surprising ferocity. Though startled by her brazenness, he relented and allowed her to grasp his hand. With his hand secured between both of hers, Mrs. Jackson studied his chest, slowly gazing up toward his neck, still avoiding his face.

While he had no intention of enrapturing her, she clearly understood he could. However, Korlemo needed answers, solutions he knew a zauber could provide.

For several minutes, Mrs. Jackson held his hand before tossing it aside. She retreated a step and chanced a sly glance into his face. Then, she laughed.

Because it sounded awkward in the previously silent room, at first Korlemo did not appreciate what was happening. But her mirth continued for several minutes before she started to cry.

Korlemo's chest heaved and his nostrils flared. His breathing deepened. He shot a grimace toward Herman, who in turn rose from his seat. His friend shook Mrs. Jackson about the shoulders. She slunk from Herman's grasp. In time, she regained control of her emotions. Her teary face curled into a mocking smile.

Furious, with a fluidity that probably appeared to her instantaneous, Korlemo strode up to her. His breath was ragged. He knew his eyes burned hellfire red. "You mock me at your peril."

Once Mrs. Jackson stopped laughing, she wiped her eyes. Throwing back her shoulders, she beamed into his face. "You will die."

His brows zigzagged a question across his forehead. "What do you mean? I cannot die."

"In your dream, the flowered sapling represents a woman. This woman will wound you. Then, she will kill you."

In a flash, his arm shot forward. Like tentacles, his fingers clutched her throat. He snapped her neck before she swallowed her words. The zauber's head slumped backward like a wilted plant.

Korlemo's eyes blazed. He squeezed until her suffused face purpled, and her neck pulverized like a squashed tomato. Blood spurted along the chiseled hardwood floors from where his clawed fingernails punctured her carotids.

Allowing her body to slump to the ground, Korlemo licked blood from his fingers. *Fool.* He stepped over her corpse.

Herman should be happy no blood stained the Persian rug. Not bothering to look back, he said, "Clean that up."

Servants entered the study at Herman's direction. Two removed the dead zauber, while others cleaned syrupy blood off the floor.

"Play for me," Korlemo ordered, standing before the windows overlooking the backyard.

His comment was not directed at anyone specifically, but he noticed Herman direct a young woman to rise from her knees. His friend guided her to a grand piano near the wall farthest away from the fireplace.

Yielding to his demands, the young woman sat at the piano, her moon-shaped eyes questioning his orders. Herman placed a sheet of music before her. Searching at first, with time she found her way along the ivories. She induced the fine instrument to play Chopin. Music drifted around the room, ascending toward the cathedral ceiling.

Once his shoulders relaxed, Korlemo's elongated frame retracted to its prior form. His canines receded. Minutes later, he moved away from the windows and regained his seat before the fireplace. His bloodied hands reached for the decanter.

Sipping bourbon, he called out to Herman. "Get me another zauber."

"Yes, Korlemo."

"And a towel."

A clean glass was brought to him and filled with more bourbon. One of the servants provided a rag, and Korlemo cleaned his hands. After several sips, he ordered the young woman playing the piano to leave. She fled without a glance in his direction.

Ocher-hued flames flickered before his eyes. He surmised the zauber had cursed him with that erroneous prediction because she knew he would kill her.

With a chuckle, he sipped his liquor. He knew he could not die. Not according to the ka'trete between him and Zorulo. He had negotiated his soul in exchange for immortality.

Staring into the blaze, he thought back to that cloudy, overcast day. The encampment where his warriors returned his mortally wounded body. In the tent where he lay dying, there had been a different zauber beside him. At his command, she had summoned a dubwana, Zorulo. With that demon's help, Korlemo achieved everything he had ever desired—revenge, success, and power.

Notwithstanding her allegiance to him, Korlemo eventually had ordered the zauber killed. To preserve his secrets, he had told himself. In truth, she had also displeased him.

A millennium had passed. The irony of now summoning another zauber was not lost upon him. For the first time in at least a hundred years, he became apprehensive. His fingers tapped against his glass.

He remained seated before the fire long after the last blued embers cooled, contemplating the steps he must take to ensure his longevity. If Herman could not find him a reliable zauber …

Sighing, he rose. Perhaps he had remained in Kentucky too long.

CHAPTER 3

MUSIC BLASTED FROM THE bar's stereo system. Three bartenders served drinks to patrons while above their heads two flat-screen televisions blared out sports commentary. It was Friday night and standing room only.

Seated on a stool in the corner of the bar, Jason sipped his beer and observed the crowd. People laughed and drank, oblivious to the chilly Kentucky evening.

He spotted a woman dancing alone near pool tables located in the rear. Alannah Myles's *Black Velvet* floated out of the audio system as the lithe woman's sensual hips swayed to the lyrics.

Jason's powder-blue eyes followed her dancing around the crowded bar. Everything and everyone disappeared into the background, except her.

Between the throngs of patrons, Jason watched the short cotton dress billow around her thighs. Jet-black hair framed her olive complexion and accentuated her red lips. Like a feather, she floated back and forth between the tables, laughing down at a woman seated in a nearby booth. Unconcerned about the overflowing crowd, the bar became her private dance floor. Throughout the evening, several men approached her and were rebuffed.

Her undulating hips left Jason hypnotized. He accidentally knocked over his glass. While mopping beer off the bar top—either aroused from alcohol or his libido—Jason could no longer resist her allure.

At about five-feet-eleven inches tall with sandy brown hair, a decent physique and freckled face, he calculated better-than-average odds of a positive reception to his advance. Having only been in Bowling Green for the past two weeks, the local bar scene was new to him. With no close friends in town, he would appreciate her companionship.

He caught her eye while approaching the pool tables. Sashaying in his direction, she favored him with a feline grin. Jason introduced himself and offered to buy her a drink. Instead, she helped herself to his beer.

For Jason, gazing into her emerald-colored eyes, the bar noise muted. Time slowed. The dancer stood close to him, her nipples brushing up against his chest. With his drink in her hand, she pivoted on her tiptoes and returned to the table where her friend waited.

The cadence of her gait invited him to follow. He joined her in the padded booth, nodding across to the friend as he slid onto the bench.

"Hello, I'm Jason," he said, greeting the unsmiling woman. She accepted his handshake but didn't provide a name. Not that he cared.

The dancer, who also declined to give her name, snuggled up against him.

"So, where are you from?" he asked, extending his arm along the headrest behind the green-eyed beauty.

"Ramsey," she said with a slight smile. "You?"

"Mississippi. I moved here for work a couple weeks ago."

Her green eyes lit up like a "Go" signal light. She winked at her girlfriend. "Well, let me personally welcome you." She waved over the bartender.

Jason ordered a round of drinks. While engaged in small talk, he reflected on how well things were going.

An hour later, he suggested they retire to somewhere private. The upturn of her chili-red lips matched the heat of his blooming libido. She accepted his offer, dragging him playfully from the booth. Her buttocks teased against his pelvis as she piloted him out of the bar.

Unfamiliar with the neighborhood, Jason accepted her directions, steering his car to a patch of woods positioned next to a freeway overpass two exits south of the bar. He drove to a secluded spot and parked as instructed.

Streetlamps dimly lit the area, creating a hallowed yellow glow. March coolness seeped inside the car once the engine stopped.

His companion's perfume wafted around the car, peppering the electrified air with anticipation. Before he could set the emergency brake, she sprang onto his lap.

Kissing preceded their disrobing. He fumbled to lift her dress. She unzipped his pants. Her heavy breathing exploded in his ears. Naked, she rode his lap in a sexual frenzy. Musk of their ecstasy mixed with her perfume. Dizzy from sensory overload, Jason climaxed.

Her appetite unabated, his date dragged him into the rear of the car where their copulation spilled over onto the back seat. Jason was delighted to continue their tryst.

Cracked windows allowed in cold night air. Occasional freeway noise drifted inside. Overcome by the sounds of their passion, Jason hadn't heard anything until gravel crunched outside his window and a car braked.

Their coitus interrupted, Jason's head jerked up to peek outside. From the steamy window, he watched the dancer's friend from the bar sauntering over to his car. For a moment, he considered inviting her to join them. Her deep scowl suggested she wouldn't be interested. Instead, he dismounted his lovely companion and searched for his clothes.

Sprawled against the back seat, his green-eyed friend remained naked and exposed. Her painted toenails rolled up and down his bare chest. "Don't get dressed. It's easier if you're naked."

The friend arrived at the car door right after Jason slipped into trousers.

Speaking through the cracked window, the friend addressed his companion. "Are you done yet? I'm hungry."

"Almost. Can't you wait?" she snapped. The dancer's attention returned to Jason. She grinned.

He glanced at her. *So beautiful.* Though he appreciated a one-night stand, he didn't want an audience.

"Here." He handed her the cotton dress.

She sat up, rubbing her jeweled fingers along his sweaty neck and back. Licking her fingers, her tongue swept across her engorged lips.

He winced. Was she a freak? Whatever. It was worth the sex.

"Maybe we can get together some other time."

"But there won't be another time."

Fine with him. He wasn't looking for a commitment. Handing her a piece of silk underwear, he grabbed his shirt from the floorboard. With one arm in a sleeve, his head poked out from the top of the shirt. He froze, shocked by what he saw.

The gorgeous woman next to him disintegrated into something unbelievable. That once smooth, supple body morphed into a rough, hairy frame. Her face contorted and mutated into an elongated snout with sharp protruding teeth.

Jason blinked repeatedly. He gawked, paralyzed in disbelief. A lanky werewolf had replaced his gorgeous companion and now lay in the back seat.

Snapped out of his inertia, Jason dropped her bra and reached for the door handle. He stopped. Out the cracked window, he observed the friend completing her own transformation. *Another werewolf! Shit.*

Recoiling from the door, he bumped up against the former green-eyed beauty. He leaped into the front seat, attempting to escape.

Hairy paws clutched him around the chest. Razor-sharp nails pierced his torso. Jason screamed. Rivulets of blood dribbled down his chest, raining down onto the car's floor mat.

Kicking and punching, he tore at her fur. Anything to stop her from hauling him toward that razor-toothed mouth. His blows proved worthless against her viselike grip. He yelled, screamed, and cursed. But she overpowered him, bringing her snout alongside his face. She bit down on the side of his head and chewed off his entire earlobe.

Jason shrieked, increasing his assaults against her head and chest. Blood gushed from his wounds. His previously pristine car became bathed in blood. He summoned all his strength to fight her off.

Blood dripped into his left eye. From the corner of his right eye, he noticed the friend opening the car door. While he wrestled with the green-eyed werewolf, the friend advanced and joined their ménage à trois.

As she bent down near his leg, Jason kicked her in the nose. She swatted his foot away and bit down on his thigh. Hearing his femur crunch between her teeth left Jason faint. His leg went numb, and he became weak.

Pain exploded along every fiber of his body. In agony, he teetered on the edge of consciousness. Before he passed out, he viewed blood spurting from his hip. His mind registered that the werewolf hit an artery as his peripheral nervous system shut down. He no longer fought.

Disconnected thoughts filtered across his mind. His body slipped into shock. The last thing he felt was the lurching of the car. His eyes rolled back, viewing darkness. Before tonight, he didn't believe werewolves existed.

CHAPTER 4

IN A SMALL TOWN nestled close to the Smoky Mountains, Makeda lay in bed. Bitter cold frosted the windowpanes. Sunlight streaked through the blind's narrow slats. While she gazed up at the ceiling, sunrays warmed her face. Aromas of bacon and fresh bread tickled her nose.

At age twenty-three, she still resided in her childhood home. In Black Ridge, North Carolina, northwest of Asheville, she lived with her parents, a pack of dogs, and two of her older brothers.

After completing her nursing degree, she traveled, exploring the country and making more money in six months than she could in an entire year in Asheville. Her decision to forgo medical school for nursing had been correct. Not that she harbored any doubts. If she intended to join the mwindaji, killing monsters across the United States, she would need money and flexibility.

Living at home was comfortable, convenient, and inexpensive. Though she refused to admit it publicly, she enjoyed being around her family. Her brothers Peter and Thomas had probably remained home for the same reason. Unlike her though, they worked in the family trade building furniture.

Not quite ready to get up, Makeda flung off the sheets and peeked out the window. A light snow dusted the earth. Birds chirped in the surrounding trees. A brown squirrel sat at the base of a tree. *Shouldn't you be gathering nuts?*

She sat on the edge of the bed, trying to recall her dream last night. It would be more appropriate to call it a vision—or a thought. Either way, she struggled to recall it. Minutes passed, but nothing came to mind.

Since her return from Haiti, the visions had increased. She started sensing things, discerning simple everyday objects in a bizarre, surreal manner. Bizarre odors, remarkable colors. This recent resurgence of visions and voices …

Everything changed after Haiti—in herself and the environment. A shift in the atmosphere. Even in Cape Fear, she detected a difference. She shivered and snuggled back underneath the covers. Makeda knew she had heard a scream in her head before it registered in her ears, like a presentiment.

She sat up, loosening the braids in her hair. Lessons from her great-grandmother circled in her mind. Makeda remembered few of the stories Big Mama had shared, and most she didn't understand. The family matriarch had died while she was in grade school, before Makeda finished her lessons or learned much sorcery. Why hadn't she paid closer attention?

Goose bumps erupted along her arms. A sense of foreboding washed over her. Her vision blurred. Closing her eyes, Makeda gripped the sheets, forcing down bile rising in her throat. Seconds later, the feeling passed. Unsure what had happened, Makeda figured she was simply hypoglycemic and needed to eat.

As she slumped out of bed, whining and scratching from the other side of the door increased. A pack of dogs—shepherds, Labs, and a mutt—leaped onto her as she exited the room, vying for attention. She petted, coddled, and comforted each dog in turn as she made her way down the hallway and into the living room.

Styled like a log cabin on the outside, the inside of their family home was eclectic chic. Family photos and potted plants accented the natural wood tones. A stone fireplace sat opposite but askew from the front door. Mission-style furniture adorned with flowered cushions decorated the living room, which poured into an open kitchen.

At the table, her parents ate breakfast. A newspaper covered all but Peter's eyes. The dogs abandoned her side and encircled the breakfast table, awaiting scraps.

Makeda kissed her parents, then considered breakfast options. Bacon, eggs, grits, fresh bread, and coffee. Everything looked good—except the coffee. Running a pot under the tap, she filled it with water to make tea.

She chewed on grapes and dropped a piece of bacon onto her plate. Usually, she didn't eat until closer to 10 a.m., preferring brunch to breakfast.

Both early risers, her parents had probably been up for hours. Her dad because of his long career in the military, and her mom from years as a grade-school teacher.

Makeda noticed her mom's glare.

"What's wrong?"

"Nothing. I'm not sure what to eat."

Mom continued to stare.

Makeda perceived Mom trying to peer inside her head. Since they were both zaubers, she knew it was possible. With her stance steady, Makeda held Mom's gaze and cleared her mind.

Apparently satisfied, Mom smiled. "Try a biscuit."

"You need to eat something," Dad said, before shoveling a spoonful of grits into his mouth. "Keep up your strength."

Not looking up from the paper, Peter said, "She's strong enough. I can smell her from here." He used the paper to fan the space around him.

"Smell this." She threw half a biscuit at him.

One of the dogs snatched it midair and gobbled it whole.

With the palm of his hand, Peter encouraged her to come over. "Want some of this?"

"You want some of this?" She stuck her chin up.

The dogs barked at their play fighting. Mom walked around the kitchen table and opened the back door leading out onto a rear porch. While Mom herded the dogs outside, Makeda bantered with her brother.

"Hurry up, son," Dad said. "We need to finish that sofa. It's gotta go out this week."

"Right." Peter folded the newspaper, picked up his fork, and resumed eating.

Makeda smiled. "Yeah, hurry up. Get back to work."

"Do you ever work?"

"I work tonight. Third shift."

"About time you did something," Peter mumbled.

Dad brought his plate to the sink. "I don't like you working late. Why can't you work day shifts?"

Hot water hissed from the tea kettle. Makeda dropped a tea bag in a mug and doused it with water. "I'm a temp, Daddy. I work whatever shifts they give me."

"You need to get a full-time job. Get some benefits." He kissed her cheek. "Maybe now you'll consider going back to medical school."

With a sigh, she dropped sugar cubes into her mug. "Then I wouldn't be able to travel with the mwindaji."

"Good." Without looking back, he grabbed a coat from the closet beside the front door and exited.

For half a minute, Makeda stared at the door before returning to her tea. Dad complaining about her decision not to attend medical school wasn't new. His comment caused more irritation than surprise. But he didn't understand the unique gifts she brought to their group.

Setting the tea kettle on the stove, Makeda searched for a spoon. The utensil drawer stood a few feet away but she spied a spoon someone left on the countertop.

One of the first skills she learned from Big Mama was telekinesis. Since her great-grandmother died, she had rarely used sorcery. Mom forbade it, even disallowing kasi kasi, a form of telepathy where they communicated via their minds.

But sometimes a zauber felt lazy. A little telekinesis wouldn't hurt. Why walk when she could command the spoon to come to her?

She peeked at the back door where Mom played with the dogs. Peter had returned to reading the paper. Dad was in the barn, and Thomas in bed. *No one would know.*

Her left palm opened, and she wiggled her fingers. Two feet away, the spoon rocked back and forth along the countertop but didn't move. She'd become rusty. That's what happened when you didn't practice, and she hadn't in years.

She concentrated and repeated the attempt, fluttering her fingers faster and with more force. In a flash, the spoon zipped toward her. It moved too fast for her to catch it. It struck her chest, bounced off her robe, and clinked onto the ground. Makeda bent down to retrieve the spoon. When she stood upright, Mom was standing inside the kitchen back door. *Damn.*

Neither spoke.

Mom glared but didn't move. Though staring at Makeda, her mom addressed Peter. "Son, shouldn't you be out in the barn with your dad?"

"Yeah, Mom." Peter set down the newspaper and rose. After placing his plate in the kitchen sink, he left by the front door.

Until the door closed, neither woman moved. Makeda held her breath and waited. It didn't take long.

A beat after the door clanked shut, Mom bustled into the kitchen. "I knew you were up to something."

Makeda rolled her eyes and exhaled. "All I did was grab a spoon."

"No, you used sorcery."

At the sink, Makeda rinsed off the spoon and stirred her tea. "It's not a big deal. I simply used it to get a spoon."

"You don't understand. Using maji—especially when you don't know what you're doing—is like sending out a beacon." Mom lowered her voice. "Alerting other zaubers to your presence."

She squared off with Mom. "Well, I would know what I was doing if you would teach me."

Mom snatched her by the arm, glancing at the door as if Peter might return. "Lower your voice. *Shato kwasi ke te banu?*"

Tears pooled in Makeda's eyes. "Yes. I want them to know what I am—who I am. Why can't they know? Why do I have to hide?" A stray tear dripped down her cheek. Her appetite disappeared, and she set the mug in the sink.

Mom leaned her head on Makeda's shoulder. "I know it's hard. I do. But it's not safe."

"If they knew we were zaubers, do you believe they wouldn't love us?"

Makeda allowed Mom to guide her to the kitchen table, where they sat across from each other. Mom slid the breakfast items aside and rested her forearms on the table.

"It's not that simple. Mwindaji blame zaubers for the monsters. They believe zaubers should be killed along with werewolves and vampires. We aren't witches. We aren't magicians. Zaubers practice sorcery, which is more powerful. Sorcery scares people."

"It's not right. With our powers, we can help mwindaji kill monsters. We could locate Korlemo."

"A zauber created the monsters, Makeda."

"No, a demon did."

"And who summoned the demon?" Mom scowled, gesticulating as she spoke. "Only a zauber could call up a demon strong enough to curse us with monsters like werewolves and vampires."

"One zauber. One person's mistake doesn't make all of us evil."

Mom's palms slammed down on the table, hurtling a piece of toast from a saucer. "A powerful zauber who summoned a demon that created human-eating monsters. One zauber who made a horrendous mistake."

"You think I would make a mistake like that—let someone use me?" Makeda heard her voice tremble.

Mom lightly squeezed her hand. "Sorcery is dangerous. Even masterful zaubers can miscalculate—or be deceived. A lapse in judgement can have dangerous consequences."

"But if I practiced. If someone taught me how to use my skills—"

"No." The pressure on Makeda's hand tightened. "I lost my mother to sorcery. I won't lose you too."

Tears streaked down both women's faces.

After a slight pause, Makeda moved closer to Mom. "I can control it. Use maji to help the mwindaji. Be a zauber like Big Mama."

"You don't understand." Mom bit her bottom lip. "Yewande didn't die from old age."

Makeda's tears stopped. Her mouth hung open. Before Mom could elaborate, Thomas entered the living room.

Scratching his behind, he asked, "Any breakfast left?"

CHAPTER 5

OVERCAST SKIES CAST A somber mood. Crystal chandeliers lit the room but didn't improve the ambiance.

Sylvia's body tensed. In bold font, the newspaper headline proclaimed a mutilated body had been unearthed off Interstate 65, north of Bowling Green. Anxiety sped her gaze across the inked lines of the article.

Once the maid cleared away the dishes, Sylvia folded the paper, stretched across the table, and found Papa's hand.

His gray eyes smiled back as he patted her hand. "Finish your breakfast."

As chief medical officer of Lebanon Memorial Hospital, Sylvia had many responsibilities. Recent unauthorized activities in their ajabu community had compounded those burdens. Discovering another death in neighboring Bowling Green increased her worries.

Papa's rheumatic fingers tenderly enveloped her hand. "Svie, what's wrong?"

Her head inclined toward the paper lying on the table. "There was another death. This time in Bowling Green."

He retrieved the newspaper, turned it over, and read the front-page headline. Silent minutes passed until he folded the paper and set it aside. "So, another death. It doesn't concern us."

"Did you read the description of the body? Werewolves did that."

"How can you be sure? Bindimèn butcher each other every day."

"No human ripped that man apart like the article described. I bet it was Jackie and her friends."

He snapped his fingers, signaling the help for more coffee. "You'd better be sure of your facts. You cannot accuse Jackie Baptiste without proof. Besides, that child has been through a lot."

"What? Because her mom died?"

"Svie." Papa grimaced. "Be nice."

"Mama died while I was young, but I'm not whoring around town killing bindimèn."

"Language. I will not have you speak about Herman's daughter disrespectfully. Some girls need a mother more than others."

"Jackie's sister turned out fine."

Her father slurped coffee. "Some children are more delicate. If Jackie's mother had lived—"

"She'd be a worse trollop." Sylvia snickered. "Mrs. Baptiste was an indulgent mother. She refused to believe anything bad about Jackie. The entire family spoiled her."

"That's because she became dangerously ill as a child. She almost died."

"Oh, Papa, please." She sighed.

Over the next half hour, they silently finished breakfast.

"Is there something else?" he asked.

"No, I'm just tired."

"You work too hard. I will tell Herman you need rest."

"I can't rest. The sheriff found another mutilated body in Ramsey last week. He's been asking a lot of questions, even investigating prior deaths."

After slathering apple butter onto a bagel, Papa slid the condiment jar toward her. "Have you spoken with him?"

Absently pushing aside the apple butter, Sylvia considered his question. From the little she had learned about the sheriff, he didn't seem like a person she could manipulate. Young, educated, and respectable, Sheriff Wilson had moved to Ramsey less than three years ago. He was promoted into the position after the prior sheriff retired and left town, never to be heard from again.

"No, that wouldn't be wise," she said. "He's an outsider. I'm not sure we should trust him. I don't understand why Mr. Beaufort appointed him sheriff in the first place."

Butter dripped from Papa's thin lips. "They needed to fill the position. No one else wanted it after the former sheriff retired."

"Mr. Beaufort should have chosen someone we could control."

Her gaze drifted out the window as her thoughts reverted to the transient found nearly decapitated with his organs removed and body exsanguinated. Their ajabu had become reckless, refusing to conform to the rules, and killing bindimèn inside the county—without disposing of the bodies. Their wanton behavior drew the attention of the authorities.

She wondered if Mr. Beaufort held any sway over the sheriff. If law enforcement pursued an inquiry into Ramsey's suspicious deaths, their entire ajabu community would be at risk. Making a mental note to call the district attorney, Sylvia hypothesized the consequences of eliminating the sheriff.

Outside, dark clouds gathered as a storm coalesced in the sky. The weather aligned with her thoughts.

Unfortunately, she'd been unable to persuade the quorum that the unsanctioned behavior endangered their community.

They considered her concerns exaggerated, comforted that the coroner had ruled each death accidental. Ajabu leadership decided not to intervene.

After wiping his mouth, Papa regarded her. "Perhaps Herman could speak with Korlemo about their conduct."

Picking at the edges of a bagel, Sylvia eventually dropped it onto her plate. She chose instead to sip coffee. Arabica bean spices washed over her brain, refreshing her composure. "Korlemo doesn't care. He's stuck in the past. He still believes in the old ways."

Papa's silver brows lifted. "Old traditions matter."

"Only to those who abide by their covenants. Young people don't care about traditions. They don't respect Korlemo as our leader anymore. They choose their own paths."

He pointed an arthritic finger at her as his head shook. "They are wrong. Korlemo honors the ka'trete."

She squeezed his hand and rose, kissing his deflated cheek. No sense in correcting him. He wouldn't understand. Ancient traditions ended long ago. Only Papa and a select few still cared about or respected them.

"Werewolves and vampires aren't concerned about their origins anymore. They go about their lives any way possible. They fear the mwindaji more than they respect Korlemo."

"That's not true. Korlemo is our leader. He takes care of us. He always has, and always will."

Papa will go to his grave observing Korlemo as our creator. Not wanting to argue, Sylvia excused herself and left.

Once belted into the car, she reflected upon recent events. Whatever the sacrifice, she wouldn't allow a few bad actors to destroy their program at Lebanon Memorial.

CHAPTER 6

ON HER BED, EATING a pint of mint chocolate chip ice cream, Makeda realized it wasn't going to be enough. In undergraduate school, she took a psychology course. It explained the dynamics of the mother-daughter relationship. But Mom was taking it to the next level, outright avoiding the subject of Big Mama. It was starting to piss Makeda off.

Then, she wasn't allowed to accompany the mwindaji to New York City to follow a lead on Korlemo. If Dad understood what she was capable of … *Forget it.* She gobbled more ice cream.

Every time she broached the circumstances surrounding her great-grandmother's death, Mom changed the subject. Once, Mom brazenly declared it was none of her business.

Big Mama made up for the absence of a grandmother. Unlike her brothers, Makeda hadn't known her grandmother, who died before she was born. Maybe that was why Big Mama had such a strong bond with her. She took Makeda everywhere, shared stories about their family—how they descended from a long line of zaubers—and legends about the mwindaji. Her great-grandmother found special moments to teach her sorcery.

Formal lessons started when Makeda turned three. Kasi kasi—what she called hush speak as a child—became her favorite. If they couldn't be together, they could still talk. At least, until Big Mama died.

While the family gathered for the wake, Makeda had fled to the comfort of her great-grandmother's bedroom. Lying on the bed, with comforters cocooning her in a floral embrace, she heard a voice inside her head. To her delight, she discovered they *could* still communicate. Death had not destroyed their connection—Mom did.

Their last conversation had been on a school day. Instead of getting ready, Makeda had spent the morning talking with her great-grandmother.

"Will I ever see you again?" she had asked.

"One day. If you are obedient and follow your lessons," Big Mama had said. "Last night, did you practice the spells I taught you?"

"Yes, but—"

A shadow fell across the bedroom floor. Mom had entered, yanked Makeda off the bed, and forced her to repeat an incantation that ended further communication with Big Mama. Her sorcery lessons ceased.

From that moment forward, Makeda stopped being a zauber. She didn't know anyone who could teach her sorcery. After a while, she had abandoned it.

Now, she wanted it back. Even before her trip to Haiti, she'd desired to relearn sorcery. Her medical work on the island simply strengthened her resolve.

A knock sounded on the bedroom door.

With a mouth full of ice cream, she mumbled, "Go away."

"Dinner's ready," Thomas said.

"I'm not hungry."

Not a minute later, he knocked again.

"Go away."

The door handle jostled.

She set the pint on her bedside table, got up, and unlocked the door. "What?"

Thomas entered the room and flopped on her bed.

After retrieving the pint of ice cream, Makeda continued eating.

"You're being a brat."

She stuck her tongue out at him and licked the spoon.

"That's not healthy."

"Really? Coming from a man who ate a box of Twinkies last weekend."

He slid across the bed and sat beside her. "Look, I'm upset about New York too, but you don't see me pitching a fit."

Dropping the spoon into the empty ice cream container, she placed it on the dresser. "I want Dad to trust me. I don't know what to do to make him understand I can help."

"He trusts you, but you're his daughter. He worries about you."

She clutched a pillow to her chest. "I know, but it's not fair. I'm as good a fighter as Peter."

"I know how you feel. I'm a good fighter too, but Dad always chooses Peter over me."

Though she loved Thomas, Makeda knew he was nowhere as good as Peter—or her. He tried hard, but Thomas was a klutz, always getting injured. Truth be told, he seemed content to take second place to Peter. She loved each of her brothers. Peter was her role model, Daniel her comrade-in-arms, and Thomas her heart. She gave him a hug.

He kissed her on the cheek. "Let's go eat."

"I just finished this tub of ice cream."

"So? I've seen you eat more than that."

She punched his arm and followed him into the kitchen. "How long are they gonna be gone?"

"Don't know. Dad said a few days, maybe a week. It may take a while to follow up on Daniel's information."

"Hmm."

Last month, Daniel had discovered a connection between Korlemo—an ancient vampire who had been the nemesis of the mwindaji for centuries—and a hospital in Kentucky. Their ancestors hunted the vampire through the ages and across continents. They exterminated many vampires and werewolves along the way, but not Korlemo, who over time acquired money, influence, and strength.

The last confirmed sighting of Korlemo had been in Europe before the start of the second world war. While everyone else focused on the Nazis, the mwindaji scoured a decimated Europe for the vampire. Not until close to the end of the war had they discovered he lived in France. Under the alias Jacques Corneau, Korlemo resided in a small village east of Cahors.

German occupation of the country made travel difficult. The Vichy governed the southern part of France. Another hurdle was the mwindaji's African heritage. Their inability to blend into the populace hampered their progress. By the time the Allies stormed beaches in northern France, Korlemo had used his influence to flee.

The mwindaji didn't know whether Corneau fled the country, the continent, or both. In the 1940s, tracking people across the fluid borders created by war impeded their search. By 2010, technology made it easier to track individuals—even back to the war.

Daniel had located associates of Corneau with corporate offices in New York City. Further investigation revealed an investment firm regularly sent considerable amounts of money to a small hospital in Ramsey, Kentucky.

While Dad, Peter, and two other mwindaji drove to New York to investigate the lead, Makeda was relegated to staying home, eating ice cream in bed while feuding with her mom.

At the dinner table, her frustration simmered, but not far enough beneath the surface for Mom not to notice. Table conversation came from Thomas describing his newest video game. Makeda glanced surreptitiously at Mom, who deflected her gaze.

While Thomas droned on, Makeda employed kasi kasi.

'How long are you going to ignore me?'

Mom continued to eat and converse with Thomas.

Makeda knew Mom hated video games. As children, they were forbidden to play them. Mom conversed with Thomas about the games to irritate her.

'I'm not going to stop until you answer me.'

"Thomas, I liked the table you finished yesterday," Mom said. "We should get a good price for it."

Makeda's left eyebrow arched. 'Why won't you answer me? I have a right to know.'

Still facing Thomas, Mom replied, 'No, you don't. Now stop it. You're messing with powers you don't understand.'

'Then explain them to me.'

Mom's head made a slight turn.

When Thomas rose, Mom did as well.

"Thank you for doing the dishes, Thomas." With that, Mom retired.

Sulking out of the kitchen, Makeda followed her into the living room, intending to speak with her. But for some reason, she relented, decided to leave it alone, and collapsed onto the couch.

Makeda stared at the fireplace and considered how to reconnect with Big Mama. *Why did I ever stop practicing sorcery?*

Those skills would prove invaluable to the mwindaji. She had to remember what she'd been taught. Her eyes closed.

'*Bajinu, mbabire.*'

Minutes ticked by as she repeated those same two words. Before she drifted off to sleep, her head snapped up. Like a shock, something flashed into her head. A startled Makeda toddled forward, tumbled off the couch and onto the floor.

Thomas laughed. "What's wrong with you? You act like something scared you."

She gripped her temples, trying to still the spinning room. After climbing off the floor, Makeda leaned against the couch. Someone answered her. A voice spoke inside her head.

Her pulse raced. Ignoring Thomas, Makeda sprinted down the hallway toward the bedrooms. Like a crazed woodpecker, she rapped on her parents' bedroom door. She tried not to scream.

"Mom. Please."

The door cracked open. The rippling expression across Mom's face reflected Makeda's fear. Mom hauled her inside the bedroom. After locking the door, Mom sat her down on the bed.

"What's wrong? What happened?"

"I called out for Big Mama, and someone answered."

"Who?"

As she sank into the pillowed edge of the four-poster bed, Makeda's confidence wavered. "I ... I don't know. The words weren't in English, or Baoumali. I got scared."

Mom glared. "I told you not to play with sorcery. You don't know what you're doing. You could get hurt."

She grabbed hold of Mom's hands. "Then teach me."

"No."

"Why not?"

"Because it's dangerous, and ..." Mom walked away, mumbling, "I can't."

Makeda's mouth opened, but Mom spoke first.

"I don't know how."

She swiveled on the bed, scrutinizing her mom. For a half minute, Makeda studied the woman she both loved and respected, wondering if Mom was trying to deceive her—lying to keep her away from sorcery.

"What do you mean, you don't know how? Big Mama was one of the most powerful sorceresses ever. You told me people came from across the country to learn from her."

"She was, and they did."

The quick reply made Makeda question Mom's veracity. She didn't challenge her, but instead waited.

Mom swallowed a deep breath, then said, "I don't know how—or why—but zaubers are born to their abilities. You can improve your skills over time, gain talent with experience. But if you aren't born with potential, you can't go far."

Questions crisscrossed Makeda's brow. "What are you saying?"

"My skills as a zauber are limited to kasi kasi. But—" Tears gathered in Mom's eyes. She cleared her throat as a smile lit upon her face. "Your grandmother was a beautiful, gifted zauber. But none of her daughters acquired those skills."

"You *did*."

"Only kasi kasi. I can barely move objects."

Mom rose and picked up a framed photo off a copper-colored dresser. The black-and-white photo displayed a young woman with a toddler riding her hip. "You remind me of her, you know. Daniel resembles her the most. He has her quiet grace. But you ... You inherited her spirit, determination, and hard head."

"I wish I knew her."

Mom admired the photo a moment longer, then returned it to the dresser. "She would have loved you."

"I'm sorry." Makeda kissed her mom and gave her a side-hug. "I know you don't like to talk about it, but how did she die?"

"Sorcery." Mom strode aimlessly around the room.

Perched on the edge of the bed, Makeda's gaze followed her mom's journey. She listened for each word, spoken and unspoken.

"Your grandmother was a true zauber—always practicing. She wasn't as talented as Yewande—your great-grandmother—but she held her own. Mama believed sorcery could solve anything. The proper herbs, a well-placed incantation. She believed a true zauber didn't need medicine."

Tears slid down Mom's cheeks. She trod a path back and forth in front of the bed.

"So, when she developed cancer, Mama didn't go to a doctor. She performed healing spells, sought out new herbs, cast forgotten incantations—even sought out other zaubers."

Makeda fidgeted, eager for information and afraid Mom's openness would end prematurely. She regretted it caused pain, but she wanted to learn as much as possible.

"I didn't know zaubers could heal."

"Zaubers have different abilities, different skill sets."

"Big Mama couldn't heal her?"

"Stop calling her Big Mama. No, Yewande wasn't a healer."

"Didn't Big—Yewande tell Grandma to go to the doctor?"

"Like I said, she was as stubborn as you are."

Makeda managed a tepid grin.

"By the time Daddy convinced her to go to the doctor it was too late. The cancer had metastasized. She died within a month of seeing the oncologist."

At that, Makeda stood and hugged her mom, long and tight. Minutes passed as they held each other. Mom sobbed, and Makeda dried the tears with her shirt sleeve.

"That's why you don't want me to practice sorcery? That's why you didn't want Yewande to teach me?"

Mom pushed her away and dropped onto the bed. "No, that's not why."

The strong retort startled Makeda. She sank onto the bed next to Mom. "Then why?"

"When I was little, Yewande would come to our house. She'd take me and my sisters out for walks, into the woods and park. But she spent extra time with me." Mom gazed forward, avoiding Makeda's scrutiny.

"When I got older, she tried to teach me sorcery—not simply kasi kasi but real maji—but I couldn't do it. No matter how hard I tried, I couldn't. After that, it was as if I became nothing to her. She didn't come around like before."

Mom pivoted on the bed and peered deep into Makeda's face. "Whenever my sisters or I had a child, Yewande would show up. She'd examine y'all like you were scientific specimens, stare into your eyes, feel your hands, place her head to your chests, trying to see if any of you had potential. She did this to every child in our family. If she didn't notice anything special in you, then she never gave you a second thought."

Makeda squinted and thought back. She tried to reconcile Mom's comment with the great-grandmother she loved and adored. "Is that why you tried to keep me away from her?"

At first, Mom glowered. Half a minute passed where she simply glared at Makeda.

"I resented that she loved you because you had a gift. She wanted to take you to live with her—to teach you to be a zauber like her. I refused. You were my daughter, my child.

I wanted you to be normal, grow up with your brothers in a real family—n mot simply be her student."

Makeda's eyes glistened.

"I guess I was also jealous. You had skills I wanted. The same gifts my Mama had."

Tears poured down Makeda's face as she squeezed Mom's hands. She climbed into Mom's embrace. In time, she moved away.

"So, what do I do? How do I figure out who's talking to me?"

"I don't know. I can't help you, and I don't know another zauber I trust to teach you."

Glad for the moment of open communication, and hoping it would continue, Makeda broached one more topic. "How *did* Yewande die?"

Straightening her back, Mom's demeanor changed. She rubbed her arms as if cold.

"Mom?" Makeda asked, her voice wavering.

Wiping her face with the back of her hand, Mom slipped off the bed. "I don't know."

Before Makeda could utter a reply, Mom sniped, "I *don't know*. Yewande was secretive. She didn't share her business with me—or the family. All I know is it involved sorcery."

Could she trust Mom regarding Big Mama?

"How do you know?"

"I was there when they found her. She'd been degloved—over her entire body. Skin pooled under her like a loose dress. Her limbs were wrenched out of their joints. It—she resembled a sack of broken bones. It was ghastly." Mom shuddered.

"Someone—something—snapped her back, arching her spine upward, like an inverted V. The ends of her hair were singed. Her face—there was no face, only openings where her eyes should have been. Her teeth had been knocked out. The house was ravaged, furniture overturned, objects destroyed. Large bloody scratches carved along the floorboards."

Makeda gawked. Her voice stammered. "Didn't the police believe her death was suspicious? Did they investigate?"

"No. Your dad knew Yewande was a zauber. He contacted friends in law enforcement. Since the house was locked up tight, and nothing had been stolen, the case was closed. We buried her quickly. After that, no one talked about it."

"I don't understand. Who could kill Yewande?"

"Exactly. Anyone strong enough to kill Yewande ..." Mom sat beside her. "Leave it alone. There are things about zaubers you don't understand."

Gazing into Mom's puffy, red-rimmed eyes, Makeda knew she had no intention of abandoning sorcery. It was her legacy.

She wanted to use sorcery to fight alongside the mwindaji. It gave her an advantage. But first, she had to learn how to be a zauber, which required Yewande.

CHAPTER 7

WITH ONE EYE ON traffic, Peter glanced at the speedometer. It was difficult enough navigating Interstate 95 north, but tension among the mwindaji made the trip longer. They had left North Carolina as a party of four. After another argument about searching for Korlemo, the other two mwindaji returned home. Too bad Thomas wasn't here. But Makeda would've insisted on coming if he had.

Peter's attempts at small talk with his dad were rebuffed. What little conversation had occurred was brusque. Eventually, he left Dad to his own preoccupations and reflected on what brought them to the city that never sleeps.

According to legend, Korlemo was born on the western lands of Africa. A monster created from the machinations of an evil zauber and a demon. Peter grew up on frightening tales of the murderous vampire.

Before he joined the mwindaji, Dad shared a secret. He had told Peter that since childhood, his one desire had been to personally kill Korlemo. With every mission the mwindaji undertook, Dad hoped to destroy his adversary.

Most of the mwindaji knew of Dad's personal vendetta. The schism it caused resulted in the resignation of several members. Year after year, Dad had been disappointed, unable to locate any sign of Korlemo. Peter understood half of his job was to find the ancient vampire, and the other to keep Dad's zeal from getting himself or another mwindaji killed.

His younger brother, Daniel, had discovered associates of Korlemo headquartered in Manhattan. By hacking into company databases, Daniel identified large sums of money transferred monthly to a small hospital in Kentucky for almost fifty years. Review of the Manhattan business's corporate filings revealed an operation that appeared legitimate.

***

Once they arrived in New York City, Peter and Dad staked out those Manhattan offices. Surveillance revealed different personnel arrived in the evenings under heavy security.

Days passed where they learned nothing new except where free bathrooms were located and the best takeout joints. On the third day, they rested in a park while checking in with the other mwindaji back in North Carolina.

With the phone on speaker, Dad provided a concise report on what they had uncovered—nothing.

Given the late hour, the large number of people milling around the park surprised Peter. He continuously scanned the area, sure a monster lurked around every tree. Perhaps he was on edge because of the lack of progress they had made. He pulled a hoodie up over his head and asked, "What next?"

Dad sipped from a steaming cup of coffee but said nothing.

Over the phone, one of the mwindaji asked, "Why don't you guys head back? There's nothing there."

"We'll give it one more day," Dad said. "If we don't pick up a lead, we'll head out."

***

Later that same evening, with a crescent moon high above in the clear sky, Peter watched a man in a business suit, surrounded by two muscular men, exit the Manhattan offices and enter a stretch limousine.

He tossed his burger aside and elbowed Dad awake.

"Here we go."

While Dad wiped sleep from his eyes, Peter trailed the limousine away from glitzy New York City. They meandered down domesticated New Jersey suburbs. Outside New Vernon, the limousine drove up to the keypad of a residence in an exclusive enclave. After entering a code, the driver proceeded past a large wrought iron security gate.

Driving slowly past the house, Peter noted the location as Dad scribbled the address in a notebook.

Once the limousine cleared the entrance, Peter doubled back. He parked their RV about three hundred yards down the road between bushy hedges. He watched for signs they'd been spotted.

When traffic cleared, he and Dad left the RV and approached the property. They scaled the fence and dropped behind lush bushes lining the perimeter. But that was as far as they got.

From behind the bushes, Peter heard jingling approach— then panting. He peered between the hedges. Large shadows raced toward them. Rottweilers.

With alacrity, he used his hands as a step and assisted Dad up and over the fence. Growls and barks increased in intensity. Peter glanced back and saw dogs bearing down on him.

"Come on," Dad said.

Peter sprang onto the fence and hauled himself over in one step. But he didn't immediately land on the ground. Something snagged his hoodie. Before he could reach up, a loud rip preceded his falling. The hoodie had caught on a piece of metal and torn.

Paws scraped the ground and parted the hedges. From between the fence's iron rods, Peter watched the Rottweilers' snapping jaws as they charged forward. Seconds later, he hustled to the truck behind his dad.

Once in the RV, he secured his seat belt. "What now?"

Binoculars pressed to Dad's face as he scrutinized the residence. "Isn't there a national park somewhere around here?"

Mwindaji didn't bring smartphones on missions because they could be tracked. Peter popped open the glove box and located a mapping device. It took a few minutes, but once the device activated, Peter identified their location.

"The Great Swamp National Wildlife Refuge is nearby. We can camp there."

"Let's go."

After scanning the rearview mirror, Peter pulled away from the shoulder of the road.

Until distance made it futile, Dad kept the binoculars pinned to his face and surveilled the property. While Peter drove, Dad updated the mwindaji.

Peter gripped the wheel and glanced over at Dad. His pulse thrilled at the idea they finally had a decent lead on Korlemo.

CHAPTER 8

COLD SEEPED THROUGH THE thin sleeping bag where Peter dozed in the RV. His eyes fluttered open. He yawned, stretched his neck, and rubbed stiffness from his shoulders.

Chattering birds perched on the hood of the RV.

Last night, they had camped outside the national park. Though Peter appreciated not having to sleep in a truck, their quarters were still cramped. The assertive smell of brewing coffee encouraged him to crawl out of the sleeping bag.

In a tiny makeshift kitchen, Dad had prepared breakfast. Wearing readers, he held a newspaper in one hand and a cup of coffee in the other.

"Morning, son. Hungry?"

"Yes, thanks." Peter wiggled his back, massaging his aching shoulder where his hoodie caught on the metal fence last night. He drank coffee and stared out the window. Nature was beautiful, but he wanted a bathroom.

Dad folded the paper under his arm. "If you're looking for restrooms, they're near the entrance beside the visitor center."

Ten minutes later, Peter returned to the camper and finished breakfast. "What's on the agenda for today?"

"That house is our one lead. We'll head back there." Dad spoke without taking his eyes off the newspaper.

Because of the security gate and dogs, for the next two days they failed to access the property.

One morning, while Peter whittled a figurine from a piece of wood, Dad spotted an advertisement for a landscape laborer. He pointed it out to Peter, who recognized the name of the company from a truck parked in front of the residence they surveilled. It was a chance to investigate the house, but since the other mwindaji were back in North Carolina, if trouble arose, they would be on their own.

"What do you think?" Peter asked.

"It's a chance to get on the property. But you'll have to be careful. Try not to stir up a hornet's nest."

***

From outside, the Lonnie's Landscape Solutions sandstone building resembled an adobe home more suited to the American Southwest. Peter took a second survey of the surroundings before entering the establishment.

A bell rang as he strode up to a dour-faced woman seated at the front desk.

"Who do I talk to about a job?" he asked.

Chomping on chewing gum, the woman peered over the magazine. "You looking for work?" Her jaw clicked as she chewed.

"Yeah. I'm new to the area. I read your ad in the paper." He held her gaze as she sized up his six-foot-two-inch, two-hundred-thirty-pound frame.

"Here. Fill this out, and I'll need an ID." She handed him paperwork and a clipboard.

Because of his clean record, they hired him on the spot.

Over the next two days, Peter worked at various properties in northern New Jersey before the crew finally arrived at the residence he and his dad had under surveillance.

As their work truck entered the heavily guarded estate, Peter sized up the exquisitely manicured gardens. Beyond scenery, he memorized camera locations and other security measures. Based on his experience from breaking into buildings, this security system was impressive.

He hopped off the truck with the other guys and grabbed his tools. The sun had barely risen when they began work.

Trimming hedges brought Peter into proximity of the house. As he weeded flower beds, he recorded the security defenses on his leg using a pen.

Two stories of grayish-brown bricks formed a classical Tudor facade. Heavy draperies covered the large windows in the front and sides of the home, preventing him from viewing the inside. Lack of tall shrubbery near the house would make a stealth approach difficult.

Around midday, the crew took a break. They were permitted entrance into the home by way of the garage. Under the pretense of relieving himself, Peter joined a queue forming beside the bathroom. As the line grew, he drifted to the rear.

He glanced around. On the other side of a spacious kitchen, Peter observed a locked heavy door. *Did it lead to a basement?*

Once he completed a short survey, Peter abandoned the queue and circumvented the kitchen. Occasionally creaky wooden planks had him continuously scanning the area. After a quick peek around, he sneaked over to the door. Well-oiled hinges gave him a false sense of security as the unlocked door inched open. Before he could descend into the basement, a large hand slammed the door shut.

Peter started and jumped back. How the hell didn't he hear the guy approach? He receded from the door and prepared an excuse. As he cleared his throat, he gazed up at the body attached to the hand. Taller than him by half a foot, the guy's large arms complemented an enormous neck. Recessed eyes were overwhelmed by a heavy brow and broad, jutting chin.

Peter's throat tightened. His hand instinctively reached for the gun he kept strapped to his waist. Nothing. That morning, he had discussed carrying a weapon with his dad. They decided it was too risky. Now, he wished he had brought a gun, or a machete. Having slain enough monsters, he knew this dude was a werewolf poorly disguised as a human.

His retreat continued. Because he was unarmed, fleeing was the only option.

"Sorry," he said. "The line was long, so I was looking for another john."

The guard groaned but didn't respond.

As Peter inched backward, in tandem, the guard advanced forward with clenched fists. A deep scowl stretched along his brow.

In haste, Peter rejoined the queue and waited his turn. After using the facilities, he resumed work outside.

At the end of the shift, Peter returned to the landscaping office with the crew. While the other workers unloaded the truck, he considered how to get back onto the property.

Mr. Aaron, the landscaping manager, stuck his head out the office door. "Crawford, get in here."

Long and angular, the manager resembled an ascetic monk, sans the robe. Peter watched him stomp behind the desk, remove a small metal box, and count out twenty-dollar bills.

"Mr. Munroe said you were snooping around the place," Mr. Aaron said, pausing as he glared down his angular nose. "You're done." After handing over two hundred dollars, he sat back down and returned to his paperwork.

Gazing down upon the manager's shimmering, balding head, Peter understood no explanation would be accepted.

He counted the money and departed. Down the street, he called Dad to pick him up.

Once Peter was inside the RV, Dad asked, "Well?"

"Werewolves."

Dad's gaze widened as he turned toward Peter.

"Careful," Peter said, observing the upcoming traffic light turn red.

Brakes squealed, and the camper slammed to a stop partially in the middle of the intersection.

"Sorry."

As they headed for the national park, Peter explained what had occurred.

"So, you think there are others?"

"Yeah. That guy's not by himself. I wish I could've gotten into the basement."

"No, it's best you didn't. You might not have made it out."

Peter nodded. Dad was right. Not bad for a day's work, though. He got what they wanted, what the mwindaji needed, proof they were on the right track. Where there were werewolves, there would be vampires. The former often acted as sentinels for the latter.

Once he showed the park attendant their pass, Dad headed for their assigned lot.

While Dad made dinner, Peter called the mwindaji. "Hold on." He placed the phone on speaker.

"So, you guys didn't see any vampires?" a voice over the phone asked.

Peter frowned. "No, but they're there."

"You don't know that," a different voice said.

"It doesn't matter. How many werewolves did you find? Is it worth the whole team coming up there?"

"Of course, there are more werewolves," Peter said. "I didn't have time to count them."

Hamburgers sizzled in the pan. Dad cooked as the mwindaji debated.

Peter's stomach grumbled, and his head ached. "We haven't identified the size of this nest, but it's worth exploring."

Dad placed burgers on a dish in the center of the table. Biting into one, Peter gave him a thumbs-up.

A voice over the phone asked, "Can we vote?"

Although Dad led their group, the mwindaji voted before approaching a target. To Peter's disappointment, the team did not agree with his assessment. At least Thomas voted with him.

A voice over the phone said, "We'll wait on hitting the house until we get more data."

"Let's check out the hospital in Kentucky first," a different voice said.

Discussion continued for another fifteen minutes. After he hung up, Peter licked ketchup from his lips and gazed across the table.

Dad's shoulders rose and fell. "You win some, you lose some. Let's pack up."

Dinner dishes were cleaned and stacked away. As they secured their supplies and prepared to leave, Peter resolved to hurry the investigation in Kentucky.

"We need to check out that hospital quick and get back up here," he said to Dad's back.

Dad finished tying down their gear and slipped into the RV's driver's seat. "Bad things happen when you rush."

Peter shot him a side-glance. He was confident the werewolf he discovered at the house was the tip of a larger iceberg. What secrets did that basement contain?

CHAPTER 9

IN THE OLD-WORLD STUDY, a clock chimed the hour. Korlemo glowered.

The zauber's lips trembled. "A woman will kill—"

Before she finished, his canines ripped apart her throat, caving in the side of her neck, leaving the esophagus exposed. Torn circulatory vessels gushed blood as the woman collapsed. In seconds, blood pooled around her head. Empty globes stared up at him from her stony, terrified face.

Korlemo stomped over her rumpled body and made his way to a chair beside the hearth. His nostrils flared, stung by a pungent stench. The zauber must have urinated right as he squashed her neck. A sneer curled at the corner of his lips.

With his head bowed, a servant waited beside the fireplace. Korlemo waved him over. "Clean up that mess."

Without questioning the command or raising his head, the servant fell to the ground and wiped foul liquids off the wooden floors.

A security guard entered the study and stared down at the zauber lying abandoned on the ground. With his foot, he tapped the body. "What do you want us to do with it?"

Tossing his hand in the air, Korlemo dismissed the question. "Remove her."

During Korlemo's exchange with the zauber, Herman had sought shelter near the large windows facing the backyard. Korlemo thought his friend would faint when he chomped into the zauber's carotid. Despite being a lupasteri, Herman had always been squeamish around blood.

Approaching the guard, Herman avoided looking down at the butchered zauber. "Take her out and bury her in the woods."

Another guard, stockier than the first, entered the study. He joined the first guard standing near the zauber. "Can we have her?"

Simultaneously, Korlemo replied "yes" as Herman said "no." The former chuckled.

"Do what you want. She served her purpose."

"Thank you, Korlemo," the first guard said.

The stocky guard bent down and broke off one of the zauber's fingers. Crunching loudly, he chewed on the digit, spitting out a polished fingernail into his hairy palm.

Herman blanched and turned away.

"Fetch my wine," Korlemo said to no one in particular.

Still diverting his gaze from the dead zauber, Herman snapped his fingers, summoning the help.

A dragging noise was the only sound in the study as the guards slid the corpse along the floorboards. A servant trailed behind, cleaning up the zauber's effusions.

Korlemo scowled into the fireplace. The dead woman had been the third zauber commissioned to interpret his dream, *and* the third to predict his death. He needed to figure this out—and soon.

Had a curse been placed upon him? Could it be Zorulo, impatient to claim his soul?

His latest victim had been a novice. She had not recognized him, but nonetheless, her prediction resembled the others. A woman would kill him.

Flames flickered in the grate. Warmth circulated around the room, reminding Korlemo of another hot evening. A millennium ago, he had encountered another woman. Humid smells of the African heat flooded his nostrils. Korlemo tasted the bile that had refluxed in his throat that evening during the battle. A woman warrior had threatened him, causing ...

No, he would not reflect upon that evening. It was long ago, in the far distant past. That battle had been unimportant because in the end, he prevailed and avenged the Ibori name. His ancestors' name.

Firelight dimmed. Korlemo licked away remnants of the zauber's blood from his lips.

Like a mouse, Herman placed a decanter and a glass beside his right hand before scampering to an adjacent chair.

Minutes passed as Korlemo drank. He needed to unravel this puzzle. Push away the alarm growing in him to flee Kentucky.

To his annoyance, Herman fidgeted in the chair. Korlemo's nerves were prickly. His anger, like a bubbling kettle, threatened to burst forth. He didn't wish to release his ire upon his friend. He needed Herman—at least for now.

Having lived in Kentucky for such a brief time, Korlemo had grown comfortable in these new surroundings. Only a thousand-year-old vampire considered half a century a short time, but it still felt recent to him, unlike Nintoubo, the home of his birth.

He and his tribe had journeyed away from West Africa around the time King Kankan Musa began a pilgrimage to Mecca. For the past six hundred years, they lived in southern France. Nestled in the fertile valley around Cahors, they had been safe and content until the inconveniences of war.

They had survived the Great War unscathed, thriving off an abundance of flesh produced by the carnage of warring republics. The second war proved not as fortuitous to their interests. Nazis tramped across Europe, parading through Paris before encroaching upon the rest of France. Due to the foresight of his dear friend and Herman's father, Frederic, their families escaped the turmoil.

They arrived in America with other refugees fleeing the conflict. Korlemo took an immediate dislike to New York City. Frederic's love of horses brought them to Kentucky.

A wary Frederic developed a system to provide for their families in perpetuity. That foresight allowed them to live in comfort without risk of persecution. Their security though may have come to an end.

Each night, haunting dreams continued to intrude upon his peace. Korlemo refused to accept the prediction of his impending demise—at the hand of a woman, no less.

"Did you wish me to hire another zauber?" Herman asked.

"I wish you to find me the right one." He brooded, swirling his goblet.

"I can't tell them what to say."

"They lie, try to take advantage of me. These zaubers believed they could trick me into being afraid, get me under their spell." He consumed the rich burgundy fluid. "I cannot die. Zorulo swore it."

Over the rim of his glass, Korlemo peered at Herman, daring his friend to contradict him. The ka'trete with Zorulo guaranteed him a long life, wealth, and victory over his enemies. True, Korlemo could not die a natural death, but Zorulo had not stated he would *never* die.

For a millennium, he had attained power, destroyed his enemies, and lived surrounded by abundance. Korlemo snickered.

How could anyone suggest a woman could kill me?

His breathing deepened as his gaze traveled over to his friend. He viewed fear reflected in Herman's gaze. "Get me another zauber. Not a seer. I need a sorceress who can cast spells and understands dubwanas."

"*Dubwanas?*"

"Demons!" Korlemo roared.

Herman's face twitched as he stood. "Yes, of course." He departed.

Korlemo refilled his glass, determined not to be defeated by anyone, let alone a woman—not again. He also had no intention of becoming a slave to Zorulo. A spell caster could keep the dubwana at bay and signal any approaching danger.

He would have to remember not to kill the next zauber. A grin spread across his lips. If this was Zorulo, running would serve no purpose.

A woman. *What woman could kill me?* It was impossible. Unless …

The glass shattered in his clenched hand.

CHAPTER 10

IN THE CRAWFORD FAMILY home scents of roasted meats salted the air. Dinner had ended, and people slowly gathered in the living room.

Seated on the floor, surrounded by their family dogs, Makeda stroked a shepherd's coat. The dog reclined on her lap as she listened to the discussion. Logs in the fireplace crackled beside her.

Whittling a scrap piece of wood, Peter said, "We should go back to New Jersey. I identified a den of werewolves there. We don't know anything about Kentucky."

Makeda watched, wondering who would win: Peter, Dad, and Thomas versus the other mwindaji.

"Daniel said a lot of money is being transferred to this hospital in Kentucky," her cousin Aaron said, stroking his pencil mustache. "I think it's worth investigating before we make a move in New Jersey."

Seated next to Aaron, her cousin Keenan nodded in agreement. "I thought you said you blew your cover."

Peter sat erect and ceased whittling. "I didn't blow anything. I said they might've gotten suspicious."

"It doesn't matter," Uncle John said, setting a mug down on the coffee table. "We need to be sure. We don't want anyone hurt." His eyes circled the room before resting upon her dad.

Though he was not a blood relative, she called John Hill uncle. His soft-spoken nature belied his military background.

Mwindaji on his father's side, Uncle John met her dad when they served in the military. After they retired, the two Vietnam vets traversed the U.S., together with their respective children, exterminating monsters.

Conversation stalled.

Makeda repositioned herself, and the dogs adjusted to her movements.

Peter resumed carving.

Before he left the living room for the kitchen, Uncle John said, "If we go to Kentucky, we'll need someone inside the hospital."

"I'll do it," Makeda and Peter said in unison.

She shooed away the dogs and climbed off the floor. "Peter, I'm a nurse. It makes more sense for me to be the source inside the hospital."

"I don't want you in the hospital by yourself," Dad said, before eyeing Peter.

Twirling the knife in his hand, Peter placed the carving on the ground by his feet before closing the flick knife. "I'll go. I can get a job as a janitor or something."

Also seated on the ground, Nyesha smiled up at Makeda. "I could get a job too. Girl, it'll be fun. You and me leading a mission."

They shared a high five.

"Nyesha, you have to stay home with Mom," Keenan said. "I have a meeting in San Francisco with my agent."

Since her uncle—Nyesha and Keenan's father—died, her aunt refused to remain home alone. Makeda knew her aunt wouldn't tolerate all her children being away at the same time.

"I'll go," Raymond said, momentarily dragging his attention away from the game player.

"No," her dad, Uncle John, and Peter said simultaneously.

Raymond shrugged his shoulders and returned to the game.

Makeda loved Raymond, Uncle John's son, but he was usually too busy smoking pot or playing video games to be interested in much else. Though he could be relied upon to do what he was told, he lacked initiative.

"What about you, Aaron?" her uncle asked.

Stroking his mustache, Aaron said, "Sorry, Uncle John. Work's busy right now."

She understood his difficulty getting time off during the week. Aaron lived in Charlotte and worked in banking.

Because Peter jumped up from the chair, the dogs startled and scampered around the living room.

"Let's vote again," he said. "We know there are werewolves in New Jersey. Let's check it out first."

"The question is whether our vampire is there," Uncle John said.

Zeke sighed. "This again. Why are we chasing after one vampire when we've identified werewolves in New Jersey?"

Uncle John glared at his son.

Dad stood. "Let's vote again. Who's for New Jersey?"

Peter's countenance fell as three hands raised. The only people who voted for New Jersey were him, Dad, and Thomas.

Makeda smiled. "So, it's decided. I'll lead the mission in—"

"I'll lead," Peter said, slumping back onto the chair and picking up the carving.

"It makes sense for Makeda to lead," Nyesha said. "She's a nurse."

Several of the mwindaji voiced their opinions. Chatter ping-ponged around the room.

A frown zigzagged across Makeda's forehead as she prepared to argue.

Dad must have noticed her expression because he fore-stalled any argument by raising his hands. "Okay, guys. Peter will lead. Makeda, you get on service at the hospital. Everyone clear?"

"Clear," Peter said, smirking at her.

Makeda side-eyed Peter, but he was conversing with Thomas and didn't notice.

People stirred. Some entered private side conversations, while others went into the kitchen for more food.

Heat swelled in Makeda's heaving chest. Her brother's filial protection was stifling. The more Dad pushed her away from the mwindaji, the more she would resist. She planned to ferret out Korlemo and show her potential despite her family's objections. Maybe use her zauber skills.

'Bajinu, mbabire.'

CHAPTER 11

IN HER MINIMALIST OFFICE at Lebanon Memorial Hospital, Dr. Sylvia Senegal sat behind a sizable metal desk, pondering upon the upcoming meeting. Her head throbbed thinking about it.

For fourteen years, she has functioned as chief medical officer for the hospital, keeping it operational despite difficult financial times. Other hospital systems tried to coax her away, but she always declined. Hospital administrators requested to observe Lebanon's governing practices, wanting to duplicate her success.

Sylvia did not encourage visits. She barely had patience for OSHA, Joint Commission, and the other regulatory bodies with which a hospital must contend. Lebanon Memorial had achieved something unique, she asserted. It could not be duplicated.

How Lebanon Memorial remained viable in the era of declining reimbursements, she refused to divulge. The hospital's accomplishments made her both revered and feared in the Ramsey medical and lay communities alike.

Presently, her biggest obstacle came from outside the medical center. The deceased vagrant the sheriff's office discovered last week was one of several bodies unearthed in the county within the past month. It caused her much perturbation because she believed the rogue ajabu activity was associated with Jackie Baptiste.

From the moment Herman Baptiste hired his daughter, Jackie had become an albatross to Sylvia's peaceful management. Unfortunately for Sylvia, Baptiste was the hospital's chief operating officer. Out of respect for him, she tolerated Jackie. Their families had known each other for years—centuries to be exact. Sylvia respected the Baptistes, except their youngest daughter.

Now, Jackie had become her problem. In addition to her tardiness, Jackie treated the hospital staff with contempt. She ignored the supervisors' directives, and more significantly, her extracurricular activities brought dangerous attention to Ramsey. Attention that endangered the livelihoods of not only the Baptistes but their entire community. During the last quorum, Sylvia had omitted mentioning Jackie's involvement in the unsanctioned killings, preferring not to embarrass Baptiste.

Time passed as she glanced out the window, oblivious to the budding leaves on the cusp of spring. Her shoulders tensed as she steeled herself to deal with Jackie—again.

This time, the billing supervisor, a bindimèn, exasperated with Jackie's poor performance, requested she be terminated. Though Sylvia would delight in firing Jackie, Baptiste would go ballistic. There had to be a way to control Jackie and curb her deviant behavior.

The desk phone rang.

"Yes." Sylvia listened as the office assistant announced the arrival of her nemesis. "Send her in."

A sulking Jackie entered.

"Sit down," Sylvia said.

Jackie slammed the door closed and plopped into a chair positioned before the desk.

With measured breaths, Sylvia calmed herself as Jackie slouched in the seat and used another chair as a footstool.

"Yeah?"

She ignored Jackie's attempt to goad her into an argument by glancing down at paperwork on her desk. "According to Mr. Mackey, you've been late every day for the past month."

Creamy olive skin gave a haunting negative space for Jackie's sparkling green eyes. With the physique of a dancer—absent the discipline—she smirked and tossed back her long, jet-black hair.

"So, what? He's lucky I show up at all."

Sylvia paused and regarded Jackie. She wanted this pest gone—from the hospital, Ramsey, and her life. Over the past three months, she had collected information on Jackie's exploits. When would it be most beneficial to make Jackie's trysts public? Should she caution Jackie? Perhaps threaten to inform Baptiste if she didn't stop. In that moment, Sylvia reached a decision.

"Mr. Mackey wants to fire you, but I've decided to place you on probation."

Jackie gaped as Sylvia continued.

"You'll work the evening shifts, run quarterly reports, check deposits, and prepare the weekly EOBs."

After her statement, Sylvia returned to the paperwork on her desk. She kept her face down, fighting to suppress a grin.

Jackie vaulted out of the seat, smacking her palms down on the desk. "What? Are you crazy? I'm not staying in this mausoleum all night."

With a lilt in her voice, Sylvia smiled. "You will if you want to work here." Her plan had two paths to success. Either Jackie would quit and leave Lebanon Memorial *or* she'd work nights, ending her evening escapades. Either way, Sylvia won.

"I'm not doing it. Forget it," Jackie said, glaring down at the top of Sylvia's head.

"You'll do it, or you'll quit," Sylvia said folding her hands. "We're done."

"Humph. We'll see what my dad says."

"Oh, he'll love it. Finally, he'll be able to keep track of you."

Jackie hissed. "You bitch. You can't stop me from doing what I want." Her polished fingers elongated into claws. She snarled as her teeth grew into fangs.

Sylvia glowered, bumped her chair backward with her legs, and completed her own transformation. Unlike the sleek were-wolf Jackie became, Sylvia transformed into a beast—dwarfing Jackie in size and ferocity. Her jaw thrust forward, and fangs descended. Sylvia's fingers became talons. Her conjunctiva yellowed, and a mouth full of enormous teeth garbled her speech.

"How dare you threaten me."

Jackie gawked. With several deep breaths, she reversed her metamorphosis. Without apology, she retreated from the office, shutting the door firmly but without noise.

Still hovering over the desk, Sylvia's breathing slowed but her body trembled. She sank into her chair and swiveled around, staring into the woods. Installed for privacy, tinted windows had hidden their transformations.

The encounter with Jackie spoiled the scenic view of the woods and wildlife. Minutes elapsed as Sylvia fought to regain her composure.

Birds soared across the clear blue sky. Squirrels raced up majestic leafy trees. Her chest heaved less, and her pulse moderated. The bucolic scene restored her balance, and she began plotting.

Jackie was in no way an intellectual, but Sylvia hadn't realized how reckless the tramp had become. One way or another, she vowed to eliminate Jackie—completely.

CHAPTER 12

WHIRLING FROM AUTOMOBILES ON the nearby interstate seeped through the thin walls of the hotel lobby.

"Here's your key," the man at the registration counter said, handing over a piece of plastic resembling a credit card.

Zainabu accepted it and walked into the waiting elevator, along the way observing the décor.

Inside her hotel room, she placed a small suitcase on the dresser and gazed out the window into the parking lot below. The surroundings still dazzled, such a contrast from Kondoro, the largest city nearest the African village she called home.

She relaxed into a large, cushioned chair. Before she could extend her legs along an ottoman, a mist developed in the far corner of the room.

Zainabu's jaw clenched, and she stood. Chewing on the inside of her jaw, she faced the solidifying cloud.

In under a minute, it assumed the form of a large, bloated face, speaking in a flat baritone. "Any problems getting to the hotel?"

"None."

"Good. Do you understand what to expect?"

"Yes, Zorulo. I studied your directions. I take a bus to ..." Zainabu consulted a map. "Ramsey. Then order a car—"

"I'm not talking about *how* to get there. Do you realize what will happen when you face him?"

"I can handle—"

"No, you can't. Follow my orders exactly or I'll ship you back to that cesspool you call home."

"Understood." She shifted her weight between her legs. "What about that cry?"

"Ignore it."

"But the zauber."

"I said forget it." His voice roared as the facial image enlarged.

Zainabu bit the inside of her cheek as her heart fluttered.

"Don't disappoint me."

Ten seconds later, the cloud disappeared.

For the next five minutes, Zainabu stood in the room, checking the area until she was sure Zorulo had departed.

She resumed her seat in front of the window, gazing out beyond the parking lot into trees lining the property. Zorulo wouldn't ruin this moment. This was the first trip she'd made to America. Zainabu intended to relish it, no matter how short it might be.

Her hands shook as they rested along the chair arms. *Steady.* This next week would define her future. She thought about home.

Resentment toward her family still festered, preventing her from mending their estranged relationship. Zainabu's parents dismissed her ambitions. Their lineage consisted of many zaubers, but her parents asserted she hadn't any talent and instead should marry.

Regardless, Zainabu sought guidance from her aunts. They questioned her sincerity and commitment to their tutelage. Because they refused to mentor her, Zainabu taught herself witchcraft and learned sorcery from other zaubers.

Pouting, she glanced out the window. The last thing she had told her parents before she left home was that she would become the most successful witch to ever come from their village. She determined to do whatever was required to realize that dream. *Anything.*

CHAPTER 13

FOR THE PAST WEEK, Makeda had searched each medical floor in Lebanon Memorial Hospital she could access. Nothing she uncovered hinted at Korlemo's location. Two floors evaded her scrutiny: surgery and psychiatry. Her first shift schedule prevented her from investigating Human Resources—the other place she missed.

When Peter failed to secure a job with the hospital, Makeda gloated but then realized searching the facility had become her sole responsibility. Working full-time on the medicine floor made it twice as difficult. Though glad she'd become the de facto leader of their mission, she needed help.

"Makeda."

Framed in the doorway of the medical supply closet was her nurse supervisor. The imposing woman, built like a linebacker, was born with perpetual scorn across her forehead.

In seconds, Makeda gathered an IV fluid bag and tubing. She pivoted around to face the charge nurse.

"Yes? Did you need something?"

Feet a half foot apart and arms crossed over her double-D bosom, the charge nurse asked, "What are you doing in here? Your patient needs her IV *and* she's due for her medication."

"I'm on it," she said, holding up the equipment in her hands and exiting the supply closet.

An hour later, Makeda had completed the medication infusion and took her break, deciding to scope out the hospital lobby.

Downstairs, she spied a hallway extending beyond the gift shop and away from the center of the hospital. She staked out the vicinity, waiting until the area cleared. When no one was around to notice, she sneaked down the passageway.

The poorly lit gray walls lacked any décor. At the end of the long hallway stood two imposing doors. Makeda proceeded forward as noises from the hospital lobby drifted behind. Tile floors punctuated her steps, magnifying the sound in her ears.

A scent of mahogany drifted from the impressive doors. No label identified the room. She decided to peek inside but discovered it was locked. *Damn.*

After surveying the entrance, she determined the hospital probably used the space for conferences. Locked doors created mystique—and Makeda craved secrets.

With her eyes closed, she touched the massive doors and inhaled their mahogany essence. In seconds, a sensation of moroseness washed over her. Like she was in a dream, her body felt tossed about as if in a cyclone. A new astringent odor met her nostrils. Makeda became queasy, and her mouth dry. Suddenly, a scene flashed into her mind—no a memory.

Transported back to the jewel of the Caribbean, Makeda recalled disembarking in the capital city of Port-au-Prince. That January, she had traveled to Haiti to help with the humanitarian effort following the earthquake. Overwhelmed by the suffering she witnessed, Makeda committed to remaining in the country for a full month—guilty about not staying longer.

Her high school French proved useless because most of her patients spoke Creole. One patient in particular touched her heart. A frail older woman named Nadege. The elderly woman suffered multiple injuries during the quake. The most serious was a head wound from falling debris. Despite her age and trauma, the octogenarian survived.

Through an interpreter, Makeda spoke daily with Nadege, encouraged by the woman's progress. A language barrier couldn't impede their affection for each other. Their last encounter, though, had been unusual.

"How are you today?" she had asked, tucking the older woman's thick braids under a head scarf.

"*Mèsi pitit mwen,*" Nadege had said, bringing Makeda's hands to her heart.

She knelt beside the cot. "Don't thank me. I'm glad you're better."

Clouded lenses fixed upon her. "*Ou se yon pitit dou. Ou se yon bon mambo.*"

Makeda waited for the interpreter, who for some reason hesitated.

"Is there a problem?" she had asked.

Nadege craned her head off the pillow, also regarding the interpreter.

For probably the millionth time, Makeda wished she had learned Creole. Listening to the two women converse, she deduced the problem involved the word *mambo*. As the discussion proceeded, she noticed her patient become distressed.

On a shaky elbow, Nadege pointed a reed-thin finger at the interpreter. Then she gestured toward Makeda.

"She says you're a good nurse," the interpreter had said, lowering her gaze.

Nadege relaxed back upon her pillows, apparently satisfied.

Dubious about the translation, Makeda had no time to dwell upon it. She kissed Nadege's wrinkled cheeks.

A crinkled charcoal face beamed back at her, as Nadege's arthritic hands caressed her cheeks. "*Beni ou, se pou Bondye Gid ou. Asire w ke ou sèvi ak pouvwa ou pou bon.*"

"She says may God bless you."

When Makeda glanced over at the interpreter, the woman stared at her feet.

Even without understanding Creole, Makeda had realized Nadege said more than the interpreter relayed, but what could she do? Still, the event had bothered her. Before she left Port-au-Prince, she asked another interpreter what mambo meant. He confided it meant healer, or witch.

Standing before the massive conference doors, Makeda wondered what Nadege had said. To her disappointment, the following day her elderly patient had been transferred to a different section of the hospital. Despite searching, she never saw Nadege again.

"Hello."

Makeda's stomach bounced up into her throat. She spun around and found a towering man with a deadpan, impassive face gazing at the doors.

He spoke in a flat bass voice. "What are you doing here?"

While recovering her composure, Makeda pointed at the conference room. "I was appreciating these beautiful doors. What type of wood is this?"

"Mahogany. They are beautiful, *and* expensive." After a moment admiring the doors, his gaze shifted back toward her.

Her shoulders tensed as Makeda realized their isolation from the rest of the hospital. An odor itched her nose. It wasn't the wood, but for the moment she couldn't place it. She studied the stranger.

His lanky arms were too long for his torso, almost marfanoid. With his pale face and disjointed features, she considered the possibility he was a vampire. But it was daytime. They were inside though, and away from sunlight. *Possible.*

Yewande had taught her about other monsters, koleo and biloko. Maybe not as prevalent as werewolves and vampires, but as deadly. *Time to leave.*

"I should get back to work." She maneuvered around him, hustling toward the lobby. Using the gift shop windows, she checked to see if he pursued.

His gaze followed, but he remained in front of the massive conference room doors.

Witch or a healer. *Had Nadege—*

"Hey."

Makeda grabbed the hand that landed on her shoulder and twisted the wrist. A second later, she glanced at the person's face. "Michael." She released his hand.

"Nice way to say hello," he said, rubbing his hand.

"Sorry. You scared me." She inspected his wrist. "Let me see."

He chuckled. "What are you doing to your patients that makes you afraid of them?"

His wrist was red but not swollen. She released it, but he held her hand.

"What are you doing here?" She frowned.

"I thought we could have lunch together. Is that okay?"

"Of course."

Side by side, they entered the hospital cafeteria adjacent to the lobby.

On her first day working at the hospital, Makeda met Michael. Since then, they spoke daily and occasionally ate together in the cafeteria. Though she hadn't asked, Makeda believed Dr. Neil Bones told Michael about her.

Michael and the doctor were good friends. She'd seen them in the evening playing dominoes in the cafeteria.

While they waited in line to place their orders, the hospital loudspeaker announced a code blue.

"I have to go. Did you come by specifically to see me?" she asked.

"Dr. Bones had an autopsy report I needed, but I did want to have lunch with you." He smiled, shifting his hat farther back along his forehead. "Are we still on for tonight?"

"Yes. I'll call you."

All thoughts about Haiti receded from her mind as she rushed to the ER. She would figure things out later. It might be important.

CHAPTER 14

EACH DAY AT TWILIGHT, Peter tramped through the woods around Ramsey, often staying out until morning. The forests were home. Organic smells from damp earth, the cacophony of animal vocals, and a visual canopy of stars brought him peace.

Since arriving in Ramsey, he had developed a routine. While Makeda worked in the hospital, he scoured the town for any signs of their vampire. This part of their assignment was monotonous—especially since he'd been unable to secure a hospital job. Leads required time to yield information. As a hunter, he understood patience.

Exterminating other monsters mattered, but destroying Korlemo would be like winning a championship, bagging the largest buck. He wouldn't be returning to North Carolina until he either found their vampire or proved it was nowhere near Ramsey. Proving a negative would be difficult.

The woods around Ramsey disturbed him. They were unusually quiet. There weren't the usual stray animals that littered every countryside, not even ubiquitous cats. It was the first, and only, abnormal thing he had discovered about the town. Otherwise, Ramsey was a quintessential small southern town. Right down to the central square bandstand—absent a confederate flag or statue, he was delighted to discover.

Peter decided to spend this evening's sojourn somewhere new. West of Cave City, on the southern edge of Mammoth Cave National Park, he found an ideal spot.

He stepped over spring saplings, upset he hadn't convinced the mwindaji to first scout the house in New Jersey. Only Dad and Thomas voted with him. He should've tried persuading Makeda instead of antagonizing her. He smiled, doubtful she would've had better luck convincing the other mwindaji than he had.

Through the underbrush, his movements were deliberate and guarded. He listened to pitter-patter from small animals scurrying between the trees. Crisp night air enveloped him, leaving him refreshed despite the long hike.

Eager to find animals more interesting than opossums, he carried his rifle, pocketknife, and crossbow. Not that he expected to find any game, but it paid to be prepared.

A breeze wafted above the trees, rustling leaves. Above the treetop canopy sat a high, bright moon. Visibility was excellent.

Two weeks had passed, and they hadn't located any sign of Korlemo—or any other monsters. His thoughts returned to New Jersey as he prepared his arguments for returning.

His boot hung in midair as he detected a disturbance in the brush. His gaze pierced the vegetation. Peter moved stealthily. Up ahead, he detected a slight movement.

Strange sounds grew louder, more pronounced. Peter zeroed in on the location but was still unable to identify the noises. He inched closer, proceeding lightly until he got a clear view.

Past the brush, he noticed two animals engaged in making Shakespeare's metaphorical beast with two backs.

A grin crept across his face. To respect their privacy, he headed in another direction. Before completing the pivot, he hesitated. Though not a voyeur, a sensation compelled him to take another peek. The animals seemed large for coyotes.

Peter locked eyes with the smaller creature, whose glistening green eyes grasped on to his. Incrementally, he examined the animal's face. The snout appeared too long and narrow for a fox—or a wolf. Wolf. *Werewolf.*

His body tensed and his eyes enlarged. In front of him were two werewolves sharing a sexual embrace. The larger werewolf hadn't detected his presence, but its partner kept its gaze positioned on him.

With stealth, Peter removed a rifle from its pouch, leveling it at the carnal exhibition ahead. Though his heart raced, his hands were steady. As he cocked the weapon, the smaller creature assumed a defensive position.

When the rifle exploded, the smaller werewolf collapsed onto the ground, bringing its partner into firing range. Gunshot reverberated throughout the forest. Both werewolves released earsplitting howls. Birds took to the air, land creatures scampered to safety.

As he advanced upon their position, Peter prepared another shot.

In a flash, the smaller werewolf scuttled away, leaped between the trees, and plunged deeper into the woods.

Focused on the larger creature, Peter reached the clearing. An undulating growl escaped from the wounded werewolf. The lycan rolled around, writhing on the ground, soiling itself with blood and debris.

He estimated the werewolf stood at least seven feet tall when upright. Blood and tissue exuded from a cavernous wound in its splintered chest. Crying and moaning on the forest floor, the creature morphed into human form. Anger sparkled in its eyes, but gradually its gaze dissolved into doe-like fear.

Peter lowered his rifle until he detected a movement on his left. Another werewolf was out there. After a glance toward the creature moaning on the ground, he followed the other werewolf's trail.

As time passed, Peter realized he was being led farther into the woods. With no idea how many werewolves were in the area, he reversed direction and decided to leave the other lycan for another day.

Mwindaji preferred to dispose of their kills to avoid detection from law enforcement—and other monsters. Tonight, he didn't have that luxury. Alone in the woods with at least one werewolf unaccounted for, Peter returned to his truck.

Once inside, he laid the rifle down on the adjoining seat and pulled away from the graveled shoulder. Leaves in the wooded area fluttered. Movement disturbed the brush near the spot he had vacated a moment prior.

In the rearview mirror, Peter spied a hulking shadow looming near a burnt oak tree. A long howl rang out from the woods, shaking small branches.

Not eager to confront another werewolf, Peter accelerated. Ten miles down the road, he called Black Ridge.

"Hey, Dad, guess what I found." He relayed his adventure in the woods.

Wiping sweat from his brow, he wondered if Ramsey would prove more interesting than he initially thought.

CHAPTER 15

AS A NURSE, MAKEDA welcomed monotony. Routine hospital patients with stable medical conditions. However, that day the medicine floor had been a pain in the ass. A testament to the opioid epidemic plaguing the country.

In the past week, she'd become acquainted with Lebanon Memorial's regular addicts. None of their current patients on the medicine floor succumbed to the disease, but she understood a few unfortunate souls never left the ER alive. Instead, they received a one-way ticket to the morgue.

Tomorrow, Dad and Thomas would arrive in Ramsey. Peter's discovery of werewolves increased the probability Korlemo lived nearby. The ancient vampire's association with the hospital remained a mystery, though. Makeda wanted to find him first.

She felt her leadership in the investigation dwindling. For the first time, Dad had allowed her to conduct a mwindaji mission. Well, not really, but she had been able to assume control in his absence. But once he arrived, she would be demoted back to following his directives.

So far, the hospital failed to yield any leads. Nothing Makeda heard or saw pointed toward Korlemo. Somehow, she had to gain access to the administrative offices.

Makeda massaged her tense neck. She decided to take a break and visit Dr. Bones. The pathologist had interviewed her for the nursing position. They had developed a friendship. One day she hoped to borrow against that relationship. You never knew when you might need a friend.

Unable to locate him in the pathology department, she decided to check the morgue. Its off-white cement walls were as cold as they were depressing. Calling out his name, she opened the door.

A cloud of disinfectant and formaldehyde choked the air. Overhead flickering fluorescent lights cast deep shadows along the concrete walls, heightening the room's drab appearance. Straining to see with the poor lighting, she scanned the room.

"Dr. Bones?"

"Over here, Makeda."

Hunched over a partially draped corpse, Dr. Bones held utensils while another physician in scrubs on the opposite side held a recorder. Together, the two men examined a body displayed on a stainless-steel slab.

Approaching the cadaver, Makeda noticed a pool of sediment and tissue collected around the drain at the foot of the table. She grimaced.

"I came down to see how you were doing."

Dr. Bones had shared with her before that few people came to the pathology department on purpose. She sensed a loneliness in him and made an effort to visit.

Despite his dry, straightforward personality, Dr. Bones thrived in the morgue. Here, he discussed pathology slides, prepared specimens, and dissected cadavers. His enthusiasm disturbed her, but at the same time endeared him to her. The pathologist reveled in his craft.

Because Dr. Bones also served as the county medical examiner, Makeda feigned interest in forensic science. She figured that explanation would account for her interest in corpses. Under the subterfuge of expanding her education, she obtained details about recent deaths in Ramsey, hoping for a lead to Korlemo. She felt a slight twinge of guilt for misleading the pathologist. Occupational hazard.

Makeda didn't believe she was causing any actual harm. She was quite fond of him and he seemed to appreciate their talks. It gave him license to lecture on his interests.

With a gloved hand, he waved her over. "Come here and look at this liver." With a razor-sharp scalpel, he made an incision in the fascia, peeling away layers of fat encasing the pitted organ. Expertly, he removed the desiccated liver, displaying it on the steel table.

She braced herself. The oppressive stench proved decomposition started well before the deceased arrived at the morgue.

"You see these nodules?" Clearing his throat, Dr. Bones prodded purplish lesions on the liver's surface.

Familiar with his distinctive habit of clearing his throat before delivering a long monologue, Makeda settled into listening. Giving obligatory "oohs" and "ahs," she waited for an opportunity to ask about any new arrivals or unusual deaths. Internally, she shook her head. Things she did for the mwindaji.

"I have some excellent tissue slides I took off a patient last week."

Only a pathologist mentioned human tissue slides and cadavers in the same sentence as "*excellent*".

He sliced a piece of tissue from the left lobe of the liver, placing it in a container of fixative. "Remind me to show them to you after we finish."

In the background, a faint sound of sirens interrupted their conversation. A message came across the radio about a corpse. Three sets of eyes switched away from the cadaver toward the doors, which led to the receiving bay. The warning signal increased in pitch.

A flat grin crossed Dr. Bones's lips. "Looks like we have another guest. Time to prepare another bed."

Another one of his personal colloquialisms. She returned a polite smile at his joke. The other pathologist moved away to prepare another table, Makeda presumed.

"You should stay and watch the autopsy. It'll help you with your studies. Practical applications," Dr. Bones said.

Makeda was at the end of a twelve-hour shift and had no interest in spending the evening dissecting a corpse.

"I can't stay tonight, but I'll come down to see the slides another time." She departed, returning to the medicine floor before Dr. Bones cleared his throat again.

***

After completing her shift, Makeda staggered outside. She noticed the sheriff's cruiser parked in front of the morgue.

A light breeze blew raindrops onto her face. The mist wet her hair as she glanced in the direction of the morgue entrance ramp. A half-dozen police vehicles were positioned alongside an ambulance.

Red, flashing headlights eerily spotlighted the doors. Torn between going home or viewing the dissection, fatigue won. Makeda drove home.

Between visions disturbing her sleep and attempting to locate Korlemo, she was beyond fatigued.

CHAPTER 16

INSIDE HIS SON'S ROOM, Enu marched over to the CD player while glaring down at Fatou sprawled across the bed. He turned off the music, silencing—according to the CD case—*Gangsta's Paradise* by Coolio.

His son sat up, his lips formed into an argument. Enu forestalled any protests.

"That music is disturbing your uncle. You need to be more considerate."

"Why, Father?" Fatou tossed aside the magazine he was reading. "He has no consideration for us."

Enu sat on the edge of the bed, placing his hand on Fatou's shoulder. "You do not understand. Korlemo is our father—our leader. He deserves loyalty and obedience."

Fatou slunk from his embrace and restarted the CD player. Music again floated throughout the room, but at a lower volume. "We are his family, not his servants. He can treat Herman like a slave, but not us."

"Do not say such things. He loves us."

Striding up to him, Fatou's brows creased. "My uncle doesn't care about anyone. Not even his *own* family. He sold his soul to avenge his pride and cursed us for eternity."

"He made a great sacrifice for us."

Though Enu opened his arms to embrace him, Fatou turned away.

Instead, Enu waved his arms around the room, pointing out the stereo system, an enormous television, and game systems encompassing an entire wall. "Look at what you have. Electronics, an extensive wardrobe, without having to raise a finger. You have more than you could ever want."

"Except my freedom and a regular life." Fatou plopped back onto the bed and retrieved the magazine.

Enu frowned. "Would you trade this life to live like a bindimèn?"

Only the sound of pages turning filled the room. A full minute passed before Fatou spoke. "I don't know. Living forever isn't so great if you can't do what you want."

At the bedroom window, Enu stared at his son's back and considered. He stood aside and drew back the heavy drapes, careful that sunlight did not fall on him or Fatou.

He remembered sunsets, how the sun warmed his skin. Sweat beading on his forehead then cooling in the African breezes. Many moons had passed since sunrays warmed his ebony skin. Perhaps Fatou had a point.

He shook away those thoughts and again turned off the music player. Before Fatou could protest, he held up his hand.

"I need to speak with you about your nighttime excursions."

A gentle grin splayed across Fatou's lips, but he remained silent.

"Do not lie to me. Herman complained about young people killing vagrants around Ramsey. It must stop. Dr. Senegal is concerned. It has been mentioned at quorum."

Fatou yawned and perused the magazine. "Quorum is stupid. It doesn't mean anything. Besides, I am not a child. I have lived for hundreds of years."

Enu lowered his voice, punctuating each word. "You are my child. And quorum is the government of our community.

There, the leaders of our tribe decide our future."

"Get real." Fatou leaped off the bed, bypassed Enu, and turned on the CD player. "Uncle Korlemo decides our future."

"Nevertheless, these deaths have garnered the attention of the bindimèn. Our safety is threatened."

Engrossed in the magazine, Fatou ignored him. Rhythm pulsed from the speakers.

Lowering his head, Enu left the room, noiselessly shutting the door. As he walked down the hallway, he realized Fatou spoke the truth. Enu knew Korlemo controlled his family's future. Pretending ignorance of that fact made life tolerable.

As Enu returned to his apportioned section of his brother's mansion, he contemplated Fatou's words. Was freedom preferable to eternal life?

CHAPTER 17

BECAUSE THE WINDOW SHADES were drawn, the living room was dark when Peter entered. He yawned and pulled the shirt over his head.

Makeda had left early that morning for work.

Using the remote control, Peter clicked on the television and watched the news while preparing breakfast. After eating and cleaning the kitchen, he grabbed his gear and departed.

He had a suspicion werewolves used the cave systems for shelter, or sport. Either way, he intended to check it out. Not that he required more proof, but Dad wanted Korlemo. In truth, Peter simply appreciated caves. Spelunking, like hunting, centered around nature.

***

When Peter arrived at Mammoth Cave National Park, he paid the entrance fee and registered for a cave tour. He opened his bag for the park ranger to inspect. Because they checked for contraband, Peter hid his retractable lance in the strap of the backpack. He would prefer to carry a gun, but at least he had some protection—in case.

Since arriving in Kentucky, Peter had completed several cave tours. He learned their routine. This one resembled the others.

At the beginning of the tour, park rangers herded partici-pants into one of the larger cave chambers. As an informational guide droned on, overhead lights were extinguished, plunging the room into complete darkness. People made silly noises. Children cried. In those few moments of darkness, Peter slipped away.

Once he left the group, Peter turned on his headlamp and journeyed into the unauthorized section of the caverns. Despite the dampness, the temperature felt comfortable. In a few minutes, he traveled far enough away from the group that he no longer heard the rangers. Increasing the headlamp's intensity, Peter relaxed and explored.

Without incessant lectures from the rangers, the cavern noises were perceptible, adding a nuanced atmosphere to the experience. Smooth rock walls displayed a myriad of colors and formations. Treacherous stalactites dripped water onto the ground, making the surface slick. Already Peter had bumped his head on two of the rocky projections.

Water drizzled rhythmically, soothing his thoughts. Comfortable in his hike, Peter's thoughts flowed to his girlfriend, Brenda. They had dated since high school. Both of their families insisted they complete their education before things progressed. Although Brenda left North Carolina to attend college, when she returned their relationship resumed. In a clothes drawer at home, Peter had squirreled away enough money to buy her an engagement ring.

He considered taking a piece of rock home as a gift. While thinking about Brenda, Peter tripped over a stalagmite and slipped. Unable to break his fall, he tumbled off the walkway and down into the cavern. His headlamp flew off. Everything went dark.

He couldn't see his hands. Fortunately, only his ego was bruised. Peter retrieved a lighter from his pocket, assessed the surroundings, and ascertained where he landed.

On hands and knees, he searched the ground for his head-lamp. Crawling along the cave floor, he realized a Bic lighter wasn't a good illuminator. *Note to self: get a better backup light.*

Then he remembered his cell phone. Within minutes, he found the lamp. With the headlamp in place, Peter peered over a precipice extending farther below into the cavern. Scattered along the bottom were objects of varied shapes and configurations. Bulkier pieces drew his attention. He adjusted the angle of the lamp and scrutinized the area again. *Bones.*

Hundreds of bones were scattered in pieces, others more assembled. Despite his limited expertise, Peter recognized the skeletal remains were human. He crept away from the cliff's edge.

A noise—not exactly a squeak—crooned above his head. It sounded more like a flutter. Either way, it was time to move. Scratching noises amplified to a shriek.

Peter's pulse soared. Sweat oozed down his back. After a deep breath, he glanced up at the pathway from where he had fallen.

The damp, smooth walls proved impossible to scale free-hand. Using a small cord from his backpack, Peter searched for something to latch on to and scale the wall. Enormous stalagmites loomed above and looked ideal.

Fluttering sounds increased in pitch. Bats.

Peter's shoulders relaxed. *Might as well take a picture for Thomas.* When the next group of bats flew overhead, he snapped a picture with his phone. *Those were some big ass bats.*

Hairs rose on the back of his neck. Something was wrong. *Move.*

After forming the cord into a lasso, Peter hurled it up toward the walking path. It made a thud on the ground and slunk back down. A howl echoed around the cavern. His blood froze. *Hustle.*

His fingers trembled as he made another toss. This time, the cord caught on to a piece of stalagmite. Once he evaluated its safety, Peter scaled the side of the cavern using whatever crags or crevices possible.

Howling inside the cavern decreased in intensity, but the air shifted. Peter detected something approaching. He didn't plan on being around when it arrived. Three minutes later, he arrived at the summit.

While he inspected his scraped hands, the torn twine slid past him and down below. Gripping the edge of the pathway, Peter gathered his strength and swung his leg over the edge of the wall. The momentum created allowed him to hoist his body over the ridge and onto the pathway.

Lying supine, Peter's chest heaved as he gazed upward.

Bats soared overhead. The headlamp spotlighted the flying mammals hanging upside down. Peter rested while he and the bats stared at each other. A movement in the cavern below attracted his attention. Gingerly, Peter peered over the rim. He startled backward as a pale face met his.

At first, Peter noticed intense velvety red eyes set against a vacant countenance. The vampire seemed to float in space.

Peter scrambled to his feet. He peeked down the pathway from where he had left the tour group. In the seconds it took for him to turn around, the vampire landed on the walkway less than ten yards away. A crooked scowl spread across its face. The headlamp glistened off its menacing, pointed canines.

Retreating a step, Peter reached into his pack for a weapon. His head banged against a stalactite. *Dammit.* He tottered on the slick ground and floundered, trying to regain his balance.

During his distraction, the vampire pounced. Its outstretched arms lunged for Peter's neck, knocking him down onto his back. The vampire loomed over him as its mouth opened wide. Peter slapped a large silver cross across its face and rolled aside.

Smoke wafted off its skin. The vampire jerked upright, screaming. An acrid smell emanated from its melting, burning flesh. Its elongated, curved fingers probed the area of molten tissue.

Peter vaulted to his feet and ran.

With surprising fluidity, the vampire flitted in front of him, blocking his escape.

For a second, Peter was disoriented by its rapid movement. He faltered as his mind frantically reviewed his options. His sweaty shirt clung to his chest. His heartbeat hammered in his ears.

A cocky grin spread across the bloodsucker's lips right before it attacked.

In one motion, Peter slid the lance from his backpack and thrust it into the vampire's chest. In under a minute, the monster dissolved. Waiting only long enough for the creature to disintegrate, Peter fled.

The atmosphere compressed. Electricity buzzed around the cavern. Bat chatter ricocheted off the walls.

Peter sped up.

A faint blush of light materialized ahead. He discerned the park rangers' voices. Realizing he was near the tour group, Peter chanced a peek at his rear. Two vampires were gaining on his position. As the distance between them shortened, the vampire closest to Peter sneered.

Unnerved at the taunting, Peter swallowed hard. Torn between anger and fright, he chastened himself for not being better prepared. If werewolves were in the area, so were vampires. A mwindaji couldn't afford mistakes.

Peter's fingers tightened around the lance as he raced down the pathway. His legs ached, but he pushed harder.

When the rangers turned out the lights in the cavernous room, Peter removed his headlamp and slipped back into the sanctioned tour area. Wiping sweat from his face, he stowed his weapons in the pack.

As the room lit up, he intermingled with the other attendees. Peter glanced back down the pathway. Sanguine vampire eyes haunted the space, hovering in the air as their bodies disappeared. Eventually, they retreated into the caverns. Like a maw, the cave gaped, ready to consume anyone careless enough to enter unprepared.

Once safely in his truck, Peter called Dad. "Have you guys left yet?"

"Not yet. Did you enjoy the cave tour?"

"Yeah." Peter viewed the picture he had snapped in the cave. "Tell Thomas I have a surprise for him."

As he suspected, his photograph captured more than bats. Now they had actual proof of vampires in the area.

But where was Korlemo?

CHAPTER 18

In the Ramsey rental home, Makeda lay in bed. She peeled open one eye to check the time. The clock read 1:00 a.m. *What woke me up?*

She needed sleep. Dinner with Michael lasted longer than expected. He had become a delightful diversion, but one she could ill afford.

Makeda planned to check out Human Resources to secure conclusive evidence of Korlemo's affiliation with the hospital before her dad and Thomas arrived.

Twice, Peter had tried—and failed—to get onto the fifth floor where the administrative offices were located. As she contemplated how to gain access, sleep arrived.

Unsure of the hour, when Makeda awoke this time, the air was oppressive. Her breathing quickened as if the room contracted. She tried to sit up but couldn't move.

In her periphery, a shadow formed. Near the bed, an irregular, shadowy shape wriggled along the wall. She struggled to rise. Her brain fired signals off to her body, ordering her limbs to obey, but there was no response. *What the hell?!*

Her gaze widened. Attempts to move her limbs proved unsuccessful. She was paralyzed. As that reality solidified in her mind, she slowed her breathing. *Don't freak out.* It was simply a hypnogogic experience and would pass. She'd had them before.

Minutes passed. Unable to move, Makeda studied the shadows along the wall. Piecemeal, the shadowy figures merged.

She blinked rapidly to clear any film that might be altering her vision. No, what she viewed was real. The shadows started to consolidate, forming a more defined shape.

She remembered stories Yewande told her about emis and bdomas, good and evil spirits, respectively. *Please let this be an emi.*

Bile rose in her throat. She flailed against the mattress—at least internally. Again, her body rejected her directions. In her head she screamed and tussled.

While she fought to move, the shadow acquired a human form. With a kyphotic back and bent arms, it peeled itself off the wall and approached the bed.

Makeda's heart sank. Understanding her impotence, she forced herself to concentrate. *Relax, stop struggling, embrace your weakness.*

Her eyes closed. She recited a spell Yewande taught her. Internally, she sensed the exact moment when the apparition hovered over her. After a beat, she flung her eyes open and glowered at the ghost. The intensity of her glare was her sole weapon. To her surprise, the apparition retreated.

Suspended in the air about a foot away from the bed—to her horror—it spoke. *'Fè atansyon. Li se isit la Sèvi ak fòs ou yo. Li tou pre.'*

Although she couldn't decipher what was said, Makeda recognized the language as Haitian Creole. *Who would speak to her in Creole?*

The faceless apparition continued. *'Sèvi ak ladrès ou. Sèvi ak yo.'*

'Who are you? What do you want from me?'

Bang. Bang.

Someone beat upon her door. The hinges creaked.

With a glance toward the entrance, the spirit evaporated.

Pounding on the door increased.

"Makeda!" Peter shouted from the other side of her bedroom door.

Though she heard him, she still couldn't move.

"Open the door!"

Afraid he would break it down, Makeda struggled to rise. But before she regained control of her body, the door crashed in. As soon as Peter burst into the room, the trance lifted. Makeda's body bolted upright, but her movements remained sluggish.

Peter ran to her side, partially lifted and shook her. "Makeda?"

For once, she appreciated his overbearing watchfulness. Her chest heaved as she gasped. She trembled and clutched on to his chest. Secure in Peter's arms, she scanned the room for any spirits.

Rocking her gently, he draped her thick, curly hair behind her ears and studied her face. "You okay? What happened?"

She opened her mouth to speak but uttered nothing.

"I heard something moving in here and I thought that skinhead across the street broke in," Peter said.

As each second passed, Makeda regained her bearings. Finally, she shook her head and found her voice. "It was a nightmare. I'm okay." Her pulse moderated, but she still clung to him.

"This is too much for you. When Dad gets here—"

She pushed off his chest and unwrapped herself from his arms.

"I'm fine." Scooting off the bed, she staggered to her feet. "I was spooked. Something in the morgue must have upset me."

Disbelief reflected in Peter's somber gaze. Mwindaji encountered horrible things all the time. Makeda knew he would doubt anything in a morgue could compare to the horrors they'd witnessed.

"I'll grab my tools and fix the door." He started to leave, then swung around. "This isn't a competition. If something's wrong, you can tell me." Without waiting for a reply, he left.

***

In the bathroom, Makeda splashed water onto her face and stared in the mirror at her blood-shot eyes. Memories of her great-grandmother swirled in her mind. People said she resembled Yewande. Makeda was in grade school when she died. It was the first time she had lost someone she loved.

After the funeral, Makeda rested in Yewande's bedroom. Wrapped in homemade quilts, she felt cradled in her great-grandmother's arms. One evening, she dreamt the nonagenarian sat on the edge of the bed, comforting her.

'*Te kato buzungu,*' the voice had said. '*Iteka moliku chane.*'

Those Baoumali words—the language of the zaubers—had both excited and calmed her. Yewande told her not to worry; she would always be with her.

More than ever, Makeda regretted closing her mind to her great-grandmother. These visions were becoming stronger, but she didn't understand or know what to do about them. She missed Yewande, and more importantly needed her.

The telepathic messages were in Creole. Nadege was the only person she knew who would speak to her in Creole. But the apparition had been faceless. Could her Haitian patient be responsible for the messages? They had shared an unusual bond.

At the sink, Makeda stared into the bowl. She realized things changed after Haiti—looked different, smelled strange.

She had chalked it up to the amazing experience of working in Port-au-Prince. *Could it be something else?*

If Nadege understood kasi kasi, she would have to be a zauber—or at least a witch. Makeda recalled the incident with the interpreter and the word mambo. Nadege must have recognized she was also a zauber.

From the intensity of Nadege's words, it didn't sound like a social visit. What could be so important? *More to the point, how can I decipher the messages?*

After disrobing, Makeda stepped into the shower, vowing to accomplish two tasks right away: learn Creole, and practice more sorcery. Hot water splashed against her tense muscles. Makeda extended her neck, allowing water to stream down her face.

Peter's hammering the bedroom door back onto its hinges prevented her from completely relaxing.

How to reach Yewande?

As heat loosened her body, a troubling thought coalesced in her mind. If Nadege went to the effort of contacting her, something was terribly wrong. An ancient vampire might be the least of her worries.

CHAPTER 19

IN THE STUDY, PAPERS covered Korlemo's desk. He sipped bourbon from a crystal goblet while reading financial reports. A minute ago, he had noticed Enu standing beside the study door. His jaw grinded.

"What are you fretting about now, brother? Come in or go away. You distract me."

Herman had dropped off the financial reports yesterday evening. Though not proficient in economics, Korlemo understood enough to realize his bank accounts contained a healthy balance, more than sufficient for his present needs.

Enu took a seat beside the desk.

Setting aside the papers, Korlemo examined his brother. Though younger than him, Enu looked older. Gray peppered his short afro. Wrinkles, like spokes of a tire, radiated from the lateral corners of his eyes.

"You need to feed. You're showing your age."

Enu craned his neck across the desk, reading the documents. "I have no interest in, as you say, *feeding*. I receive more than sufficient nourishment from our weekly allotment."

"How can you be content having nourishment doled out to you? Come with me tonight. There will be more than enough to satisfy us both." Korlemo knitted his fingers together behind his head and reclined into the plush chair.

Enu frowned. "How long can this continue? The bindimèn are suspicious."

Behind the rosewood desk, Korlemo stood and paced before the bookcase. "Bindimèn are stupid. Besides, we control Ramsey. There is nothing to fear."

"The sheriff is investigating recent deaths. Sylvia says—"

"What Sylvia says is unimportant," Korlemo said, raising his voice and leaning into Enu's face. "She is paid to keep our secrets. If necessary, she will eliminate the sheriff."

"Money is always your solution. One day, that answer will come up short." Frowning, Enu moved to the coffee-colored sofa facing the expansive manicured lawn.

"Money solves problems." Korlemo dusted a speck from his dress slacks. "If you do not feed, you will age yourself into an early grave. You hardly resemble a younger brother."

"I am not afraid to die. Sometimes, I feel I have lived long enough."

Korlemo threw back his head with a loud guffaw. "Of course you do. You refuse to be satisfied. What do you desire that you do not have?"

"This is not the life I envisioned. Too many years have elapsed. I have seen more death than one man should."

With a chuckle, Korlemo returned to his desk. "Well, I plan to feed tonight." He noticed Enu's grimace. "Are you bothered that I enjoy sucking the life out of bindimèn?"

Shaking his head, Enu began to depart.

"Wait. I require another musician. The last pianist … disappeared." The grin across Korlemo's face grew as he uttered the last word.

Enu groaned. "I cannot continue to replace the help, brother. People talk. We are far from town. Many laborers refuse to work in the country—not to mention tolerating our particular needs."

At the sideboard, Korlemo prepared himself a drink. "Ridiculous. Offer them more money."

"With you it will always come to money," Enu said, gesticulating and raising his voice.

In a whirl, Korlemo swung around, baring his teeth. "It is your duty to see to my needs. Figure it out. I want another musician." He watched Enu as he drank.

Though his brother remained impassive, Korlemo knew Enu would obey. Despite his personal feelings, Enu remained loyal. The last words of their mother, as she took her dying breath, had been for Enu to obey Korlemo—and he had.

Relaxed by the liquor, Korlemo wondered if he should order Enu to find him a zauber. Then he remembered the interpretations from the last three sorceresses, and his mood soured. Women had figured prominently in his life—though not positively.

Where was Herman? They needed to discuss their arrangements. Kentucky was becoming less welcoming.

CHAPTER 20

TOWARD THE END OF her shift on the medicine floor, Makeda received a call from a friend in Human Resources.

"Hey, Jeff. What's up?"

"One of the third-shift surgery nurses called out. The unit will be shorthanded if I can't find someone to fill in. Are you interested?"

Although it meant working twenty-four hours, she agreed. Surgery and psychiatry were the two floors she had yet to examine. Both were secured 24/7, with access limited to assigned hospital personnel. Only immediate family members were permitted patient visits.

At the end of her medicine shift, Makeda trekked up the staircase to the third floor.

Not bothering with personal introductions, the charge nurse detailed Makeda's duties, giving her an impromptu tour around the unit, explaining where the medications and supplies were located. Makeda received her patient assignments while contemplating where to search first.

The charge nurse said, "The third-shift supervisor will be here in an hour. Until then, you can familiarize yourself with the floor."

"Thanks, but I'll grab dinner before the shift begins."

Instead of going to the cafeteria, Makeda decided to visit Dr. Bones, see if anything noteworthy happened—suspicious deaths, corpses with teeth marks in their necks.

In the morgue, Dr. Bones was at the sink, cleaning up. Apparently ready to depart.

"Hello," she said.

He glanced up a second before returning to cleaning instruments. "You missed a great case the other day, Makeda. If you want to understand forensics, you need to live in the morgue. You can't expect to learn if you don't attend class."

"I know. Next time, I promise."

After placing instruments inside a cabinet, he walked over to a wall of small gray doors. He unfastened one of the locks and pulled out a long stainless-steel drawer. It creaked along rusted rails. An acrylic beige cloth draped over a body.

Cold from the freezer billowed past her. Makeda watched him work.

With professional zeal, he explained their newest arrival while moving the corpse to a steel table. "The police discovered this man in the woods south of town."

Though familiar with dead bodies and their odors, Makeda recoiled at the appearance of this specimen. Breathing through her mouth, she approached the table and examined various cuts and tears along the torso and neck. Torn muscles surrounded the abdominal cavity. Rough irregular edges framed an empty expanse.

She pointed to the torso, flayed open with a typical Y-incision. "Were these caused by the autopsy?"

"No, those wounds were post-mortem."

Postmortem? That suggested the person died and then was gutted. She studied the corpse again. Its head lay on the right shoulder, essentially decapitated. She sensed Dr. Bones observing her as she inspected the deceased. She bit the inside of her lip and guarded her emotions.

"The body was eviscerated after death," he said. "Hunters unearthed him. Police identified him as a drifter, a known drug addict."

After gloving, Makeda picked up a stainless-steel probe from an assortment of instruments on the countertop, examining the ragged-edged tissues framing the abdominal cavity. The absence of blood left the hollowed space a pasty yellow tinge. Skin tissue had faded to gray. Muscles were now a muted red.

"Where are the organs?"

Dr. Bones removed his glasses, cleaning them with gauze. "The sheriff's department didn't locate any organs. The liver, kidneys, spleen, heart—all gone. Coyotes probably ate them."

As he droned on about the opioid epidemic, his voice diminished into white noise. Makeda's attention was riveted on the corpse. She found the head most unsettling.

The deceased's ear hung limply, askew from the rest of the head. Severed vessels radiated outward from the neck at incongruent angles. She shuddered at the savagery that left the man's throat exposed.

Faced away from her at the sink, Dr. Bones resumed cleaning instruments while commenting on the ills of society. "He was probably intoxicated. The drug screen is pending. Coyotes attacked while he was unconscious. He wouldn't be able to fight them off. Scavengers picked him apart."

Makeda doubted his assessment. The death appeared suspicious, especially now she knew werewolves and vampires inhabited the area. While his back was turned, she gave careful attention to the jugular area, trying to identify anatomy among the damaged topography.

Once Dr. Bones finished washing the instruments, he removed his glasses and cleaned them again. "I ruled the death an accident. Another unfortunate casualty in this epidemic."

Seemingly comfortable with his assessment, he hummed an unfamiliar tune.

While bending over the corpse for a closer inspection, Makeda glanced at her watch. "Oh, no. Sorry, I have to go." She dropped the probe onto the tray.

Leaving the morgue, she jogged across the lobby. The hospital was winding down. Staff and visitors alike were departing. She took the stairs two at a time and managed to arrive at the surgical floor on time.

Once on the surgery unit, Makeda proceeded to the nursing station. Patient rooms were located on the right side of the hallway, with a supply room on the left. A mirror image hallway was on the other side of the supply room with corresponding patient rooms.

A U-shaped countertop encircled the nursing station. Computers and chairs were positioned around the area where medical staff completed their documentation. Weaving her way behind the counter, Makeda introduced herself to the third-shift charge nurse.

The woman had nonexistent lips and beady eyes. "The surgical floor gets *very* busy during third shift. If you have any questions, let me know. And under *no* circumstances are you to go back into the operating suite."

Five yards behind the nursing station stood two imposing stainless-steel doors, secured with a key card entry. The warning drew Makeda's gaze toward the entrance and teased her curiosity. Instantly, her mind contemplated how to get on the other side.

"You'll be working out here on post op," the nurse said.

Makeda's brow rose. "There are surgeries scheduled tonight?"

The nurse nodded. "All surgeries at Lebanon Memorial occur at night."

Highly unusual, but Makeda didn't comment. She intended to use her assignment on the surgical floor to search for evidence of Korlemo.

"I should check on my patients."

A quick circuit around the floor showed it to be a typical hospital unit with linoleum floors, drab beige walls, and aggressive, bright, overhead fluorescent lights. Incessant sounds of machines beeping, televisions blaring, and families conversing confirmed it. Makeda detected nothing different from the other hospitals where she had worked. She introduced herself to her patients and returned to the nursing station to enter patient vitals into the electronic health record.

Kitty—short for Katherine—had introduced herself during sign-in. Already, Makeda realized she was the nicest nurse at Lebanon Memorial.

Kitty whispered, "Makeda, would you cover for me while I go to the bathroom?" Before she left, Kitty explained that her patient with the ostomy bag needed a dressing change, but she would complete it when she returned.

"No problem, I'll take care of it."

After the dressing change, Makeda noticed the other nurses were preoccupied. Their faces were buried in patient charts, cell phones, or both. *Time to check out the OR.*

She hurried toward the locked doors but was interrupted by a call for help. In a patient room two doors from the operating suite, Makeda found an elderly patient holding a call button.

Reclined in the hospital bed, Rose was enveloped in blankets and a homemade quilt. Her white fluffy hair contrasted with her ruddy cheeks.

Barry, Rose's husband, kept vigil in a chair on the left, watching television while firmly grasping her hand. They appeared well positioned for a night of television and popcorn. The room, cluttered with discarded food containers, smelled of liniment and grease.

Rose's glass-blue eyes beckoned. "Would you move this IV for me, sweetie?"

"Yes, ma'am." In under a minute Makeda obtained the items required and examined the site. She stopped the IV drip while making small talk and securing the stop valve.

Rose and Barry watched attentively.

"It itches," Rose said, scratching her antecubital area.

Lightly tapping on Rose's hand and wrist, Makeda searched for a better IV site. A nice plump vein popped up, and Makeda prepped the skin.

Barry turned down the volume on the television. "Where yah from, young lady?"

"North Carolina."

The needle pierced Rose's skin, and she winced. "Where'd you get the name Makeda?"

"My great-grandmother. It's Ethiopian for the queen of Sheba."

Rose smiled, patting the Bible on the bedside table. "We know about her from the Bible. Don't we, Barry?"

His double chins jiggled. "You don't have an accent. Do yuh?"

"No." Makeda explained that because she attended school up north, she had lost her southern accent. In truth, she never had one. None of the Crawford children did. Their work took them across the country. An accent brought unwanted scrutiny.

Once she completed the IV, Makeda cleaned the area and prepared to remove the old line. She frowned, noticing two puncture wounds in Rose's left antecubital. Careful to remove the tape without damaging the paper-thin skin, Makeda inspected the site.

"Don't worry, sweetie. It always takes a lot of pokes to get an IV in me. Right, Barry?"

Her husband chuckled. "That's right."

Not wanting to alert the couple that something was amiss, Makeda grinned, pretending to accept their explanation. "Would you like me to remove the dressing from your neck too?"

"Oh, yes, dear. Thank you."

It took a moment, but Rose settled back onto the pillows and craned her neck to the opposite side, providing an unhindered view of the area below the mandibular angle.

With a better visual, Makeda removed the dressing and discovered more puncture wounds.

"Rose is full of holes." Barry laughed.

His wife giggled.

To continue the charade, Makeda smiled. But she didn't believe it to be the joke the couple thought. Repeated attempts to gain intravenous access in the same location was unusual. *Besides, why would Rose require intrajugular access in the first place?*

It was generally reserved for critically ill patients, specific monitoring, or patients receiving medications requiring a central line. None of that applied to Rose. It didn't make sense.

Right then, Makeda didn't have time to ponder the implications. She removed the old dressings. Once she secured and cleaned the sites, she departed.

Seeing no one in the hallway, Makeda tiptoed toward the steel doors leading to the operating suite. When she stood a foot away from the keypad, heavy, mechanized doors swung open. She hopped aside as two nurses in scrubs and wearing face masks wheeled a patient out on a gurney. Intravenous lines were forgotten as Makeda tended to patients.

An hour passed. Fluorescent lights dimmed as dinner trays were removed. Visiting hours concluded. The surgical floor, though, became busier.

What operating suite functioned at night? For emergencies, of course, but not routine procedures.

Not long after visiting hours ended, surgical staff wheeled patients out of the operating suite every thirty minutes. The unit hummed with activity until dawn.

Makeda had never experienced anything like it. However, the patients she examined appeared fine. Nothing untoward seemed to have happened to them as far as she noticed. The nurses managed their cases like they would at any other medical facility.

Rose's IV site still disturbed her, though. Intrajugular access was a difficult procedure, prone to infection or injury to the surrounding vessels. Patients that ill were usually transferred to intensive care.

Hours passed before the floor quieted. Makeda and the other nurses returned to their documentation. Before she had time for a break, sign-out arrived. She never had an opportunity to view the operating suite. Accustomed to a slower third-shift routine, she was exhausted.

Once she finished charting, Makeda slipped down the hallway. She wanted to send Peter a text about when she would be home. Before she hit send, a patient cried out for help. Though not one of her assigned patients, because the other nurses were occupied, Makeda decided to help. *Shouldn't take long.* Since she couldn't view the operating suite, she was ready to leave.

Inside the patient room, Makeda switched on the overhead lamps. Lighting sputtered, casting the room in shadow. Her eyes required a moment to adjust.

In the hospital bed, a woman of generous build with rumpled brown hair and blond highlights moaned and tossed. From the doorway, her face appeared pale but animated. Makeda strode up to the bedside and switched off the call light, scrutinizing the woman's shimmering eyes.

The woman's voice was low and croaked, "Help me."

Palming the patient's clammy wrist, Makeda calculated her pulse and respirations.

"Help me, please." During her pleading, the woman grabbed Makeda's scrubs and squeezed her breast.

"I'm going to help you," Makeda said, wincing and extricating herself from the woman's vicelike grip. She gritted her teeth and tried to calm the woman. There would be a bruise, but she managed to salvage her breast. "Hold on a moment. What's the problem?"

"They're trying to kill me."

Great. She immediately regretted coming into the room. From a medical chart hanging at the end of the bed, Makeda checked to see if the woman had mental health issues—or maybe hallucinations from the anesthesia. Nothing. Running on fumes, she mustered the little compassion she had left.

"I'm here to help you."

The name tag on the woman's wrist read Susan Topper.

Makeda hoped her voice sounded soothing because her heart wasn't in it. "Who's trying to hurt you, Susan?"

"Not here. In there." Susan pointed her chin toward the door. "The doctor. He tried to kill me. They're all trying to kill me."

"Okay. Tell me what happened." Makeda straightened the bedsheets and checked the IV, reading the name of Susan's medication. An antibiotic, but no psychotropics.

"The doctors. When I went in for my surgery."

Pulse steady. No tachycardia or dyspnea. Makeda continued her examination. "Go on."

"The vampire …"

Once Makeda heard the word *vampire*, nothing else registered. Her brain did a double take, missing the next few words. She asked Susan to repeat herself.

"… vampire. When he placed the mask over my face—"

Dumbfounded, she hovered over Susan. "Who, the anesthesiologist?"

"Huh? Who?" Susan stared back with shimmering eyes. "Yeah—I guess. He thought I was asleep, but I wasn't. His face got closer, then he bent to the side. I thought he was checking my breathing, but he bit me in the neck—and I screamed. And someone said, "She's awake." The vampire stood up, and I saw blood dripping from his teeth. My blood!"

"Look, tell me everything—quick. And try to be quiet."

Susan had her complete attention, but Makeda needed to get more information fast. Her shift had ended. Soon, the first-shift nurses would arrive.

Their heads huddled together as Susan explained what occurred in the operating room. Susan detailed how she screamed and fought until someone held her down and shoved the mask over her face.

Susan's eyes filled with tears. Her pale face appeared sunken under those enormous eyes. When she grabbed Makeda this time, she assaulted an arm.

"Please. You've got to help me."

Makeda understood her desperation. She'd encountered

many vampires but couldn't image the terror of being under their control.

The first problem was how to get Susan out of the hospital. Makeda's mental faculties were stretched, but she managed to formulate a plan—at least for Susan.

What about the rest of the patients? Could this be an isolated incident? The evidence from Rose's IV sites negated this being a one-time occurrence. Was this evidence of Korlemo? Her head ached. She needed to alert the mwindaji.

As she spoke, Makeda retrieved Susan's purse from a side drawer. "Call your husband. Tell him to come to the hospital *now*. Say it's an emergency, but you can't explain over the phone."

While detailing the plan, Makeda explained she would stay until Susan's husband arrived. Once they left the hospital, Susan could tell him what occurred. They should go straight home. Makeda would have her brothers escort them to another hospital.

At that moment, the door opened.

The first-shift nurse entered and marched up to the bedside. She interposed herself between Makeda and Susan, reading from a typed list.

"Hello, Mrs. Topper. I'm going to be your nurse this morning."

"I'm staying with Mrs. Topper until her husband arrives," Makeda said, ignoring the nurse's behavior. She circled around to the other side of the bed and held Susan's hand.

"That won't be necessary. I can keep her company."

Susan clutched on to Makeda with both hands. "I want her to stay."

From the way the nurse stomped out of the room, Makeda knew the discussion wasn't over. But she had more questions.

Her gaze turned from the door where the nurse exited to discover Susan had drifted off to sleep. Makeda understood Susan was exhausted *and* traumatized, but she needed answers.

A vampire in the operating room explained why the hospital conducted surgeries in the evenings. Vampires using an operating room to drink patients' blood sounded farfetched, but possible. If Susan was correct, Makeda needed to verify the hospital's complicity and identify the bad actors involved.

A scowling nurse supervisor returned with the first-shift nurse in tow. The nurse supervisor said, "Makeda, your shift's over. It's time for you to go."

Susan startled awake and reached out for her again.

Hard lines around the supervisor's mouth gave Makeda little choice but to offer an explanation. She peeled Susan's fingers off her forearm and motioned for the nurses to accompany her outside.

"I need a minute." Makeda glanced back toward Susan. "I promise I'm not going to leave."

Once she was sure Susan could see her from the doorway, Makeda lowered her voice and faced the supervisor. "Mrs. Topper was hallucinating. I calmed her down by promising to stay until her husband arrived."

The first-shift nurse stepped forward. "You don't know what you're doing."

Makeda gave the nurse a mere side-glance, still facing the supervisor. "Maybe not, but I do know my presence made her better. When her husband arrives, I'll leave."

The supervisor's gaze jostled between Makeda and the first-shift nurse. "What happened?"

"I don't know," Makeda said. "She wasn't my assigned patient. I was trying to help."

The first-shift nurse huffed down her nose. "We can deal with Mrs. Topper. You need to go."

"I'll leave when her husband arrives." Makeda pivoted on her heel, returned inside the patient room, and stood guard beside Susan, who had fallen asleep.

The nurses left.

Makeda uttered a Baoumali phrase and flicked her wrist. The hospital room door shut. She then woke up Susan. "Give me your information."

Though she needed to contact her family, Makeda didn't want Susan to overhear the conversation. After sending Peter a text, her gaze fell across the IV line in Susan's left antecubital. Her eyes drifted up to a dressing over Susan's left jugular. There wasn't enough time to remove them, but she knew they would resemble Rose's IV sites.

A quick peek at her phone showed Peter hadn't replied. *Was he out in the woods?*

Next, she texted Thomas. It was early, but if he was up, Thomas would be in front of the television set.

After what felt like an eternity—but was closer to a half hour—Susan's husband arrived. His shirt was unbuttoned and not tucked into his pants. His droopy gaze struggled focusing. He hugged Susan, stifled a yawn, then asked what happened.

Sidestepping his question, Makeda addressed Susan. "Remember what I told you. Insist on leaving against medical advice. Go home. My family will meet you there and take you to Bowling Green."

If vampires lurked in the hospital, they wouldn't let Susan go if they knew she could recount what happened in the operating room.

Makeda gave Susan's husband a stern glare, holding his gaze, hoping to confer the importance of her words. "Get

Susan out of here. When you get home, wait for us. We'll protect you."

The husband frowned and scratched his stubbled chin. He glanced from her to Susan. "But she just had a hysterectomy. She can't leave."

Makeda understood his confusion, but there wasn't time. "Susan will explain everything *after* you leave."

Before departing, Makeda slipped a palm-sized silver crucifix from her pocket into Susan's hand. She had to trust Susan would convince her husband to follow directions. With no weapons, and exhausted from working all night, Makeda was little use to them if it came to a fight with the staff.

Susan accepted the gift and gripped it to her chest.

"Do exactly what I said, and you'll be fine." Makeda left.

***

After clocking out, Makeda rushed to her locker and retrieved her purse. Too much in a hurry to wait for an elevator, she sprinted down the hospital stairs. Where the hell were Peter and Thomas? She had to alert them.

In her Honda, she raced down the two-lane road toward the rental house.

Dawn had crested over the thick tree line as she navigated the small, narrow roads. She scanned the rearview mirror, making sure no one followed. Unfortunately, the morning drive had more perils than vampires. Sirens rang out as blue-and-red lights danced above the police cruiser behind her.

Damn.

Makeda maneuvered onto the shoulder, striking the steering wheel, and mumbling another curse word. Because she had sped out of the hospital parking lot, she couldn't call anyone. On the passenger seat, she glimpsed her phone. Peter had texted back. Too late to answer now. With a glance in the rearview mirror, she knew this wouldn't be a simple ticket.

Sheriff Michael Wilson approached her driver's side window. His hat sat low, shading his eyes. Lips pressed together, pad in hand, he acted official today. In a flat tone, he said, "Roll down your window."

Even as he prepared to write her a ticket, she enjoyed his deep voice. His muscular frame leaned against her door. She wondered if he was upset that she had cancelled their date.

"License and registration."

She complied, regarding him as he scribbled on a pad.

"Do you know how fast you were going?"

"No. I'm sorry, I don't."

"You were flying around some blind curves there. You could've killed someone, or yourself."

He was right, but she didn't care. She made no attempt to reply. Getting home was her primary concern. His gaze bored into her profile, but she looked at the road straight ahead.

He tapped his pen against the pad. "You know this ticket is over four hundred dollars."

She gripped the steering wheel. "I made a mistake. I said I'm sorry."

He crouched down level with her face and stared.

She didn't flinch.

"What's going on, Makeda?"

The concern in his voice was genuine, but she needed to move things along. "I had a difficult double shift, and my last patient was a mess." *The truth, but not the complete truth.*

He stood up, but his gaze remained locked on her. "Look, I'm gonna let you off with a warning this time since your license is clean. But be careful. We get a lot of accidents on this road."

He rapped on the car roof, then stepped away.

She should've thanked him, but she was too glad to be free. Cautiously, she pulled away from the shoulder. In the rearview mirror, she watched his cruiser turn and head in the opposite direction. When he cleared the curve, she stepped on the accelerator and sped home.

CHAPTER 21

THE SUN HADN'T PEEKED over the horizon before Susan's phone call woke Larry from a deep slumber. He'd planned to stop by the hospital later that morning and visit her before going to work at the garage. Instead, her frantic call for help brought him to the hospital earlier than intended.

He dropped their kids off with his parents, who lived next door. In under a half hour, he had arrived at Lebanon Memorial.

With his help, Susan heaved herself out of bed. Larry watched her struggle to dress.

"Su, this is crazy. You just had surgery."

"I don't care. I'm not staying here. Get my bag." Sweat glistened across her forehead.

In her scrunched face, Larry saw determination—and fear. He didn't know what caused it, but right then, he didn't want to argue. After packing her items, he began to carry her.

"No," she said, "get a wheelchair. There should be one by the entrance."

When Larry returned to the room, he found his wife arguing with a nurse.

Susan teetered on the edge of the bed, clutching a pillow to her abdomen. "I don't care. I'm leaving."

He circled around the nurse and assisted Susan into the wheelchair. She swapped the pillow on her lap for the suitcase. While hunched over the bag, Susan nodded toward the door.

The nurse crossed her burly arms over her chest and blocked the exit. "You can't leave unless the doctor discharges you."

"Watch us," Larry said, wheeling around her and departing.

On their heels, the nurse followed, yelling for them to stop.

At the security doors exiting the unit, they encountered another nurse. Frizzy, graying blond hair stood up on end around her forehead, giving her a shocked appearance. This nurse stood with a wide stance, centered in front of the doors.

"Mrs. Topper, this is ridiculous. Please, let us help you back to your room. We can discuss any concerns you have about your treatment. I've already called the doctor. You're only hurting yourself."

Taking his cue from Susan, Larry wheeled out the doors and toward the elevators without responding. Before the elevator doors opened, he heard one of the nurses call for security. He removed a cell phone from the pocket of his jeans and called his in-laws.

"Meet me at the hospital entrance," he said before hanging up.

A doctor and nurse rushed into the elevator before Larry could hit the button to shut the doors. They accompanied Larry and Susan down to the lobby. During the short ride, the medical duo requested that Susan return to her hospital bed. They listed possible complications if she left against medical advice.

Susan stared at the wall and ignored them.

"At least tell me why you want to leave," the doctor asked. "What happened?"

She refused to explain.

The doctor glared at Larry, who glanced down at Susan.

Kneeling beside her wheelchair, the doctor said, "Mrs. Topper, let's return to your room. We can discuss this like reasonable people."

Susan simply shook her head, still avoiding his gaze.

Larry's stubbled, freckled face leaned in toward the doctor. "We ain't going back."

As the elevator doors craned open, he charged forward, causing the doctor to leap aside. Larry zipped through the hospital lobby with the wheelchair clearing their path.

The doctor called after them, "Mrs. Topper is too weak to leave. You're placing your wife in danger. If you care about her, you'll stay."

Though he acted like he didn't hear what the doctor said, Larry *had* listened. He thought about what he was doing. Susan had major surgery. She didn't understand medicine. He didn't understand medicine. Although he had no idea what was going on, he trusted his wife.

To him, Susan was still the bubbly teenager he fell in love with in high school. They married right after graduation once he landed a mechanic job. Within a year, they had the first of their two children.

Susan was the bedrock of their family, confident, not anxious—even as a teen mom. The panic he heard in her voice that morning chilled his lanky frame. Nothing had ever frightened Susan—until now.

At the automatic doors leading outside the hospital, another person blocked their escape.

"Mrs. and Mr. Topper, I'm the hospital ombudsman. My name is …"

Larry tuned the woman out as he scanned the parking lot for his in-laws. He had no idea what an ombudsman was or what they did. All he cared about was getting Susan home.

The ombudsman offered them a concession to appease Susan's concerns if they returned to the hospital room.

A beeping horn from a tan minivan announced the arrival of his in-laws. With the ombudsman momentarily distracted by the noise, Larry propelled the wheelchair out the sliding doors.

At the minivan, he handed the suitcase to his father-in-law. "Help me with Susan."

A doubled-over Susan pressed her balled-up coat to her abdomen. She shivered. A small trickle of blood ran down her forearm where she had pulled out her own IV.

Larry threw his jacket over her shoulders, lifted her from the chair, and placed her into the back seat.

With a shrill cry, the ombudsman waived a document in front of the car window, trying to get Susan's attention. "If you insist upon leaving, Mrs. Topper, you have to sign this document."

Susan stitched her lips together and turned away from the window, religiously rubbing a crucifix the Black nurse gave her. Her lips trembled.

Larry heard her repeatedly mumbling something. He studied her lips, trying to decipher what she said. It was a prayer. *What in the hell made my wife suddenly find religion?* At best, they were agnostic. The last time they attended church was for a friend's wedding.

While he considered Susan's praying, the ombudsman shoved a document in his face. Like a fly at a picnic, the paper waved before him.

"If your wife won't sign the form, then you can, Mr. Topper," the ombudsman said, handing him a pen. She placed the document on the hood of the van. With a spindly finger, she instructed him where to sign.

Larry's brow wrinkled as he hesitated and read over the form.

His father-in-law crept up beside him. "Don't you sign nothin', boy."

A fog lifted, and Larry snapped to attention. "Go home, Dad. I'll be right behind y'all." He trotted over to his pickup truck, got in, and followed his father-in-law out of the lot.

With the form in her hand, the hospital ombudsman stood alone in the hospital parking lot.

In the rearview mirror, Larry observed the sullen look on her face. He knew there would be hell to pay. It didn't matter though. In his gut, he knew he'd made the right decision. Susan had been in danger, and he got her out just in time. *But from what?*

CHAPTER 22

ON THAT SATURDAY MORNING, Sylvia had no pressing engagements. She had slept in. The week had been trying, and she needed rest. She rolled out of bed and logged on to a yoga app.

Soft light streaked across her mat from an open window. In the middle of mountain pose, her phone rang. With a tap, she ended the shrill ringing and read the screen. Human Resources. A call from the hospital on the weekend couldn't be good.

"Dr. Senegal. I'm sorry to bother you, but it's an emergency. A patient left the surgical unit this morning against medical advice."

Sylvia's jaw tightened.

Minutes elapsed as the caller detailed what had unfolded.

"Get me the surgeon on call last night." She muted the yoga app and waited outside on the patio deck with her sandal-clad feet propped up on the metal railing as she gazed up into the graying morning sky.

"Here he is," the Human Resources person said before switching over the call.

A bored baritone voice came on the line. "Good morning."

Her foot tapped against the rail. "I would like to speak with Dr. Ruphert."

"I'm sorry, but he's not available. May I take a message?"

"No, you may not. I need to speak with him now. Wake him up."

The voice maintained a consistent timbre. "That would not be possible. Do you wish to leave a message?"

His terse reply aggravated her already brittle disposition. "You wake him up, or I'll come over and get him up myself."

"I would advise against that. It would not be … prudent."

Though unafraid, Sylvia didn't need any further drama right then. She hung up and thought about who to contact instead. The anesthesiologist. Dr. Joffy wouldn't be pleased to hear from her either, but at least he would be easier to rouse. He answered her call on the second ring.

"Joffy, this is Sylvia. What happened in the OR last night?"

He sighed.

She settled back into the lounge chair, waiting for his explanation.

"Sylvia." He coughed and cleared his throat. "I know I made a mistake with the anesthesia, but I immediately corrected it."

"Apparently not." She explained to him a patient left the hospital that morning AMA.

Joffy unleashed a litany of expletives. "I … I didn't know. How could I have made such a stupid mistake?"

She reached for a pen to take notes while he admonished himself. After half a minute, she calmed him down. She needed answers, which required him to focus.

"Enough, Joffy. Tell me everything."

"I did the procedure the same way I always do. I swear." Which he did several more times before he continued. "I gave Mrs. Topper the same dose of anesthetic I give all patients."

"Perhaps you should have given her more."

"Mrs. Topper is overweight, but not more than the average adult male. The dose I gave her should have been sufficient."

"But it wasn't."

Conversation paused. She wanted him to squirm.

His voice wavered. "Sylvia, it's not unheard of for a patient to have an idiosyncratic reaction to a medication. Some patients aren't anesthetized even when given an appropriate dose. Once I realized Mrs. Topper was still conscious, I increased the dosage. She went under, and we completed the procedure."

"But not before she witnessed something," she emphasized. "What did she see?"

"I don't know. Whatever it was disturbed her enough to leave the hospital first thing this morning." Her pen drummed against the table as she considered how to proceed. "What would she be able to remember after receiving the anesthetic?"

"Well, anesthesia can induce short-term memory loss. I used ketamine for the induction. It works by producing dissociative amnesia, which causes the patient to dissociate pain and memory regarding perioperative events. Patients can have temporary delirious and hallucinogenic episodes associated with ketamine. If a patient is conscious after the induction, it's likely they would confuse or distort reality."

She listened to his discourse, making notations on a legal pad. To herself, she said, "So it's possible to attribute anything Mrs. Topper saw to a hallucination." Seconds later she remembered Joffy was on the line. "What happened from the moment they wheeled Mrs. Topper into the OR and until she left?"

He stated that the staff transferred Mrs. Topper to the surgical table. He inserted an IV and placed the mask over her face. He directed the surgeon to proceed. Before the hysterectomy began, Dr. Winters came in for a feeding. While Dr. Winters was sucking away, the woman sat up.

Sylvia's head shook in disbelief, but she didn't interrupt. The tapping of her pen increased.

Joffy's voice rose. "I couldn't believe it. As soon as I realized she was awake, I pushed her down onto the table and increased her sedation. I held the mask over her face until she went under."

"Did she say or do anything else?"

"She screamed and slapped Dr. Winters. But we got her under control in seconds."

Enough time for the woman to remember something.

Sylvia needed to know how reliable a witness this Susan Topper could be, check her medical records for any history of mental illness or drug use. Mrs. Topper's account had to be discredited if Sylvia hoped to get the situation under control.

The mobowou in Ramsey had adapted to having their blood feedings provided to them. Most didn't know how to hunt anymore. Hospital patients were now their prey, presented to them as willing patients, consenting to the recommendations of their physicians. The organization worked like a well-oiled machine. Their ajabu community depended upon the hospital—and her.

As soon as the call ended, Sylvia dressed. In the bathroom, she styled her thick black hair into a tight bun at the base of her neck. Large hazel eyes complemented her light brown skin. Once satisfied with her appearance, Sylvia headed for the hospital.

***

At Lebanon Memorial Hospital, Sylvia directed the Human Resources staff to get the surgical nurse supervisor into her office ASAP, *and* the charge nurse from last night. *If I can't enjoy Saturday morning, why should anyone else?*

The computer loaded while she sipped coffee.

Sylvia managed a staff of approximately twenty-five medical providers—mostly ajabu. The werewolves and vampires had unique requirements. They made no requests for financial bonuses or trips to exotic locales. They requested security, privacy, and nourishment. Sylvia made sure they got it.

When Lebanon Memorial's blood bank supplies depleted and the staff needed to be fed, Sylvia devised a system to provide an endless supply of sustenance. Fresh meat and blood to satiate their hunger. The medical staff ordered labs or surgical procedures when necessary to accommodate the appetites of their community.

Last night's mistake could destroy everything. Sylvia worked hard to ensure the program functioned as Frederic Baptiste intended. It would not fall apart under her management.

A knock sounded on her office door.

"Come in."

Sylvia glowered. "Sit down. You're the first-shift nurse supervisor."

"Yes, Dr. Senegal." The woman trembled, teetering on the edge of a chair.

Good. Fear was a useful advantage.

"Tell me what happened this morning." No time for niceties. The sooner she obtained answers, the sooner she squelched the problem.

Brushing frazzled graying hair off her forehead, the nurse said, "I don't know. When I got to the floor this morning, the nurse assigned to Mrs. Topper told me the third-shift nurse refused to leave."

"Something *must* have happened. What were you told in sign-out?"

Seconds passed as the nurse supervisor referenced her notes. "Mrs. Topper had a hysterectomy. Surgery went as planned. An IV antibiotic and pain pump were ordered and started before she left the OR. Nothing concerning was reported at sign-out.

The problem was this nurse who refused to leave."

"What's her name?"

"I don't know. If you ask me, the problem was that nurse. She hadn't worked on the surgical floor before." Again, the supervisor searched the records. "Here it is. Her name is Crawford. Makeda Crawford."

Sylvia dismissed the nurse supervisor once she extracted all pertinent information. She called Human Resources again.

"Get Makeda Crawford in my office *now.*"

"She's gone home, Dr. Senegal. Do you—"

"Call her."

CHAPTER 23

SILVER COTTON-LIKE CLOUDS THREATENED rain in the late morning sky. After her brothers and Dad left for Susan's place, Makeda showered and collapsed into bed. She slipped into stage-three sleep as her head hit the pillow.

From beneath the covers, she heard her cell phone humming. She watched the phone shimmy atop the mattress, too tired to answer it. The vibrating phone slowly eddied into silence.

Again, she drifted off to sleep. Three more cycles of this occurred before Makeda answered the phone. She croaked out a woozy, "Hello."

From the phone a voice asked, "Is this Makeda Crawford?"

She propped herself up on pillows. "Yes."

"Hold the line. Dr. Senegal would like to speak with you."

That woke her up quick. Makeda knew she would have to account for what happened on the surgical floor, but she'd hoped administration wouldn't investigate until after the weekend. She straightened her back and swung her legs over the side of the bed.

It was imperative that she not say anything to jeopardize her nursing position. The vampires that assaulted Susan might be associated with Korlemo. Even if they weren't, they had to be destroyed.

Ramsey residents were being preyed upon by people entrusted to protect them. Their safety depended upon her and the mwindaji.

She yawned, rose, and shuffled down the narrow hallway into the kitchen. While she waited for Dr. Senegal to come on the line, she made tea. A strong voice blared across the phone, causing her to spill the water.

"Miss Crawford, explain what occurred this morning on the surgical unit with your patient, Susan Topper."

She recognized the voice. Although the medical director's reputation preceded her, Makeda hadn't expected her to be hawkish. Heat radiated from the tea mug warming her hands as Makeda delivered her prepared statement.

"After I gave sign-out, I was leaving when a patient called for help. I entered the room and found Mrs. Topper sobbing. She wasn't my assigned patient. I helped out because the other nurses were busy." Makeda leaned against the countertop and sipped tea. "Mrs. Topper was hysterical. I settled her down and agreed to stay until her husband arrived. When he came, I left."

"What did Mrs. Topper say to you?"

"Not much. She kept repeating she wanted her husband and complained about the pain. I guess the surgery was worse than she expected."

"Anything else?"

Makeda kept her responses deliberately vague, not wanting the doctor to suspect Susan recalled the vampire attack. But she also had to provide a legitimate reason for her actions.

Stirring sugar into her tea, she pretended to be thinking. "Umm, no. I promised to stay—that calmed her down. I worried she'd cause a scene and disturb the other patients."

Neither woman spoke.

Dr. Senegal didn't prod, and Makeda offered nothing else. The latter drank her tea and awaited further questions.

After a significant pause, Dr. Senegal asked, "Did Mrs. Topper do anything to suggest she was hallucinating?"

"She tried to climb out of bed and insisted on leaving after her surgery. I didn't want to risk her doing anything dangerous—she could've hurt herself."

In the silence, Makeda felt the doctor ruminating over her story. The scenario was plausible, but she needed Dr. Senegal to accept it. The Toppers needed time to flee, and Makeda needed to maintain her cover.

"Thank you for speaking with me."

Makeda jerked the phone away from her ear as the doctor slammed down the receiver.

CHAPTER 24

EARLY SATURDAY MORNING, KORLEMO sat before a cold hearth, considering last night's events. Heavy drapes covered the windows, blocking the sun. Recessed lights between the ceiling rafters threw shadows around the room. European furniture with ornate carvings decorated the space, more situated to a French country manor than rural Kentucky.

He should be more upset about the incident in the operating room last night. In truth, the experience was exciting—unexpected and spontaneous.

As time progressed, the novelty of living in Ramsey had dulled. Too many years had elapsed since he acquired sustenance from a conscious victim. Blood from a living specimen tasted different, richer. Having devoured the vital substance for centuries, Korlemo considered blood as a chef would umami. For him, the satisfaction came from the chase.

Years ago, his dear friend Frederic Baptiste designed a program whereby their tribe feed off hospital patients. Even now, Korlemo could hear Frederic's voice of caution. In twentieth-century America, vampires required a more reliable source of victims, Frederic had warned. Mindful of this guidance, since relocating to Kentucky, Korlemo had practiced restraint and consented to the system conceived by his friend and now managed by Sylvia.

However, yesterday evening when that woman rose from the surgical table and fought him … A long-forgotten passion awakened. He considered whether to let it go dormant again.

When Korlemo relocated to the United States, he had been cautioned about evolving customs—not simply in America but worldwide. Technology jeopardized their anonymity and security. At the time they fled France, World War II was ending, and technology was in its infancy.

Frederic had sensed the changing environment. As the war progressed, he grew more apprehensive. Soon, the conflict became as destructive as the Great War. The First World War benefited their lifestyle. With carnage everywhere, their activities blended into the turmoil plaguing Europe.

The Second World War presented greater obstacles. Their sanctuary in southern France had been disrupted. Hitler circumvented the French Maginot Line and trampled across northern France on his way to Paris, displacing the French government. In 1940, the Vichy government was established in southern France.

As a result, more people moved around the countryside surrounding his home near Cahors. At the time, he'd assumed the alias of Jacques Corneau, a man known and respected as French nobility. His status afforded time and insurance against the Nazi invasion. Maquis rural guerilla bands were also active around their province. For Korlemo, being discovered by the resistance would be as deadly as the Nazis.

Rumors had circulated about aristocracy captured by the German SS and forced to give up their wealth to the Reich through blackmail, ransom, or torture. Several of their ajabu compatriots had been assassinated, and other more unfortunate souls became specimens in their captors' gruesome experiments. A mobowou like himself would not evade detection long under German imprisonment. They needed to relocate, and fast.

By 1942, Hitler assumed control over France. Frederic arranged for their families to flee out of Bordeaux, and from there they traveled to America. They reached the fateful decision to relocate to the Kentucky countryside after Frederic convinced Korlemo that a large city would be unfavorable for their activities.

Vast open countryside allowed them to roam for miles without encountering bindimèn. Though dissimilar to southern France, Kentucky provided similar seclusion. Korlemo became a big fish in a small pond. Money and influence were easier to peddle.

Cultural differences also helped. People were polite and inviting but respected privacy. Kentucky had been a good choice.

As the war ended and America climbed out of the Depression, Frederic installed their households into Ramsey's new community, creating a more permanent solution to sustain their families. He had the idea to use the hospital to supply all the blood and bodies they would ever require.

There would be a small risk. They had to interact with the community. Not a problem for lupasteri, but mobowou had limitations. Hospitals were open twenty-four hours a day, every day of the week. The mobowou would work evenings.

His friend designed the system, Korlemo financed it, and the community consented. For the past fifty years, they'd controlled the hospital's governance. His tribe, and their ajabu community of lupasteri and mobowou, lived a comfortable life.

Last night, a desire renewed in him. Would he be able to suppress it again?

His nose twitched. For several minutes, Herman had stood outside the doorway, but Korlemo refused to let him disturb his reflections. Now he waved Herman inside.

"Come in, friend. I was remembering your father. He was a great man."

In seconds, Herman scurried across the study into a chair alongside Korlemo's.

"Your father was a clever man. Frederic appointed bindimèn to the hospital board with positions of prominence, but no authority. We control everything." He chuckled. "Do they understand the purpose of their hospital?"

Stretching his feet forward toward the hearth, Korlemo did not expect an answer. From his periphery, he observed Herman hanging on his words, knowing the man enjoyed stories about Frederic. Korlemo poured more liquor from the decanter and reclined into his seat. A pleasurable silence stretched out as he imbibed.

Their subsistence on the hospital proved prudent but prosaic. Korlemo struggled to understand how to recapture those emotions from last night. *How to experience adventure while maintaining security?*

Korlemo remembered how the woman's sweat tasted mixed with her blood. It was delicious. The power he experienced when his teeth pierced her skin made his pulse quicken. He longed for that initial metallic tang from warm blood that gradually became sweetness.

That slurry the blood bank provided had a citric aftertaste that made his stomach churn. Blood from surgical patients often gave him a headache. Korlemo hungered to savor lifeforce ebbing from a conscious victim.

Herman's voice trembled. "I apologize, Korlemo, but Sylvia would like to speak with you. She's left several messages with your assistant."

"There is nothing to discuss. What happened is past." He grimaced, suddenly irritated by Herman's timidity.

What Sylvia considered a mistake, Korlemo considered a blessing. He had traded adventure for security and become defunct. Killing was gratifying. Instead, here he was—Korlemo—holding out his hands like a beggar waiting for his divvy.

"Last night, when that woman rose up, a desire awakened inside me. Sparring with her, matching my strength against hers."

Before he stood, Korlemo placed his empty glass on a small table. "Vitality will once again flow through my veins. I will no longer participate in this charity program."

Herman gaped, gripping the arms of the chair. "But Sylvia's afraid we might've been discovered."

"That is not my concern. Sylvia is remunerated handsomely to guarantee our protection." He started to depart.

In a rush, Herman leaped from the chair and followed. "But—"

With eye-blinking fluidity, Korlemo swiveled around quickly, catching Herman off guard. His eyes became slits.

"I am Korlemo! Father to all mobowou *and* lupasteri. I created the ajabu. I will not be bothered with trivialities. If Sylvia stands in my way, it will be her misfortune."

He stormed from the room, leaving a stunned Herman in his wake.

CHAPTER 25

SYLVIA STARED INTO THE mug of inky fluid. The coffee had cooled. With disgust, she set the cup aside and reconsidered Crawford's story.

It was plausible. Joffy had explained it wasn't unusual for a patient to hallucinate following anesthesia. She could find no fault in the nurse's actions. But Sylvia still had a dilemma. Susan Topper had to be dealt with. Their program required secrecy. If that woman recalled the incident in the OR ...

Action was required before Mrs. Topper informed her family about what occurred. It would be best if this became a simple medical malpractice claim. Legal would need time to negotiate a settlement with the family, though. *Can I risk waiting for a legal settlement?* There were more drastic measures she could take.

Sylvia tilted back into the chair and swiveled around to face the window. A fine mist clouded the air. Half an hour elapsed as she stared outside, contemplating how to proceed. By then, the sun had dissipated the mist.

No reason to wait.

She brought up a contact listed on her phone by a simple exclamation point. The best way to eliminate the problem was to eliminate the Toppers.

Mister Exclamation Point answered.

CHAPTER 26

ONCE THEY ARRIVED HOME, Larry opened the minivan door and instantly regretted taking Susan from the hospital. He recoiled at her appearance. Those previously blooming chubby cheeks of hers were sunken. Her ghastly, pale complexion glowed in the shadows of the van.

His mother in-law touched Susan's face. "You look terrible."

He saw worry in his mother-in-law's droopy eyes.

His father-in-law placed a fresh piece of tobacco in his mouth. "Why'd you take her outta there? She ain't well."

Larry ignored them and eased inside the van. Tears gathered in his eyes. He whispered to Susan, "Baby, I … You don't look good. We gotta leave. We can't wait for the nurse."

Susan's body shuddered as sobs racked her frame. Her voice quivered. "We must. She can protect us."

"Protect us from what?"

"From the vampires," Susan said, her eyes boggling against her ashen face.

What the hell?

Larry's head reared back as he viewed his wife. He brought her trembling hands to his lips. "Su, there's no such thing."

She jabbed her neck, extending her head in the opposite direction. "Yes, there is. He bit me on my neck. Right here." Her gaze widened and fixed on to his.

Larry rubbed his head and reconsidered the woman he'd wed ten years ago. It was clear something bad had happened in the hospital. But right now, he needed to get Susan medical care. He'd figure out what occurred later.

He directed his in-laws back into the minivan, leaving the keys in his truck. Once he buckled into the driver's seat, he sped off.

Susan cried, "We need to wait, Larry. Her family's gonna come with us."

"I'm not waiting for no one. Lebanon's the only hospital in Ramsey. We gotta hurry if we wanna get you to Bowling Green before traffic gets bad."

Despite her pleas, Larry refused to wait. In the rearview mirror, her protestations met his frowning brow. Her blanched, hollow face reflected at him. *What the blazes happened last night?*

Yesterday afternoon, he had dropped her off for what was supposed to be a routine hysterectomy. Because Susan suffered from heavy menstrual bleeding and cramping, her gynecologist recommended the procedure.

Though Larry hated the idea of surgery, Susan told him that since he didn't have to deal with the bleeding, he didn't get to decide. He couldn't argue with that. He had stayed at her bedside until visiting hours ended, not expecting to return the following day to break her out.

His father-in-law spat tobacco juice into an empty soda can. "Why aren't we going to Cave City? It's closer."

"Bowling Green has the teaching hospital."

Larry steered onto Cumberland Parkway, calculating the trip should take about an hour.

Nestled in blankets and pillows, Susan rested in the seat and sipped soup her mother had prepared.

As the asphalt road spread before him, Larry reconsidered Susan's comment about a vampire. He hadn't heard of a vampire doctor before and had no idea what she meant. Whatever happened to Susan was the hospital's fault. He'd make them pay for hurting her.

His mother-in-law tucked blankets around Susan. "I had the woman surgery, and ain't nothin' happened to me."

"I can't believe the surgery did this. What'd they give her, boy?"

"I don't know, Dad. I wasn't there."

"You should've called Dr. Lincoln," his mother-in-law said, crunching on saltines. "She a good doctor. She'd figure it out."

Dr. Lincoln had come highly recommended, and he knew Susan trusted her. But Dr. Lincoln didn't do the surgery. Instead, she'd referred Susan to a Dr. Ruphert. Larry first met him the evening of the surgery. He should have checked the guy out first. He wouldn't forgive himself if something bad happened to Susan.

Rolling, windy clouds threatened rain, but none fell. Trees lined the highway, swaying as their minivan whistled along. In the rearview mirror, Larry checked on Susan and at the same time spotted a pickup truck behind them. Tinted windows hid the driver's face as the vehicle sped up.

Most vehicles on the road were eighteen-wheelers. A caravan of semi-trucks traversed the opposite side of the two-lane road.

Larry gripped the wheel with both hands to withstand the drag from the trucks. Because his attention was on the semis, he hadn't noticed the pickup truck had caught up with him and was now riding his bumper.

His father-in-law adjusted the side mirror. "He wants to pass you."

"I know. The turn off's a couple miles ahead." Larry frowned and accelerated.

"Try getting over on the side there."

That stretch of highway narrowed, giving Larry little room to maneuver onto the shoulder. He scrolled down his side window, motioning with his hand for the driver to go around. Despite his gesture, the truck made no effort to pass. Before Larry could roll up the window, a jolt struck the back of the minivan.

"What the fuck?"

"Larry!" His mother-in-law reached out to steady Susan.

"Son, be careful," his father-in-law said, stretching the seat belt over his potbelly.

"I'm trying, Dad." Curse words dribbled under Larry's breath. He snuck a peek at Susan before his eyes scanned the roadway for an exit.

She gawked, staring out the side window.

On the other side of the highway, semis streamed past. A sign advertised the passing lane in a quarter mile. Larry hit the gas. Their van lurched forward.

The passenger truck kept pace with them. Seconds later, it rammed the minivan again.

With a snap, Larry's neck whipped back. Out of the corner of his eye, he viewed his father-in-law struggle to fasten the seat belt. He glanced down at the speedometer, which read ninety miles per hour.

Like a jab, the truck struck again, but this time it maintained contact, pushing the minivan toward the center yellow lines.

Unable to outrun the truck, Larry clenched the steering wheel, trying to reach the shoulder.

With a loud crash, the truck slammed into the minivan, propelling it across the highway. The minivan careened over the double yellow lines.

While his in-laws screamed, Larry fought to regain control. He viewed the grassy roadside yards away, wrenched the steering wheel hard, and aimed for the shoulder. He said his own agnostic prayer, hoping to reach the opposite shoulder of the highway before …

Larry slid the van behind an eighteen-wheeler, but not before another imposing semi bore down upon them. He managed to get the minivan pointed toward Ramsey as the second semi clipped the van's passenger-rear panel.

Screeching tires and crushing metal exploded around him, followed by a brief suspension of sound. The minivan veered off the highway, flipped on its side, and spiraled into brush before coming to rest against a knotted pine tree.

Then darkness.

***

Unsure how much time had elapsed, Larry awoke to find himself suspended between the seat and airbag. The minivan had crashed on its flank with the passenger side settled on the ground.

It felt like a million tiny knives pricked his face. Larry shook glass from his brown, unkempt hair, straining to see through blood trickling down between his eyes. A glance toward the passenger seat revealed verdant grass slick with morning dew.

What happened to the door? And where was his father-in-law?

A large gash in Larry's left arm had a strange object protruding from it. His conscious mind refused to admit it was bone. With considerable effort, he pivoted in the seat.

"Su? Susan. You okay, babe?"

A tremulous voiced answered, but Larry couldn't distinguish the words. When he managed to touch Susan's hand, he panicked. Her cool skin resembled plastic.

Like a kid in a jumpy house full of plastic balls, Larry punched the airbag, fighting against it to reach Susan.

From outside the van's window, Larry heard footsteps.

"Hello."

Above the road traffic, Larry heard a voice in the distance.

In an oscillating voice, someone asked, "Hello? Hello? Can anyone hear me?"

Thank God. "Yeah. Over here," Larry screamed.

"We're coming for yah, guy."

Minutes later, firefighters extracted Larry from the minivan and secured him onto a portable stretcher. EMS carried him up to the road. Fire trucks, ambulances, and police vehicles crowded the roadway. Flashing lights illuminated darkening skies.

Travel on Cumberland Highway ceased. Police officers directed vehicles around the accident.

EMS attempted to slide him into the ambulance. But Larry clung to the door with his right hand. "I'm not going without my wife."

Paramedics assured him they had retrieved Susan. A glance around the ambulance door confirmed their statement.

Larry watched paramedics carry Susan up the incline, still wrapped in blankets.

"Be careful. Yesterday she had surgery."

A police officer questioned him about the accident, requesting a description of the truck. Larry described a Dodge Ram, double cab, dark gray. Due to the tinted windows, he hadn't seen the driver.

Paramedics adjusted Susan into the ambulance. Once they were both secured inside, they were evacuated from the scene.

Before he relaxed onto the gurney, Larry demanded to be taken to Bowling Green.

Road rage proved more deadly than Susan's make-believe vampire. He entwined his fingers with hers, resting his head on the stretcher.

CHAPTER 27

TWO HOURS AGO, SYLVIA returned home from the hospital. After exchanging her suit pants for sweats, she reclined on a velvet settee and began reading a book.

A piece of shiny dark chocolate hovered inches from her lips when her cell phone rang. She popped the chocolate into her mouth and answered on the second ring.

"Yes?"

A curt voice said, "It's done."

"You sure?"

"A semi hit the car, slamming it into a tree. Nobody could survive that. They're dead."

She licked remnants of chocolate from her fingers and ended the call. It *had* been more expedient to dispense with Susan Topper. Rarely did Sylvia make the decision to draw innocent blood, but the program at Lebanon Memorial was a priority and her responsibility. She would do whatever necessary protect it.

Helping herself to a glass of wine, Sylvia wished the situation with the rogue killings in Ramsey could be resolved with similar efficiency. But she had a plan to deal with that problem too. A tiny grin crossed her lips, along with another piece of chocolate.

CHAPTER 28

CLOUDS LOOMED IN THE gray sky as cold air fluttered her long, draping cloak. Zainabu approached a formidable stone fence. She shivered, but from nerves, not the temperature.

Through the fence, she viewed an enormous house—more like a castle—set back about half a kilometer from the road. It was the most beautiful home she had ever seen.

She sensed footsteps. The entire mission depended upon her presentation. If she failed, she could be sent back home—or worse. Her jaw clenched.

Wearing a tan uniform, a man bustled up to the fence. He held a baton in his right hand with a firearm secured at his waist. He towered in front of her with only the stone fence between them.

"This is private property. Get lost," he asserted, tapping the fence with his baton.

From his scent, Zainabu identified him as a lupasteri. Her eyes widened and fastened on to his gaze. She bored deep inside him, beyond his eyes, touching his consciousness.

"*Chekate.*"

He blinked rapidly and started to turn his neck.

Sweat erupted along her spine, but Zainabu persevered. Two minutes later she entered his mind. Once she controlled him, her voice—deep and sure—said, "*Da nga.* I need to speak with the owner of the home. Take me to him—now."

At first, the man didn't budge. He was fighting to regain control. But Zainabu had gained access to his mind and wouldn't relent. Her gaze widened and pupils enlarged. She strengthened the trance and repeated the command.

Like an automaton, he removed a bulky key ring from his coat pocket and unlocked the gate. He stood aside, allowing her to enter.

To her surprise, he escorted her past the large house. They walked in silence for five minutes until …

Zainabu gaped.

An even larger house stood a kilometer behind the first. Spires extended from turrets at opposite ends of this mansion. Careful not to trip on the stone driveway, Zainabu followed the guard, maintaining a close distance while she surveyed the grounds.

It amazed her someone could live in such a grand estate. Her fists clenched, she needed to temper her amazement. She had a job to perform. The most significant one she ever had— or would have.

Through the front entrance of the mansion, the guard brought her into a two-story foyer. Zainabu gazed upward, marveling at a chandelier as tall as herself.

Not more than a few minutes elapsed before a slender gentleman joined them. His soulful eyes welcomed, but she detected suspicion in his aloof manner. Though soft, his scent identified him as mobowou.

"Who are you?" he asked.

She extended her hand, which he accepted. "I am Zainabu Toure. You are not the owner of this home. I need to speak with the owner."

With a slight slant of his head, the man studied her. "How do you know that?"

A small grin creased her lips. "An influential man would not meet a stranger in his home without an introduction. Please tell the owner I am here with an answer to his dreams."

The man gawked, momentarily, then left.

Half an hour later, a servant led her into a large room to wait. Zainabu admired the stone fireplace encompassing almost an entire wall at one end of the room. On the opposite wall, an immense floor-to-ceiling bookcase overflowed with periodicals, novels, and ornaments.

Sunlight splashed across the wooden floors as she pulled back the drapes. Out the large windows, she viewed an expansive yard. Zainabu smiled at a tiny squirrel nibbling on a nut near the window.

The study door opened.

"Shut the drapes!"

Startled by the booming voice, Zainabu released the curtains, closing out the sunlight. Her heart raced. She swallowed three deep breaths. *Calm down.* A second later she turned and faced the door.

Whatever she expected, he wasn't it. The man with the soulful eyes now stood next to a tall, solid man. They shared a close resemblance, but this second man had a strong, overpowering, scent. Her nostrils flared. She inhaled.

An irony odor of blood flooded her senses. With guarded steps, slowly she approached him, giving herself time to overcome the initial shock. She couldn't believe it. This was Korlemo. *Remember your instructions.*

Zainabu sized up the vampire. "I am here to interpret your dreams."

Korlemo glared. "Who are you?"

"My name is—"

"I know your name. Who are you?"

"Recount your dream, and I will prove to you who I am."

For half a minute, he stared at her.

It wasn't easy, but Zainabu maintained her composure.

"Be seated."

She sat on the couch facing the study door. He sat opposite her, and the man she met at the front door, who now introduced himself as Enu Ibori, remained standing.

Crossing his legs and extending his arms along the back of the couch, Korlemo said, "The dreams begin differently, but end the same. Last night was particularly disturbing. I was back in Nintoubo, the village of my people, walking with my son. A small girl arrived, and my son left my side to play with her. The girl was evil, a dubwana—I recognized this immediately and called my son back. But the girl led him away. I chased after her."

Korlemo's hand squeezed the arm of the couch. The crunching sound was the single noise in the room for a quarter of a minute. His gaze locked on her face.

She didn't interrupt, nor move in any way to distract him.

He cleared his throat. "When I captured the girl, I turned her over to my soldiers to be burned alive. They tied her to the stake, and flames surrounded her. I started to leave, but before I could depart, something grabbed my leg. The girl had become a woman and she was pulling me toward the flames."

His temples twitched. "I clutched at the ground, tried any means possible to stop from being hauled into the fire. No one helped me. My soldiers vanished. Before I awoke, I noticed the woman sneering at me from inside the flames."

Zainabu paused, giving the appearance of evaluating his dream. Once she believed enough time had passed, she breathed deeply and raised her hands.

"Your dream is a metaphor. The woman represents the life giver." She paused for effect. "Woman gives life and can take it away."

She watched as the vampire's lips curled. Afraid he might lash out, her shoulders tensed.

"Zorulo," Korlemo said, rising and pacing the room.

"Correct." Her body relaxed. The vampire had reached the desired association.

"I knew it." Korlemo's hands fisted.

Zainabu rose and started to depart.

"Wait, zauber." Korlemo glided up to her as if on water. "I believe we can help each other. Spend the evening. I am sure we can reach an agreeable settlement."

She bit the inside of her cheek, hiding her pleasure. "I'm sure we can."

CHAPTER 29

FROM INSIDE THEIR TRUCK, Peter watched as Dad and Thomas spoke with a short gray-haired woman at the front door of a small tract home. Several children circled around her legs.

This neighborhood was nicer than the run-down area where their rental house was located. Yards had green grass, and discarded toys didn't litter the lots.

As soon as Makeda returned from work and told them what occurred at the hospital, they jumped in the truck and headed over to the Toppers' home.

Peter noticed a pickup truck in the driveway.

Dad and Thomas returned, wearing solemn expressions.

"What?" Peter asked as they climbed inside.

"They already left," Dad said, securing his seat belt.

Peter frowned. "I thought Makeda told them to wait."

"What can I say? They left." Dad stared out the window.

Peter handed Thomas a phone. "Try calling them. Maybe we can catch them on the highway."

He drove back toward the rental house. A minute later, from the rearview mirror, he saw Thomas shaking his head.

"No one answers. It goes to voice mail."

From the corner of his eye, Peter looked across the truck. "Now what, Dad?"

"I don't know. If what Makeda said is true—"

"You don't believe her?" Peter asked, before his gaze cut right, observing traffic.

Dad hesitated.

"I believe her," Thomas said.

Peter grinned. "What's wrong, Dad? She wouldn't make it up."

"Of course not, but she … she might be mistaken."

"How could she be wrong about something like that?" Peter drove past the hospital, giving it a weighty glance.

"I'm saying, if she's correct, how many vampires do you think it would take to run something like that in a hospital?"

Thomas leaned forward into the front seat. "Maybe it's not the entire hospital. Maybe there are a few vampires."

"Or only one," Dad said, staring out the window.

Nearly back to the rental house, Peter asked, "So, what're we gonna do about it?"

Dad glanced into his wallet. "Drive back to the hospital."

"What do you have in mind?" Peter asked, his brow furrowed.

"Chest pain." Dad grinned, showing Peter his medical insurance card.

CHAPTER 30

WITH A QUICK GLANCE right and left, Peter strode into the lobby of Lebanon Memorial Hospital, trying to slip past the information desk and reach the elevators. During his job interview, he'd surveilled the building and evaluated their security system. He remembered the hospital installed cameras on each floor facing the elevators, but none *in* the elevators.

He hoped the hospital had less security staff working on Saturday mornings. Unfortunately, volunteers worked every day. As he feared, the person at the information desk spotted him.

The smiling woman waved him over. "Sir, can I help you?"

As he walked over to the desk, he plastered a grin over his mouth. Because of his slow gait, another visitor got there before him. While the man chatted with the volunteer, Peter peeked at the patient roster displayed on the volunteer's computer screen. He found a promising name and decided to use it.

The rosy-cheeked volunteer finished with the other gentleman and turned her attention toward Peter. "Sorry about that. Now, how may I help you?"

"I'm here to see a family friend. The name is Rogers."

Taking her seat, the woman tilted her screen away from Peter and reviewed the list. "Okay. Let me see if we have a Rogers." Glasses hung from her neck by a chain. The woman squinted at the screen for a half minute before putting them on. "Yes. I found her. Mrs. Rogers is on the medicine floor."

She scribbled his name on a visitor's tag. "There you go. Make sure you keep it on, or security will get you." She beamed at Peter, a laugh behind her eyes.

He smiled. "Oh, yes, ma'am." As he hurried to the elevators, he heard her giggling.

There were two elevators, and from his memory, they were quite small. He allowed a couple and their kids to enter the waiting elevator, choosing to take the next one. They thanked him and herded their brood inside.

When the next elevator arrived, Peter popped inside and rapidly pushed the close door button. A woman at the information desk started in his direction. The doors closed as she began running. Peter caught the frown on her face as the elevator doors shut.

Not sorry. He needed the elevator to himself. The instant the doors closed, he texted Thomas.

I'M IN

Now, he had to get to the surgery floor and verify what Mrs. Topper told Makeda happened in the operating room. Without proof … Mrs. Topper could've been wrong.

With a swoosh, the elevator doors opened onto the third floor. As Makeda stated, the mechanized doors were secured with a card key reader. Peter had grabbed Makeda's security card before he left to find the Toppers, but he knew she didn't have access to the surgical floor.

He tilted his ball cap low over his eyes. With his head down and turned away from the cameras, he swiped the card across the key reader. A red light flashed. After a quick scan of the area outside the surgical unit, he hopped on the elevator. *What next?*

Out of ideas, he rode the elevator down to the first floor. He trusted Makeda's judgement. If she believed Mrs. Topper was attacked by a vampire, then the woman had been attacked. But how? And what could they do about it? They couldn't storm the hospital searching for monsters.

Once he exited the elevator, Peter waved at the volunteer. She smiled back but was occupied helping visitors. He sauntered over to the gift shop, giving passing glances at the paltry items on display. Should he buy something for his girlfriend?

He'd never been to Kentucky. Brenda would appreciate the gesture, but not from here. This stuff was crap. He admired a snow globe with a horse inside. While turning it upside down, Peter noticed a hallway leading toward the back of the hospital.

Makeda had mentioned a large, locked conference room. Bored with the gift shop, Peter decided to check it out.

Though poorly lit, the walkway was spacious and ended at thick wooden doors as impressive as Makeda detailed. His hand lightly caressed the wood. He inhaled its scent. He loved mahogany and considered things he could create from it.

He returned to the task at hand, jostled the door handle, and discovered the room was locked. Unlike his sister though, he came prepared.

In a second, Peter removed a lock pick set from his jacket and in another fifteen seconds had the door open. After a quick glance around, he slipped inside, shutting and locking the door behind him.

Peter surveyed the partially lit room. A placard on the wall read it could hold three hundred people. Auburn-colored wallpaper surrounded wide-planked dark wood floors.

In the center of the room, Peter made a full circle, sizing up the space. *Beautiful.* From his backpack, he removed a camera and snapped off a series of pictures.

At the front of the conference room was a stage. Peter touched the deep purple velvety curtains framing the platform. But a glance at his watch told him he needed to hurry. Dad and Thomas were in the ER, close by in case he needed assistance.

He sprinted for the exit, then stopped. *What if I recorded what happened in the room for Makeda?* She'd love that.

He wriggled the backpack off his shoulders and removed a portable camera he used to record his nature walks. *Too bad it wasn't on when I came across those werewolves.*

With a knife, Peter removed the grating over the air return. He found string and a few other odds and ends to form a mount for the camera. Once the grate was secured in position, he exited the room.

In the elevators, he received a text from Thomas.

YOU OK? DAD READY TO GO

Peter sent a text in return.

NO GOING TO 5

When everyone had exited the elevator, Peter pushed the button for the fifth floor. The doors opened, and he encountered a scowling guard.

His feet barely stepped onto the fifth floor when the man ran up to him. Peter braced for a hit, but the guard stopped inches before making contact.

"What're you doing here?" the guard asked, jabbing a thick finger in his face.

Peter stepped back. Not simply because the man stank, but because he believed the guy was a werewolf. Thick brows shaded the guard's goatlike eyes. His uniform appeared ready to tear apart at any moment, like the Hulk.

"I was looking for my friend," Peter said. "She's on the medicine floor."

"Wrong floor. That's second."

Peter pushed the elevator door button repeatedly. "Sorry. My mistake."

The guard leered.

Tense minutes passed before the chime alerted Peter the elevator had returned. He rushed inside. A knife wouldn't be enough against that werewolf. *Next time, bring gun.*

After the doors closed, Peter exhaled and pushed the hold button. He used the railing along the side of the elevator car to haul himself up through the emergency opening leading into the elevator shaft.

This time, when the elevator doors opened, Peter gazed down on the occupants from a small opening in the panel. *But, now what?*

The occupants departed.

Peter jumped down from the elevator shaft and pushed the button for the fifth floor. When the doors opened this time, he didn't see the hulking guard. He hopped out before the doors closed and ran to the opposite wall. He spotted the camera, but there wasn't anything he could do about it—except to hurry.

Around the corner, Peter spied an entrance to the administrative offices. He waited until the camera rolled to the opposite side of the hall and raced to the office door.

With practiced agility, he used the lock picks. Ten seconds later, he was inside. *Hurry.* The guard could return any minute.

Down another hallway in administration, Peter located a door that read *Chief Operating Officer.* In a hurry to get inside, he didn't notice the wiring along the doorframe. As he entered the room, an alarm blared. *Shit.*

Peter raced back down the hallway and into a different administrator's office. He tried to ignore the blaring alarm and concentrate on how to escape.

Outside the main door leading into the administration wing, the elevator pinged.

In under a minute, from a gap beneath the door, Peter viewed feet. He inched away from the door. *Would they search all the rooms or just the one where the alarm went off?*

An echo of doors opening and closing confirmed his worst fear. They were checking each office. This room was too small to hide in, and it didn't have a closet. *Window.*

As Peter lifted the window sash, it squeaked. *Dammit.*

He peeked outside. A foot below the window was a ledge. At a half foot wide, it would have to do. Peter tightened his backpack straps and placed his knife in the front of his belt.

He shimmied out the window and onto the ledge. With care, he closed the window and tiptoed over to another. It was locked. *Double damn.*

From the corner of his eye, he spied someone in the room he had left. His pulse raced, thundering in his ears. At that moment, his cell phone vibrated. He clung to the wall, not moving an inch. He dared not check the room again.

Peter flattened his body against the stone wall of the building as he searched for a way to climb down. A few minutes passed before he moved along the ledge, careful to avoid birds nesting in the recesses.

He made it to the edge of the building where a metal drainage pipe extended from the roof to the first floor. Like a kid at a park, he slid along the pipe down to the ground.

Bent over, huffing and sweating, he called Thomas while smacking dust from his clothing.

Thomas answered on the second ring. "Hey, where are you? Dad got discharged. We're in the truck."

Peter hustled toward the visitor parking lot. "I'll be right there. I had to do a Spider-Man to get away from a werewolf."

"What?"

"I'll explain when I get there. Makeda definitely found something."

CHAPTER 31

NIGHT HAD DESCENDED, COOLING Makeda's bedroom. Spread-eagle on her stomach, her body was encased in bedcovers. After speaking with the medical director, she had fallen asleep.

Her cell phone hummed. In no hurry, she peeked at it, expecting to see a number from the hospital. Instead, the screen displayed Michael's name and number. She smiled and disentangled herself from the bedsheets.

"Hello."

"Hey. How are you feeling?"

"Fine." She tossed the blankets onto the floor and adjusted the t-shirt she slept in.

"Sorry. Did I wake you?" He didn't sound apologetic.

"Yeah, but it's fine. I should be getting up anyway." She winced as her bare feet touched the floor, searching for her slippers.

"Good. I thought we could get something to eat."

Previously, she had tried—without much conviction—to discourage him from asking her out. Michael was a nice distraction—but she needed to focus. If they grew closer, she might be tempted to explain her true motives for being in Ramsey. Telling someone you tracked and slew monsters was a major buzzkill.

She realized he awaited an answer. *Would it hurt to relax a little?*

"Sure."

"Great."

Dating the sheriff wouldn't be the worst decision she'd ever made. At age twenty-three, she was entitled to bad choices. She had a lifetime to redeem herself and handle any fallout. Right now, she was hungry. Michael provided stimulating conversation and was easy on the eyes. Even monster slayers enjoyed eye candy.

She rushed into the bathroom, considering what to wear.

***

They met at Thai House restaurant in downtown Ramsey, off Main Street. Michael offered to pick her up, but Makeda felt it prudent to keep him away from the house. She didn't want Michael inquiring about what her dad and Thomas were doing in town—or worse—him meeting them.

Tonight, she simply wanted to enjoy a good meal and conversation, maybe fantasize about more than a platonic relationship with an attractive man.

In front of the restaurant, Michael stood grinning like the Cheshire Cat. His warm brown eyes appraised her as she approached. He wore a long-sleeve button-down shirt, which accentuated his muscular chest.

She smiled. "Hi."

"Hello." With his hand positioned in the small of her back, he guided her inside.

Her skin tingled from his touch. Warmth spread through her body. She wore sling-back heels with a blouse revealing minimal cleavage—classy conservative. With the heat he was generating, she wouldn't need the off-white cashmere sweater she brought.

With only four other diners present, in short order they were seated. Michael chose a table in the back, providing them a modicum of privacy.

After placing her order, Makeda settled into the pleather booth. She wondered if he would mention her earlier speeding—not an example of her best conduct.

"How's it going at the hospital?" he asked before tasting his soup.

"It's fine." Also savoring the soup, she considered prodding him for information about the recent deaths in Ramsey. Instead, she inhaled the broth's salty aroma, allowing steam to drench her face. "How's work?"

She observed his full lips as he ate.

"Not bad. Occasional vandalism, or speeder. You know, the usual." His wicked side-grin gave a hint of pearly white teeth.

Her back straightened as she pretended to be offended. "I'll have you know, I've never had a speeding ticket."

"That doesn't mean anything. I didn't give you a ticket either. Doesn't mean you weren't speeding."

Food arrived, interrupting their banter.

Once the server departed, she said, "I'm a safe driver. I was simply tired after working a double shift."

"Umm-hmm. Everybody's always in a hurry. You have to be careful. Those roads are curvy. Accidents happen." He spoke between bites of his pad Thai.

When his lips puckered around the straw, she fantasized about what it would feel like to kiss them.

He wiped his mouth with a napkin. "We cleared up an accident on Cumberland this morning. A family headed to the hospital. Well, they ended up having an ambulance escort for two, and a hearse for two others."

Her fork dropped as she zoned in on what he said. "An accident? This morning? Where?"

Michael's gaze bored into hers. His fork hung in midair. "On Cumberland Parkway. The family was headed to Bowling Green hospital. Someone slammed them into oncoming traffic. An eighteen-wheeler clipped their minivan."

"Who? Do you remember their names?"

Right after Makeda spoke with Dr. Senegal, Thomas had called. He explained that when they arrived at the Toppers' home, the family had already departed. Makeda thought the danger existed only in the hospital.

Michael's stitched brows regarded her. "Topper."

"Susan and Larry?"

He nodded. In his sheriff's voice, he asked, "How do you know them?"

"Susan Topper was my patient."

His shoulders relaxed and he resumed eating.

Conversations from the other tables floated between them.

Makeda gazed beyond him, reflecting upon what he had said about accidents happening all the time. Her appetite evaporated. She glanced up and noticed him studying her.

He reached over the plates and took up her hand. "I'm sorry. Did you know them long?"

"No. I met them today. This is terrible."

"Larry and Susan survived. They were transported to Bowling Green. Her parents didn't make it."

Makeda's eyes closed as she inhaled the scents of peppers and cilantro. The accident upset her. Her goal was to protect Susan. *Fail.* Time for more details.

"You said Larry was speeding?" She knew Susan couldn't have driven.

After spearing a piece of shrimp, Michael's fork hovered

in front of his mouth. "Not his fault. According to witnesses, the truck behind him was in a hurry. Where the road narrows, the truck tried to pass on the graveled shoulder. It clipped the minivan, pushing it into oncoming traffic. Bad timing. Big rigs travel along that stretch of highway all day."

"Did the guy stop?"

"No. Cleared out quick. We'll never locate the driver. When he finds out he killed two people, he won't be coming forward. Besides, only a jackass does that kind of thing."

She couldn't disagree with him about that. However, she feared this involved more than someone being a jerk.

The hospital administration would question Susan's precipitous departure. Moreover, the vampire who assaulted her would worry about exposure. *Was the hospital complicit in the accident?*

Again, she got lost in her thoughts. A minute later, she discovered Michael staring at her. The man possessed smoldering good looks and a taut jawline. His smile did something to her. When she reached for her fork, she realized he still held her hand. He lightly rubbed his thumb along her fingers before releasing it.

She missed the warmth of his calloused fingers. Her mind drifted into imagining what those hands would feel like caressing her—

"So, what brought you to Ramsey?"

"Nursing."

"Did you consider medical school?"

Makeda regarded Michael. *How much should I share?* "I did, but it was too expensive. My parents offered to help, but—"

"You didn't want to burden them with debt."

"Exactly." She nibbled on her entrée. "Your turn. What brought you here?"

167

He set aside his plate and folded his hands. "I completed my undergraduate degree in business, then—"

"Business? I thought cops usually majored in criminal justice."

"I thought a degree in business would help me with investigations. Crime is usually about sex or money." He flashed a toothy grin.

"And you already know about sex, right?" She laughed.

He shrugged and they both laughed.

An unspoken invitation twinkled behind his eyes, which she longed to accept. It would be easy to give into his allure. They were both young, educated, and available.

A glance around the restaurant alerted her that they were the sole occupants. The bill had been placed on their table, neglected by their immersive conversation.

He picked up the check, then finished his drink.

She offered to split the tab. When he refused, she didn't insist. He dropped three twenties on the table, and they rose. Again, his hand cradled her lower back as he guided her out of the restaurant. She delighted in the warmth of his touch and wondered how the evening would end.

Two years had elapsed since Makeda's last relationship, which terminated after her brothers caught her boyfriend cheating. It still hurt.

"Did ... did you like dinner?"

"It was okay, but I've had better Thai food."

His awkwardness comforted her. To know all six feet, five inches of him was as uncomfortable as she was felt good.

They ambled toward her car. Night had fully enveloped Ramsey. Only their cars and those of the employees remained in the lot. Dim lighting heightened the energy between them.

A cool breeze brought their bodies closer together. Their arms brushed against each other. *A prelude of things to come.* She wished.

"Can I call you tomorrow?" he asked.

"Sure." She sounded like an immature schoolgirl.

A goofy grin spread across his face. Flirting. Her heart floated.

Anticipation grew as the distance from her car decreased. If he didn't make a move soon, she would reach up and plant a kiss on his generous lips.

Beside her car, his deep brown eyes plunged into her core. No words were spoken. As he leaned in, his cologne left her intoxicated. For a moment, she became dizzy with excitement. Her lids closed. Lightning sizzled up and down her spine. She had wanted to taste his lips from the moment they met.

Their foreheads touched. Her breath slowed. Light at first, his kiss soon increased in intensity. Their lips melted into each other. Minutes later, they parted.

Cool air calmed her racing heart. For a moment, they remained nose to nose, basking in each other's warmth.

He brushed his face against her cheek. Then he gave her a quick peck on the lips. "Until tomorrow." He stepped forward and opened her car door.

By the time she eased out of the parking lot, he had entered his double-wide truck. He followed behind her toward the rental home.

She knew he lived on the opposite side of Ramsey. That he drove across town for her safety touched her. She appreciated his gesture. Perhaps tonight she would dream of something pleasant. No werewolves, vampires, *or* sorceresses.

CHAPTER 32

INSIDE PETRA'S APARTMENT, JACKIE'S foot tapped along the floor. A week of inactivity left her eager to hit the bars. She watched Petra—not her best, but only friend—dress. Petra had agreed to accompany her tonight, bar hopping in Bowling Green.

Incapable of saving money or paying bills, Jackie lived at home on the large Baptiste estate north of Ramsey with her dad and three brothers. Residing at home didn't deter her from living on her terms. According to her mom, ajabu were beyond bindimèn laws—especially lupasteri. Since her mom died, her dad remained willfully ignorant of her extracurricular activities, content to have his youngest child safely at home.

She checked her watch and huffed. "Hurry up."

"I'm coming," Petra said, sliding into three-inch heels.

Jackie left the apartment with Petra close behind.

On Interstate 65 South out of Cave City, Jackie thought about that bitch Sylvia ordering her to work evenings. A week had passed since she ate out. Ramsey's charm had dulled long ago. She preferred to fraternize away from home—alternating between Cave City and Bowling Green. Rarely, she had traveled as far as Nashville, but Jackie preferred to stay in Kentucky—in case she got into trouble and required her dad's influence.

In a little over half an hour, her Jaguar reached Bowling Green. Jube's Bar, located on the city outskirts, seemed like a good place to start their evening.

Jackie parked and strutted toward the bar. She thought about the guy she had been canoodling with in the woods when the hunter happened upon them. Her late, unlamented friend had associated with this group.

She hadn't told anyone about the fate of her paramour. This would be the first time she met anyone from that group since the incident occurred. As far as she was concerned, her date should have been more careful. Shit happened to werewolves screwing in the woods.

The spring evening was chilly. Because they'd dressed to attract attention, she and Petra wore no protection against the weather. Petra, a thin—bordering on skinny—hazel-eyed blond who wore her hair straight down her back with a light touch of makeup, shivered as they entered the bar.

Air thick with a yeasty stench bombarded them. Raucous laughter and conversations drowned out the music. Popcorn and peanut shells littered the floor with an occasional cigarette ash. Cruising through the crowded bar, Jackie and Petra quickly became the center of attention.

Aware of the onlookers, Jackie glided to the rear of the bar, heading for the pool tables. Several bikers saluted, and she grinned in acknowledgment.

A bartender wearing a sleeveless white t-shirt belched as he handed Jackie and Petra each a beer bottle—on the house, of course.

She and Petra joined a group of women standing near a pool table. Jackie selected a cue from the wall and sized up the table.

An older biker named Maxwell was leaning against a wall nearby. He caught Jackie's gaze. She grimaced and returned to playing pool.

At five feet, seven inches, shorter than Jackie even without her heels, Maxwell was stout with a sullen face, weathered by the sun. His protuberant abdomen, stocky arms and legs were covered in blue jeans, and a hoodie shadowed his face. He trod over to where the women played pool and motioned for Jackie to join him.

She rolled her eyes and continued with the game.

A minute later, his thick fingers pushed down Jackie's pool cue as she attempted a shot.

Her green eyes narrowed. She dropped the cue and—

"Hey, dude. Cut it out. Leave her alone." A man from the bar pushed Maxwell aside and away from Jackie.

She favored the interloper with a dazzling toothpaste-ad smile as she evaluated his clean-cut, fresh appearance. In seconds, she identified him as a bindimèn, not simply by his scent, but his actions. Only someone who wasn't ajabu would intervene. No one else in their crowd came to her rescue. They knew she could handle herself.

Jackie discarded the pool cue and slithered up to him. "Thank you."

"You're welcome. My name's Roger."

"Nice to meet you. Why don't you and your friends join us?" Her arms entwined around her new beau's waist.

Roger and his friends accepted.

She led him away, glaring at Maxwell over her shoulder in mocking amusement.

Maxwell's angry scowl followed. He retreated against the wall after sending Roger an intense glare.

Jackie unabashedly flirted with Roger, suggestively bending over the pool table and asking him to help her hold the cue. After banking a shot, Jackie rubbed up against him, pressing her ass into his groin. She felt him rise against her hips. A smile grew at the corner of her lips. She would be eating tonight.

Roger whispered into her ear, "Can I have your number? I'd like to see you again."

"The evening isn't over yet." She nibbled on his earlobe. *Umm.* Though tempted to take a nip, she resisted. The establishment discouraged dining on bindimèn inside the bar.

A minute later, Roger escorted her outside.

Cold air assaulted them at the door. Jackie nuzzled against his body, relishing the vitality flowing under his tanned skin. Even the odor of stale beer and piss in the graveled parking lot didn't assuage her appetite. On the way to his car, she clung to him, allowing him to fondle her.

Skulking in the shadows, Maxwell tromped in front of them. "Jackie, we need to talk. Now."

She read the impatience wrinkled across his face but had no intentions of surrendering her evening repast.

Roger pulled her slightly behind him. "Look, dude—"

Maxwell's bulky arm flew out and snatched Roger by the neck, lifting him several inches off the ground.

Though he was taller and younger than Maxwell, Jackie knew Roger couldn't match a werewolf's strength.

Her arms folded across her chest as Roger's face flushed red, then purple. He scratched in vain at Maxwell's hand. They aroused the attention of the bar patrons. Associates of both men ran toward the scene.

The bar owner stepped outside and yelled, "I'm calling the cops," before rushing back inside.

Jackie stomped her foot. "Stop it." She marched forward and stood beside Maxwell. "I said stop it."

Amid yelling and taunts from onlookers, Maxwell snarled and hurled Roger against a car, causing a dent.

Roger crashed onto the hood of his own car and slunk to the asphalt. He curled into a ball, coughing and spluttering. His friends ran over and helped him up.

Ever the gentleman, Roger inelegantly stumbled over to Jackie. "Are you all right?"

She tousled his hair. "Go home. I can handle this."

"Come with me."

"Maybe some other time."

Roger and his friends climbed into their cars, driving off yelling slurs. Most of the patrons returned inside once the hostilities ended.

As she watched her meal depart, Jackie bolted over to where Maxwell waited on his motorcycle. She glared into his wrinkled face. "What the hell do you want?"

He climbed off his bike, grabbed her by the elbow, and led her away from the throng.

She shook him off and waited.

"What happened to Dirk?" he asked.

Her vacuous emerald eyes gaped. Jackie puckered her bloodred lips. "What do you mean?"

He lowered his bushy brows and stepped closer. "What happened?"

It disappointed Jackie to find him immune to her allure. "We ran into some trouble."

"Who?"

"I don't know."

He advanced.

"I don't know!"

Rubberneckers loitering in the parking lot watched.

Maxwell paused, waiting until their audience returned to prior activities.

Jackie crossed her arms. "It happened so fast. We were interrupted." She didn't elaborate. Maxwell understood why Dirk left with her that evening.

"There was a shot, and I got the hell out of there. When I stopped to look back—no Dirk."

She stood there, daring him to ask another question. But there was nothing more to be said.

CHAPTER 33

MAXWELL WATCHED JACKIE SASHAY back into the bar. Music blared out the open door, casting a harsh yellow light along the graveled driveway. He returned to his motorcycle and considered what she had said.

Jackie didn't care about Dirk. He just happened to be the most available dick that night. But Dirk was Maxwell's friend. They traveled the roads together for years, covering each other's backs. When Dirk went off with Jackie that night, Maxwell figured the guy deserved some fun.

They had run into her at a club in Cave City. Jackie flirted with Dirk. Usually, she paid him no attention. Whether bored or horny, she had allowed Dirk to grope her all evening. Tired of watching them, Maxwell—and probably the rest of the bar patrons—were thrilled when the two left.

The next day, when Dirk didn't show up, Maxwell searched the woods around the bar. South of Mammoth Cave National Park, he found Dirk's body with a gaping bullet wound in his chest. If someone happened upon them in the woods, Maxwell knew Jackie wouldn't break a nail to help Dirk.

What he couldn't understand was why anyone would be in those woods at that time of night. It could've been a coincidence, but he didn't believe that. He figured someone was after Jackie and Dirk got caught in the crossfire. She had burned a lot of people.

Of course, there was also that cockamamie scheme in Ramsey. Maxwell knew about the screwball arrangement the werewolves had of eating hospital patients. One night at the bar, Jackie got drunk and told everyone about it. She said her family believed it was more civilized than running around the woods looking for food like dogs. *Insane.*

Apex predators like werewolves and vampires shouldn't have to feed off accident victims and surgical patients. The whole thing sounded obscene. It didn't involve Maxwell, though, so he didn't care—unless it got his friend killed.

He wanted to know more, but questioning Jackie would be useless.

He climbed on his motorcycle and rode off. He'd have to find out what happened to Dirk on his own, and he knew where to go to get answers.

CHAPTER 34

MARCH IN KENTUCKY VACILLATED from spring to winter each day. Michael zipped up his jacket and shut the truck door. He tramped across the woods, stamping his feet against the rock-hard ground, glad he had remembered to stuff gloves in his coat pockets before leaving home.

He yawned, missing the warm comfort of his bed. Like fog, his breath dangled, suspended in the morning air. Mentally, he counted how many months until summer arrived. He couldn't remember Georgia ever being this cold. He slogged carefully around trees and joined his deputies huddled together over a corpse.

One of the deputies said, "Morning, Sheriff."

"Morning. What have we got?"

A different deputy pointed to a group of men gathered off to the side, shouldering their rifles. "Hunters found the body about fifteen minutes ago. They've been out since three this morning."

"Any identification?" he asked.

"No, I searched the body," the deputy said, providing further details about the scene.

Everyone stared down at the frozen body as portable lights illuminated the misshapen corpse.

Thirty minutes ago, Michael slept in heated bliss. Foremost in his thoughts was his date last night with Makeda. Now, he stood in the bitter predawn morning examining a disfigured corpse found by hunters in the woods south of Ramsey.

He knelt for a closer inspection. Deep gashes around the neck left the body nearly decapitated. Intestines spilled out over the sides of the body cavity. Despite his lack of a medical degree, Michael identified several missing organs.

With a flashlight, he followed a trail of bodily remains extending away from the deceased and scattered among the ground cover. He cleared a small area of debris with his foot and identified shoe and paw prints. The tracks testified to animal activity in the area.

His breath came out as white puffs of air as he stood upright. He addressed his deputies while still surveying the scene. "Make sure to check out those animal tracks. See if you can find any … any pieces of him."

One of the deputies followed the tracks, while another interviewed the hunters. Paramedics assisted other deputies in zipping the deceased up into a thick black body bag. In twenty minutes, the paramedics had departed.

A full sun crested above the tree-lined horizon, making the morning dew glisten in prisms of light. Wishing for an early summer, Michael stomped his boots to get blood flowing to his toes. After giving orders to his deputies, he departed.

On the way to his vehicle, he said, "I'll be at the station." Once in the truck, Michael changed his mind and drove to the morgue.

***

Dead bodies didn't bother him, but dead bodies in morgues did. When he approached those doors, Michael told himself there was nothing sinister inside. It didn't help, but at least he could concentrate on the words and not the source of the odors.

Outside the morgue doors, he inhaled a chest full of air and then entered.

Overhead fluorescent lights flickered above dingy gray-tiled floors. *Ignore the lighting and focus on the investigation.*

Low—high—low, the light fixture created a strobe effect that did nothing to alleviate his discomfort. Michael's stomach gurgled. He remained near the doorway, as close to the exit as possible.

Being frozen blunted the funk of decomposition, for which he was grateful. Regardless, the pungent scent of disinfectant, in addition to whatever other fluids surrounded dead bodies, had him on the verge of heaving.

"What do you think, Doc?" he asked.

Glasses hung on the edge of Dr. Bones's nose as he hovered over the corpse, reading paperwork. "I haven't thawed the guy out yet, Mike. Give me a chance to examine him. Where's the crime scene report?"

"The guy was found in the woods off Bryer Road. There was minimal blood at the scene. I located evidence of animal *and* human activity. No weapons were located on site. No identification on the body. He's most likely a transient. I recognized needle marks on his arms."

The doctor walked over to the counter and set down the paperwork. "Thanks for the summary. I received the body five minutes ago. Come back later, and I'll give you my assessment."

"Fine."

Not taking his eyes off the deceased, Dr. Bones spoke to Michael's retreating back. "I'll call when I'm done."

Eager to leave, Michael waved over his head to the doctor and exited.

Too tense to return to the station, he stopped at the Main Street Diner for breakfast. With a steaming cup of coffee in front of him and food on the way, Michael reflected on the two bodies discovered earlier that month.

The sheriff's department had uncovered a total of five bodies in the past two months. This corpse had been butchered like the others. *A serial killer?* Possible. Statistics were against it, but it would be prudent to keep all possibilities in mind.

Officially, Dr. Bones had certified the deaths as accidental overdoses. Unfortunate consequences of illicit drug use compounded by homelessness. Michael disagreed.

The idea of a serial killer made more sense. If he was correct, then the state authorities should be contacted. But without any of the deaths officially classified as a homicide—or a death under suspicious circumstances—Michael would have a difficult time persuading the state to investigate.

Caffeine registered in his brain, and his tension melted. Now he could concentrate. He consumed eggs and sausage while calling Makeda.

Yes, he was on duty investigating a potential homicide, but as sheriff he was on call day and night. He had to take advantage of personal time whenever he could get it. Right then, he wanted Makeda. On the third ring, she answered.

"Good morning," he said.

"Morning."

"Too early?"

"No, I finished a run around the neighborhood."

"Good. Interested in going for a ride?"

Even before she agreed, he told her he'd be at her door in five minutes.

CHAPTER 35

ONCE MICHAEL HUNG UP, Makeda finished braiding her hair. In the hallway of the rental home, she smelled breakfast. Bacon sizzled and popped, filling the air with enticing aromas. In the tiny kitchen, she snatched a piece of bacon from the tray before her brother could.

Peter smacked the back of her hand. "That was mine."

"It was." She smiled and ate the bacon.

He lurched at her, as if about to give chase.

Dad placed a plate of pancakes and more bacon on the table. "Sit down, Peter. If we're going hiking, we need to leave early."

Thomas stumbled into the combination living room—kitchen as he finished dressing. He collapsed onto a chair at the table and started piling food on his plate.

"Morning." He started eating.

At the stove, Makeda waited for water to boil. "What are we doing about the hospital?"

"Nothing, baby girl," Dad said.

She grimaced. "Nothing? They're attacking the patients."

"We don't know that. Peter couldn't get onto the surgical floor."

"But I identified vampire marks on her neck."

"Makeda—"

"What do you want us to do," Peter interrupted Dad, "go and shoot up the surgical floor?"

"We can't let them feed on patients."

"There's no proof. The one piece of evidence we have is from a patient, who won't answer our calls," Dad said.

Water boiled and the kettle hissed. Makeda prepared tea and considered what Michael had said last night about the car accident. She had tried calling Susan. After over a dozen calls and texts, Susan's husband answered and told her not to call them again—ever.

Nauseated, she regretted eating the piece of bacon. After dumping her tea in the sink, she went to the refrigerator for water. "But we have to do something."

"We will." Dad rose from the table and kissed her temple on his way to the sink. "First, we figure out what we're up against before calling the rest of the team. We don't know what to tell them yet."

Her brothers set their plates in the sink too.

Thomas asked, "Sure you don't want to come with us?"

"No. I already exercised this morning." She nibbled on the edge of a piece of toast.

"Later," Peter said before closing the door.

***

Makeda glanced at her watch, calculating how long ago she spoke with Michael. Five minutes had become twenty. Her intention had been to spend Sunday morning alone practicing sorcery.

Instead, she ran into the bedroom and dressed. After slipping into a down jacket, she waited outside the rental home.

From around the street corner, Michael's smile shone like a beacon. Her pulse quickened as his F-150 double-cab truck pulled into the driveway. She was becoming quite attached to that smile.

As she climbed inside the truck, she detected a heaviness in his stiff manner. Despite his smile, Michael acted preoccupied.

"You're up early. Work again?"

"Yeah, some hunters discovered a body this morning. I've been up for a few hours." The smile disappeared. He reversed down the driveway and onto the main road.

She had hoped this would be a pleasurable visit. But if another body had surfaced, she wanted details. The adage about mixing business and pleasure occurred to her, but she didn't have much choice. Like him, she had a job to do.

"Is your brother up? I haven't had a chance to meet him."

"He's not here. Maybe you can meet him when we get back."

Of course, he would be curious about her standing outside in the cold rather than allowing him to come to the door. She had no interest in introducing Michael to her family. They would give her a hard time, and she didn't want trouble.

She gazed out the side window. "Where are we going?"

"I'm taking you to my favorite place in Ramsey."

They drove in silence with no pressure to speak. It was comfortable. Being with Michael seemed natural.

In a short time, he turned into the Florin Park entrance. She'd run there before. It contained a well-cultivated garden with a beautiful central lawn. Veterans' Memorial rose garden reigned as her favorite destination in the park.

Because it was too early and cold for most people, only two other vehicles were parked in the lot. Before she could exit, Michael had walked around the truck to help her out. She appreciated his attention to tradition.

They proceeded down the sidewalk and into the gardens. Michael gazed distantly ahead.

What's with him?

Makeda touched his arm. "Are you okay? Is it about the dead bodies?"

"Yeah."

"If you want to talk—"

"How was your run?"

His interruption was brusque. Clearly, he didn't want to talk about work. For now, she would appease him.

"Nice. I like running early. I have the trails to myself."

His body drifted closer. "Be careful out there. I wouldn't want anything to happen to you."

Though he held her gaze, she realized his thoughts were elsewhere.

Makeda heard a squirrel scamper up a tree. Behind her, a bird glided on the air. She watched it without turning around. *How?*

Michael brought his body closer. Their arms grazed each other. She noticed him observing her.

"I'd like to spend more time getting to know you."

She glanced up at him, reading sincerity in his intense gaze. Makeda blushed. She'd been trying to get information out of him to locate a vampire, and he was trying to start a relationship.

When he extended his elbow, Makeda linked her arm through his. They traipsed around the park.

"Do you have a boyfriend?"

"No."

"Do you want one?"

Her forehead wrinkled. She focused on a duck waddling along the water's edge. "I don't know."

"Were you ever married?"

"No."

He raised his eyebrows. "Engaged?'

"No."

He gave her a side-glance. "Did you *ever* have a boyfriend?"

She chuckled. "Yes."

"What happened?"

"I didn't have time for a relationship." No need to tell him about her brothers' interference.

"I don't believe that."

Before facing him, she took a deep breath. "It's true. I wasn't ready for a relationship. Work and my career came first." She unlinked her arm from his, needing distance to breathe. "I like my work. It's more important to me right now than anything."

When Michael looked into her eyes, she didn't waver. After a moment, they resumed walking. His arms dangled at his sides. She placed her hands in her jacket pockets.

"You're settling down here in Ramsey, right? This isn't a temp job, is it?"

"Michael, I like you, but I can't promise how long I'll be here." *Damn.* She hated to lie.

"I understand."

They completed another circuit around the pond. This time, when he reached for her arm, he snuggled her in close and whispered into her ear, "I'll take every minute I can get." He kissed her forehead.

They returned to his truck.

Once inside, Makeda was surprised when he didn't exit the parking lot. Instead, he moved to a secluded area behind some trees. The engine idled. She grinned, wondering what he had in mind.

Michael fumbled with the console display. "What type of music do you like?"

"Most types. I usually listen to R&B at home."

He located a radio station playing Peabo Bryson's *I'm So into You*.

"You set that up." She laughed.

He also laughed. "No, honest. It came up on its own."

As he leaned forward to read the display, she tried to see if the song came from the radio or a playlist. Their heads bumped. But before she could apologize, he kissed her on the lips. Surprised at first, she quickly warmed to his affection. She broke away first.

"When was your last relationship?"

He studied the floorboards. "When I started this job. My girl came up for a visit and ended things before she left. I thought she loved me enough to go anywhere. I guess rural Kentucky was one step too far."

Makeda squeezed his forearm. "Sorry."

"I was too at first, but I suppose it would have been something eventually."

She leaned back and gazed out the windshield. "Love is always chastening."

"You think so?"

"Love makes you look at yourself as not fully complete. There's something another person has that makes you whole. You never realized anything was missing until you fell in love." She gave him a side-glance.

"Someone has something that makes a more perfect you. While you're together it's wonderful. But when it ends, you understand how imperfect you are."

He glanced out the windshield. "I hadn't thought of it that way." Reaching for her hand, he asked, "Tell me more about you?"

"You go first."

Softly massaging her fingers, he slid closer. "I work out, watch sports. Like to eat out, but can cook—if I have someone to cook for." He smiled and inched closer. "I enjoy playing cards. I don't like rock music, and I'm the youngest in my family. Your turn."

"I'm also the youngest. I cook, but I don't barbeque. I like rock music, but not heavy metal. I don't watch sports. I like going to the movies—but nothing where a dog gets killed. It makes me cry."

His right eyebrow rose. "Seriously?"

In return she arched her left brow. "Seriously."

Laughter enveloped them as Michael lifted Makeda onto his lap. "Well, I'll never make you cry."

This time when he kissed her, Makeda melted into his lips. It felt ethereal. Only a few minutes elapsed before beeping disturbed their interlude. She checked her phone, thinking it was one of her brothers. But it wasn't from her phone.

With a resigned sigh, Michael pulled his cell phone from his coat pocket. He cracked open the steamed-up truck windows, then answered the call.

Makeda slid off his lap and attempted to bring order to her disheveled self. Cool air stung her hot skin. She listened to the one-sided conversation, noting a change in Michael's demeanor.

He hung up and slid under the steering wheel. His profile displayed a furrowed brow and grim, flat lips. His eyes stared out the windshield.

"Let me take you home."

"What's wrong?" She buckled her seat belt.

"I have to go by the morgue. Dr. Bones finished the autopsy." He waited until she belted in before exiting the lot.

Makeda needed details, especially if it related to monster activity around the hospital.

"I can go with you. Dr. Bones often shares his autopsies with me."

He side-eyed her. "You sure? I mean ... It's a morgue—with dead bodies."

"I'm a nurse. I've seen worse than dead bodies."

CHAPTER 36

AT THE MORGUE SINK, Dr. Bones was cleaning equipment as Makeda and Michael entered. The former removed his glasses as they exchanged greetings.

"Hello, Dr. Bones," Makeda said, walking up to the stainless-steel table where the deceased had been washed and dissected. She noticed the pathologist regarding her closely as she followed behind Michael.

Once he finished wiping his lenses, Dr. Bones pulled a sheet off the body. Michael flinched.

Although it had been washed and defrosted, the corpse appeared no less gruesome than other dead bodies she had seen. A large, cavernous hole replaced the abdominal space.

The doctor retrieved a stack of papers from his desk and handed them to Michael. "I've completed my report. The deceased died from natural causes. Wildlife devoured the body postmortem."

Michael stared at him.

A palpable tension rose between the two men. Peripherally, she noticed Michael remove his hat.

Makeda was interested in the deceased and allowed Michael and Dr. Bones to hash out their disagreement. She found a probe on the counter and examined the corpse.

Michael rubbed his face from the top of his head down to his chin. "Doc, that makes no sense. You're telling me a man happened to die in the forest, and some coyotes or hogs ripped his neck apart like that?"

"This wasn't an ordinary man. His body aged prematurely from being homeless. He was an addict, probably intoxicated when he passed out. If he was under the influence of drugs, he wouldn't have been able to fend off predators."

Dr. Bones turned on a computer. "I sent off blood, tissue, and eye fluid for a tox screen. It'll tell us the level of inebriation. The true cause of death will most assuredly be drugs."

Michael joined the pathologist at the desk. An argument erupted about the autopsy conclusion.

Makeda perceived Dr. Bones observing her, although Michael's body blocked most of his view.

"There's an opioid epidemic, Mike, or haven't you heard? This type of death is common here."

A frowning Michael squeezed the brim of his hat. "There were different-size footprints around the area—not from our victim."

"Did you check those prints against the hunters?"

"The prints weren't fresh. And before you mention animal tracks, the prints were from something larger."

"A pack of wild animals could do a lot of damage."

Michael raised his voice. "Addicts don't get their throats mangled. Those marks on the bones, they look like something hacked them. And what caused the slashed muscle tissues?"

"I told you animals ate him *after* he died."

"And what, took the organs back to their den for a late-night snack? Addicts don't die like that."

Dr. Bones's face reddened. His neck muscles stretched taut. "They do when they die in the Kentucky woods, or maybe you're unfamiliar with accidental deaths—can't distinguish them from an actual homicide. After all, you've only been sheriff for two years."

Michael flushed.

Makeda marveled that Michael maintained his composure. There probably would've been a lot more screaming and cursing if she hadn't been present.

As she leaned over the cadaver, she used the probe to separate skin around the neck. Frayed tissues splayed open, displaying broken structures—torn and mutilated. Identifying the anatomy proved difficult with the severed muscles. She laid the neck muscles aside and located the esophagus and trachea, then traced back to the carotid and jugular vessels.

From the bottom of the head, the esophagus dangled. She couldn't locate the thyroid gland, which made her curious. The left earlobe made a good landmark. The probe peeled back torn skin where Makeda identified the frayed jugular vein and pinpointed the carotid artery. From the jugular foramen, she followed the artery where it exited the skull back to where the external carotid artery entered the chest cavity.

Carefully, she repeated the process until she found what she sought; two puncture wounds in the artery at the neck below the submandibular angle. The butchery of the neck was intended to disguise those signature puncture marks. *Why didn't Dr. Bones notice those puncture wounds?*

Perhaps he had. If so, what was his conclusion? Either he thought the wounds insignificant and ignored them, or he knew the significance and wanted to cover it up. She couldn't ask Dr. Bones in front of Michael. Once satisfied with her findings, Makeda focused on their discussion.

"It looks suspicious to me. I'm thinking of calling in the state investigators."

His face now beet red, Dr. Bones asked, "Why? Because you can't do your job, or because you don't think I can do mine?"

Michael's body stiffened. He slammed the hat on his head. "Look, I'm sheriff. If I believe something's wrong here, I'm authorized to call in the state medical examiner. Get your report and toxicology screen to me as soon as possible. I'll make my decision after that."

With a gesture, Michael motioned for Makeda to join him. She met him at the exit doors.

His long strides brought them to the truck in seconds. Anger radiated off him like the heat their kissing generated in the park. She gave him space. They drove to the rental home in silence.

In the driveway, Michael placed the truck in park and sat there. His hands clenched and unclenched on the steering wheel.

Seconds passed. Makeda hesitated, unsure whether to leave or talk. Finally, she reached for the door handle.

Michael stopped her with a gentle touch of her arm.

She reclined against the seat and waited.

His haggard eyes regarded her. "I'm sorry you had to see that."

"It's okay. I'm used to doctors behaving badly." Her heart broke for him, understanding his frustration. *He has no idea what caused those injuries.*

He kissed her lips. Their embrace continued for several long blissful minutes before they drew apart.

After helping her out of the truck, Michael escorted her to the front door.

"Is your brother home?"

She poked her head inside. "Nope."

Michael's grin told her he realized she was avoiding their meeting. If he knew what happened to the last man she dated, he'd understand. "Maybe next time."

"Sure."

In the doorway, Makeda watched him steer the truck toward town. She regretted holding out on him about what she'd discovered at the morgue. Maybe she did him a favor. Knowing monsters existed was a heavy burden, even for a sheriff. Maybe especially for a sheriff.

CHAPTER 37

THE HOUSE WAS EMPTY. Her dad and brothers hadn't returned from their hike. Makeda changed out of her clothes and roped her braids together under a head scarf. She made herself a snack and rehearsed incantations.

After another hour passed and they still hadn't returned, Makeda decided to go for a walk. She wanted to clear her mind and practice sorcery. Because of the chill, she tossed a light jacket over her Malcolm X t-shirt. Makeda grabbed her backpack and locked the door.

The smell of burning trash clung to the air like the stench from the North Charleston paper mill she remembered from visiting Uncle John in South Carolina. Homes in this neighborhood had never known better days. Chipped paint littered yards off wooden homes neglected for decades. There were no sidewalks. Derelict vehicles and plastic toys speckled overgrown yards.

Across the street, a group of neighbors huddled around a pickup truck, smoking and drinking. One of the men leered and saluted her with a beer can and middle finger.

Makeda whispered a short incantation.

The man tripped and fell beside the truck. His companions laughed as he crawled off the ground. Before he regained his balance, Makeda jogged away.

As far as she knew, they were the only African Americans living on the street. If others were around, they kept well hidden. After a short distance, she veered off the street and jogged into the woods.

Despite the bright sun high in the clear sky, the woods remained cool. The ground was gentler on her feet than the asphalt. Thirty minutes in, she stopped for a break. She surveyed the area, making sure she was alone.

Once certain of her seclusion, Makeda dropped the backpack and removed several weapons. If she wanted to use sorcery to kill monsters, she had to practice. Holding a throwing star in each hand, she commanded them to strike a tree ten feet away. Both stars fell to the ground. *Damn.*

Again, she concentrated on the throwing stars, directing them to rise into her hand. They didn't move.

She tried an incantation Yewande taught her. With her hands at her sides, she commanded a pile of rocks to rise. A few of the stones teetered, then rolled over. After several attempts, she managed to slide the stones but couldn't overcome the laws of gravity.

'*Bajinu, mbabire.*'

Seconds after the thought left her mind, a message exploded in her head.

'*Fè atansyon. Li se isit la. Sèvi ak fòs ou yo. Li tou pre.*'

Makeda spun around. "Who's there?" She strained but detected no one in the vicinity.

Once more, she recognized the message was in Creole. It had to be Nadege. Unfortunately, Makeda understood little of the language.

She incorporated into kasi kasi the few Creole words she had learned and repeated them in English. '*Nadege, mwen pa pale kreyòi. Ki sa ou te di? Tampri, ede m.* I don't speak Creole.

What did you say? Please, help me.'

For a few minutes Makeda waited for a reply. She wriggled her cold fingers to stimulate the circulation. She mumbled a different phrase from her lessons with Yewande. '*Ubumi. Chekate. Ubumi.*'

She gasped. The scattered rocks shot into the air, floating several feet off the ground before crashing back to earth. A throwing star hovered in the air, one in front of each of her hands. Her fingers spread wide, then she flung the stars into a nearby tree. They embedded into the wood as splinters sprinkled on the ground.

Makeda raised her hands, manipulating her fingers as if she played a piano. The stones soared into the sky. She admired how high they flew above the treetops, twisting and twirling them to her delight.

A message came into her mind that she associated with the mind-voice of Nadege. '*Mwen prai voye èd.*'

She understood the word *help*. While Makeda was distracted, her arms fell to her sides. In tandem, the rocks descended.

About to be pummeled, Makeda threw up her hands. The stones ceased their precipitous descent, floating inches above her head. With a flick of her fingers, she tossed them aside.

Panting, Makeda wiped sweat from her forehead, musing over Nadege's message. Her attempt to learn Creole online had helped. *How long would it take to learn more?*

She picked up a machete and tried to wield it with her mind. Half her attention focused on the weapon, while the other half wondered what Nadege was anxious to contact her about. Whatever it was, she intended to be prepared for the next message.

Her head ached, but she managed to swish the machete, though without any power. With the tip of her sneaker, she cleared a small patch of ground and sat down. Using the backpack as a pillow, she rested.

Animals scampered in the brush. She observed rabbits, a squirrel. Once, she thought she spied a deer. Birds chirped and flitted between the trees. Makeda took a nap.

Less than an hour later, she dusted soil from her buttocks and stood. As she considered what to try next, a voice entered her mind.

'Can you hear me?' it asked.

Makeda's gaze searched the area while her mind answered the voice. 'Yes. Who is this?'

'Nadege asked me to speak with you. I'm Tamara, a family friend.'

The elderly woman had understood her message. For the first time since she arrived in Ramsey, Makeda felt like she'd made progress.

'Nadege senses danger in Ramsey. A powerful man threatens you.'

Makeda frowned. She'd met several influential men at work, including Dr. Bones. 'Can she be more specific?'

A minute elapsed.

'No. Ramsey is dangerous. You should leave.'

Impossible.

'Thank you, Tamara. I appreciate you relaying the message. I'm still working on my Creole—and kasi kasi.'

'I understand. It takes a while, but be careful. You're broadcasting your thoughts to everyone.'

'I don't remember how to do it. Can you help me?'

'Direct your messages to the intended party—not the entire neighborhood. By broadcasting your thoughts into the air, everyone within a certain radius can hear you.'

'I don't understand.'

Tamara proceeded to give her an impromptu lesson. 'Concentrate. Visualize the person you want to address.'

Makeda followed her directions.

'Close off any parts of your mind you don't want to share. Then push your message forward.'

Makeda grimaced, trying to duplicate Tamara's actions. 'It's hard.'

'Not really. Like anything, it takes time. Different parts of our brain perform different functions. The temporal lobe is designated for speech—others for thought or emotions. Keep the areas separate. During kasi kasi, focus on one activity. Close the other parts of your brain.'

'I don't get it.'

'Consider a computer. Have you ever had someone access your computer remotely—for a repair or something?'

'Yes.'

'Let's say you grant them access to your computer to fix a software program, but you leave your email open. Then they could read your emails, right?'

'Right.'

'This is the same thing. In kasi kasi, you're opening your brain, and anyone can access your mind. You want to limit access. Otherwise, another zauber could read your thoughts, memories, secrets. Understand?'

'Yes. I'll try again.'

'Practice. It's important. Have you ever wondered how magicians read people's minds? Someone grants them access. If other zaubers can do it, you can too. Remember, concentrate on the person you wish to speak with. Close your thoughts to everyone else.'

Thanking Tamara again, Makeda collected her weapons and headed for the rental house.

While tramping in the woods, she considered how to prove to her family that monsters preyed on the hospital patients. More importantly, she needed to figure out how to protect them.

Before she got to the house, she decided to borrow against the friendships she'd made. And if that didn't work …

How far would she go to protect the patients?

CHAPTER 38

AN ENORMOUS RUSTIC METAL chandelier lit the dining room where Korlemo remained seated with Herman, whom he had invited over for dinner. Family members had departed a half hour earlier.

Now, servants scurried around, clearing dishes off the twenty-foot-long dining table. After the light repast, Korlemo and Herman ended the tranquil evening with a nice wine.

Their spacious homes stood yards apart, situated on an isolated hundred-acre parcel of land in northeast Ramsey. Black oak trees surrounded their estates and provided a wholesome, natural barrier from onlookers. Korlemo possessed the larger home, lavish even for a physician. But of course, he was more than a doctor—so much more. His fortune had increased over centuries.

Following the meal, Korlemo and Herman retired to the study, where they relaxed and engaged in light conversation about Ramsey politics. The hearth warmed the space, spewing a yellow-orange glow around the room. Animal heads occupied corners of the study. Impressionist art adorned the walls.

Cognizant of Herman's sensibilities, Korlemo understood his announcement would cause distress—and he needed Herman at his best. His safety, their safety—but most importantly *his* safety–depended upon it.

"Did you enjoy your meal, my friend?"

"Yes, thank you." Herman sat opposite him in a leather chair.

Korlemo's fingertips formed a steeple as he leaned forward. "Herman, you are my dearest friend. I have known you since you were born."

Wiping perspiration from his brow, Herman nodded.

Unsure what distressed his friend, Korlemo had other concerns. He swirled wine in his glass while studying Herman. His scrutiny made his friend squirm more.

"I have trusted you with my life. You have more than honored your commitment." He paused and sipped wine. "I have decided to leave Ramsey."

Herman bounded off the chair. His cheeks puffed out as he stammered. "But you've been safe here for over fifty years. Why would you want to leave?"

"I have tired of this regimented life and want a change." Korlemo's eyes widened, recalling the incident in the operating room. "I need to hunt."

"My father designed this program for you. To keep *your* family safe. How can you find it unsatisfactory when it meets your needs?"

"Irrelevant. Besides, information has come to my attention that requires my departure."

"Does this involve that zauber?"

"She is a brilliant sorceress, and correctly interpreted my dream."

"How do you know her interpretation was accurate? We know nothing about her."

"I know enough. She explained how my dream about a woman killing me was a metaphor—because a woman could never kill me. The zauber said this woman represented a creator, someone capable of bringing forth life. Zorulo, of course. That dubwana wants me dead."

"Then if there is no danger for you here, why do you insist upon leaving?"

"Herman, you do not listen. The dream referenced Zorulo. However, the zauber had a vision last night warning of danger here in Ramsey. He has sent someone to kill me."

Korlemo placed his empty glass on a side table. "I have remained here too long. The zauber advised I leave immediately. I am delegating that responsibility to you, my friend. My household needs to evacuate."

"You don't appreciate the difficulty in moving our families."

"Then move my family first. You can join us later." Korlemo stood, glancing down upon Herman before he departed. "I want you with me—to handle my affairs."

"You can't rely upon other werewolves to protect you like they do here. The ka'trete has disintegrated. The world has changed. Werewolves and vampires have changed. Ajabu live independently among bindimèn, hiding in the open. They answer to no master. I'm afraid you're stuck in the past."

"Your job is to carry out my commands." Korlemo placed his hand on Herman's shoulder. "I want to leave as soon as arrangements can be made." He left.

***

A fire smoldered in the hearth. A servant entered the room and turned on the overhead lights, then extinguished the remaining embers.

Herman remained seated. An argument would be futile. Korlemo clearly was in no mood to listen—not that he ever was. As a smoky blue hue glowed over the embers, Herman stared into the hearth, reflecting upon the evening.

When Korlemo invited him to remain after dinner, he worried the discussion would involve his daughter. Though relieved not to be reminded of Jackie's transgressions, he had no idea his patron wished to leave Ramsey.

The zauber's influence on Korlemo left him blindsided. Herman had planned to investigate the woman, but time was not on his side. He must speak with Enu, get his impression of the zauber.

Several hours passed with Herman seated in front of the fireplace. Long after midnight, he finally rose and returned home. He had plans to arrange.

They had influence in Kentucky, but he couldn't guarantee similar security somewhere else. Could he replicate a similar scenario outside of Ramsey on such a short deadline?

Rushing caused mistakes. Herman had to get it right. Not only was Korlemo's life at stake, but their entire community.

CHAPTER 39

A NORTHERN PRESSURE SYSTEM settled over Ramsey last night and brought a surprise cold snap. Peter drove his dad and Thomas out to Mammoth Cave National Park. Dad wanted to get out of the cramped rental house. They agreed a hike in the woods would be good for everyone.

Peter had to admit he'd been a jerk to Makeda about her patient. He considered apologizing but thought it would set a bad precedent.

At the park, he decided not to use the authorized entrance. The public entrance was another mile north. Instead, he steered off the highway and down a secluded dirt path perpendicular to Carpet Hill Road.

"Is this where you parked?" Dad asked.

"No, it's farther down. I'll show you where I encountered the werewolves."

They bounced down a potholed road before parking under an oak tree scarred with a large burn at the base of its trunk.

While they gathered their gear, Thomas read a pamphlet about the park Peter got from the visitor center.

"Dad, did you know Mammoth Park has one of the longest cave systems in the world?"

Peter snatched the brochure from Thomas and tossed it into the back seat. Thomas pushed him aside and searched for the brochure.

"Cut it out, guys," Dad said, strapping a backpack over his shoulders. "Let's go."

After locking the truck, Peter led them into the woods.

Tall trees and dense foliage provided a canopy that blocked much of the sunlight from reaching the forest floor. It kept the piney air brisk. Although it was alluring, Peter didn't find the scenery as appealing as North Carolina—but of course he was biased. Over three generations of their family had made the North Carolina Smoky Mountains their home.

He hiked at a brisk pace, eager to show where he had encountered the werewolves.

Headphones covered Thomas's ears as he played on a game controller.

Dad snatched the headphones off. "You need to hear the woods to appreciate them."

Peter smirked and shook his head. Thomas smacked him in the back.

About twenty minutes into their walk, Peter pointed to a small clearing surrounded by tall pines.

"Over there. I didn't have a chance to bury him because of the other werewolf." His brow creased. Now, the area lay vacant.

"You sure it was here?" Dad asked.

"Yes." Peter scanned the area, examining the soil for animal activity. "Maybe a coyote hauled the body away."

"Or a bear," Thomas said, clutching his machete.

For a moment, no one spoke.

Dad knelt, examining the ground and picking up leaves. Then he studied nearby branches. He brought the debris to his nose, turning it over in his hands while staring into the woods.

Likewise, Peter stirred the dirt with his boots, searching for signs of how the body was removed. It had been about a week since he killed the werewolf, but he noticed recently disturbed foliage. His gaze swept the area.

Animals scuttled along the woods. Things seemed peaceful and serene, but Peter noticed Dad's hand hovering over the machete hooked to his belt.

With a grunt, Dad dusted dirt from his hands. "It looked like … Doesn't matter. Let's go, guys."

This time Dad led their journey into the woods. Thomas was right behind him, and Peter brought up the rear.

They skirted the established trails, wanting to avoid people—especially the park rangers, since they hadn't paid the entrance fee. Around noon, they stopped to eat. Thomas played video games. Peter found a random piece of wood to whittle. Dad napped—to rest his eyes, he said.

**

Two hours later, Dad woke up and they marched back to their truck.

A large round sun descended over the late evening. Peter admired the clear sky, swishing a flick blade in his hand.

Thomas dropped the headphones in his backpack. "Do you think there are bats here, Dad?"

"Watch where you step and stop worrying about bats," Peter said, charging in front of his brother.

"The bats are probably closer to the caves, son."

A wide-eyed Thomas scanned the sky. "Too bad. I would've liked to see some bats."

More broken branches and disturbance in the soil became apparent during their trek. Peter studied the forest floor, falling farther behind his dad. "Look at those footsteps. Someone's walked here."

"Yes, I noticed," Dad said.

Close to dusk, Peter calculated another half hour before they reached the truck. After glancing at his watch, he noticed something stirring in the trees.

With a hand raised, Dad stepped forward and signaled for their caravan to halt. He placed two fingertips to his lips, alerting them to remain silent. In a slow 360-degree turn, he surveyed the area.

Because he was focused on the sky, looking for bats, Thomas careened into Peter's back.

As a hunter, Peter understood different types of quiet, some natural, others deliberate. Forests had a certain type of peace, but this silence sounded intentional. There was no movement. No birds flew. No animals scurried.

Dad used hand gestures, signaling them to spread out and get down. He retrieved a gun from the side of his pack and proceeded forward.

Peter squinted. Twenty yards ahead, on the trail, he saw a werewolf.

The glowering werewolf stood a few yards away from Dad. Under six feet tall, the beast had thick brown-black hair jutting out at various angles from its body. Oval, bulging, yellow eyes sat alongside an elongated snout with drooling fangs. Long, hairy arms with clawed, clenched limbs hung at its sides.

Prepared for the creature to leap forward at any moment, Peter loosened the crossbow from his backpack.

Instead of pouncing, the werewolf spoke. Its words slurred with dripping saliva. "Was it you? Did you kill Dirk?"

Peter's attention ping-ponged from Dad to the werewolf.

The lycan crept forward. "Did you?"

Dad stood his ground, staring straight ahead. A yard away from Dad, the werewolf leaped to the right as Peter's arrow sailed forward. Before the arrow met its target, the werewolf bounded into the woods. Peter sprinted after it, but the creature was too fast and disappeared into the forest.

Winded and panting, Peter circled back to Dad and Thomas. Before he arrived at the trail, a swoosh of air flurried the branches above his head. It gave him an idea.

Strapping the crossbow to his backpack, Peter climbed up a giant tree. From his perch, he observed and waited.

A moment later, on the trail, a howling lycan flew at Dad. Although smaller than the prior werewolf, this monster looked no less frightening,

In a crouch, Dad fired his rifle. Two projectiles slammed into the creature's chest. Like a dead weight, it crashed to the earth.

On the same trail, Thomas rushed toward Dad with a crossbow in one hand and a machete in the other. Before he reached Dad, tree branches rustled above Thomas's head. A lycan landed on his back.

Another werewolf bore down upon Dad from the left—one hundred and eighty degrees from the prior assault. Pivoting on his back foot, Dad fired twice, hitting the werewolf center mass with each shot.

Thomas screamed and fell forward. The werewolf clung to his back, lashing at the backpack—the one thing preventing it from tearing off Thomas's head. As the monster clawed Thomas's right chest, Dad ran to his side.

A second later, Peter lobbed an arrow laterally into the creature's chest. The werewolf rolled off his brother's back as he readied another shot.

Blood splattered the side of Thomas's face. He wiped pieces of tissue from around his eyes and attempted to stand.

On the ground, the lycan rolled in the dirt, shrieking. It plucked the arrow from its chest, screamed, and threw it at Thomas before scrambling away.

As the monster fled, Thomas climbed to his knees and fired a projectile into its back. A low thud escaped as the werewolf slumped forward onto the forest floor.

Dad reached Thomas. "Here, son. Let me help you." He lifted the pack from Thomas's back and helped him to a nearby tree.

Like a seesaw, Thomas breathed heavily.

Peter observed blood oozing briskly from his brother's wound. He wavered between helping Thomas or waiting for that other werewolf. Where was it?

With Thomas's rear protected, Dad rummaged in the pack for something to cover the gash. He worked fast. They hadn't brought many medical supplies, more concerned with food and drinks than dressings and antibiotic ointments.

While Dad worked, Thomas held a weapon in each hand. A wadded-up t-shirt became a compress as Dad applied it to the wound.

Once blood no longer dripped down Thomas's side, he laid down the machete and hugged Dad. "Thanks."

From his perch on a low-lying tree limb, Peter spied movement in the branches above their heads. Unable to identify anything because of the foliage, he waited for an opportunity to get a clear shot.

Soon, the rustling drew Thomas's and Dad's attention. They glanced up at the same moment a werewolf descended from the tree. Dad rolled right and Thomas left.

An arrow sailed between them, hitting the tree trunk.

Shit. Peter's shot missed the werewolf.

Large teeth twinkled in the setting sunlight. Peter watched the monster leering down upon his brother. The lycan swiped at Thomas's face. Before the creature could connect, Dad struck the werewolf in the back with a machete.

Scurrying backward, Thomas abandoned the spot where the monster collapsed on the ground at his feet.

Branches shook. A roar pierced the forest. The original werewolf they encountered on the trail thundered toward Dad.

In a precipitous retreat, his dad tripped over a tree root and fell on his buttocks. Since his machete was stuck in the other werewolf's back, he was unarmed.

Thomas reached for a crossbow and aimed. But Peter fired his weapon first, shooting an arrow into the monster's upper thigh.

The creature's eyes narrowed as it removed the arrow and hurled it aside. It rushed toward Dad, leaping with curled talons raised in the air.

This time Thomas discharged an arrow, piercing the right side of the lycan's head. Despite those injuries, the werewolf continued forward, apparently unaware of the fatal blow.

Peter jumped down from the tree, entered the clearing, and discharged another arrow into the werewolf's back.

Seconds passed. Gradually the lycan slouched to the ground, its body crumpling into a heap.

Thomas sank down and wiped his forehead.

Giving Thomas a thumbs-up, Dad limped over and slapped Peter on the back.

With a pained sigh, his brother tried to rise. "Guys, I need help."

"Stay down, Thomas—rest a minute. We need to clean up this mess," Dad said.

Together, Peter and Dad gathered the bodies and rolled them onto a tarp. Once Dad checked Thomas's wound, they set off, dragging the tarp containing the werewolves through the forest.

"There should be a deep hole or ditch around here somewhere," Dad said, leading the way.

The sun had set, and dark was quickly overtaking the forest. Peter secured his headlamp to light their path.

It took another twenty minutes, but they located a sinkhole. By then, the werewolves had shriveled back to human form. As they rolled the bodies over a precipice, Peter noticed a chest tattoo on the heavier man that read *Maxwell*. After disposing of the lycans, Peter glanced into the hole but couldn't see their bodies nor the bottom of the cavern.

Dad secured Thomas's dressings, and they trekked back to the truck. Thomas was too weak to climb inside, so Peter assisted him into the cab while Dad secured their weapons.

"Well, that was quite a walk," Dad said, strapping on his seat belt.

Peter gave him a side-glance and put the truck in gear. A pothole swallowed the front tire of the truck.

"Ow! Watch it." Thomas grabbed his side.

"Stop whining," Peter said.

Kicking the back of the driver's seat, Thomas yelled, "Careful!"

In the rearview mirror, Peter glanced at his brother. "Do you want me to drive fast, or let you bleed to death?"

His brother seemed to consider his options, until the next pothole.

"Bleed to death. Bleed to death. Slow down. No more potholes!"

CHAPTER 40

EARLY MONDAY MORNING, THE phone in Sylvia's office rang. *Problems already?* She was going to need more coffee if this was how the week was going to begin. Setting down her half-empty cup, she picked up the receiver.

"Yes?"

Her assistant said, "Dr. Senegal, you have a call from a Dr. Tobias at Benton Alliance Hospital. He insists on speaking with you immediately."

Benton Alliance was in Bowling Green. Sylvia couldn't imagine why a doctor from there would need to speak with her. She removed a legal pad from her desk drawer and selected the line with a flashing red light.

A crisp, blunt voice said, "Dr. Senegal, Susan Topper is my patient. I'm trying to get her medical records from your facility. We've faxed release forms, but your medical records department refuses to send them over."

Sylvia's body tensed. She listened, but her mind was elsewhere. Alfred Baptiste had been mistaken. Susan Topper had survived the crash. Drumming her fingers on the desk, she tried to stall.

"How is Mrs. Topper? We were concerned when she left the hospital AMA. She'd suffered a reaction to the anesthetic and started hallucinating. Is she feeling better?"

On her legal pad, Sylvia scribbled a note to direct the nurse supervisor to document in the medical chart how Mrs. Topper acted unusual in post-op.

Despite her questions, Dr. Tobias refused to provide details on his patient's disposition.

"Well, our surgeon hasn't finished his notes. The records should arrive by the end of today."

"You can't make it sooner?" Dr. Tobias asked.

She assured him the medical records would be sent posthaste.

After ending the call, Sylvia ordered her assistant to arrange an emergency meeting with the hospital board of directors. Their quarterly ajabu quorum was scheduled for Wednesday, but the situation with the Toppers needed to be addressed now.

Twirling her graduation ring on her finger, she cursed the stupid men screwing with her life. First, Joffy made a mistake with the sedation. *Moron.* Then idiot Alfred Baptiste failed to eliminate the Toppers as directed. Worst of all, Herman Baptiste, and his nymphomaniac daughter … The pen snapped between her fingers.

Like always, she had to fix other people's mistakes. She brought the coffee cup to her lips and realized it had cooled. She grimaced. Setting the cup aside, she took up the phone and called the hospital's counsel. After speaking with the legal department, she reclined in the chair and massaged her temples.

The law firm would dispatch associates to Benton Alliance to reach a settlement with the Toppers—payment would require their silence.

Sylvia planned to mention the incident at quorum. After a moment's reflection, she decided to revisit the issue surrounding the deaths in Ramsey. Maybe she would go for broke and share the salacious details about Jackie.

That would require further contemplation. Upsetting Herman Baptiste could possibly cause more problems than she could handle. First, more coffee.

CHAPTER 41

LAST NIGHT, MAKEDA STITCHED up Thomas, reassuring him that his liver wasn't damaged. He kept insisting the blood looked different. The third time he claimed his liver had been injured, she considered using a sleep incantation to knock him out. Instead, she gave him fifty milligrams of diphenhydramine and he finally slept.

At work Monday morning, the medicine floor started out busy and remained consistent throughout the day. Two hours before her shift ended, Makeda received a call from her friend Jeff Carson, who worked in administration.

"I've got a few minutes," he said. "Want to see the psychiatric unit now?"

"Absolutely. I'll be right there."

After concocting a story about her brother requiring inpatient treatment, Makeda had requested a tour of the psychiatric floor with the pretense of having him admitted. Carson had agreed to help.

The psychiatric floor remained the one medical unit she hadn't explored. Now that she knew about vampires in the operating rooms, Makeda wanted a complete perspective of the hospital. She needed to know whether the problem was confined to the surgical unit. Taking the stairs two at a time, she hurried up to the fourth floor.

Outside the unit, Carson waited with a key card. Locked doors shielded the area from prying eyes.

"Sorry for the rush," he said. "Dr. Senegal ordered an emergency board meeting this week, and everyone's scrambling to get things in order."

Out of breath, Makeda took a second to answer. "No, this is great. Thanks."

He waved his card before the reader. Mechanized doors parted and they crossed the threshold.

Unlike other medical floors, psychiatry encompassed one large open space. Individual patient rooms lined both sides of the unit. Near the entrance, positioned off to the right, was a nursing station.

While Carson searched for a nurse, Makeda proceeded down the unit. She reached for her cell phone, intending to take pictures.

Gray textured walls framed dilapidated linoleum floors. Thrift store landscape pictures clung to the walls. Downcast lighting gave the expanse a dispirited aura.

She scrutinized the area, gathering as many details as possible. High up in a corner of the wall, a red light from a security camera blinked. She turned away, continuing her survey.

There was no day room on the unit. Where did the patients congregate, or families visit? All the patient room doors were closed. The open floor space was vacant.

A foreboding saturated her mind. Makeda reached for a wall as the room swirled. Its intensity increased. She recognized sounds as her throbbing head became thick. While she watched Carson conversing with the floor nurse, a voice spoke inside her head.

'Petit pran prekosyon.'

Her teeth gritted. 'Not now, Nadege.'

In a flash, the presence evaporated, and her head lightened. Before she could continue her scrutiny of the unit, a security guard stepped out of the nursing station. He interposed himself between Carson and the nurse.

An earthy funk tickled her nose. The smell didn't resemble typical hospital odors. It could be from soiled linen. She had smelled something like it before on the medicine floor.

Carson glanced at the guard. "Makeda is one of our nurses from the medicine floor. She would like to check out our accommodations."

Trying to imagine how she would feel with a mentally ill brother who required hospitalization, Makeda's shoulders slumped. She sighed. After working ten hours, her fatigue made it easy to appear sad.

"My brother needs inpatient hospitalization. If he could stay at Lebanon Memorial, I could keep an eye on him."

The nurse's thick arms covered a generous bosom. "We don't have any available beds."

Frowning, Carson glanced from Makeda to the nurse. "That can't be right. I verified the census this morning. Three rooms should be available."

No one spoke. Makeda and Carson stared at the nurse.

A pounding fractured their stalemate. Everyone pivoted toward the source of the noise, which originated from a patient room.

Makeda shared a questioning look with Carson before proceeding in the direction of the clamor.

With a side step, the security guard barred her progress.

"What was that?" Carson asked.

The nurse glowered at him. "Don't worry about it. It's one of the patients. You know they're crazy here, right?"

Makeda took an instant dislike to the nurse, whose attitude was inappropriate for someone caring for mentally ill patients. She was concerned about the guard's proximity and retreated a step and bumped up against another guard.

"No beds," the scowling guard said. His booming voice brokered no doubt.

When she spun around, that peculiar scent filled her nostrils again. Now she understood the significance of those odors. Makeda inched away.

Carson's face flushed. "Now look here—"

"It's fine," Makeda said, laying a hand on his shoulder. "I can find another place for my brother."

Surrounded by two guards—one a werewolf—and a hostile nurse, Makeda decided it was time to leave. She hauled Carson by the arm toward the exit. He started to object, but she gave him a hard glare. Only once they were outside the unit did she relinquish his arm.

"Did you see that dude?" Carson asked. "He needs a complete makeover—ugly would be a step up for him."

She agreed and thanked Carson again before they exchanged goodbyes.

Carson took the elevator up to Human Resources. In contrast, Makeda jogged down the stairs toward the medicine floor. She considered how to access the operating rooms and psychiatric floor to get more information about what was going on. Lebanon Memorial had a systemic problem.

Inside the stairwell, a shape materialized in the corner of her eye. At first, she thought the security guard had followed her. Swiveling around, she found no one there. Whatever she thought she saw had disappeared.

Her hand touched the doorknob leading onto the second floor when a pressure gripped her forehead. She became discombobulated. Makeda leaned against the railing and collapsed onto the steps. Her eyes closed as she waited for the agony to abate.

Once the pressure burst, a portrait unfolded in her mind. A man of medium complexion with short, wavy black hair wore a rustic colored mudcloth—a Malian cotton fabric—outfit. Makeda studied the image, but it vanished as fast as it emerged. Her headache dissolved with the picture.

Makeda stumbled to her feet, cradling her head. *Why are spirits reaching out to me now?* Was there a relationship between Ramsey and these visions?

It didn't make sense. Lebanon, monsters, visions. *How will any of this help me locate Korlemo?* Perhaps it had nothing to do with the vampire.

Something had to give. Makeda had no one to confide in. No one she could speak with about these visions. Nadege communicated with her, but those dreams ... The visions originated from someone else—somewhere else.

Makeda doubted they came from her great-grandmother. Yewande would use kasi kasi. Feeling a burgeoning headache again, Makeda stopped thinking about the possibilities and returned to the medicine floor.

***

At the end of her shift, Makeda trudged across the employee parking lot. Though she had viewed the psychiatric floor, she didn't obtain any concrete information to share with the mwindaji.

She'd learned enough to understand Lebanon Memorial had a serious monster problem, but would it persuade the team to intervene? And if they did agree, how could the mwindaji cleanse the hospital of monsters without harming the patients?

Her cell phone vibrated as she entered her car.

"Hello?"

"Makeda, how about dinner?" Michael asked.

Better judgement would've been to decline his offer. But how many chances did a zauber get to spend an evening with a handsome man? Makeda needed to unwind, let down her guard for a few hours.

"Where?"

"My place."

She heard a smile in his reply, but was unsure about going to a sexy man's home in her current state of mind. Michael assured her that he would be on his best behavior. She hoped not. Life was full of bad decisions—at least Michael would be a pleasurable one.

***

Following his directions, Makeda arrived at the house before Michael. The quaint bungalow was in a nicer neighborhood than her rental. Fifteen minutes elapsed. *Where was he?* As she pulled out her cell phone to call him, Michael arrived in a sheriff's cruiser.

Not until that moment did Makeda consider her attire: scrubs and a ponytail. Too late to make herself more presentable. She came au naturel.

Inside the cozy home, they passed by the kitchen and entered the living room. An open floor plan revealed soft gray walls with recessed lights.

Makeda explored the bachelor pad. Michael's intoxicating cologne scented the air. An oversized black leather couch faced a sixty-inch television hanging above a brick fireplace. Built-in shelving along the wall surrounded the television. Vinyl record covers plastered the walls: Chaka Khan, Stevie Wonder, Marvin Gaye, and Earth, Wind & Fire displayed as art.

Family photos featured prominently along the mantel. A younger, thinner Michael paraded in his police uniform at a graduation ceremony. Another photo showed him hugging two smiling people on each side of him—his parents, she presumed.

In the kitchen, Michael unbagged the food containers. Makeda helped set the table with glasses and cutlery.

He kissed her cheek and held out her chair. As they dined on takeout, Makeda noticed the absence of his smile.

"Any more bodies surface?"

His hound-dog eyes gazed at her. "Let's talk about something else."

Conversation reverted to current events.

Michael pushed his food around for several minutes, without interest, it seemed. This wasn't the evening she desired. He retrieved a bottle of wine from the kitchen. Makeda declined and requested a soda.

He looked tired. She wanted to comfort him, for them to comfort each other.

"I noticed your graduation pictures. Your parents must be proud."

"Yeah." His downcast eyes rose, made brief contact, then drifted away.

Her brow wrinkled. "Michael, what's wrong?"

Tossing down his fork, he picked up the glass. "Nothing. It's … My parents weren't thrilled with my career choice."

"Are they ever?" She grinned.

He rubbed his forehead and gave her a tiny grin. "They expected me to become a businessman in our small town, not move out of state for a career in law enforcement. I'm over thirty, unmarried, and living away from home. To say my parents aren't pleased would be an understatement."

Makeda leaned back in her chair. "My dad hasn't forgiven me for dropping out of medical school."

The conversation stalled as she pursued her own thoughts.

She looked up and noticed Michael observing her.

He smiled and gathered her hands into his. "No more talk about work, or family." He kissed her fingers, then rose and cleared the table. "Hope you liked dinner. I didn't have time to cook."

"It was fine." Makeda finished her soda, then helped him clean up.

"Next time I'll grill something. Maybe your brother could join us." He winked.

Makeda ignored his comment—he was teasing her—and cleaned dishes. Not until music floated inside the house did she realize he had left the kitchen. She dried her hands and followed him into the living room. If he wasn't cleaning up, neither was she.

"Michael, I need to go."

Al Green's *Love and Happiness* crooned from the speakers. Michael held out his arms, inviting her to dance. His lips wore an enticing smile.

She slipped one hand into his and rested the other on his shoulder. His arm slid around her waist, and they glided in harmony with the sensual beats. Their bodies swayed to and fro.

Inebriated by his scent, Makeda's body swooned. With each melody of Al Green's vocals, their bodies migrated closer together. Rhythm surrounded their embrace.

Her tension drifted away as she floated in his arms. Like diving off a cliff into the ocean, she wanted to give in to the temptation of him. She knew she should leave before they reached the danger zone. Gazing up into his face, she placed her hand on his chest. Her mouth formed the words, but her lips fumbled.

He brought his face down next to hers, and their lips connected. Marvin Gaye's *Let's Get It On* drifted around the room. Wrapped in his muscled arms, she was lifted and carried to the couch. Makeda rested on his lap. Their lips never parted. The sounds of their heavy breathing made her heart race.

Sometime later, a vibration drummed against her leg. Her cell phone hummed. She broke their embrace and read the screen. Peter. Her gaze fell across her watch. *Damn.*

She jumped off Michael's lap and adjusted her scrubs. Her feet slipped into her sneakers as she answered the call.

"I'll be home in twenty minutes," she said, hanging up before Peter replied.

"Who was that?" Michael asked, buttoning his shirt.

She disregarded his question and gathered her hair into a ponytail. *Where is my hair clip? Screw it.* She sprinted for the door.

It was past midnight. In five hours, she had to return to the hospital. More importantly, she didn't want her overprotective brother to come looking for her.

In under a minute, she rushed out the door and into her car. If she wasn't worried about Peter, she could reflect upon the beautiful evening she spent with Michael. She wasn't in the mood to deal with her brother. Remembering how he treated her last boyfriend, Makeda didn't want him anywhere near Michael. A glance in the rearview mirror made her stomach lurch.

Michael followed in his cruiser.

Her jaw tensed. *Damn, damn, damn.* She clenched the steering wheel. At the rental house, as soon as the car engine shut off, the front door opened. Peter.

Locking the car, Makeda ran for the front door—*get Peter inside*—before Michael turned down the street. *Too late.*

At the end of the driveway, Michael parked the cruiser. He strode up the graveled pad sporting a wide grin. Peter's stern expression hinted at an unwelcome reception. She tried to push him over the threshold, but he resisted. Makeda wished she knew a spell to make him go inside.

An oblivious Michael extended his hand. "I'm Sheriff Michael Wilson. Nice to finally meet you. I want to apologize for keeping Makeda out late."

Peter accepted the handshake but continued mean mugging. "What were y'all doing?"

Makeda's face pinched into a frown. She shot Peter a glare, which he ignored.

Michael's gaze jockeyed from her to Peter. "We had dinner and lost track of time. Won't happen again."

Makeda gritted her teeth and jabbed Peter—hard—in his side. Her brother glared at Michael but didn't speak.

"We had dinner—that's all," Makeda said, tugging at Peter's arm.

"Again, my fault. I should have watched the time."

Peter glared, making no attempt to converse with Michael.

With wide eyes, Makeda angled her head to the side, hinting for Michael to leave.

"Again, nice meeting you. Perhaps we can all get together for dinner soon." Michael left.

Holding the door open for her, Peter followed Makeda inside. As soon as they crossed the threshold, an argument ensued.

Makeda's finger flew in his face. "I told you before to stay out of my personal life."

"Y'all weren't talking this late at night."

"What I was doing is none of your business. I don't comment about your long weekends at Brenda's place, do I?"

"That's different."

"No, it's not."

"You're my sister. Besides, we both know you have poor judgement when it comes to men." Peter proceeded down the hallway leading to the bedrooms.

Makeda grabbed the shoe off her foot and considered hurling it at his back. *How much damage could a sneaker do?*

Her temples pulsed. Half a minute passed before she placed the shoe back on her foot and went into the kitchen for water, then retired to her bedroom.

As she undressed, she reflected on the evening. For a moment, while Michael held her in his arms, she contemplated telling him about the monster activity afflicting the town. But he had established a comfortable life here in Ramsey. Perhaps it was better he didn't know.

Makeda crawled into bed. She cared for Michael and would make sure no harm came to him. Within five minutes, she was sound asleep.

CHAPTER 42

BESIDE THE WINDOWS INSIDE the study, Zainabu peeked outside. Heavy drapes blocked the brilliant sunshine. She followed the discussion between the brothers. It reminded her of a tennis match she'd watched on television during her layover in London.

Enu asked, "Korlemo, why do we need to rush? You must give Herman more time."

Herman sat near the fireplace, wiping sweat from his twitching brow.

She noticed his furtive glances. Once she caught his gaze and gave him a curt smile. He quickly averted his face.

"Korlemo, please," Herman said. "These arrangements are delicate. With more time, I can arrange sufficient accommodations for *all* our families."

Standing before the fireplace, Korlemo glared down at Herman. "I will not wait. My family will leave immediately. You can follow later."

Herman turned droopy eyes upon Enu.

"Brother, what you desire cannot be accomplish in this limited time frame. Give our friend the opportunity to move you comfortably."

Korlemo ignored Enu's comment and strode to the large desk in front of the bookcase. "Herman, your father accomplished much more than I am asking of you, in far less time. I trust you will not disappoint me."

Enu joined Korlemo at the desk. "This is ridiculous. Why this urgency because of a dream from a stranger who portends danger for you? Because of this, you demand we uproot our families and flee from an unspoken threat."

As he conversed, Enu glared in Zainabu's direction. Those deep black eyes held her gaze. She returned his attention with an equal measure of intensity, gracing him with a timid grin.

Zainabu understood Enu didn't trust her. His displeasure was not her concern though. Korlemo's mattered. In short order, she'd discerned the dynamics of the household. Though the brothers were similar in appearance, Korlemo was superior in force.

Enu stopped eyeing her and continued his argument.

"Enough," Korlemo said, turning toward Herman. "I want to leave immediately. Make it happen." He stormed from the room.

Gazing at his feet, Herman's face twitched.

With a sigh, Zainabu started to leave.

Gliding in front of her, Enu's liquid speed confirmed his vampiric nature. He blocked her departure. Minutes passed as he studied her face. Though uncomfortable, Zainabu maintained her composure. She shifted from one foot to the next— eager to leave, but not wanting to exude fear.

He gravitated forward. His proximity made her sweat. The coppery blood scent of him upset her stomach. She forced herself to appear at ease.

"In our village," Enu said, "the old people spoke of a legend. It said if you murdered a zauber, she would be reborn in the form of a child. When the child matured, she would avenge her death."

Feeling judged, Zainabu recoiled.

His eyes pursued her, peering deep inside, as if he searched for something—or someone.

Zainabu bit the inside of her lip. She refused to cede to him the advantage and restrained herself from hurling a litany of incantations and spells upon him.

Enu's voice deepened. "In your eyes, you remind me of someone long dead. If you are her—" He shook his head. "No. It is not possible. I do not know who you are, but I know what you are. You have deceived my brother, but know this— I understand you wish him no good." With unnatural speed, he left.

A second later, Herman darted for the door, departing on Enu's heels.

After they left, Zainabu decided to remain in the study. She settled into Korlemo's chair near the fireplace. A smile crept across her lips. She beheld the enormous room with its lavish furnishings, appreciating the embellished fixtures and rare paintings. She relished being in such opulence. Things were proceeding better than she had planned.

Now, she lived in a mansion. Korlemo rewarded her with more money than her parents would ever attain in their lifetimes. But she had to be careful. Korlemo was no stooge, and his temperament vacillated like the changing tides.

Suggesting he leave Ramsey had been a risky move, but Zainabu thought it wise. It threw him off-center. She wanted to remove him from everything offering him security. For her plan to succeed, she needed him to rely upon her counsel alone. By declaring she had a premonition of impending danger— though she had no such thing—she had persuaded the vampire to leave his sanctuary.

The art of divination eluded her. She couldn't predict the future or interpret dreams, but with Zorulo's help, she had. The demon led her to Korlemo, but she had plans for them both. Extending her legs forward toward the fireplace, she laughed.

"What are you doing, you silly girl?"

With alacrity, Zainabu sat up. At the door stood a curvaceous, dark-skinned woman.

"Well?" The woman zipped over to the chair where Zainabu sat as if carried on the wind. "Answer me."

Moving slowly, Zainabu rose. "I am a zauber hired by—"

"I know *what* you are," the woman snapped. "Why are you sitting here laughing to yourself?"

"Excuse me." Zainabu circled around the woman and proceeded toward the study doors. Before she could exit, a hand grasped her around the throat.

"Be careful," the woman hissed. Her index finger stroked the side of Zainabu's chin. "I am Korlemo's wife. No maji will protect you from me."

With effort, Zainabu glared into the woman's face, defiantly standing firm.

The woman released her grip.

Zainabu exited the room with her head high.

***

Once she left the study, Zainabu hurried upstairs. She locked the bedroom door, listening to see if Korlemo's wife followed. Minutes passed.

Inside her spacious bedroom, Zainabu twirled around, astonished at her good fortune. The bedroom was larger than the entire home she shared with her parents and brother. She sank her bare feet in the plush rug.

A month ago, she lived in a tiny village and spent her evenings dreaming about escaping to Gamali, Mali. Now she lived in America, in a mansion. Compared to her prior living arrangements, it was a castle.

Her grandmother had conferred their ancestors' oral histories into written words, and Zainabu studied everything she ever wrote. When her aunts had discovered she dabbled in forbidden maji, they ostracized her. People in their village shunned her. If they discovered she worked for a vampire …

She lay on the bed and gazed up at the ceiling, recalling what it took to get here. To say she sold her soul to the devil would not be far wrong. Zorulo demanded a high price. Fortunately, she formulated a strategy to eliminate the demon. First, though, she had to contend with Korlemo.

By colluding with Zorulo against Korlemo—Zainabu went from zero to infinity in one transaction. Relaying the interpretation was easy. She simply used Korlemo's arrogance to her advantage. The translation accomplished its purpose, allowing Zainabu to wrangle her way into his home and confidence. As advisor to Korlemo, she could acquire money, influence, and power.

Everything was fine until she heard that cry. A stupid zauber crying for her grandma. *How pathetic.*

Zorulo had also heard the zauber's pleas. He had warned Zainabu to avoid the woman but refused to explain why. She thought the lady was mental, assuring Zorulo she could deal with the naïve zauber if necessary. The idiot didn't even understand kasi kasi. Anyone within fifty kilometers had heard her whining.

A heavy presence descended upon the room. Zainabu sat up and scanned the area. Pressure filled the room, drawing out the air. Her breathing slowed. She waited for Zorulo's apparition to manifest.

An ash-colored cloud materialized in the middle of the room. Within seconds, the cloud morphed into the form of a bindimèn.

Zainabu crossed her legs and prepared to provide an update on her progress.

Zorulo's form hovered inches above the ground. "My dear. It's been too long. Why haven't I heard from you?"

"It's been three days."

"Have you broached the topic with him yet?"

"No, I'm working on it. I need time to develop his trust. He was pleased with my interpretation of his dream."

The apparition's artificial smile dissolved into a grimace. "Don't forget our deal. I will not wait long."

She swallowed hard. "I understand."

"Good. Do not test my patience. I've waited too long to retrieve Korlemo's soul. A thousand years was more than a son of a chieftain deserved. Make sure you follow my instructions. I will not be deceived by a mere witch."

Zainabu clenched her fists, creating indentions where her nails dug into her palms. "I suggested he leave Ramsey immediately."

"How does that coincide with my plans?"

"Moving will remove him from his security. He'll be more dependent upon me."

"Was that your reason for the suggestion?"

"I heard that zauber again. She mentioned a warning. I couldn't interpret everything she said, but I thought one of the words sounded like *help*. She might threaten our plans. Of course, I could eliminate her."

Zainabu's countenance remained neutral as Zorulo digested the explanation.

"She is stronger than you think. Besides, I didn't bring you here to battle a zauber. Your job is to entrap Korlemo and deliver him to me."

"Who is this woman? What do we know about her?"

"We? You presume too much. Forget the zauber. She's inconsequential to our arrangement."

"How do you know?"

"I know. Listen to me and stay away from her."

"Why does she bother you? If she's not a threat, why do I have to avoid her?"

"She has no footprint—no trail—but manifests an atmosphere about her I do not understand."

Zainabu grinned. "You can't be afraid of her."

"Do not forget who you are and why you are here. There are places worse than that wretched village you grew up in where I could send you. I am your master." Shedding his bindimèn body, Zorulo dissolved into a gaseous form. His presence grew inside the room, filling the space. The light fixtures flicked off, and the room darkened.

For a moment, Zainabu averted her eyes, feigning obeisance. "Yes, Zorulo."

His gaseous form lessened. The force in the room diminished, and the air cleared. The lights zapped on.

"I'll keep an eye on the zauber. You concentrate on Korlemo." His form dissipated.

Once sure he had departed, Zainabu exhaled. Something about the zauber bothered Zorulo. It didn't make sense. The woman was a moron. Zainabu could easily kill her. However, she needed Zorulo to deceive Korlemo. For now, the stupid zauber lived.

The drapes swooshed closed as Zainabu pulled the strings taut. Again, she made sure she was alone before sneaking into the closet.

Her hand adoringly caressed the royal blue wallpaper embossed with gold fleur-de-lis. Once she locked herself inside the wardrobe, she unpacked a book hidden inside her suitcase.

Waving her hand across the surface of the tome, Zainabu whispered an incantation.

The unlabeled cover fell aside, opening the book. She took great care turning the delicate vellum pages. With a flutter of her fingers, she found the desired section of the book. She caressed the written incantations of her ancestors as translated by her grandmother.

She had secreted the journal from her parents' home before she escaped. Skimming along the pages, Zainabu read a passage about demons. She sat cross-legged on the floor, reading spells on how to bind demons.

CHAPTER 43

WEDNESDAY MORNING, MAKEDA FOUND the hospital routine less cumbersome. She had spent Tuesday evening discussing with her family how to proceed in Ramsey.

Peter suggested they attack the monsters they had discovered and then return to New Jersey. She wanted to disinfect the hospital of whatever monsters haunted the medical floors. As usual, Thomas aligned with Peter. Dad remained undecided, believing they were missing something. He preferred to wait for further confirmation. Also, she knew he hoped to find Korlemo.

In the hospital, her medicine patients were on the mend. Work that day had been mundane. She managed time for a lunch break. Since she couldn't explore the surgery or psychiatric floors, she detoured to the pathology department to speak with Dr. Bones about the corpse unearthed on Sunday.

The overhead lights in the morgue flickered their strobe illumination around the drab chamber. Disinfectant stung her nostrils. Nothing had changed, except Dr. Bones was absent.

She spoke with the assistant pathologist, who stated Dr. Bones called out sick for the entire week. Sunday—from what she remembered—he hadn't looked ill. Not sure what to make of his sudden absence, Makeda headed for the cafeteria. She was sure Dr. Bones knew something about the monster activity in the hospital. But what was his involvement?

In the lobby, Makeda witnessed a bevy of people. Everywhere she looked, cooks, maintenance staff, and security personnel bustled around the medical center. People engaged in various activities, carting chairs, tables, boxes of assorted items, headed for the conference room with the enormous mahogany doors. Workers scrubbed the lobby in earnest. This level of activity was unusual for Lebanon Memorial.

Picking her way along the crowd, Makeda noticed new, more professional security personnel patrolling the floor. In addition to the activity, she noticed that pungent earthy smell again. Werewolves.

From her vantage point in the cafeteria, Makeda observed the activities. She spotted Kitty seated at a table with several other nurses. Discarding her meal tray, Makeda decided to find out about the hullabaloo.

She waved. "Hey, Kitty."

"Hi, Makeda," Kitty said. "Pull up a chair."

"Thanks." She sat down between Kitty and a nurse with a yellow bandana. "What's going on in the lobby?"

The older nurse wearing the bandana said, "The quorum's meeting tonight."

Makeda's brows knitted. "They need security for a meeting?"

Kitty's eyes danced with excitement. "Oh, yes. Our most important community leaders will be here tonight."

Chewing on lettuce, bandana nurse said, "It's a big deal here."

"They meet a few times a year," Kitty said.

Bandana nurse leaned across the table, lowering her voice. "I heard they're going to discuss what happened on the surgery floor this weekend."

The other nurse at the table shook her head. She set down her coffee cup and looked down her nose at bandana nurse. "I heard it was about Mr. Baptiste's daughter. They found her banging someone in the administration offices."

Wide-eyed, Kitty gawked. "No."

Makeda looked away as bandana nurse spoke again with a mouth full of food.

"Uh-uh. Jackie's been screwing her way around Lebanon since she started here. They wouldn't meet about that." The nurse swallowed then faced Makeda. "It's their regular quarterly meeting."

After assimilating the information, Makeda thanked them and left. Amongst the throng of workers in the lobby, she attempted to steal a peek into the conference room. The massive mahogany doors stood agape. Muscled guards patrolled the area. She couldn't come up with an excuse to get a closer view inside—besides, the odor bothered her.

Back on the medicine floor, Makeda rushed to finish her patient care, anxious to complete her shift. After work, she intended to check out Peter's camera and have a private seat at the meeting.

Peter had provided an outline and pictures from his prior excursion. Now she'd get to view the room in action.

***

Her phone rang as she pulled into the driveway. Michael.

Now was not the time for fooling around. Makeda kept the call brief, telling him she didn't feel well. When he offered to bring her soup, she declined. She hated lying, but she wanted to watch the video.

Once inside the rental home, Makeda couldn't figure out how to activate the camera. No one was home, and Peter wouldn't answer his phone. In the end, she called Daniel, who had the camera operational by the time her dad and brothers returned.

Dropping takeout food containers on the table in front of her, Peter asked, "What're you watching?"

"There's a meeting in the hospital conference room tonight," she said. "Daniel got the camera working for me."

Peter peered over her shoulder and viewed the screen. "Why didn't you call me? I could've done it."

She shot him a glare. "I did call. You didn't answer."

Thomas walked behind her to view the screen too.

After checking his phone, Peter grinned and pulled her hair. "While you're waiting, comb your nappy head."

"I will when you do something about your ugly face." She smacked him in the back.

Thomas chuckled until Peter smacked him in the arm. As they play-fought, Makeda removed items from the bags. Everyone carried their food into the living room to watch the game except her. Alone at the kitchen table, Makeda stared at the computer screen and ate takeout.

Dad balanced a plate on his thigh. "Let us know if anything happens."

On the video, Makeda watched staff bustle around tables, arranging utensils and centerpieces. Peter had positioned the camera opposite the massive wooden doors. A dais featured prominently on the screen. The room was breathtaking.

"Remember there's no audio," Peter said, chewing on a chicken leg.

Makeda hated that she couldn't be onsite. While eating, she imagined what secrets the room held.

CHAPTER 44

BEHIND THE PODIUM SITUATED in the large conference room, Sylvia surveyed the audience. Seated at a table immediately below her were Papa and Herman Baptiste.

This evening, in front of the people she cherished most, she would play a calculated move. It would either solidify her position at Lebanon Memorial or destroy her reputation throughout their community.

She raised a glass. Her gaze encompassed the room. "Welcome to spring quorum."

Light applause followed.

"We have urgent issues to discuss tonight, but first I would like everyone to take a moment to thank Mr. Herman Baptiste for his continued service to our community."

Most people stood. The applause was more substantial and continued for almost a minute. Baptiste stood and gave a short bow. Before he regained his seat, Sylvia noticed he shot her a side-glance.

She pretended not to notice and addressed the congregation. "Mr. Baptiste has spirited our community through difficult times. He has provided our families with security and prosperity. The leader of each household was provided a binder when they arrived. It contains the financial statements for the prior quarter."

Over the next hour, Sylvia detailed the hospital's finances. In time, the attention of the audience waned. She decided it was time to broach more sensitive topics.

She stood straighter. "There is a delicate subject we need to discuss." From her periphery, she noticed Baptiste's body stiffen. "Friday evening, we experienced a complication in the operating suite. Dr. Joffy addressed the situation, but not before a patient became cognizant of our activities."

As she explained what transpired, her foot tapped against the stage floor. "Unfortunately, I only received notification of this lapse the following morning. By then, the patient had fled the hospital. I contacted Alfred Baptiste to handle the situation. Perhaps he would like to explain his participation in these events." She yielded the podium.

A grimacing Alfred came forward. "Sylvia told me to extinguish the problem. I wasn't successful." He quickly abandoned the podium.

Following his pittance of an explanation, Sylvia regained the platform, sending him a sharp glare. She expected more personal chastisement from Alfred.

"The patient is now at Bowling Green hospital, probably intending to sue us."

"Let her," an audience member shouted. "We can pay her off."

The comment garnered laughter from several participants in the room.

Another person said, "Yeah. Medical malpractice—the new lottery."

Sylvia allowed the chuckles to subside. "That is not the point. We cannot afford any untoward attention on the hospital. Frederic Baptiste established this program at Lebanon

Memorial to allow us to live in comfort, free like bindimèn. Scrutiny from the authorities could unsettle our affairs."

Her finger rubbed along her graduation ring. She glanced down at its intricate carvings, remembering the strength of her tribe reflected in the three brilliant jewels. "We must be vigilant. For the past year, we have experienced multiple breaches in protocol by individuals in our community."

Again, her gaze fell on Baptiste. His eyes bored into hers, bristling at the comment.

She said, "Dead bodies have surfaced in Ramsey over the past two months. The sheriff has opened an investigation. We cannot afford rogue activity in our neighborhood."

One of the attendees stood and asked, "Who is doing this, Sylvia?"

She hesitated. An uncomfortable stillness descended over the meeting.

Her papa stood and placed a hand on Baptiste's shoulder. "Herman, why are you making this difficult for Sylvia?"

Baptiste rose, trembling. "Difficult for her? You believe this is difficult for *her*?" He glowered at Sylvia. "How dare you bring this topic up at quorum."

Before she could reply, Papa said, "This is where it belongs. We are family. The enterprises of your daughter and her associates have brought police attention to our community."

Dr. Ruphert raised his hand. Sylvia recognized his request to speak with a nod.

Standing beside his chair, Dr. Ruphert said, "Herman, don't blame Sylvia. Your daughter has been out of control for years. We credited her conduct to the foolishness of youth, but Jackie's behavior has escalated, bringing an undesirable element into Ramsey. We won't tolerate it. You need to deal with her licentious conduct or—"

"Or what?" Puffing out his chest, Baptiste's face elongated as his changeover to werewolf began.

Hissing in return, Dr. Ruphert's hands and arms elongated as he made his vampiric transformation. His posture became more erect. The doctor grew half a foot in height and bared his incisors. He taunted Baptiste, using his fingers in an invitation. "Come on over, you old dog, and give it a try."

From her position, Sylvia watched the room descend into chaos. Transformations occurred everywhere as the participants took sides. She remained in bindimèn form and attempted to regain control of the room. Her firm rebukes and commands were ignored.

Baptiste and Dr. Ruphert swore and snarled at each other as attendees struggled to keep them apart. Smaller arguments developed throughout the room.

As if propelled by a breeze, Korlemo floated up to the dais. With a wave of his hand, he motioned for Sylvia to be seated. With a slight bow of her head, she acquiesced.

Korlemo surveyed the room. His mere presence returned peace to the auditorium. Most participants reverted to their bindimèn forms. Everyone resumed their seats. After calm returned, he spoke.

"There is nothing to be gained from this dispute. Herman is an indulgent father—no fault there. The actions of Jackie have been nothing more than juvenile antics. If Sylvia or anyone else has evidence to the contrary, let them present it now."

With a measured pulse, he perused the room. Every eye tumbled before his. Once Korlemo scanned the entire space, his and every other gaze rested upon Sylvia.

Time to play her ace.

Sylvia retrieved a folder from a briefcase and handed it up to Korlemo. As he skimmed the documents, she watched.

Once finished, Korlemo gave her a slight nod before pursuing a different refrain.

"Jackie's actions will be dealt with by her family."

Sylvia noted the significant glare he gave Baptiste, whose countenance darkened from the reproach.

Turning his attention toward the audience, Korlemo said, "I will take this opportunity to make an announcement of my own. I have decided to leave Ramsey."

Sighs and objections rang throughout the room.

With raised hands, Korlemo quelled the murmurings. "Per our agreement, I will continue to provide financial resources for the hospital and the ajabu families in our community."

Rumblings and discussions resumed as he abandoned the dais.

Sylvia eyed him. She stood in his path and chanced to touch his arm. "Why, Korlemo?"

He addressed not her but the congregation. "Ramsey has become distasteful to me. I wish to return to the life I knew before."

"But this arrangement has brought us safety, unmolested by bindimèn," an attendee said.

"Yes, my friend. Safety, but no vivacity. I and my family will be leaving."

The attendee collapsed onto the seat as if his legs failed him.

There seemed nothing left to do but conclude the meeting. Sylvia sighed. "I will arrange another meeting to discuss the changes that will occur with Korlemo's departure."

No gavel banged; none was required. Sylvia, like the other attendees, she assumed, was exhausted. People dispersed at their leisure. Members encircled Korlemo, asking about his plans. Some sought advice, others made small talk. Sylvia watched him indulge them all. He replied to their concerns without revealing his true intentions.

Wondering what brought about this sudden decision, Sylvia eavesdropped on his conversations. She scrutinized the vampire, detecting his pleasure at the obsequious conduct of their community toward him. Under his regal bearing, she believed, lay apathy, visible in the negligible smile teasing at the corners of his lips and in the empty platitudes he offered in response to the participants' worries for their future.

Sylvia doubted Korlemo would honor his financial commitment. He was pure vampire, a mobowou in every sense of the word. In his voice, she heard a vacant mocking interest. The leaders didn't hear it—couldn't see it—but she did.

A mobowou didn't survive centuries by being concerned about the welfare of others. No, Korlemo was up to something, and she needed to uncover what it was. If he left, the money left. What would happen to their community?

***

On the drive home, Sylvia considered what occurred at quorum. As medical director, the hospital's solvency was her responsibility. Their community's subsistence depended upon the hospital's success.

Moreover, she feared for the financial stability of her family. Above all else, her loyalties lay with them. Somehow, she had to confirm Korlemo would continue funding the hospital—and the ajabu families.

Once home, she showered and crawled into bed. Down cotton sheets provided little comfort. After several hours of tossing and turning, she rose and hastily dressed. Lebanon Memorial held the answers she desired. That was where she needed to be.

***

In the predawn hours, she drove back to the hospital. She entered the ER, where two patients waited—one stretched out across chairs, sleeping. Sylvia explained to security she would be in her office—which was mostly true. First, she would scour Baptiste's desk for financial records.

The empty hospital lobby echoed her footsteps along the corridors. In the silence, she heard the elevator gears engage as it delivered her onto the fifth floor. After scanning the hallway, she hurried to the administrative wing.

From habit, her finger rubbed against her ring. She entered the security code into a touch screen pad outside Baptiste's office, disengaging the alarm. Out of caution, she didn't flip on the overhead light. Inside, she used a flashlight to search the room.

Supporting the hospital wouldn't be a financial burden for Korlemo given his substantial wealth. Sylvia had little confidence though that he would adhere to their current arrangement. Her family's ties with the Baptistes extended back centuries, but the Senegal family had no personal attachment to Korlemo—no familial bloodline.

Baptiste kept the hospital financial affairs sequestered from her. Years prior, he had provided her with a key and access code to his office when he became ill—in case of an emergency. She considered this an emergency.

Korlemo had provided no departure date. She doubted he would send a resignation letter to hospital administration. He wasn't even a doctor. His medical credentials were fraudulent, appropriated from a long-deceased physician. The state medical board had been lax in screening his application, along with several other medical staff members—not unusual. Most medical boards performed a cursory review of applicants, which their hospital's credentialing department used to their advantage.

In a metal cabinet near the desk, Sylvia uncovered a myriad of documents. As she considered where to begin, she spied a bulky leather-bound ledger hidden under a stack of manila folders. She removed the ledger and settled into a cushioned chair behind the desk.

The ledger held a treasure trove of information: offshore account numbers and notations about payments to the families in their community. Using her cell phone, she photographed the pages, then returned the binder to the cabinet. She double-checked the room before she departed.

Unsure when Baptiste would arrive, she barricaded herself in her private office. In her haste, she forgot to reset the alarm.

CHAPTER 45

IN THE RENTAL HOME, Peter yawned and propped his feet on the coffee table. "Anything yet?"

"No. Stop asking. I'll let you know if I see anything." Makeda stretched her aching shoulders. She'd sat in the dining chair for over an hour, staring at the computer screen. *This must be what it feels like to watch C-SPAN.*

The one thing she'd viewed for the past hour was Dr. Senegal speaking from the podium. In the interim, Makeda had called her best friend and braided her hair. She regretted passing up a date with Michael.

She recognized Mr. Baptiste, the hospital COO, but she couldn't get a direct visual on the gentleman seated beside him. From his profile, she admired the man's carob skin. Short, wavy, black hair suggested he was African American. An impeccably tailored suit adorned his well-toned physique. She assumed he was a physician.

Servers flitted between the tables. Attendees ate food arrayed on crystal plates and consumed beverages from goblets. Her attention, however, always reverted to the man seated next to Mr. Baptiste.

As she studied his characteristics, bile flooded the back of her throat. Her head throbbed and she became weak. Makeda grasped on to the table. She didn't want her dad to notice her being sick and have a reason to drop her from the team.

While Dad and Peter watched television—Thomas had already gone to bed—Makeda tiptoed into the kitchen for some water. After several sips, her head stopped spinning and her nausea abated.

Returning to the computer, she recognized several other physicians in the room, but not Dr. Bones. It seemed odd he hadn't attended. She presumed he must still be ill. Otherwise, he should be present at such a prestigious event.

Minutes ticked by. Her hope of learning something from the video evaporated. Stifling a yawn, she laid her head on the table.

Three weeks had elapsed, and the first mwindaji mission she led hadn't unearthed anything associated with Korlemo. They located plenty of monsters in Ramsey, but the real prize was Korlemo—at least as far as her dad was concerned. Maybe Peter was right about their vampire residing in New Jersey.

Bored with the video, Makeda considered how to access the operating suite and psychiatric floor. Perhaps she should get Peter admitted to the psych unit—he'd love that.

Dad cleaned their weapons while watching the game. Peter whittled an animal figurine from a piece of wood. A quaint domestic scene if you didn't know they hunted monsters.

On the video feed, Mr. Baptiste rose and faced off with another man. Makeda's eyes enlarged. The hospital COO morphed into a werewolf right on camera.

She waved her hands and screamed. "Oh, my ... Daddy, come here. Peter, look. Look!" Pointing at the screen, her mouth gaped.

They rushed to the kitchen table.

Peter gawked over her shoulder. "What the ..."

In his underwear, Thomas stumbled from the bedroom and joined them in front of the computer screen. Together, they stared at the video. The conference room sprouted vampires and werewolves in droves.

Dad grabbed Thomas by the shoulders. "Go get my Bible. It's in the duffle bag under the bed."

Thomas dashed off. The rest of them watched the video.

Makeda hadn't seen so many monsters in one place before. Gripping the table, she waited to see if Mr. Baptiste would fight the vampire she knew as Dr. Ruphert. From the corner of her eye, she glimpsed Dad. A chill crept down her spine. Frown lines zigzagged across his forehead—and something else. Fear. She'd never seen him afraid before.

From the bedroom, Thomas ran up to the table and handed Dad the Bible. Then he pulled up a chair and sat down beside Makeda.

She overheard Peter on his cell phone calling the other mwindaji. Makeda shuddered. How could they kill a hundred monsters?

'*Bajinu, mbabire.*'

Dad meticulously removed items from his Bible case, searching for something. With a steady hand, he set aside a picture of her mom dressed as a young bride. As his search continued, he became more animated, and his fingers trembled.

Makeda examined the items he set aside on the table.

A yellowed, frayed paper clung to the tips of his fingers. His eyes lit up. Quietly, he studied the computer. His gaze ping-ponged between the screen and paper.

Leaning forward, Makeda peered across the table at the paper, an old-fashioned, hand-drawn portrait. Her eyebrows questioned him.

"I inherited this picture from your grandfather," he said.

She already knew the answer, but Peter asked anyway. "Who is it?"

"Korlemo."

On the computer screen some semblance of order had returned to the room. The distinguished gentleman seated next to Mr. Baptiste now rose. He replaced Dr. Senegal at the podium.

Déjà vu washed over Makeda. She didn't need the portrait for comparison. This was the man from her vision in the stairwell. They had found Korlemo.

***

Pacing the living room, Peter ended his call with Zeke. "We need to go up there now, Dad. This is the closest we've ever come to Korlemo."

Peter's eagerness worried Makeda. Rushing, without a strategy or the other mwindaji, would be fatal. Her gaze gravitated toward Dad.

At the table, he held the Bible, his creased forehead a testament to his intense thoughts. "If we go there now, son, we die. We'd never reach Korlemo."

Moaning, Thomas plopped down on the couch. "There must be a hundred monsters in there."

Dad rubbed his forehead. "And taking down a thousand-year-old vampire won't be easy either."

Peter strode up to the table. "Dad—"

Makeda's chair slid back from the table. "Peter, we can't simply go up there and start shooting."

"She's right," Dad said. "The mwindaji work in secret. Our mission is to kill Korlemo, but we can't start a shootout in public. Safety is important."

"And the patients," she said. "They could get hurt." Susan Topper flashed into her mind. Makeda had failed her. When she visited the Toppers' home, Larry told her to get off his property. She had underestimated the situation in the operating suite. She was determined not to make that same mistake again.

"We have to be strategic," Dad said, speaking more to himself than them.

Peter crossed his arms over his chest. "If we don't act now, they'll scatter."

Makeda glared at him.

He ignored her and resumed pacing.

"We must be cautious in who we kill. The entire medical staff aren't monsters. We need to leave people to care for the patients," she said.

Dad finally set the Bible down and hugged Makeda. "I know you're worried about the patients, baby girl, but Korlemo must be stopped. He's our priority. If some monsters escape—"

"We aren't—"

"Sit down," Dad said, pointing at Peter. "I have to think."

Seeing Dad afraid scared Makeda more than she dared admit. He had survived 'Nam, an experience so terrifying that, although he often spoke about his time in the service, he *never, ever* mentioned Vietnam. Now he was in his sixties, and she still viewed him as a strong, invincible soldier. Nothing in this world had ever frightened him—until he saw all those monsters.

She couldn't show fear. In a soft voice, she said, "Daddy, I can discover Korlemo's identity tomorrow at work. Find out his alias, where he lives. Then we can kill him away from the hospital."

Peter jumped up again. "What about the monsters working at the hospital?"

Thomas nodded in agreement. His head snapped up and down like a seesaw.

Crossing her arms over her chest, Makeda grimaced. "I want to eliminate the monsters in the hospital too, but it won't be easy. Like Dad said, we must be selective in how we strike."

They spent the rest of the evening discussing how to eliminate the monsters in the hospital while protecting the patients.

Well after midnight, Makeda collapsed into bed. She knew tomorrow promised worse things. Was her sorcery ready? Could the mwindaji save Lebanon?

Too nervous to sleep, she closed her eyes, repeating incantations in her mind.

CHAPTER 46

AT HOME, HERMAN LUMBERED down the stairs and into the kitchen, scratching his legs where support stockings dug into his calves. The stove clock read 3:00 a.m. Putting the final touches on their exit strategy taxed his mental faculties. He started the coffee maker and prepared to review the folder Sylvia created on Jackie.

An hour later, he was sipping coffee when the front door creaked open.

Jackie hummed and staggered into the foyer. Seemingly unaware of his presence, she crept up the stairs.

A pungent stench of alcohol met Herman's nose. He slipped on the hardwood floors charging after her. "Jackie, we need to talk."

Her pace never slackened.

Herman trailed behind, but she ignored his pleas and headed straight for her bedroom. As a final indignity, she slammed the door in his face.

He pounded on the door. "Open up, right now. I'm your father. Open this door."

In answer to his shouting, Herman's sons came to his aid.

With a flat hand, Alfred slapped on the door. "Jackie, open up. Dad wants to speak with you. Open the damn door!"

Minutes passed, but no response came from inside.

Herman hung his head, thanked his sons, and directed them to return to bed. In a stooped gait, he retreated to the kitchen and reread the dossier Sylvia had amassed.

Inside a manila folder, along with other documents, lay a newspaper clipping and photo. The article detailed the murder of a man from Bowling Green. Jason Tupelo, it read, was a recent Mississippi transplant, who relocated to the city weeks before his death. Motorists discovered his mutilated body discarded off an expressway.

Frowning and shaking his head, Herman reread where the last sighting of the victim had been—a bar in Bowling Green. Witnesses placed Tupelo in the company of an unidentified woman, who was now a person of interest. Authorities sought the public's help in identifying this woman.

Anyone who knew Jackie would be able to make an identification despite the blurry photo. Given her busy social life, it was only a matter of time before one of Jackie's friends contacted the police. Herman massaged his temples and considered what he could do. He needed to protect her but wasn't sure this time he could.

Seven hours later, he finalized the arrangements for Korlemo. His bones ached from sitting in the kitchen chair all night. He decided not to go into work today. It was imperative he conveyed to Jackie the need for her to remain inside the house.

***

Later that morning, footsteps pattered down the stairs. Without a word to him, Jackie made a beeline for the cappuccino maker.

Herman observed his daughter, waiting until she joined him at the table. On the outside she resembled an angel; inside … Where had he gone wrong?

His wife died before Jackie became a teenager, but problems surfaced before then. Would things have turned out differently if Stella had lived? Though it pained him to admit it, Jackie would've been worse.

Stella at least had the decency to conduct her injudicious behavior outside of Ramsey. The last time he saw her alive, she was headed to Memphis with Dayo and several other women for an evening out. Two nights later, the police recovered Stella's body inside a downtown motel. Neither Dayo nor the other women ever discussed what occurred. Herman couldn't ask Korlemo to question Dayo—not that it mattered.

He married the woman he loved, but Stella was reckless. Jackie inherited her mother's beauty *and* disregard for authority. Fortunately, Herman was able to discipline their other children, but Jackie—

"Good morning, Daddy." Jackie set down a mug and Danish. With disinterest, she stirred the coffee and picked at the pastry. Her gaze wandered out over the back yard.

A sunny Kentucky morning held no attraction for Herman. Between Jackie's escapades and Korlemo's demands, the day looked pitch-dark.

Herman brought his hands together as if in prayer. "Jackie, listen to me. You need to leave Ramsey." He spoke softly, not wanting to antagonize her because he had no appetite for an argument.

Without taking her eyes away from the scenery, Jackie drank coffee and nibbled on the pastry.

When Herman realized she didn't intend to respond, he pelted the table with his fists, launching the pastry onto the floor. "This is serious. I can't fix it."

Jackie curled her legs up along the chair, turning blasé eyes upon him. "I'm sorry, Daddy. I won't do it again."

He slid the folder across the table, knocking over the coffee mug. Liquid spilled onto the tiled floor, a muddy river washing over the pastry.

Lazily, Jackie eyed the opened folder. As Herman watched, her gaze glided across the papers, then paused on the photo. She flipped the file closed and her attention drifted back toward him with an attitude of insouciance.

"Nice picture."

"I can't help you if you won't listen. You must leave here—now. Korlemo is leaving. We *all* will be leaving."

Her gaze widened. "Where are we going?"

"To a new place."

"Where?"

"I can't tell you, but we leave this weekend—and I want you to come."

Rolling her eyes, Jackie's arms crossed over her chest. She drawled, "Daddy—"

His hands slammed on the table as he leaped up from the chair. "No! No more discussion. You must leave with us."

Her green eyes softened, and her lashes fluttered. "Yes, Daddy."

He ambled around the table and kissed the top of her head. "I need you to stay home until we leave. Do you understand? If someone identifies you, the police will pick you up."

She bestowed an Oscar-worthy smile upon him and gave her solemn word to stay put.

Herman rubbed his bleary, bloodshot eyes and left. He failed to notice the sparkle in her emerald-green gaze.

As soon as he climbed the stairs, Jackie's cell phone came out of her pocket.

CHAPTER 47

INSIDE THE SHERIFF'S STATION, Michael removed his hat and ambled toward his private office.

A deputy waved his arms, vying for his attention. "Sheriff, we got a bulletin from the highway patrol."

Michael accepted the paper, perched on the edge of the deputy's desk, and read it.

The missive stated the highway patrol sought the identity of the woman pictured below. She was a person of interest in the murder investigation of a Jason Tupelo. Jurisdictions should forward information to Bowling Green homicide division.

Studying the picture, Michael thought he recognized the woman. Presently, he couldn't recall her name. *Someone around town would know her, though.*

He donned his hat. "I'll show the picture around Dempsey's bar, then hit some of the local shops. I have to go over to the courthouse this morning anyway." He directed his deputies to make copies and circulate the photo around town. Then he placed the bulletin in the pocket of his uniform and departed.

CHAPTER 48

BEEPING MACHINES AND FLUORESCENT overhead lights animated the lackluster décor of the hospital medicine floor. That morning, Makeda's imagination soared. Every sound—every shadow—cast a sinister impression. An atmosphere of foreboding followed each step she made. Before her imagination went absolutely haywire, duty called.

She went to answer a patient call light. Nursing routine settled her nerves. After helping her patient, Makeda hid in the supply room and called Carson.

"Hey, I need some information." In the background, papers shuffled.

"I've got that in spades," Carson said. "What's up?"

"I saw this doctor the other day. Older black man with thick, wavy, black hair. Tall and distinguished—"

"Dr. Steven Winters. Don't tell me you're falling for him too."

"What do you mean?"

"Most of the nurses in the hospital have made a play for him. What happened between you and the sheriff?"

"Nothing. I ran into the doctor last night and wanted to know who he was."

"Yeah, right. Whatever."

"Really, I'm not interested in him like that."

"Hey, I'm not judging. I've played the field myself, but you should know he's married."

"He is?"

"Oh, yeah. And his wife's a piece of work. She'd bite your head off."

Makeda chuckled. "I bet." The doctor's wife was most likely a vampire and *could* bite her head off. But Carson didn't know that. She thanked him and ended the call.

Next, she sent Daniel a text.

LOOK UP DR STEVEN WINTERS

"Makeda!"

She exited the supply closet and attended to her patients.

Later, a text alert chirped on her phone.

NO ADDRESS SEARCHED LOCAL STATE INTERNET ZERO

They'd have to find another way to locate him. If Dr. Winters, aka Korlemo, showed up in the operating room tonight, the mwindaji could follow him home. Makeda needed to check the surgery schedule—another item for her list.

Before the cantankerous charge nurse screamed her name again, Makeda returned to her patients.

CHAPTER 49

THE BUZZING OFFICE DESK phone distracted her reading, but Sylvia ignored it. Dawn crested hours ago, but there were still a lot of financial statements to review.

After the third call, she answered. "What?"

An official-sounding voice said, "The Toppers consented to a financial settlement of two hundred thousand dollars. I obtained a signed nondisclosure agreement."

After a brief discussion with the lawyer, Sylvia terminated the call. She shook her head in disbelief. *Idiots.* The Toppers hadn't realized the hospital would have paid considerably more to secure their silence. At least she completed one task. Baptiste would need to be notified, but that could wait.

Her examination of the ledger revealed Korlemo's financial assets exceeded what Baptiste had disclosed to her—or quorum. Sylvia contacted the banking institutions to verify the information. Records revealed that days before quorum, Baptiste completed several large transactions. One involved discontinuing the dispersal of monies paid monthly into Lebanon Memorial's accounts receivable. There were no further pending payments due and outstanding to the hospital. Baptiste and Korlemo planned to abscond and leave their community destitute.

Sylvia's foot tapped rapidly against the floor. The secret to Lebanon's success was the supplemental income provided by Korlemo. Without additional funding, the hospital would go bankrupt in a matter of months. Reimbursements from insurance companies and Medicare were woefully insufficient to maintain their operations. Like many rural hospitals, Lebanon Memorial would close.

Hours later, she gained a better understanding of the hospital's financial situation—and Korlemo's. She uncovered multiple withdrawals made for household items and property. Baptiste had purchased a new residence.

The clock displayed the late hour. It had taken her all day to investigate Korlemo's finances. Sylvia wouldn't have time to research this new property. With account numbers from the ledger, she conducted several of her own transactions.

She gazed out the office window while stretching her neck. A soft breeze rustled the trees. Burnt hues of the setting sun cascaded along the sky. As she appreciated the vibrant green leaves of spring, her finger grazed her graduation ring.

The phone rang.

"Hello."

"Sylvia?" The blunt tone raised hairs on the back of Sylvia's neck.

"Albert? What's wrong?"

"I received notification from the state medical board. An allegation of medical misconduct has been made against the hospital."

She exhaled. For a moment, she feared Alfred had discovered her embezzlement.

"The consumer affairs division will be conducting an emergency inspection next week."

How would the state inspection affect her plans?

Since she had no intention of remaining in Ramsey after this weekend, it wouldn't. But she needed to keep Albert and his father away from Lebanon long enough for her to flee.

"It was probably the Toppers. I'll take care of it." Cleaning up Lebanon's messes had been her responsibility for years. Well, no more. In an aside, she asked, "Albert, will you be leaving with Korlemo?"

The line went silent.

"No, I plan to stay in Ramsey."

Liar. "Thank you, that's good to know."

After hanging up, Sylvia considered what Alfred had said. It wouldn't surprise anyone that he accompanied his father. People understood if Korlemo left, Baptiste would too. But why did Albert attempt to deceive her?

Sylvia called her assistant.

"Yes, Dr. Senegal."

"Cancel the emergency board meeting for tomorrow. Schedule an administration meeting next week regarding a state health inspection." She hung up.

Over the next half hour, she arranged for the computer to send a resignation letter to Human Resources late tomorrow afternoon. Sylvia knew it wouldn't be read until Monday morning. Hospital staff shut down early on Fridays.

The rest of the evening she devoted to reallocating money Baptiste hid and redistributing those assets among new accounts established in her name. When she exited Lebanon Memorial that evening, it would be for the last time. Unfortunately, the hospital would implode. She didn't have time to dismantle their operation in an orderly manner. If Baptiste or Korlemo discovered her transgressions ...

She couldn't worry about that now; she had to hurry.

CHAPTER 50

AROUND ONE IN THE afternoon, Michael sauntered into Dempsey's bar, circulating the police photo. Despite the early hour, the bar was half-full. After speaking with several patrons and the bartender, Michael received a positive identification.

The woman in the photo had been recognized as a Jackie Baptiste. According to the bartender, Ms. Baptiste worked at Lebanon Memorial Hospital. But no one had her address or phone number.

At the sheriff's station, a public records search failed to yield any demographic information on Ms. Baptiste. Michael decided to try her place of employment.

***

In the hospital lobby, Michael waved to the volunteer at the help desk before proceeding up to the fifth floor. He briefly considered stopping on the medicine floor to speak with Makeda but realized it would be inappropriate. On the fifth floor, he exited the elevator and followed signs to Human Resources.

There, a receptionist scrutinized his badge. With one eye on him, she placed a call. After several "uh huhs," she directed Michael down a hallway.

A morose woman stood as he entered the office. The place smelled of roses and lavender. Cat photos and tchotchkes covered every visible surface. With a firm grasp, the woman received his handshake. "I'm Ms. Davies."

He accepted the seat proffered. Removing his hat, he again presented his badge. "Good morning. I'm Sheriff Michael Wilson. I need the home address and phone number of a Ms. Jackie Baptiste."

Like a rigid mannequin with a sallow yellow complexion, the unblinking Ms. Davies said, "Subpoena." Her mouth moved like an automaton as her hand opened and stretched forward. It would remain empty.

Michael had been unable to secure a subpoena. Although he knew it was required, he decided to try to obtain the information anyway, hoping the authority of his uniform would overcome any obstacles.

"It's being processed." Not a lie. He had completed the application.

Her hand retracted. "Come back when you have the form, signed by a judge."

He squeezed the hat's brim and leaned forward. "Ma'am, I need to speak with Ms. Baptiste about an important matter. If you would give me her phone number and address—"

"Her address is the most personal of information, Sheriff. It's where she lives. Our home is our castle." With her beaked nose held high, Ms. Davies glared across the desk.

Several useless minutes elapsed as Michael tried to persuade her, explaining the request involved a homicide.

Unmoved, Ms. Davies reclined in her chair. "Mr. Baptiste is a pillar of our community and should not have his trust breached by sending police to his home. I will not deviate from protocol to make your life easier. A subpoena is required, and I insist you provide it before I release information on any of our employees. Good day, sir."

Unable to persuade Ms. Davies, Michael settled into his hat and departed. The supercilious expression on her face irritated him. So prim and proper, she hadn't realized she confided in him that Jackie Baptiste lived with her father. With this new information, he returned to his cruiser.

On the way out, he spotted Makeda in the employee parking lot.

"Makeda!"

CHAPTER 51

Outside the hospital, wind pierced Makeda's scrubs. She shivered and quickly zipped up her jacket. Before she could cross the hospital parking lot, someone shouted her name. She spun around and noticed Michael jogging toward her with a large smile on his lips.

People rubbernecked, stopping their flight home to snoop.

Once he caught up with her, he kissed her cheek. "Hey, how're you doing?"

"I'm fine, but what are you doing here?"

Without answering her question, Michael led her by the elbow off to the side. Once they were away from the traffic of exiting employees, he asked, "Do you have a moment? I have a question." As he spoke, Michael guided her onto the passenger seat of his cruiser.

Inside his cruiser, he alerted dispatch to hold his calls.

Makeda's brows rose. Unconsciously, she touched her thick black hair. She wished she could have looked more presentable. *Calm down, girl. You just got off work; he shouldn't expect much.* She could've at least rubbed some petroleum jelly over her dry lips.

He asked, "Do you know Jackie Baptiste?"

She frowned. It wasn't what she expected or hoped for. "No, I don't. I've heard of her, of course."

"Why 'of course'?"

"You know, hospital gossip." Her head tilted to the right.

"What's going on?"

"She's a suspect in a homicide. I need to know where she lives. Where she hangs out." Michael placed his hat on the console and explained about the police bulletin from Bowling Green homicide. "I really want to assist in this investigation, bring her in for questioning." He handed her the bulletin and photo.

After a quick glance, Makeda handed them back. "I don't know anything about her aside from the local gossip."

His gaze widened. "Which is?"

"Which is she's the spoiled daughter of the hospital administrator. She does what she wants, when she wants, because she can. Most people at the hospital respect her father and overlook her behavior."

"What type of behavior?"

With a loud sigh, Makeda relayed what she'd heard.

"Do you know anyone she's tight with? Anyone who would know where her dad lives?"

She shook her head. "I wish I did. Why don't you give the authorities in Bowling Green her name and let them pursue it? It's their case."

Michael frowned. "Why would I do that? She's a suspect in my jurisdiction. I understand you're worried about me, but this is my job."

"I know it's your job, but it's one case. Please, leave it alone."

He studied her eyes. "You believe she's dangerous."

Clouds blew across the sun, plunging the sky into a shaded darkness. Makeda wriggled. Her breath slowed. The ticking of Michael's watch took on a larger dimension in the confined space of his vehicle. They stared at each other.

Breaking eye contact, Makeda glanced across the parking lot. "Drive over to my car."

He obliged but didn't speak. Once he brought the cruiser alongside her Honda, he parked. Michael angled his body to face her.

She licked her lips and considered how to convey concern without seeming like a nut. *How do you explain to someone monsters exist? Tell the truth.*

"Jackie is a monster."

Michael's right eyebrow rose. "You mean she's a very bad person."

"No, I mean she's a monster."

He didn't flinch. She didn't blink.

Rubbing from his forehead to the back of his neck, Michael took a deep breath. "Okay, Makeda. What type of monster?"

She inched closer to him and leaned over the console between them. "I know it sounds crazy, but I'm serious. Remember the autopsy last weekend, the body from the woods?"

He nodded.

"I examined the victim's neck. Two puncture wounds pierced his carotid artery."

"Okay."

"And you said there was almost no blood at the crime scene."

"So?"

Her left brow arched. "So? Puncture wounds to the neck, no blood where you discovered the body. Remember the savagery around the neck and the torso slashed in that gruesome manner." She tried to lead him to a conclusion he refused to make.

Michael placed his hat back on, then removed it again. His jaw clenched.

Makeda worried. She wanted to caution him, but not such that he would feel compelled to intervene.

His fingers drummed along the car's console. "Okay, I agree. An animal didn't inflict that level of trauma, a human being did. But you sound like—like you're suggesting a vampire killed this guy." Michael's sarcasm met her stoic, unwavering face.

"I know it sounds crazy, but there's something evil here in Ramsey. I've gone down to the morgue several times this month. This isn't the first body found exsanguinated with the organs removed, am I right? Tell me, what type of animal does that?"

Michael's arms shot forward as he gesticulated. "I agree with you. Something's going on here. There's a murderer at work—maybe a serial killer. But a vampire? Makeda, please, work with me. It's the twenty-first century. There are no vampires."

"Why not? Why can't monsters like werewolves and vampires exist in the twenty-first century?"

He had no response.

"Dr. Bones hasn't been at work this week. Why? I believe he knows what's going on. The question is whether he's involved or simply covering up."

"Something is going on, but right now I want to find Jackie Baptiste. This is my first big case since becoming sheriff. I need to show this town I can run a serious investigation."

Makeda understood his desire to succeed. Gathering his hand in hers, she said, "I understand you want to assist in this investigation, but make me one promise."

"What?"

"Don't go anywhere near Jackie alone. Promise me."

"I promise."

Her shoulders slumped. After she relinquished his hands to reach for the door handle, he caught her palm and cradled it in his. She settled back into the seat.

He grinned. "Now, you have to make me a promise."

"Yes?"

"When this is over, we spend some time together. Alone."

Time stretched out.

Eventually, she gave him a peck on the lips. "All right. Please be safe."

"That goes for you too. Don't share your theory about monsters with anyone. I want us to talk about it some more."

With a slight nod, Makeda exited his cruiser and entered her car. On the drive home, she thought about their conversation. *Did I do the right thing?*

She recognized disbelief on his face, but at least he would be on guard. Makeda wanted to keep him safe until the mwindaji completed their work. What she needed was sorcery—and more time to practice.

Michael drove behind her to the rental house. His instinct to protect remained strong.

She exited the car and waved to him. Part of her felt she shouldn't have confided in him. *Could I do more to protect him?* He was the sheriff, but that wouldn't make a difference against a vampire.

CHAPTER 52

As MAKEDA ENTERED THE house, Michael pointed his cruiser toward downtown and called dispatch. "Carlotta, anything going on?"

The radio dispatcher sounded cheerful. "No, Sheriff. You need more time with your girlfriend?"

Laughter erupted in the background of the sheriff's station.

Fortunately, alone in the cruiser, no one witnessed his blush. Before Makeda arrived, Michael hadn't requested privacy. "I'm good. Call me if anything comes up. Out."

A moment later, he called dispatch again. "I'll be at Dr. Bones's place. Call me on my cell if anything comes up."

It took less than fifteen minutes to arrive at the traditional mid-century ranch home. A gnarled oak tree encompassed most of the front yard.

Michael used the knocker to rap three times on the door. With no signs of movement visible from the side window, he waited. He knew the doctor lived alone. Before he could knock again, the door opened.

Wearing a sweater and slacks with glasses propped on his forehead, the doctor stood back, inviting him inside without uttering a word.

Michael stomped his feet clear of leaves on the welcome mat and crossed the threshold.

The home resembled the man; immaculate. Everything had a place. Straight ahead, glass double doors overlooked a stone porch. Dense woods extended beyond.

Michael's eyes flowed toward a large fireplace. He inhaled the scent of burning logs. Positioned before the fireplace were two leather chairs with a small table between.

At his host's invitation, Michael sat in front of the fireplace. The doctor joined him after obtaining a drink from the side bar.

Holding the glass tightly in his hands, he asked, "You want anything, Mike?"

"No, thanks. I'm good." Michael removed his hat and stretched his legs.

In that short time, his friend emptied the glass. Apparently satiated, the doctor placed it on the mantel and retrieved a deck of cards.

Michael watched the shuffling cards. "I need some information, Doc. I believe you can help me."

"You play?" he asked while distributing the cards.

"Yeah. Poker mostly. Gin. Spades." Michael unfolded his fingers and picked up his cards.

"Umm. Cards isn't like dominoes."

Michael raised his eyebrows in agreement.

"What do you want to know?"

While they played gin, neither spoke, taking up cards from the deck and discarding them in rapid succession. Brisk play was interrupted when Michael called, "Gin."

An expletive ripped from his friend's mouth. The doctor shuffled again.

Michael used that moment to survey the room. Family photos decorated the walls and mantel. Neil had shared stories about his family, which had lived in Ramsey for generations.

Once the cards were dealt, the doctor settled back.

As he evaluated his hand, Michael asked, "Where does Jackie Baptiste live?"

Neil glowered. "Now, how would I know?"

He didn't budge. More would come. Michael understood people's urge to explain overwhelmed their initial reluctance. No conversation occurred for another round of play until Michael again called, "Gin."

The doctor bit his lip. "How the hell—"

"You're distracted, Neil. Tell me where she lives." Michael tossed his cards onto the table.

"I don't know where she lives—and that's the truth."

"How about Herman Baptiste, the hospital administrator?"

Not making eye contact, the doctor repeated his denial.

For the moment, Michael let it go. Whether or not he believed it, he had more questions. "What happened to that dead guy? And don't ask me which one; you know the one I mean."

Another hand started. Michael prepared to spend the night if necessary. He needed answers. Between the hollowed-out body cavities of the deceased victims, Jackie Baptiste's possible involvement in a murder, and Makeda believing in vampires, Michael needed sane explanations.

This time Neil claimed victory. Corralling the cards into a pile, the doctor reclined into his chair and stared into the fire. When he spoke, his voiced sounded distant.

"Mike, sometimes you must make hard decisions—decisions that don't simply affect you, but other people. Doing nothing can be the hardest thing you ever do."

Michael frowned and watched his friend pour another drink. Jiggling the bottle, the doctor motioned toward him.

Again, Michael abstained. His gaze followed Neil from across the room and back to the chair.

Neil tossed his head back and swallowed the beverage. Then he stared into the empty glass as if he didn't know where the fluid had gone.

"I knew this day would come, but I hoped not in my lifetime." The doctor paused as his eyes glossed over. "You have to believe me. If I knew this would happen …"

He slammed the glass down and cradled his head in his hands. "Damn it. I knew. Everyone knew."

Was Neil crying?

For the first time since the bodies surfaced, Michael feared the pathologist could be complicit in the deaths. One of his few friends in Ramsey, Dr. Neil Bones always struck Michael as a person of principles.

"How much do you know?" Neil asked, raising his head.

"What I know is those men weren't killed by animals. I did a search. Over the past three years, in this tri-county area, dozens of bodies have surfaced with similar trauma. I didn't look any further back. I didn't have to. There's a serial killer loose in Ramsey. Even Makeda noticed the deaths were suspicious."

At the mention of Makeda's name, Neil's demeanor changed. His back stiffened and gaze focused. "What did she learn?"

"You don't wanna know."

"Yes. I do." His friend inclined forward, hands on his knees.

Confused by this sudden interest, Michael rubbed his head and face, trying to refresh his senses. He hesitated, not wanting Neil to believe Makeda was crazy. *That's how rumors start.*

Until Makeda voiced her theory about monsters, Michael considered her not simply rational, but highly intelligent.

She had also spoken to him in confidence. He was reluctant to violate her trust.

"Mike, don't think anything is too wacky. I've heard everything."

"Not like this, you haven't—not from someone like Makeda." *Quid pro quo.* Give the doctor something to get something. "Makeda thinks a monster killed those guys."

After Michael blurted it out, he was too embarrassed to look at Neil. He stumbled over his words, hurried to voice the insane theory and move forward. "Makeda noticed holes in the guy's vein—or artery. I don't remember which. That and the fact we discovered little blood at the crime scene; she concluded a vampire killed those men. She's trying to find an explanation to fit the facts."

Because Neil's attention was riveted on him, Michael continued.

"I know someone moved that body. Strung that man up by the neck and exsanguinated him. I don't know how or why, but I do know someone murdered those men. Not a monster; a simple regular homegrown murderer. Now, what I want to know from you is why you certified those deaths as accidents."

A log in the fireplace fell over, spewing sparks throughout the room. A temporary brightness flared before the room sank into a low, warm glow. With a dead stare, the doctor's blue eyes pierced his.

Craning forward, Michael's position mirrored his friend's. "Neil, your turn. Why are you covering up those homicides?"

The doctor flinched, then sat up straight. His eyes retreated toward the fire. "She's right."

"What?" Michael strained to hear.

"I covered it up because—because Makeda's right."

No amount of head rubbing would remove cobwebs that didn't exist. *This can't be happening.* Michael extended his head to rest on the back of the chair.

"Shit. What the hell is going on in this place? Is everybody insane?" The chair provided no comfort. He rose and ambled around the living room.

Neil shuffled the cards and cleared his throat. "They came during the war. You must understand, we were desperate. FDR established programs to pull the country out of the Depression, but what brought America through was the war—and it was ending. After defeating Hitler, the war shifted to the Pacific. The town knew it was only a matter of time. What would happen when the programs dried up? Ramsey had no other commerce. It wasn't even a town back then."

After returning the cards to the mantel, Neil refilled his glass. Brandy this time. At the table, he set it aside. "My dad told me a handful arrived at first. Fredrick, Herman Baptiste's father, was their leader. He offered the town help in building a hospital, to provide medical care and jobs—good jobs. You can't understand what it meant to our community. Social security had started, but back then if you didn't work, you didn't eat. The hospital provided a once-in-a-lifetime opportunity for people to support their families."

Michael grew restless, it required effort to listen. None of this explained the deaths or got him closer to Jackie Baptiste. "What opportunity?"

"My father was a farmer. After my mom died, I placed him in a retirement home where he befriended a gentleman from an affluent Ramsey family. The man told my father how Fredrick arrived from Europe. Back then the community used a barn as a makeshift hospital. It functioned as the sole medical facility for the surrounding counties. We couldn't afford a permanent doctor. Once a week, a Bowling Green physician examined patients in that barn. Ramsey had a full-time nurse, and a midwife for the mothers. Then came Fredrick Baptiste."

Neil explained the agreement was to secure funding for a hospital if the community agreed to disregard the *eccentricities* of Baptiste's family. Control over the medical center would remain with Baptiste. Once the agreement was sealed, weird things started to occur.

Gazing into his beverage, Neil said, "People noticed changes around town. Mangled deer carcasses surfaced in the surrounding woods. The feral hog population declined. Residents reported strange noises at night."

His eyes drifted around the room. "Coyotes sounded different. If you looked closely—well, no one looked, not the authorities or the town leaders. Ramsey built their hospital and had it operational by the end of the war. It served the area well and provided high-waged jobs—still does."

The doctor stroked the rim of his glass. "Then the bodies started appearing."

"What bodies?"

"Transients. No one of importance, the authorities decided. Usually, the families didn't claim the bodies. People no one missed. So, of course my dad asked his friend what he meant. Monsters. The man said the Baptistes were monsters." Neil laughed. It was high-pitched and long.

Michael flinched. When Neil began to cry, he figured the guy was drunk. He reached forward and tried to grab the glass from the table, but Neil was quicker and snatched it away.

"I'm not drunk, and I'm not crazy. Neither is Makeda." He wiped his face on his sleeve. "I didn't want her to find out. I wanted to keep her away from—from this."

Michael's eyes gaped. "This what?"

"At the time, I worked in Covington. When the Ramsey coroner died, I jumped at the chance to return home. My dad had died long ago. Things were quiet at first. No mysterious deaths surfaced until last year. During the autopsies, I discovered organs missing, excessive brutality around the necks, arteries nicked. I realized the story my father told me years ago was true."

At the bar, refilling his glass, Neil spoke over his shoulder. "My dad said if the bodies started showing up again, it would be bad. We existed with them in a sick symbiotic relationship. The system worked if boundaries existed."

"What boundaries?"

After taking a sip, the doctor sat back down. "They were supposed to use transients. Dispose of bodies in the caverns to make sure their activities remained covert."

From the edge of his seat, Michael regarded his friend in horror. "Use—they didn't use them. They killed them!"

"No, they consumed them." Casting his eyes downward, Neil considered the empty glass. "Makeda's half-right. Werewolves *and* vampires live here with us good citizens. They have for many years."

The doctor took another deep breath. "I thought it was under control, until I read about the boy killed in Bowling Green. He graduated from college last fall and started a new job. What she did to him wasn't right. We made a pact with the devil, and now—now we pay the price."

Recognizing the drunken glaze, Michael wondered how long before his friend passed out. He removed the photo of Jackie Baptiste from his pocket and showed it to Neil.

"You're suggesting this woman killed him? Look at her. How could this lady tear a man apart like that?"

"Mike, you still don't get it. She's a werewolf, son. A damn werewolf! She could tear your head off!"

Sapped of energy, Michael had heard enough. He stretched and shook his body free of whatever nonsense had enraptured his friend and proceeded toward the front door. He donned his hat and jacket. Everyone was going crazy. He needed to get home. Rest. Tomorrow, he'd figure it out on his own. As he made his exit, Neil called him back.

"Wait. You'll need these."

Michael accepted a leather container. He unzipped the main pocket and found bullets and a large cross. The puzzled look on his face was obvious.

"I don't know if they'll work, but my father gave them to me before he died," Neil said.

Securing the container under his arm, Michael left without saying a word. Not because he believed his friend, but because it was easier.

In the cruiser, he checked in with dispatch. The throbbing from his head was tremendous. He rested on the steering wheel, wishing he hadn't come. Now, he had more questions than answers. He rolled down the windows and started the car.

His closest friend in Ramsey and his girlfriend both believed in monsters. Many people believed in aliens. He supposed there could be people who thought monsters existed. *But rational people?* Steering his vehicle toward home, he hoped he had some ibuprofen.

CHAPTER 53

DELICIOUS SCENTS OF CORN bread and collard greens excited Makeda's senses when she entered the rental house. She heard grease popping and inhaled the intoxicating aroma of fried chicken. Her stomach grumbled approval. Dropping her purse at the door, she greeted her cousins.

Nyesha was the first to give her a hug. "Hey, girl. How's work?"

Makeda hugged her cousin and explained her conversation with Daniel as she entered the kitchen.

Uncle John smacked the back of her hand when she reached for a chicken leg. "Go wash up."

After a quick change of clothing, Makeda rejoined her family in the kitchen. She assembled a plate of food and joined Nyesha, already seated on the living room floor.

Dad balanced a plate on his knee and asked her, "Did you find Korlemo?"

Makeda hurriedly swallowed some greens. "No, and he's not on the surgery schedule for tonight. But we can follow him home from work after his next shift."

Aaron licked his fingers before stroking his mustache. "How long is it gonna take? I took Friday off, but I work on Monday."

Wiping his mouth with a napkin, Zeke asked, "Why are we focused on Korlemo? From the video, there must be over a hundred monsters around here. Why don't we go after them?"

Keenan rubbed the indentations on the sides of his nose where his glasses pinched. "Zeke's right. Korlemo isn't the only vampire around here. There may be worse bad dudes out there."

"Korlemo is our priority." With a solemn face, Dad set his plate on the table.

"Why? Why do we waste our time on him?" Zeke asked, crossing his arms over his chest.

"Because I said so, and I lead this team." Dad eyed Zeke. Time ticked by an uncomfortably long moment as the two men glared at each other. Each person watched either Zeke or Dad. Tension swallowed the air in the tiny home. No one ate. No one moved.

The unspoken element had been stated. Korlemo's importance tore at the fabric of their group. Prior disagreements left them minus two former members and estranged from the larger mwindaji community. Dad refused to yield then, and Makeda doubted he would capitulate now. His fixation on killing the millennial vampire was legendary, bordering on obsession.

Uncle John cleared his throat. "We know you lead the team, James. The young people just want to be included." Her uncle signaled his son, communicating something unsaid.

"Sorry, Uncle J," Zeke said.

Dad rose and patted Zeke on the back. "It's okay, son. I'm distracted. This won't be an easy assault. We're severely outnumbered."

"We need to calculate how to deliver maximum damage and kill as many monsters as possible before we're detected," Uncle John said as he watched Dad.

"We have to get Korlemo," Dad mumbled, staring down at his feet.

Makeda wanted to provide a solution. She stood. "I got it. We divide into two teams. One team goes after Korlemo, the other takes the hospital." She paused to gauge the room. Since no one spoke, she continued. "I'll lead team hospital."

Nyesha stood beside her. "I'm with you. Team Makeda."

Dad rubbed his eyes. "That's not a good idea."

"Why not?" she asked.

Seconds passed by as he fumbled to provide an excuse. She knew he struggled to find a logical, non-fatherly reason to keep her from leading the team.

"You're not ready," he said, quickly picking up his plate.

Her teeth clenched. She opened her mouth to respond, but her uncle intervened.

"I'll lead team hospital. Makeda, you'll be our eyes and ears."

She understood her uncle was trying to maintain peace, but she was furious. Refusing to look at her dad, she sat on the floor again. Her silence confirmed consent.

"I'll lead the attack on Korlemo," Dad said.

Every time the mwindaji carried out a mission, Dad zeroed in on Korlemo. It had become his sole preoccupation. *Was that what I wanted?* A life devoted to hunting and killing monsters. Being a mwindaji had to have more meaning. Of course, she was more than a mwindaji. She was a zauber. She had forgotten that for too long. A sorceress created things, restored balance and order.

Over the ensuing hours the mwindaji planned their assault. Discussions flowed back and forth, but the details were not working out. A problem remained between Makeda and her dad. While he concentrated on Korlemo, she worried about the patients. Her thoughts returned to Susan Topper, and she refused to allow another innocent person to be injured.

"The hospital's our best chance to catch him," Dad said.

"Um-hmm," Peter agreed. "If we don't attack him there,

he's going to kill more people."

With little hope of appealing to her brother, Makeda said, "Dad, the patients have ongoing medical needs. If we remove the entire medical staff, who will care for them? Besides, not all the hospital personnel are monsters."

Playing conciliator, Uncle John asked, "If we don't hit Korlemo at the hospital, what do you suggest?"

Before Makeda could answer, she received a text. "Well, its moot now anyway. I asked a friend in Human Resources to check the surgery schedule. Dr. Winters—Korlemo—called off for the rest of the week. He won't be coming into the hospital tomorrow."

During the lull, people observed their feet, the door, the floor—anywhere their thoughts could flow uninterrupted.

Brian rose and collected scattered dishes. "Then we need to hit him at his home."

"We don't know where he lives," Peter said, rising from the couch.

Dad caught her gaze. "Daniel found nothing on the COO or Korlemo?"

Makeda shook her head, racking her brain to come up with a solution. "I know. Like we discussed, we divide up into two teams. Dad's group will go to the hospital and follow Mr. Baptiste. As COO, he must know where Korlemo lives. He's probably the vampire's sentinel. Also, you guys should follow Dr. Senegal. Her father's a werewolf, so obviously she's one too."

Peter said, "I'm going with Dad."

Soon everyone chose sides. Nyesha resigned from team Makeda to accompany her brother, Keenan, who joined Dad's team.

Makeda read anxiety across her dad's furrowed brow. He didn't like her not accompanying him on the attack. Still angry at him, Makeda scorned his unease. She intended to show that despite his efforts, she would be involved in the raid.

"Brian will disable the surgical suite," she said, addressing the group. "He'll make sure no patients are operated on during our attack. We can't exterminate all the medical personnel, but we can stop further injuries."

Peter approached Brian. "I have some ideas on how you can access the surgical unit."

Dad suggested Uncle John enter the hospital by the ER. "Daniel can access their security system remotely and disable the cameras."

"We don't need Daniel. I can disable the security system," Zeke said, carrying his plate into the kitchen. He started washing up.

Makeda smiled. As kids, they called Ezekiel "Zeke the Freak." Their dads retired from the military around the same time, and the families had been close for years.

Dark-skinned, about five-foot-nine, with dreadlocks extending down his back, Zeke had wanted to be a military pilot but failed the fitness exam. Instead, he became an engineer—an exceptional one. He had a gift for building things, especially weapons. With thick, black-rimmed glasses and a nonchalant manner, he didn't appear to be much of a fighter. Zeke subverted conventional stereotypes.

"We'll let Daniel in on our plans, but you'll be responsible for disabling the security system," Makeda said.

The evening descended into multiple conversations as everyone ironed out their individual assignments. At the center of it all, Makeda conferred with each person—clarifying their instructions.

Dad piped in, "Each team is responsible for disposing of their kills. If necessary, use the sinkholes around Mammoth Park."

"Remember, safety is paramount. If in doubt, back out," her uncle said.

Makeda noticed he directed those words at Dad, whose zeal to kill Korlemo was apparent to everyone. How far would he go to kill the vampire?

Around 2:00 a.m., Makeda excused herself to rest. She invited Nyesha to crash in her room.

"Not exactly my idea of a sleepover," Nyesha said, giving Makeda a wink. "Girl, let me tell you about my date last week."

As she and Nyesha proceeded down the hallway, Makeda overheard her dad conversing with Zeke. They exchanged a bro hug.

Dad's words were thick with emotion. "Take care of her, Ezekiel."

"I will," Zeke said.

The words brought comfort. She would have to accept that Dad would always view her as a little girl.

In the bedroom, Makeda collapsed on the bed fully clothed. Despite Nyesha's rambling story, she fell asleep within minutes of her head hitting the pillow.

Makeda tossed back and forth, unable to get comfortable. Something pushed against her shoulder. She startled awake and found Nyesha gazing down upon her.

Nyesha frowned with her eyes half-closed. "You okay? Girl, you've been tossing and turning all night. I could sleep better on the ground."

"Sorry," Makeda said.

Bumbling into the bathroom, Makeda washed her face but kept the lights off so Nyesha could sleep. A small wall night-light was the only illumination.

Water dripped off her chin as she glanced into the bathroom mirror. Her pupils constricted as a bright light materialized in the lower corner of the glass. Like a spotlight, it highlighted a scene, and her gaze zoned in.

An imposing dark-skinned man argued with a shorter, petite woman. He wore tan patterned kente cloth and had a twisted, toothy grin. The woman's light yellow eyes pleaded.

Makeda appreciated a tenderness in the woman's soft facial features. With no sound, she had to interpret their discussion from movements and expressions.

The woman gestured toward the man with her hands extended forward, imploring him to do something. His brows pinched. Throwing his hands forward, he pushed the air, knocking the woman over without touching her. The woman attempted to rise and failed. Her body slammed onto the ground again. Puffs of dust rose from the sandy surface.

Clapping his hands together, the man crushed the woman's body farther into the dirt. His fingers curled as he contorted the injured woman. Her torso arched at his command. His teeth clenched as he snarled.

Terror grew in the woman's wide gaze. She raised pleading hands.

With a flip of his wrist, he spun her around, onto her knees with her back facing him. He extended her neck backward.

Makeda trembled, terrified the man would snap the woman's neck.

The tiny woman's arms flung skyward. Her lips moved rapidly as she struggled to keep her neck from hyperextending.

Makeda deciphered the words on the woman's lips. Baoumali. She recognized the incantation as one she learned in childhood.

In a flash, another figure materialized. This second woman, stately and muscular, wore a long purple dress. She approached the wounded zauber. Golden edges from her garment swept the ground. White-gray hair in locks matched her white pupils. Underneath her creased forehead her oval eyes glared.

The brawny woman made a fist with her left hand and punched the air in the man's direction. He doubled over and grasped his abdomen. He threw his hand out toward her, but the regal woman stepped aside. A wind passed, billowing her dress.

Making a backhand motion, she flung the man aside. Her dress flowed around her limbs as she marched forward, raining punches upon his body.

Coiling into a ball, the man tried to shelter himself from her successive blows. Her fingers twisted around each other like snakes. In a flurry, the man's body was caught up in a whirlwind. Flailing, he spun around in the air. The purple-robed woman threw her hands to the sides. Instantly, the man dropped off into oblivion.

Because she lurched forward, Makeda's head bumped against the mirror. *Where did he go?*

She strained to peer inside the glass. Like the end of a movie reel, the scene went black. Her eyes blinked repeatedly to see if anything materialized. From her periphery, she detected a new figure in a different part of the mirror.

This heavyset woman kneeled on the ground. In increments, her head rose. Her hands pointed forward, beckoning. Makeda studied the face. It was her great-grandmother. *Bajinu?*

Like steam, the vision evaporated. Makeda touched the glass, trying to recapture the image. She examined the mirror, scrutinized its sides—even tried to rip it off the wall.

She heard Nyesha snoring and stopped tearing at the mirror. Instead, she sat on the toilet, weeping. Makeda recalled Tamara's directions, reined in her emotions, and directed her message to her great-grandmother.

'*Bajinu, mbabire.*'

Tears flowed down her cheeks. Minutes passed. No response came.

She stood. *Should I return to medical school?* Maybe Dad was right, and she didn't have the constitution to fight monsters, at least not as a zauber.

CHAPTER 54

THE SMALL RENTAL HOME didn't give Peter many options to burn off energy. He circled the living room.

"I can't believe we're sitting here doing nothing."

Most of the mwindaji had retired to sleep. Thomas stretched out on the couch playing a handheld game system. Dad and his uncle played dominoes at the kitchen table.

"Be patient," Uncle John said.

After watching him wear a hole in the carpet for the past hour, Dad suggested they go for a drive.

In a flurry, Peter threw on a jacket, then grabbed his backpack and weapons.

"Can I go too?" Thomas asked, setting down his game player.

"We'll be back in an hour," Dad said, addressing Uncle John. "We're gonna drive around town, get some air."

Peter grabbed the keys from Dad's hand and flew out of the house.

Inky blackness clothed the sky. Dawn remained hours away. Once in the truck, Peter drove toward the hospital.

"What're you doing?" Dad asked. "It's third shift. Korlemo's not gonna be in the hospital at this hour."

"Yeah, and the COO guy won't be there either," Thomas said.

Through the rearview mirror, Peter glared at his brother. "*Et tu Brute?*" He continued toward the medical facility, avoiding Dad's gaze. "There's nothing wrong with driving by."

Dad shrugged and stared out the side window. "I guess that's all right."

After driving past the hospital—twice—Peter parked at an abandoned shopping mall down the street. He needed to do something, even if it meant sitting in a truck until morning.

"Turn on the radio," Thomas asked.

He rolled his eyes but consented and settled in to stake out the facility.

Reclined against the headrest, Dad slouched down into the seat and slept.

Peter checked his watch. It read 3:55 a.m. His brother's crunching on snack mix grated on his nerves.

"Dammit, Thomas, close your mouth."

"I am," his brother said, wiping crumbs from the front of his shirt. Thomas retrieved a pair of night goggles from under the car seat.

"What're you doing now?" he asked.

"Using the goggles Makeda bought me for Christmas." Thomas scanned the hospital parking lot.

The only audible sounds were crickets and the occasional scampering opossum. Peter cracked the windows, allowing in cool, fresh air.

An hour passed before Thomas nudged him. "Look. Over there."

Peter sat up and pulled out his own binoculars.

Dad squinted. "What?"

A sports car zipped out of the employee lot.

Peter didn't recognize the driver. "Who was it, Thomas?"

"A lady. The one onstage in the video."

Tightening his view through the binoculars, Peter said, "According to Makeda, she's the medical director, and a werewolf."

Before anyone responded, Peter started the ignition and tailed the vehicle.

"Careful, son." Dad got out his cell phone. "John? Tell the kids we left to follow Dr. Senegal. They need to get to the hospital and watch for that Baptiste guy."

The Audi made a circuitous route around Ramsey. Its journey led to an exclusive enclave of condos on the northeast side of town.

While Thomas observed the doctor, Peter kept the truck idling in a grove of trees.

"She went inside," Thomas said, surveilling the residence with binoculars.

Peter, Thomas, and Dad employed the scientific method of rock, paper, scissors to determine who would approach her dwelling.

CHAPTER 55

LIKE A FOGHORN, THE cell phone alarm blared. Sylvia slapped it off. Still woozy with sleep, she glanced up at the ceiling.

The last twenty-four hours had been a whirlwind. Using Baptiste's passwords, she transferred over five million dollars to new accounts. Korlemo would be furious, but she didn't care. Sylvia was proud of the actions she took to protect her family—at least until she informed her father.

"How could you, Svie?" he had said. "I did not raise you to be a thief."

"But, Papa, Baptiste and Korlemo hid millions in overseas accounts. I found—"

"I will not listen to these lies against our friend and bene-factor," he had interrupted.

Though Sylvia only had a few hours of sleep, she had to speak with Papa before Baptiste discovered the missing money. The COO hadn't come into work yesterday, but she couldn't trust he would be absent two days in a row.

She climbed out of bed and packed a small suitcase. There would be nothing to return to after Human Resources received her resignation letter. Not a sentimental woman, Sylvia had her personal items loaded into the Audi in under thirty minutes.

Before she left the condo, she paused to admire the ring on her finger. A gift Papa entrusted to her, instilling the importance of family. Sylvia chose a path that promised security for her family.

She placed the car in gear and headed for Papa's home. Gunmetal gray clouds gathered in the sky. Did they portend bad tidings?

Sylvia turned on the radio to drown out her pessimistic thoughts.

CHAPTER 56

FRIDAY MORNING'S WEATHER FORECAST read cloudy and cool. It succinctly captioned Herman's melancholy mood. Yesterday, he missed work to confront his daughter about her extracurricular activities. He made sure Jackie stayed home, not wanting her arrested by the authorities. In that time, he completed the arrangements for Korlemo. But there was still a lot to accomplish before they left.

Herman directed his son, Alfred, to stay home and oversee the packing. He requested his other two sons accompany him to the hospital. Three days didn't seem long enough to complete everything, but Korlemo had been insistent about Herman leaving too. Though he should feel flattered, the work thrust upon him was immense.

The situation was delicate, not only concerning his friend Gerard Senegal, but also the other families in their community. Herman had to reassure everyone Korlemo would continue his financial support, although it was untrue. Already, Korlemo had withdrawn financial support for the hospital. Soon, the money provided for their ajabu community's subsistence would cease.

A thousand years ago, their tribe journeyed across Africa and crossed the seas to Europe. They clung together for strength, support, and security against a world of persecution. Now, that relationship would be destroyed because Herman was about to deceive them—fracture the blood oath they had sworn—for the leader of their clan. Would they blame him for the subterfuge or Korlemo? Did it matter?

He wondered if they would survive but was not conflicted for long. His father had made him swear allegiance to Korlemo above all others. He had feared the time would come when he would be tested. The moment came sooner than anticipated, and at an inconvenient moment. His worry for Jackie hampered his discernment.

As he guided his Mercedes into an assigned parking spot at Lebanon Memorial Hospital, Herman was confident Jackie understood his concern—at least he hoped so. He told her about their plan to evacuate that weekend. But she had to stay home until then.

On the fifth floor, as Herman approached his office, he detected something amiss. Though the door was closed and locked, the alarm wasn't engaged. He rushed inside and headed for the safe. Within minutes, he concluded nothing had been stolen. If it wasn't a robber, why would anyone enter his office?

The alarm had been disengaged but not triggered. His thoughts returned to quorum, and then to Sylvia. She alone had unrestricted access to his office.

He stumbled over a chair and ripped open a metal file cabinet. Again, nothing had been removed. *Wait.*

Several documents appeared disturbed, and his ledger was no longer in the far corner as he always left it. He flipped along pages and noticed his placeholder had been disturbed. He slammed the metal file cabinet door.

"Damn her."

The ledger contained passwords to private accounts and other sensitive financial information. *What would Sylvia do with it?*

Herman didn't know, but he had to find out—and quick. It could threaten Korlemo's departure. He dashed from the office, looking for his sons.

CHAPTER 57

FRIDAY MORNING, MICHAEL STRODE into the sheriff's department with a renewed purpose. He placed donuts and coffee on a file cabinet.

"Good morning."

As they grabbed donuts, his deputies returned his greeting and filled him in on what occurred—or didn't—during the evening.

Once the briefing ended, Michael retreated to his office. He whistled along the way, dropping several files on his desk. Once rejuvenated with caffeine, he made phone calls.

"May I speak with the detective in charge of the Jason Tupelo homicide?" He tilted back in the chair with a cup in his hand and waited.

A minute passed before a male voice said, "I'm in charge of the investigation. How can I help you?"

They exchanged introductions before Michael gave the homicide detective the information he had collected on Jackie Baptiste. Though he refused to believe the woman was a murderer, at this stage of the investigation it didn't matter.

He said, "I haven't obtained her demographic information yet, but I've applied for a subpoena to get the hospital employment records."

"Working together, we'll get it done," the Bowling Green detective said.

After a brief discussion, the detective thanked Michael and hung up. Both jurisdictions would issue a BOLO alert—be on the lookout—for Jackie Baptiste. Bowling Green would also alert the neighboring counties.

Next, Michael called the Ramsey courthouse. Unfortunately, The Honorable Judge Henry Powell had more pressing matters on the court docket, he was informed. According to the clerk, Judge Powell would be occupied all day.

Twirling a pen between his fingers, Michael said, "Please ask him to review my request as soon as possible. I'd appreciate a return call today."

"Yes, Sheriff. I'll tell him," the clerk said.

Michael hung up and chuckled. Ramsey didn't have enough judicial matters to occupy an entire day of the judge's time. He began to appreciate the level of influence the Baptistes carried.

It would be futile to request the personal data from the hospital again without a subpoena. Michael called the district attorney's office, the mayor, and several city council members. Everyone turned him down—at least those gracious enough to take his call.

The Baptistes must know law enforcement was involved. Perhaps Michael was wrong. With the obstacles placed in his way, it appeared Jackie Baptiste might be more involved in the homicide than he thought.

Staring at his desk, he remembered something the woman at Human Resources had said about Jackie Baptiste living at home. Perhaps Herman Baptiste was the key to locating her. It would be harder to get a subpoena on him, but at least he could inform Bowling Green. He picked up the phone again.

***

The sound of Michael slamming down the phone receiver echoed throughout the station. Deputies spun around and stared at him through the open office door, but no one spoke. Michael had never lost his temper before at work—never had a reason.

Judge Powell's clerk informed him the subpoena had been denied. A photo of Jackie Baptiste leaving a bar in the company of a murdered man on the day of a homicide apparently didn't rise to the level of reasonable cause for His Honor.

Stretched back in the chair, Michael allowed his anger to dissipate while he stared at ceiling tiles. The deputies returned to their duties as he considered what to do next. His desk phone light blinked, and he snatched up the receiver.

"Yes?"

"Mike, I got a warrant for Jackie Baptiste's cell phone and her financial statements," the Bowling Green homicide detective said.

Pissed that they could get a warrant, but he couldn't, Michael took solace in the fact their investigation was proceeding. "Great. Did you learn anything?"

"Not much. Her cell phone pinged off a tower near the bar that evening but not at the time we believe the homicide occurred. It's something, though. The DA still wants her for questioning."

"It's something, at least." He rubbed his forehead.

"Hold on, Mike."

The line went silent. Michael waited.

In under a minute the detective came back on the line. "Sorry about that. We received a call from the phone carrier. The suspect's phone pinged off a cell tower in Cave City. I need to call the authorities there. It's Friday afternoon and I want to alert them before it gets too late."

"Keep me informed." Michael hung up. His fingers drummed along the desktop. He looked around the room. "Screw it."

He grabbed his hat, determined to assist in the investigation.

A deputy asked, "Where you going, Sheriff?"

Slapping the hat on his head, Michael said, "Not sure. Call me on the radio if something comes up."

CHAPTER 58

JOHN HILL ENTERED THE emergency room complaining of abdominal pain. Makeda suggested the ruse. It was a complex symptom, easy to counterfeit and hard to disprove. He needed to be admitted to the medicine floor and in position once the hospital closed that evening. His son, Raymond, was by his side as he approached the reception window.

A disinterested receptionist said, "I need you to fill out these forms *completely* and provide your ID and insurance card." She never looked up from her computer.

Once the paperwork was completed, the staff ushered him into an exam room.

Pulling out his cell phone, Raymond sent his brother, Brian, a message.

WE'RE IN

***

Scratching his back, Brian caught a glimpse of himself in the reflective panel of the elevator door. The maintenance uniform was tight, but it was the only one Makeda could find. She'd detailed the layout of the hospital. Last night, Peter and Zeke instructed him on how to disable the operating rooms.

Grouped with the other maintenance staff, Brian stood at the security doors outside the surgical floor. With a quick glimpse into his tool bag, he verified his weapon was safe.

He waited his turn to be cleared to enter. In his mind, he recited the plan.

A huge burly guard compared name tags against a roster. Sweating, Brian sized him up.

The guard glared. "Hey, you. Come here. I don't have all day."

Brian pointed to the name tag on his shirt and held his breath as it was verified.

With a grunt, the guard waved him inside.

Giving little attention to the surgical unit, Brian hustled toward the second set of security doors. A different guard was stationed outside. Again, Brian pointed to his badge and was permitted inside.

The maintenance staff got to work. While everyone cleaned, Brian carefully made his way into an operating room. There were three. *Dammit.* Makeda hadn't told him how many rooms there were—she didn't know, he supposed. He needed to move quick. She told him the surgical suite operated at night, which should give him time to work undisturbed.

Brian disconnected the oxygen supply tanks—no gas, no procedures. Zeke explained how to disconnect the electricity for the monitoring equipment. Once his act of sabotage was completed, Brian exited the last operating room to find the entire staff had already left. He rushed out of the unit.

On the surgical floor, a nurse cornered him. She had frizzy, graying blond hair. Snapping her fingers, she motioned for him to come over.

Nervously, he swallowed. "Yes?"

Her thick finger pointed at him. "What were you doing back there?"

"Cleaning—"

"No, you weren't," she cut him off. "You were goofing off. Well, I have work for you out here. Room 301. Hop to it."

She snapped her fingers once more before stomping away.

Room 301 was located near the exit. When the nurse turned her back, Brian fled.

In the elevator, he pushed the button for the fifth floor. The team wanted to obtain any available financial documents. A monetary trail could lead to other monster dens. If they could locate bank account information, it could also help fund their expeditions. Weapons and travel cost money—not to mention the price of silver.

As the elevator doors opened onto the fifth floor, Brian remembered the camera in the conference room—removing it was imperative. Depending on what occurred that evening, they might not gain access to the hospital again. He took the elevator down to the first floor and dashed to the conference room. Large mahogany doors let him know he had the correct location.

Inside the enormous room, chairs and tables were stacked against the walls at over eight feet high. Brian squirmed behind the furniture and located the ventilation shaft. As Peter described, the camera mount hung right behind the grate.

Voices approached. They grew in volume until they seemed to come from right outside the conference room. Then the doorknob turned.

Brian realized people were about to enter and hid himself behind a table and stack of chairs. He peeked between the furniture and noticed three men enter.

A gray-haired older man said, "Come in here. We can talk in private."

"What does she know, Dad?" one of the younger men said.

The older man walked farther into the room, his face twitching. "I have no idea. So far, I figured out Sylvia accessed three accounts."

Placing his hand on the older man's shoulder, one of the younger men said, "Can't you stop her?"

"I closed the remaining accounts, but I haven't had time to calculate how much she stole. This morning, I had to set up new accounts and transfer money to cover our move." The older man sighed.

"What're you gonna do?"

"Talk to Gerard. She can't get away with this."

"What are you going to say if he asks about the money?"

"I don't know. Tell him I planned to set up separate accounts for each family remaining in Ramsey. I'll think of something. Right now, we must get that money back—all of it."

As the men exited the conference room, Brian attempted to reattach the grate. In his haste, he lost his balance and knocked a chair off the stack. It crashed onto the floor. Brian froze.

The men stopped and reentered the room.

Moving farther behind the furniture, Brian could no longer see the men, but heard whispering. He believed they were approaching the wall. He became motionless, opening his mouth to further quiet his breathing. The men stood nearby, but where?

After a few minutes, Brian heard their conversation. Inching around a stack of chairs, he caught a glimpse of them at the door. A half minute passed before they departed, closing the doors behind them.

Brian exhaled and wiped his forehead. He placed Peter's camera in a tool bag. Out of caution, he lingered for a few more minutes. Eventually, he eased from behind the stack of chairs and cracked open the door.

The hallway was empty. Brian hurried to the main area of the hospital and resumed his ascent to the fifth floor.

CHAPTER 59

SITUATED AGAINST A FORESTED background, the classic colonial home was centered on a sprawling, manicured estate. Large white columns stood before its symmetrical square structure. The Audi raced past iron security gates onto a cobbled circular drive.

Dogs ran across the lawn and encircled Sylvia's car. Yelping with excitement, they accompanied her inside.

Papa gave her a stern glare before kissing both her cheeks. He shuffled into the library. "Come in here." His kiss was tender, but his voice harsh.

It was imperative Sylvia explain her actions. Korlemo *and* Baptiste planned to desert them. Their dear family friend had turned traitor.

One of her brothers was already in the library.

Last night, Sylvia had called her oldest brother, Jules, who lived in New York City. She faxed him documents from Baptiste's ledger. Jules was a CPA. Sylvia trusted he would understand her position.

Papa's eyes were bloodshot. His voice croaked. "Sit down, Svie."

She sat as directed. "Papa—"

"No." He held up his withered hand. "Nothing can condone stealing from our protector. Korlemo is our leader, our provider. I don't want to hear anything except you intend to return the money forthwith."

"Let her explain," her brother said, taking a seat beside her.

"Do you not understand what you did, child? You brought shame on our family. Pilfering, like a common criminal—and from our benefactor."

The distress on his face humbled her. In his agitation, he rose and paced before the mantel. A photo from her medical school graduation hung above his shoulder.

Joining him, she placed a hand on his arm. "Papa, I can prove to you what I say is true. Korlemo is leaving us with no money. Baptiste has depleted the hospital accounts. There is no money left for the families. I had to protect us. You taught me family comes first."

They stood nose to nose. "Herman *is* our family. Korlemo is like a father to us."

She pivoted away from him to hide her eye roll.

Her brother must have sensed her frustration. "Give her a chance."

Without prelude, Sylvia opened a folder, and copies of Baptiste's documents spilled onto the marble-topped desk. In a short presentation, she delineated Baptiste's transactions over the past week and then pointed out the depleted accounts.

"These transactions preceded Wednesday's quorum. Mr. Baptiste failed to mention closing those accounts."

"He didn't have a chance." Papa scratched his head, causing his hair to stand up on end.

"He had plenty of opportunity at quorum or before. Why weren't these figures included in the financial documents provided to the families?"

Papa's face fell as Sylvia showed the amount of money removed from Lebanon Memorial's accounts. Like the sun rising over a dew-drenched field, a change evolved in his appearance. Sylvia hoped he was convinced.

Peering over Papa's shoulder, her brother also studied the documents. "This doesn't make sense. Sylvia is right. Baptiste—"

"No." Moving away from the documents, Papa's head trembled. "Taking the money without giving Herman a chance to explain was wrong."

"When was he going to explain?" Sylvia glanced from him to her brother. "They're already leaving. I found proof Korlemo purchased another property, and furnishings."

The trilling of the house phone interrupted their discussion. They paused. A domestic entered the library and announced Herman Baptiste was on the line.

Papa picked up the phone. Sylvia listened to the one-sided conversation. A minute elapsed, and then he replaced the receiver.

"Herman has discovered your embezzlement. He's coming over now. You will return the money, and then he will explain how Korlemo will establish new accounts for the hospital and those families remaining in Ramsey."

Stepping forward, Sylvia looked him in the eye. "Baptiste is a liar. I'm not returning the money."

In a flash, he slapped her across the face, knocking her to the ground.

Sylvia gasped as her fingers gingerly palpated her bruised cheek. Tears tumbled down her face. He had never hit her before, hadn't even raised his voice in anger. Didn't he understand she was trying to protect him—all of them?

Her eyes brimmed with tears as she gazed up at him, then traveled over to her gawking brother. She crawled up the side of the desk, declining her brother's offer of assistance.

She sprinted from the room, up the stairs, into her childhood bedroom, before slamming the door.

CHAPTER 60

UNABLE TO ACCESS THE administrative offices, Brian left the hospital and returned to their camper parked in the visitors' lot.

Outside, he changed out of the maintenance uniform, stashed Peter's camera under the front seat, and grabbed his pack. He then entered the emergency room to join Raymond and his dad.

Brian watched Raymond arguing with the doctor.

Seated beside the hospital bed, Raymond stood up and raised his voice. "If something happens to my dad, I'm gonna sue y'all's asses."

Kindhearted Raymond's effort rang hollow to Brian's ears, but it worked. The ruckus over his dad's abdominal pain led the doctor to consent to an admission. Within an hour, the staff transferred their dad to the medicine floor.

***

As he stood beside the hospital room door, Brian filled Makeda in.

Makeda wasn't his dad's assigned nurse, but she stopped by to check on him. "How did it go?" she asked.

"I disabled the operating rooms—there were three, by the way."

"Sorry, I didn't know."

"No problem. I removed Peter's camera, but I couldn't get inside the administration offices. There were too many staff for me to look around without being noticed. What's next?"

She fingered the stethoscope looped around her neck. "We wait. When visiting hours end, I'll check the morgue. It'll be the best place to dispose of any bodies. Once I give you the signal, we'll go check out the psych floor."

Brian eyeballed her.

She glared. "Wait for me. I'll call when things are ready."

His dad picked up the cell phone. "I'll call Zeke, tell him to get in place."

"Tell him to coordinate with Daniel," Makeda said. "The cameras must be disabled and ER access to the hospital blocked." She left.

Speaking on the phone, his dad asked, "Ezekiel, where're you at?" He ended the call and told Raymond to get his clothes. Changed into black camouflage, his dad climbed into bed and covered himself with bedsheets. A wicked grin crossed his face. He looked at Brian and Raymond—a spark shone in his eye.

"Ready to go hunting?" he asked. Without awaiting a reply, he pressed the nurse call light.

From the speaker, a voice asked, "Mr. Hill, how can I help you?"

"I wanna speak with my doctor."

"The doctors are on their way out. It's almost five o'clock. What's wrong?"

His dad suppressed a laugh. "I wanna speak with my doctor."

"Okay, Mr. Hill. I'll see if I can locate someone for you."

"Thank you."

Ten minutes later, a disgruntled-looking physician walked into the patient room. He marched up to the bed where Brian's dad lay with bedcovers drawn up to his neck. Holding a stethoscope with one hand in his coat pocket, the doctor glared down and asked, "Mr. Hill, what do you want?"

Careful to silently close the door, Brian crept up behind the physician.

His dad said, "I have an important question."

The doctor frowned. "What?"

"Are you a vampire?"

As the question escaped from his dad's lips, Raymond sprayed colloidal silver water in the doctor's face. Skin sloughed off the man's chin. He cried out as his hand reached for the bed. Fangs erupted from the doctor's mouth, and he grew in stature. Streams of blood and chunks of tissue poured down his neck as he morphed into a vampire and leered over the bed.

Yanking off the bedsheets, his dad sank a silver spear into the monster's chest.

Choked cries diminished as the vampire's fangs retracted and his red eyes turned black. Eye sockets became hollow a moment before the creature disintegrated into a pile of sand.

Brian brought over a trash can, and Raymond helped him sweep up the remains.

Once they cleaned up the room, his dad got situated in bed again. "Ready for more suck heads?"

Brian grinned. "You've been watching *Blade* again, haven't you?"

"What about it?" His dad chuckled. "Ready?"

He and Raymond nodded in agreement.

Snickering, his dad pushed the call button again. "I wanna speak with my doctor."

CHAPTER 61

PETER PARKED THE TRUCK down a narrow access road beside the estate, positioning it to view the gated entrance. They'd trailed Dr. Senegal from her condo that morning after surveilling her place.

"Let's go," Dad said.

Peter and Thomas grabbed their gear as everyone exited the truck. They scaled the fence and dashed toward the house.

Lying on the damp, cold ground, Peter spied out the home and surroundings using binoculars. He relayed to Dad what occurred inside. "The doctor is talking with two men. We should go in now."

"Give it a minute. We want Korlemo, remember," Dad said.

"The draperies are open. I doubt he'd be in the room," Peter said. The video had thrown Dad off his game, seeing all those monsters. Peter would have to compensate and take more initiative.

"At least the dogs are inside," Thomas said.

With a smirk, Peter glanced at Thomas and started to speak when he heard car tires. He crawled across shrubbery bordering the driveway as another car sped onto the estate and screeched to a halt at the front door. Three men exited the vehicle and entered the home.

Peter eyed Dad. "Well?"

"I know. We need to move—now."

Before Peter could climb off the damp earth, Thomas alerted them to movement on their left flank. They turned around, armed and prepared for the interlopers.

A familiar bird call crowed.

Dad held up a hand, directing them not to attack.

Seconds later, Peter viewed the top of Keenan's head. Clothed in black from head to toe, including a face mask revealing only his eyes, Keenan wore their traditional hunting gear. Nyesha and Aaron followed close behind.

Squatting beside the bushes, Keenan said, "Hey, Uncle J."

In response to Peter's quizzical expression, Keenan said, "We went to the hospital after Uncle J called. That COO guy left with two other men. We followed them here."

The mwindaji adjusted their plans.

Dad said, "We'll enter from the rear. Everyone else through the front. Peter and I'll head for the basement. Thomas will meet up with you guys inside. Got it?"

"We're good," Keenan said. He, Nyesha, and Aaron fanned out, using the brush to hide their approach to the front entrance.

Peter led Dad and Thomas around the side toward the rear.

CHAPTER 62

IN THE FOYER, DOGS yapped and barked. Gerard circled around them, opening the door for Herman and his sons.

"Go ahead into the library. I'll be there in a moment," Gerard said, herding the dogs into the kitchen.

In the library, Herman sat in front of a marbled desk while his sons stood beside the door. Gerard's youngest son entered the study and joined them beside the bookcase. The four young men conversed amongst themselves.

Gerard returned to the library and sat behind his desk.

Herman leaned forward. "This is a simple misunderstanding. I can explain everything, but I need Sylvia to return the money at once."

Papers were strewn across his desk. Gerard picked up a copy of a spreadsheet. "Svie says you and Korlemo are leaving us destitute—that hospital funds have been diverted."

"That's simply not true." Herman gaped. "You know me. Our families have relied on each other for centuries. Trust me."

"Where's Korlemo?" Gerard's youngest son asked, advancing toward the desk.

Herman glanced at the young man as one would an infant but didn't answer. He gazed back at Gerard. His eyes narrowed. "Sylvia must return the money immediately or I'll call the police."

Leaping to his feet, Gerard circled around the desk. "The police! You would call the authorities on my daughter? After all the years we have disregarded the indiscretions of Jackie, you would surrender Svie to bindimèn?"

In the background, the dogs barked. Their excitement increased in pitch.

His face suffused with anger, Herman shook his finger at Gerard. "Don't you speak about Jackie. At least my daughter is not a thief!"

Gerard's apoplectic face purpled. He swatted away Herman's hand. "No, she's a whore like her mother."

Herman punched Gerard in the nose. Blood sprayed down his face. In return, he backhanded Herman. A brawl erupted as the two men struck each other until their sons intervened and managed to separate them.

Struggling to be free, Gerard shouted, "Why didn't you mention the money at quorum?"

Herman's mouth opened—in what no doubt would have been a rebuttal—but his head shattered as a bullet slammed into the left side of his face. A gaping hole obliterated the skull above his ear. Blood and tissue splattered Herman's sons. Their father's body slipped from their grasp as shots rang out from all directions.

Gerard watched his older son transform into a werewolf, turn, and take up a defensive stance. Bullets pelted his son in the abdomen, and his body slumped to the ground in front of the bookcase.

One of Herman's sons morphed into a werewolf and leaped out the window. A bullet struck him in the back.

Gerard reached forward to protect his youngest, but not before two bullets struck that son in the chest. As Gerard cradled his son's bloodied body, a bullet splintered his right chest. His gaze fell over the blood leaching across his shirt.

Noise from bullets, howling, and dogs barking added to the chaos of servants scurrying throughout the house.

As Gerard's vision diminished, he watched Herman's other son transform into a werewolf. Losing consciousness, he observed the young man complete his metamorphosis and manage to howl before a bullet sliced into his throat.

Crawling across the carpeted floor, Gerard lay beside his oldest son before everything went black. The last thing he heard was someone yelling.

"Nyesha, stay here. Watch the front door. We're going upstairs."

CHAPTER 63

PETER AND DAD SNUCK into the kitchen door beside a large bay window. A pack of dogs charged them. Dad hit them with bear spray, then shoved, pushed, and threw them outside. Peter knew his dad wouldn't kill a dog unless absolutely necessary.

Outside, the animals barked and whined, scratching at the kitchen door.

Dad raced downstairs. Peter hurried behind him, knowing his dad's determination to find Korlemo could cause him to act hastily.

***

After shooting two werewolves in the kitchen, Thomas sprinted toward the front of the house.

Nyesha motioned over her shoulder, pointing him toward the stairs. Behind his cousins, Thomas took two stairs at a time, racing up to the second floor.

On the right side of the hallway, where the bedrooms faced the front yard, he heard glass breaking. Rushing to the window, he watched a sports car fly down the driveway and out the gates. From downstairs, he recognized Nyesha's voice.

She yelled, "Y'all, they're getting away!"

***

A spacious, wood-paneled basement contained an enormous television, pool table, and arcade games. Peter explored the room with a gun in each hand, and a crossbow strapped across his back. Dad entered a wine-tasting room and exited a half minute later.

Together they examined a thick, heavy door, cool to the touch. Dad located a hidden lever alongside the trim that when pulled slid aside a large section of the adjacent wall.

Peter chuckled. "Neat. The door was a dummy."

While he watched the rear, they descended into a musty tunneled passageway surrounded by damp stone walls.

Floor lighting illuminated the space. The stairway ended and deposited them on a dirt floor inside a cavernous room. Limited furnishings included three wooden coffins occupying the center of the room.

Peter gingerly approached the first coffin, regarding the elaborate surface ornamentation. As he reached the tomb, Dad simultaneously approached the second, middle coffin.

Because the coffin lid was heavy, Peter set down his guns and heaved it aside. Inside, he discovered a lovely woman with a large black afro sleeping on a silk pillow. He'd learned a long time ago not to be transfixed by vampires. Before she could awake, Peter slipped a silver stake from his side pocket and thrust it into her chest.

Unleashing a horrid scream, the vampire attempted to rise. As she wailed and thrashed, Peter hammered the stake into her chest using the butt of his machete. Her long, delicate hands struggled to remove the implement.

At the second casket, Dad managed to slide the lid partially off. However, that vampire was already awake. It lunged from its crypt and grabbed Dad's stake. Smoke billowed from the vampire's hand, but it managed to toss the stake aside.

Dark complexioned with thick, coiled black hair flecked with gray, the vampire sneered, pulling its lips away from pointy canines. It climbed free of the coffin, leering at Dad.

Still trying to impale the vampire in the first coffin, Peter kept an eye on the other skirmish.

Sweat poured down Dad's face as he quickly unfurled another stake, but the vampire grabbed his wrist. The monster's other arm elongated and reached for Dad's neck.

Still busy with his own fight, Peter tried to hurry along the lovely vampire's death. Realizing Dad was losing the battle, he relinquished his hold on the stake, whipped the crossbow from off his back, and shot an arrow into the other bloodsucker's chest.

Dad fell back as the vampire released his wrist. It slumped into the maroon-lined coffin before disintegrating into a pile of sand. With a grateful nod, Dad retrieved Peter's arrow before sliding closed the coffin lid.

Before his vampire gained the upper hand, Peter used the butt of his crossbow to hammer the stake clear through her body and into the wooden box.

While they fought the two vampires, a third escaped from its coffin and fled upstairs.

Dad angled his head toward the staircase. "Let's go."

They bolted up the stairs in pursuit. The vampire glided up the stone steps. She outran them with easy agility. Before they reached the top, a deafening wail rang out.

In the kitchen, Peter found a tower of flames in front of the door. He backed away from the blaze.

On the tiled floor, the vampire convulsed, screaming as her body was bathed in sunlight streaming in from a large bay window. Over several minutes, flames receded to a low flicker above a pile of ashes. By the time the other mwindaji arrived in the kitchen, the flames expired as dust settled along the travertine tiles.

Wheezing, Dad bent over, cradling his knees.

Keenan massaged his uncle's back. "Was he down there?"

Dad shook his head, still short of breath.

Peter filled the team in on what they discovered in the basement.

Aaron asked, "Did you want us to gather up the bodies and hide them in the park?"

Without answering, Dad slogged over to a chair and collapsed.

Nyesha and Thomas entered the kitchen.

"We're finished," Nyesha said. "I planted two guns on the guys in the study. It should look like a domestic shootout."

Dad nodded. "Gather whatever can be traced back to us. Let's head out."

Peter and Thomas checked the kitchen. As they left the property, a few werewolves sprinted into the forest.

As his finger glided along the gun barrel, Peter glanced at Dad. "Should we go after them?"

Dad frowned. "No. We delivered major damage today. Time to move on." His flat tone revealed his disappointment.

On the way to the truck, Peter's cell phone beeped a text message. He read the screen before handing it to Dad. "It's Daniel. He thinks he found Korlemo."

CHAPTER 64

JACKIE DIDN'T LIVE CAUTIOUSLY—HER mom hadn't. When she awoke Friday morning and discovered her dad had left for work, she phoned Petra and arranged to meet up in Cave City.

Leaving Ramsey didn't bother her. She had experienced everything—and everyone—the town had to offer. Now, she desired one last orgy. Like her mom, she would savor life to the very end.

Too bad the gas station security camera captured her leaving the bar. She wasn't worried, though. If her dad's money and influence couldn't fix the problem, she could always depend upon Judge Powell.

She had known the judge since childhood, visiting his chambers as a girl whenever her dad had business at the courthouse. The Honorable Judge Henry Powell had bounced her on his knee, given her sweet treats, and let her play with his gavel. His Honor still liked Jackie to sit on his lap, but now she engaged in a different type of bouncing.

While her brother prepared their departure, Jackie snuck out of the house. As soon as she exited the interstate in Cave City, she called Petra.

"I'm here. I'll be at your place in ten minutes. You better be ready."

"I will. I'm almost dressed," Petra said.

Tossing her cell phone into a cupholder, Jackie spotted a police cruiser under the freeway overpass. From the rearview mirror, she observed the cruiser crawl behind her as the signal light changed. Executing several precipitous turns, she noticed it kept pace with her.

Jackie wasn't in Ramsey, or Cavendish County. Judge Powell couldn't help her here. In a flash, the police cruiser's siren blared on. Red-blue flashing lights converged upon her car.

She circled back toward the interstate. Her Jaguar flew up the expressway as she punched the gas. Quickly, she merged into traffic and put miles between her and the police in under a minute.

***

Gates at the Baptiste estate parted right before Jackie sped up the flagstone entrance. She drove into the garage, oblivious to people outside traversing between moving vans and the house. Staff scurried out of the way, then resumed their work as if unsurprised by her disregard for their welfare.

After parking, Jackie sprinted inside the house. Everywhere people were packing or moving furniture. She commandeered one of the servants.

"Where's my dad? Go get him."

"He hasn't returned home," the man said. Like a robot on autopilot, he returned to work before she could give any further orders.

Ripping through the house, Jackie shouted for Albert. She found him in the library surrounded by books and papers. "Where's Dad?"

With several books in hand, Albert continued packing. "He went to speak with Senegal. Where have you been? There's no way we'll be ready by tomorrow unless everyone helps. I need you to—"

Jackie left the study before he finished the sentence. Albert's yelling trailed her upstairs. Unconcerned about the chaos of moving, Jackie escaped into her bedroom and locked the door.

CHAPTER 65

BEHIND THICK CLOUD COVER, the sun began its nightly descent. Peter pulled off the shoulder onto the main road as Dad spoke with Daniel over the phone.

Squinting as he listened, Dad ended the call and turned toward Peter. "Daniel traced a call this morning to a phone registered under Herman Baptiste."

"Yeah, but he's dead," Peter said.

"We should still check the place out. The location is north of Ramsey. If it's Baptiste's home, we might find Korlemo."

Keeping his eyes on the road ahead, Peter side-glanced at Dad, who hoped to find his nemesis there. A minute passed as Peter thought it over.

"Get the directions." He glanced in the rearview mirror. "Thomas, call Keenan. Tell him to follow us. We got another lead to check out."

***

The mwindaji arrived at the Baptiste estate early in the evening. A high stone fence surrounded the property. Security gates blocked the driveway. Positioned in front of the home and garage were three large moving vans.

From their vantage point, Peter spied a small Jaguar speed past the gate. A woman leaped from the vehicle and entered the home. With the gates momentarily parted, Peter signaled with a bird call. The mwindaji rushed inside before the gates shut.

"Peter, Thomas, and I will approach the moving trucks," Dad said. "Y'all cover the rear and surround the house."

"We'll be exposed as we approach the trucks," Peter said.

"No problem," Keenan said. "We got your backs until you find cover."

"Fine," Dad said. "Peter and I will take the basement and search for Korlemo. Thomas, rendezvous with the others once they're inside. Go."

Everyone spread out.

For a half minute, Peter watched movers exiting the house and packing trucks. He waited, timing their arrivals and departures between the trucks and house. When he spied a gap in their attention, he bolted for a truck closest to the house. He flicked open a hunting knife and released air from the tires.

In that moment, someone exited the mansion. They noticed Peter, dropped their boxes, and morphed into a werewolf. On all fours, the lycan charged him.

Pop, pop, pop. The werewolf hit the ground and expired without a sound.

Saluting the mwindaji at the tree line, Peter rushed to the next van. Before he got there, shots peppered the previously tranquil evening. It took a moment for him to realize the fireworks came from inside the house.

The other mwindaji must have entered the premises. So much for their plan. Bedlam erupted everywhere. People packing the trucks stopped.

Peter's position was compromised. Several werewolves bore down upon him from different directions. He fell back toward the woods.

Dad and Thomas shot the charging werewolves. One werewolf went down with a direct hit to the torso. A second leaped onto the side of the house and somersaulted into a nearby tree.

Werewolves had the advantage in the woods, especially at night. Peter decided to take the battle inside and sprinted toward the house. He noticed Thomas and Dad right behind him.

Chaos in the house made him consider returning to the driveway. It was all-out war. Shrieking, howling. Some werewolves fought while others fled. Frantic servants scrambled, trying to get out of the way.

In the foyer, Peter saw Nyesha stab a lycan in the shoulder. Keenan finished the creature off with a stab at the base of its neck.

Thomas ran upstairs.

Dodging the skirmish, Peter and Dad headed for the basement.

***

On the second floor, Thomas checked each bedroom. At the end of the wide hallway, a door ripped open. Before he could load his crossbow, a werewolf bounded forward, knocking the weapon from his hand.

He staggered backward and removed a machete from its sheath.

Instantly, the long, slender lycan smacked it from his grip and tossed Thomas onto his back. It mounted him. Sharp, jagged teeth loomed over his face as saliva slathered down his chest.

Thomas screamed for help.

Claws grasped the sides of his head as the werewolf brought him in for a bite. His eyes closed as blood splattered across his face and chest. The monster sagged onto him.

Disentangling himself, Thomas flung the creature aside and watched the werewolf dissolve into a svelte woman with jet-black hair and emerald eyes—or eye—the other orbit shattered with that side of her head.

He shuddered.

Nyesha nudged him. "Dude, let's go."

He gave her a hug and a kiss, then continued searching the rooms.

***

Coming up from the basement, Peter and Dad met the other mwindaji in the foyer.

"We found one vampire but no Korlemo," Dad said.

Keenan ran up to them. "Uncle J, there's another house out back."

It took a second for Dad to register the words before he dashed outside. Peter chased after him.

Night had descended. Fighting a vampire like Korlemo had immediately become harder.

***

A second home was nestled less than a hundred yards away. Peter sprinted after his dad, who without hesitation ran inside the palatial home.

While Dad rushed past werewolves and servants, Peter and the other mwindaji cleared a path, shooting anyone or thing impeding him.

Peter caught up with Dad at a side door in a long hallway. He grabbed his arm. "Careful."

Dad nodded and opened the door. They checked three different doors before they located the basement. Together, they descended.

Downstairs, the layout resembled the basement in the previous home—absent a wine cellar. Dad scurried around the room, searching the walls and floor for a secret passageway.

"Dammit, I've got nothing. What've you got?" Dad asked.

Standing in the center of the room, Peter scrutinized the area and detected an irregularity between the book shelving. "I have something here." Peter tapped along the side of a bookcase.

They removed books and knickknacks, then the shelves. After several minutes, they uncovered a subterranean passageway behind the wall. Again, Dad took the lead.

The stone steps were slick with dew. How old was this passage?

Less than a half dozen wall sconces lighted the narrow stairway. More than once, Peter slipped on the wet steps. Precipitously, the stone staircase ended in a dank cave-like room. It reminded him of a root cellar.

This subterranean dwelling had more wall sconces and better lighting than the passageway. Along the far wall were four tunnels, similar to Roman catacombs.

Dad rushed to the first sepulcher, which contained a single crypt. The lid lay askew.

Peter peered over his shoulder. The crypt was empty. They checked each tunnel; two contained empty tombs, the others contained nothing.

As Dad leaned against the wall cursing, Peter photographed the lettering on the crypts. *Maybe Daniel could decipher the writing.*

Dad stared at the dirt floor.

Peter called but Dad didn't respond. He walked over and placed a hand on his shoulder. "We need to go,"

"Right." Dad followed him up the staircase, cursing under his breath.

When they exited the basement, Peter heard Dad's phone ping. He glanced at the text message.

MAKEDA HURT

His gaze widened.

CHAPTER 66

THE HOSPITAL DOORS SWISHED open and like a fish swimming against the tide, Zeke entered the lobby wearing black clothing, headphones covered by a hoodie, and a large backpack. He was confident he could disable the hospital video system. *No need to call the family wunderkind.* While staff and visitors alike exited the hospital, he strode over to the help desk.

A teenaged volunteer leaned against the desk, chatting on her cell phone while chewing gum—despite her braces.

"Hello," he said.

The bright-eyed teen grimaced but put away the phone. True to her position, she asked, "May I help you?"

As people streamed by, her gaze flitted toward the sliding doors.

"Security?" he asked.

Her soft eyes didn't question why but pointed him in the direction of the gift shop. "Make a right. Go down the hallway, then left. Continue until you reach a dead end."

"Thanks." He departed.

She returned to her cell phone as soon as he walked away.

Following the directions, Zeke arrived at a nickel-gray door. Large block letters spelled *Security*. He knocked.

A lanky man swung the door open. He glowered into Zeke's face. "What?"

"That's not how you offer assistance," Zeke said, spraying colloidal silver water into the guard's face.

Puffs of smoke evaporated from its skin as the guard morphed into a vampire. Shouting painful expletives, he lunged for Zeke's neck. Without moving, Zeke skewered the vampire in the chest with a retractable lance. The monster squeezed Zeke's throat and bared its teeth.

Straining to breathe, Zeke twisted the lance, inserting it farther into the vampire's chest. Seconds passed as the vampire's hands slumped to its sides. In under a minute, it dissolved into sand.

Zeke stepped over the pile. With his combat boots, he swirled the sand and retrieved a security badge.

He accessed the security room and studied a bank of outdated screens. An intercom and radio system were positioned off to the side. He viewed the video screens before unplugging the equipment. Once he disabled the security and video systems, Zeke called his dad.

"It's a go."

CHAPTER 67

MICHAEL DECIDED TO GO to the hospital to speak with Dr. Bones in person. When he called ahead, the staff assured him the pathologist had come in to work that morning. As he strolled across the lobby, a sea of people flowed around him. *Should've come in the back.* But he knew why he entered the front lobby.

His gaze scanned the exiting hospital staff, secretly hoping to see Makeda. He wanted to update her on the situation with Jackie Baptiste. Let her know he had kept his promise and hoped she would keep hers.

A teen volunteer waved to him. "Hey, Sheriff."

"Hello, Sally. Be safe. No cell phone while driving."

"Yes, sir." She smiled and departed.

While crossing the hospital lobby, Michael noticed a man dressed in black carrying a backpack enter the hallway that led to the morgue. He briefly glimpsed the man's dreadlocks and thought he recognized a gun strapped to the man's hip. He immediately worried about a potential workplace shooting.

The hospital lobby emptied.

Michael reached for his radio to call dispatch; unfortunately, someone else was making a call across the radio. He replaced the mic and jogged after the suspect.

"Sir. I need to speak with you. Sir. Wait. Stop!"

The guy increased his gait and rounded the corner.

For a moment Michael lost sight of the man. Panting, he also rounded the corner, but ... The guy disappeared.

Michael knew this part of the hospital included the pathology department and morgue. A half-dozen doors branched off the cement-walled hallway. He tried the first two doors along the hall, but they were locked. He checked each door until he arrived at pathology.

Located on the right side of the hallway, the pathology office stood yards away from the morgue. Leading with his gun, Michael pried the door back along its rusted hinges.

Lights were on, but no one was present. Michael conducted a cursory survey before heading across the hall to the morgue. Before he entered, he gulped air, trying to shake his apprehension. If he wanted a career in law enforcement, he would have to get over it. Michael raised his gun and opened the door.

The room was pitch-dark. He grazed the cold cement wall, searching for a light switch. Overhead fluorescent lights flickered on. The low light cast a dull yellow glow over the room. A few places remained shadowed. Formaldehyde and decay filled his nostrils. Michael scanned the room.

Fluorescent lights blinked.

He wondered when someone would fix those bulbs. The strobe effect increased his discomfort. He gritted his teeth.

At the far end of the room, Michael detected movement. Someone stood near a gurney. Until the lights came on fully, he could only view the front half of the room. The person was partly in shadow but stood behind a table. No, they were bent over a gurney. Were they examining a corpse?

A tan sheet partially covered the gurney.

Michael approached with his gun raised.

The lights stopped wavering and the room became fully lit. With his view unimpeded, Michael recognized the security uniform. He exhaled and lowered his weapon.

"What're you doing in here?"

A gruff voice matched the thick overhanging brow and goatlike eyes. The guard asked, "Who are you?"

Lowering the gun, Michael pushed his hat back along his forehead. "Sheriff Wilson. Now your turn. Who are you, and what were you doing here in the dark?"

As he spoke, Michael appraised the hulking man's pockmarked face and dirty blond—mostly dirty—hair. The guy barely fit into the uniform and didn't reply to his question.

On the gurney, Michael noticed the guard's hands were covered in blood and held a dull-colored floppy item. Screwing up his eyes, Michael zeroed in on the object. Cogitating the scene before him, he realized the guard held ... *a liver?*

With the organ still in hand, the guard sneered and advanced upon him.

Michael gawked. He raised the gun and retreated. "Stop, or I'll shoot."

Tossing the liver onto the gurney, the guard continued forward.

Not wanting to hurt the man, Michael delivered another warning.

The guard snorted and transformed.

"What the hell?" Michael froze. Before him, the guard morphed into ...

Thick hairs sprouted from the guard's skin. His head elongated, and his nose became a snout. He grew in height and girth. Longer, sharper teeth spilled out of his mouth. With a shake, the guard's hair stood up on end.

A werewolf? Michael backtracked and considered his options, confused by what he beheld.

The guard—monster—continued forward. Its arms grew longer, legs became thicker. Hunched over, it roared.

Michael's fingers tightened around the gun. He didn't understand what was going on, but he knew this thing had to be stopped. "One more step, and I'll shoot."

With a cackle, the werewolf stepped forward and roared. Its teeth glistened in the light.

Michael's first shot struck the creature in the leg. The bullet's small punch merely tossed up hairs, hardly causing any bleeding. Four more shots hit the werewolf's torso. Michael stumbled slightly backwards. Understanding his precarious predicament, he searched the morgue for another weapon.

Large talons extended as the werewolf pounced. Michael braced for a hit.

Pop, pop. Two bullets struck the werewolf, one in the head, the other in the neck—but not before its left claw slashed Michael across the chest.

The beast fell to the ground. A whimper escaped as its body slammed to the floor.

Clutching his wound, Michael stared at the dead werewolf. He bent over, gripping his chest. He flinched when a hand touched his shoulder.

CHAPTER 68

MAKEDA STOOD OVER MICHAEL, who wobbled on unsteady feet. He allowed her to assist him to a stainless-steel stool.

As if mesmerized, Michael stared at the werewolf's metamorphosis, fixated on the scene. The guard transformed from a terrifying beast back to a hulking man. Michael stammered, refusing to sit and unable to speak.

Forcing him down onto the stool, Makeda tended to his wound. She placed her gun on the countertop and searched inside her backpack for something to clean his lacerations.

"What the—"

"Exactly." She removed items from her pack.

"Makeda. What was that?"

"A werewolf. I warned you."

His head shook as she deftly treated his cuts. His voice trembled. "But it's—it's not possible."

"Well, then you have a vivid imagination because you imagined a dead body on the floor and a laceration across your chest."

She sympathized with him. It was a lot to digest at once, but she didn't have time to comfort him.

He cringed as she applied antiseptic.

Her eyes rolled. "Don't be a baby. It's not that bad."

"I—I don't understand."

Packing away the first aid supplies, Makeda retrieved her gun and prepared to leave. "I don't have time to explain right now. I have work to do. Either come with me, or I suggest you go home—or to the sheriff station."

"Wait. What work?" He grabbed her left arm.

"This is what I do. This is my real job. I kill monsters. We need to go."

"Where?"

"There are other monsters in the hospital."

This time, when she tried to leave, he grabbed her gun and blocked her egress.

"You can't go around shooting people. What if you're wrong?"

Her foot stomped on the ground. "We don't go around shooting people. We do our research. That's what I've been doing since I got here."

He gasped. "You knew about this?"

"I tried to tell you. Let's go."

Michael tossed the gun behind him onto the countertop. "No. I'm the sheriff here. No more killing until you explain this to me. *Now.*"

Makeda's fists clenched. Though she cared for him, she had things to do. If she knocked him out and left him here, he could get hurt. She needed to get to the rest of the mwindaji and complete what they had started.

She smiled into his eyes and put her arms around his waist, ostensibly to give him a kiss. He laced his arms around her hips. Holding his gaze, Makeda quickly reached around him to snatch the gun. He proved quicker and slid the gun farther away.

Her fist pounded against her thigh. "Damn it. I need my gun. We don't have time for this."

Michael's angry, furrowed brows glared down at her. "Make time."

Pissed, she tussled with him to reach the gun. While they wrestled, the morgue doors sprang open.

Framed in the doorway, Makeda viewed an abnormally tall man. Her nose crinkled. He smelled different. She was beginning to understand her zauber ability to scent out monsters. Presently, she had more pressing concerns.

The vampire fixed on her.

Makeda backed away from Michael.

Focused on her, the monster lurched forward. Michael jumped between them. With a backhand smack, the vampire slammed him up against the wall.

After smashing into the cement, Michael sank to the ground.

The vampire's eyes narrowed, and its gaze bored into her. Makeda realized it was trying to entrance her. Instead of looking away, she scowled right back. As they glared at each other, she propelled two silver stars at it in quick succession.

Like they were insects, the vampire swatted the implements aside.

Makeda reached in her pack for the machete.

Michael climbed off the floor as the vampire rocketed toward her. Inches before it reached her, a long pole burst forth from its chest.

Still holding the machete, Makeda gawked.

The impaled monster bellowed as it struggled to remove the pole. Blood gushed from its chest as it thrashed about.

Realizing the wound was fatal, Makeda stepped aside.

Simultaneously, she and Michael looked toward the door for who hurled the pole. Dr. Bones stood there a moment before removing a tissue from his pocket and wiping his glasses.

Gradually, the vampire slumped to the ground. The pole kept it from reaching the floor, reclining its body at an awkward angle. After a few seconds, the creature succumbed to its wound. In under a minute, the silver pole clanked onto the floor surrounded by a pile of dust.

Dashing around Michael, Makeda retrieved her gun.

Stepping inside the morgue, Dr. Bones regarded them. "I wanted to help."

"Thank you," she said.

He walked over to the pile of sand, swirling it with his shoe. "Anytime."

"Why did he turn to sand, but not the werewolf?" Michael asked.

The shell-shocked look on his face made her feel bad. She felt she owed him an explanation, but first she checked her gun.

"Vampires become dust because they died before they turned. At their second death, they immediately become dust. Werewolves revert to their human form. Much of the mythology around werewolves and vampires is correct. The lies surround their origin."

She returned the silver stars to her pack. "There's more work to do. I have to go."

This time Michael didn't argue.

At the door, Makeda spun around. "Dr. Bones, can you help us?"

Picking up the pole and cleaning off its surface, the doctor looked over at the dead guard. "Yes. It's about time I did something to fix this mess. What do you need?"

She pointed to the incinerators. "Would you help us destroy the bodies?"

"On it. I also have keys to the funeral crematory up the street. We can use their facility if needed. Before you leave, could you help me with this one? He's a beast."

Together, they lifted the guard onto a gurney. On the way

to the incinerators, the doctor picked up a striker saw. As they pushed the gurney, the morgue doors opened.

Makeda leveled her gun. Michael grasped the doctor's spear. Fortunately, they hesitated long enough for Zeke to raise his hands in surrender.

He removed his earbuds and Makeda heard *Jamming*, by Bob Marley, emanating from his device.

"Friend, not foe," Zeke said.

Makeda walked over and gave him a hug. "Zeke, where have you been?"

"Killing bad guys." He put his headphones back on and sang to the music.

She grinned. "Really?"

"You're lucky I didn't come in singing *I Shot the Sheriff*."

Her cell phone pinged. Glancing at it quickly, she read Uncle John's message.

DEAD BODIES WHERE?

Angry they didn't wait for her instructions to proceed, she called him. "Cover the bodies with sheets and bring them down in the service elevators." She gave directions before he rang off.

Makeda started to leave again when the doctor suggested they check out the refrigerator.

Dr. Bones cleaned his glasses again. "I don't know what's in there, but I've heard rumors."

With Michael and Zeke in tow, Makeda departed for the lobby. She eyed Zeke. "Are the doors from the ER locked?"

He nodded. "We're good."

With his right eyebrow raised, Michael glanced at her. She explained they needed to block access to the hospital while they searched for monsters.

They found the cafeteria empty. Following behind Zeke, Makeda entered the kitchen and studied the refrigerator's locking system.

"Who places a lock on a refrigerator?" Michael asked.

"People with something to hide," Makeda said, studying the locks.

"How do you expect to get in?" he asked.

Before she could answer, Zeke shot off the locks.

Covering his ears, Michael turned his body away from the flying debris.

Makeda picked up the spent rounds before entering the refrigerator. Nothing could have prepared her for what she found.

Displayed on the shelves were various body parts. Arranged like items in a butcher's freezer, they were efficiently prepared and labeled: organ meats, offal, limbs, brain, eyeballs. The labels also identified the remains as human, goat, cat, dog ...

Michael and Zeke circled around the refrigerator. Michael's eyes were as large as saucers. Zeke lowered his weapon and gaped.

In the middle of the refrigerator, Makeda turned in a circle, examining the various shelves. She became nauseated and left. Michael and Zeke exited a minute later.

In the lobby, they met up with Raymond, who said "Dad and Brian took the bodies to the morgue."

They returned to the morgue.

Makeda counted eight bodies stacked on the floor. "I told you not to start until I gave the signal. What if patients—"

"Makeda, I'm sure they'll be fine," her uncle said. "Let's go."

Understanding arguing wasn't prudent, she left it alone.

"This is unbelievable," Michael muttered and collapsed onto a stool.

Her uncle angled his head in Michael's direction.

"Uncle John, this is Sheriff Michael Wilson. Michael, this is Uncle John, Raymond, Brian, and you met Zeke."

Her uncle nodded at him, then addressed Dr. Bones. "You gonna be all right, Doc? Can you get rid of these bodies by tomorrow?"

"It'll probably take until Monday, but no one will be here before then," Dr. Bones said.

Michael removed his hat, wiping his forehead. "Why, Neil? I don't understand."

Dr. Bones frowned. "I'm not going to make excuses. What could I do? Who would've believed me? Those who knew were paid to keep quiet." Looking at Makeda, he said, "I wish you had told me what you planned. It would've helped to know I wasn't alone."

She shrugged. "Like you said, who would believe werewolves and vampires had taken over a hospital? It's hard to know where people's alliances lie." She tapped her uncle on the shoulder. "We need to head up to psych."

"What about the fridge?" Zeke asked.

They decided to move the refrigerator contents to the morgue after they investigated the psychiatric floor.

Dr. Bones shook his head, his expression forlorn. "This community needs Lebanon Memorial. Things will be bad enough when the authorities prosecute Jackie for that boy's murder."

"Jackie! I forgot." Michael jumped up and ran out of the morgue.

Makeda followed, stopping him with a touch of his arm.

A tiny grin teased at the corners of his mouth. "Come with me."

"I can't. We're not done here." Removing a gun from her waistband, Makeda handed it to him. "Take this. Guns with silver bullets work better against werewolves."

"And the vampires?"

"Not as well, but it'll slow them down."

"I'll remember that." He smiled.

As he moved closer, her body tensed. She worried he would kiss her in front of her cousins—she wouldn't hear the end of that.

Instead, Michael accepted the gun. He stepped aside, saluted the Hills, and sprinted out of the hospital without looking back.

Makeda watched him drive away before she swung around. "Let's go."

While they climbed the stairs up to the fourth floor, no one spoke.

She heard Zeke's music, *Chase the Devil*, by Max Romeo. *How appropriate.* Now, if only they could catch him.

CHAPTER 69

IN THE HOSPITAL STAIRCASE, Makeda grasped the door handle leading onto the fourth floor. Suddenly, a heavy presence enveloped her. Like slogging in the humid summer heat, her movements slowed. The air was thick, her limbs leaden. A presence settled in her mind. She glanced around, searching for a vision or apparition.

'Prekosyon.'

The word flashed in her mind. Makeda held on to the knob, trying to retain her balance.

Zeke touched her shoulder. "Makeda?"

Like a Florida rain shower, the presence evaporated. Cracking open the door, Makeda glanced at him.

He nodded.

Confident the cameras had been disabled, they ran to the secured doors leading into the psychiatric unit.

"Ready?" she asked.

Uncle John cocked his gun. "Go."

Makeda swiped the access card across the entry pad—she'd lifted it from Carson earlier that day—and watched the beige doors swing aside. An odor assailed her nostrils before the doors completely opened. Her zauber skills were manifesting after years of inactivity. Did zaubers have a scent? She would have to ponder that later.

Together with Brian, she approached the nursing station. Zeke steered around them and proceeded farther down the unit with his dad and Raymond.

A nurse exited the station wearing scrubs. She approached Zeke. "Excuse me, but this is a secured unit. Where are you going?"

With his headphones blasting reggae music, Zeke ignored her and marched forward.

Brian tapped the nurse on the shoulder. As she swung around, he sprayed silver solution in her face.

The nurse screamed as her skin bubbled. Elongated fingers preceded the eruption of canines protruding from her snarling mouth. Skin sloughed from her forehead to her chin, exposing moist pink tissue.

As he strode around Brian, Raymond thrust a spear into her chest and held tight until she decomposed.

At the same time, Makeda entered the nursing station and was immediately thrown out of the room, crashing into the opposing wall. She scrambled to her feet, grasping her machete with both hands.

A vampire charged out of the nursing station. With supernatural speed, it avoided Makeda's slashing machete. It hissed at her and ran toward the exit doors. The vampire flashed a badge across the door security reader. Before the doors swung open, Uncle John propelled a lance into its back. The vampire disintegrated.

Her uncle retrieved the spear. "One less suck head."

Using her feet, Makeda toed the vampire's badge but didn't pick it up.

After Raymond retrieved a key ring from inside the nursing station, he and Zeke unlocked the first patient room.

Like a bat out of hell, a man burst from the room and charged down the hall.

Zeke managed to spray the right side of the guy's neck as he ran past. The liquid created no reaction. Raymond grabbed the man by the shoulders and restrained him against the wall.

In a tattered hospital gown, the man's gaunt, disheveled body was tattooed with scratches and sores.

"Get off me. I've got to get out of here. Let me go," the man said, struggling.

"Wait up, guy. We got you," Zeke said.

The man gaped at Zeke. "You're crazy." Despite his diminutive appearance, the man managed to push Raymond aside and scramble toward the exit.

Makeda raised her hands and stepped in front of him. "Wait, let me look at you. Make sure you're okay."

"No way." He shoved her out of the way and darted for the door. "I have to get out of here."

"Wait. We can help you," she called after him.

"I'm not staying here." He mumbled, "I'm leaving before they drain me again."

Straining to understand what he said, Makeda's left eyebrow arched. "Before they what?"

At the secured doors, the man scooped the badge up off the floor, wiped sand off with his gown, and flashed it at the screen. Before Makeda could question him further, he fled.

Brian shrugged his shoulders and tilted his head toward the opposite side of the hallway. Makeda followed him. She unlocked the patient room closest to the exit.

Glancing inside the room, she gasped at the macabre scene. Despite the limited lighting, she viewed a woman strapped to the corners of a bed by her arms and legs, lying supine with three vampires on top of her.

As Makeda entered, the door squeaked. The vampires stopped feeding and glared at her and Brian.

The vampire at the woman's feet soared off the bed and charged them. Moving swiftly, it caught Brian off guard and flung him into the wall. Before Makeda could react, the vampire escaped.

With her attention on the fleeing vampire, she turned around to find another monster lunging at her. This female vampire wore scrubs with its hair pulled back into a ponytail.

Makeda thought the vampire resembled one of the nurses assigned to the medicine floor. *For the past month, I've been working among werewolves and vampires.*

When the vampire-nurse stood a foot away, Makeda thrust a silver lance into its upper chest. The wound unfortunately wasn't fatal.

The vampire hissed, pulled the lance out of its chest, and retreated. As Makeda prepared for another attack, the creature ogled her. With crooked jagged teeth only a shark could admire, the vampire grinned. Blood dripped from its mouth.

Repeatedly, she jabbed at the vampire, but its movements were swift and elusive. Makeda failed to land one successful blow. Each attempt she made, the vampire-nurse negated.

In her periphery, Makeda spied Brian wrestling with the third vampire. That breach in attention left her vulnerable—enough time for the vampire-nurse to slash her left arm.

Blood sloshed down her side, and she dropped the lance. Cradling her shoulder, Makeda viewed ripped muscles and a hint of bone. Her jaw clenched. The pain was intense, but she wasn't done yet.

Neither was the vampire. With a wide, toothy grin, the monster licked its lips with an elongated, red, snakelike tongue.

Makeda grimaced and realized she needed a different tactic.

With a deep breath, she released her shoulder and brought her arms down along her sides—ignoring the burning pain. Wriggling her fingers, she made a fist and uttered an incantation in Bauomali.

Rapidly, the vampire slid toward her. The monster's grin enlarged as it advanced.

Damn. Understanding her mistake, Makeda splayed her fingers wide, repeated the incantation and pushed. This hurled the vampire back against the distant wall. In seconds, Makeda surged forward and sank her machete into the vampire's throat. Blood splattered the walls. The metallic stench from its putrid breath washed over her.

Partially decapitated, the vampire's frowning head lolled to the side. Its flailing arms tried to grasp Makeda but connected instead with the wall. In half a minute, the monster slumped to the ground.

After watching it disintegrate, Makeda pivoted around to discover Brian gaping at her. Her stomach sank. He had observed her using sorcery.

"Um, I can explain."

Before she could, however, her uncle and Raymond entered the room.

Then she remembered the woman on the bed. Makeda rushed to her side, lightly tapping the woman's face. Puncture wounds covered her body. While Makeda checked vital signs, she asked, "Can you hear me?"

Tachycardic and dyspneic, the woman moaned.

"She's in shock," Makeda said, looking at her cousins. "Help me lift her up."

"What about you?" Brian pointed toward her arm.

"Don't worry about me; get her." Clenching her teeth, Makeda evaluated the woman's wounds with her uninjured right arm.

Brian zipped open her backpack and found material to dress her wound. "Take off your jacket."

He and Uncle John attended to her shoulder while Raymond lifted the injured woman from the blood-soaked mattress.

Once they bandaged Makeda's shoulder, she assessed the woman again.

Makeda said, "I don't have anything at the house to help her."

"She needs a hospital—a *monster-free* hospital," Brian quipped.

"We'll have to go to Bowling Green," Makeda said, eyeing the injured woman.

"We'll get you both help," her uncle said.

In the hallway, they found Zeke talking to a man.

"Did you check the entire floor?" she asked.

"All clear. Those who could walk—left. I got your vampire before it escaped. There's only this guy and your lady."

Appraising the man, Makeda evaluated his hospital gown. Unruly, shaggy brown hair partially hid his cornflower-blue eyes. He appeared in moderate health, though, with no visible wounds.

She asked, "Who are you?"

"Robert Beaufort. Bobby to my friends."

His calm manner and lack of emotion disturbed her— considering what she'd witnessed in the patient room with the three vampires. "How did you get here?"

"The psychiatric unit served as a food source," Robert said.

"You don't look like you've been eaten on," Zeke said.

He didn't appear to be sucked dry like the woman Raymond carried, Makeda noticed.

Robert ran his hands through his hair, making it more untidy. "They couldn't hurt me. My family wouldn't allow it."

Zeke frowned. "Who's your family?"

"The Beauforts control Ramsey. My brother is the district attorney."

On their way out of the hospital, Robert explained how he left Ramsey after high school, traveled the world, and only returned two years ago. Once back home, he became privy to Lebanon Memorial's secret.

"I told my brother I would go to the police if the program wasn't discontinued. Before I could contact the authorities, his thugs locked me on this floor." Robert stared vacantly in the distance. "That was eighteen months ago tomorrow."

Settling the woman into the RV, Raymond said, "And I thought our family was mean."

"Keep her warm," Makeda said. She heard the weakness in her voice.

"Don't worry about her," Uncle John said. "We're taking you both to Bowling Green. Bobby, why don't you help us come up an excuse to explain this lady's condition to the doctors."

While Raymond drove, her uncle reclined in the passenger seat talking to Bobby, who sat in the chair behind him. Brian sat in a swivel chair opposite Bobby.

Makeda lay on a bench across from the injured woman. She watched Brian's profile as he faced Bobby.

'Are you okay?'

Scanning the RV, Makeda searched for an apparition. She honed in on the voice. 'Who is this?'

'Brian.'

Even as her uncle and Bobby talked in the background, Makeda focused on Brian's voice. 'You're a zauber?'

'Yeah. Not like you, but I know kasi kasi.'

'Why didn't you say anything?'

'The same reason you haven't.'

'Does anyone know?'

'My dad.'

'He's all right with you being a zauber?'

'I'm not much of a zauber. I guess he figured speaking in my head wasn't a threat.'

'Who taught you?'

'No one. One day, I discovered I could speak to people telepathically. Later, I read some stuff about it on the internet. I've never had a real conversation with anyone. Occasionally, someone would say hi to me. That's all.'

'It's nice not to be the only one.'

'Where did you learn that stuff you did in the hospital?'

'I ... figured it out.'

She viewed the doubtful look on his face.

'My great-grandmother died before she could teach me much of anything.'

'Your great-grandmother was a zauber?'

She nodded. He must have seen the weariness in her eyes.

'Get some rest. We can talk later.'

Her eyes shut.

CHAPTER 70

WIND TOSSED LEAVES ACROSS the hospital parking lot. As he buckled into the cruiser, Michael checked in with dispatch.

"That you, Sheriff?"

"Yes, Carlotta. I've been at the hospital. Did I miss anything?"

She informed him about a message from Bowling Green homicide.

"Put 'em through." Michael drove toward the station.

The homicide detective explained they had obtained a warrant to apprehend Jackie Baptiste but couldn't get the district attorney in Cavendish County to cooperate.

In the middle of an intersection, Michael executed a U-turn and sped toward the district attorney's house.

"Don't worry. I got this."

***

Michael found the district attorney's house lit up like a Christmas tree. Apparently, there was a party going on. Sounds emerged from what he perceived was an orchestra. Parked cars lined the driveway and continued down onto a side street. Music and laughter drifted out the windows.

Zipping up his sheriff's jacket, Michael draped the badge around his neck, plopped on his hat, and marched up to the front door.

When the housekeeper greeted him, Michael strode around

her without preamble. Inside, he found the district attorney seated at a large table with his wife and guests.

Walter Beaufort hailed from one of the oldest and most established families in Cavendish County. He stood awkwardly as Michael entered the dining room. His artificial tan did little to hide the red fury blooming across his face. Beaufort glared at him under frowning brows. It would've looked more menacing if the eyebrows hadn't been manicured.

Placing his napkin down on the table, Beaufort asked, "Sheriff, what's the meaning of this?"

Michael held up his hand and gave Beaufort his best "don't mess with me" face. "I suggest we have this conversation in private." He gave Mrs. Beaufort and their guests his apologies.

The district attorney led him into a study. Beaufort stomped inside and placed his palms flat on the enameled surface of an enormous desk.

Michael shut the double doors behind them.

As soon as the doors closed, Beaufort raised his voice. "How dare you interrupt—"

"Shut up," Michael said. He removed the subpoena from his jacket pocket and tossed it on the desk. "Sign that."

Beaufort lifted the document as if it was contaminated, then skimmed it.

With a crooked grin, he said, "I'm not signing this tonight. We'll discuss it on Monday."

"I've seen the refrigerator." Michael's expression remained flat.

His words hung in the air. The implied threat was evident in Beaufort's gaping mouth. Neither spoke as they sized each other up.

Sitting down heavily on a chair, Beaufort gazed up at him. "I'm not sure what you mean by that comment, Mike, but I suggest you think before you—"

"Before I what?" Michael hovered over the desk and slid the document closer to Beaufort. He removed a pen from its stand and handed it over. "Sign it or I'll make sure every one of your very important guests learns about the contents of those hospital refrigerators."

He displayed his cell phone for Beaufort to view. Although he'd snapped pictures of the refrigerator contents, Michael secretly hoped he didn't have to show them to anyone—ever.

The machinery was working behind those cornflower-blue eyes. Michael had called the district attorney's bluff. Beaufort had no idea what he knew—or more importantly—what he could prove.

In a snit, Beaufort snatched the pen from his hand, signed the document, and shoved it toward Michael. He dropped the pen on the desk and stomped away.

Michael reviewed the document—a warrant for Jackie Baptiste to be detained and questioned. He validated the signature was in the proper location and placed it in his jacket pocket. Then did he headed for the door.

Beaufort spoke to his back. "Your career is over, Mike."

He spun around. "I don't give a rat's ass what you do to me tomorrow, but tonight, I'm going to pick up Jackie Baptiste for questioning."

After what he experienced in the hospital, Michael wasn't intimidated by Beaufort's threats. He would deal with any reprimands from the department later.

Inside the cruiser, Michael called the homicide department in Bowling Green. He'd wait for them at the station—not simply because of his promise to Makeda, but also because he wasn't eager to experience anything like what occurred in the morgue again, especially not alone.

CHAPTER 71

SYLVIA'S PLANE LANDED ON time at JFK Airport. The flight from Cincinnati International Airport took about three hours. She deplaned and headed for the taxicab queue.

While waiting in Cincinnati, she had called Jules. He had reviewed copies of the financial records she obtained from Baptiste's ledger. She knew he would believe her. In addition to being a certified accountant, he was already suspicious of Korlemo. It was the main reason he relocated to New York.

Years prior, her brother had quarreled with their father about Baptiste's fidelity to Korlemo. Papa refused to hear any slander against his friend. Their disagreement became heated.

Refusing to yield, Jules moved to New York. He never returned to Ramsey, or Kentucky for that matter. Papa had to travel to New York if he wanted to see his oldest son. Jules predicted Korlemo would be the death of them. Sylvia hadn't dreamed his forecast would come true.

When shooting started at Papa's home, Sylvia vaulted out of her bedroom window and sprinted for the car. In under four hours, she arrived at the Cincinnati airport and caught a flight to New York.

Standing on the doorstep of her brother's Manhattan condo, Sylvia trembled. When the door creaked open, she threw her arms around Jules and cried.

He brought her inside. "It's okay, Svie."

She lugged her suitcase over to the sofa and caught a view of herself in the foyer mirror. Sylvia looked a fright; swollen red-rimmed eyes, frizzed hair, wrinkled clothes. She collapsed onto the couch and cried more.

Her brother gave her space. After a half hour, Jules placed a glass of brandy in her hand. Sylvia's fingers shook as she brought the amber fluid to her quivering lips. Once she emptied the glass, she felt calm enough to speak.

With his arm around her shoulders, Jules sat beside her. "I can't believe this. When you told me about Baptiste's betrayal—I wasn't surprised, but I still couldn't believe it. How could he leave the families destitute?"

"You read the documents I sent?"

He nodded. "Why would he do it?"

"Korlemo. If he had a choice, Baptiste wouldn't have betrayed Papa and abandoned the ajabu."

"Had?" Jules frowned.

Sylvia had neglected to inform her brother about what occurred at the house—afraid to acknowledge what she knew to be true.

"Baptiste is dead." She hesitated a moment. "So is Papa."

Jules's jaw tightened and eyes misted.

Dissolving into another fit of tears, Sylvia explained what happened to their brothers and Baptiste's two sons.

"The mwindaji?"

"I don't know." She blew her nose. "Baptiste kept a lot from us."

Jules hugged her tighter.

Reluctantly, Sylvia unwound herself from his embrace. "I have to go."

"Why?"

Scared sober, she wiped her face. "When the authorities

discover my embezzlement—and Baptiste's death—they'll come after me. I'll be arrested."

Immediately, Jules perceived the gravity of her predicament. He contacted an associate. A few calls later, he had obtained a new passport and persona for Sylvia. He handed her a piece of paper where he had scribbled information.

"This is a friend. If you can't reach me, he'll help you."

"Is this a burner phone?" she asked, glancing at the paper before slipping it into her purse.

"Yes. Contact me as soon as …"

Time passed as they discussed the arrangements. Before Sylvia could rest, a non-descript car arrived and drove her back to JFK.

Not until she boarded the plane could she rest. Had Korlemo escaped the melee? If he did, she had better not get too comfortable. He would be coming for her.

CHAPTER 72

SUNDAY MORNING MICHAEL DECIDED to visit Makeda. Incidents over the past two days had kept him busy. When he spoke with her over the phone last night, she was in pain and partly sedated. Their conversation was brief.

When he reached the rental property, two trucks were in front of the house in addition to Makeda's Honda. Michael parked on the street, slapped on his ball cap, and trudged up the graveled driveway.

Zeke and Raymond loitered outside. Leaned up against the vinyl siding, Raymond smoked a joint. Michael acknowledged Zeke with a nod and glanced toward Raymond. A surprised Raymond dropped the blunt on the ground and stomped it into the gravel.

Laughing, Zeke said, "Smooth, bro." With *Positive Vibration* by Bob Marley blaring from his headphones, Zeke sauntered away.

From inside a pickup truck in the driveway, Brian waved.

"Don't worry about it, man," Michael said to Raymond, before striding over to the truck and shaking Brian's hand.

From the house's front door, Michael saw John Hill exit, walking next to another man, whom he presumed was Makeda's father.

Mr. Hill patted the other man on the back. "Don't take it hard, J. We'll get him next time."

When the two men noticed him, Michael exchanged greetings. "Good morning."

"Sheriff," Mr. Hill said before turning to the other man. "J, this is Sheriff Michael Wilson. Sheriff, this is James Crawford, Makeda's dad."

Michael removed his cap. "Nice to meet you, sir."

"Morning." Mr. Crawford shook his hand, then continued conversing with Mr. Hill.

From tidbits of their conversation, Michael learned that the Hills were leaving. He stood aside as the men exchanged goodbyes.

Mr. Hill addressed his sons. "Time to go."

Zeke trotted to the RV parked at the corner across the street.

Raymond attempted to climb into the truck with Brian, but Mr. Hill locked the doors, talking to Raymond through an open window.

"Oh, hell no," Mr. Hill said. "You ride with Zeke. I'm not smelling skunk shit all the way back to Charleston."

Watching Raymond and Mr. Hill argue, Michael tried not to laugh.

As the argument continued, Peter came outside, laughing out loud as Raymond pleaded his case—to no avail.

John Hill scrolled up the window as Brian reversed down the driveway.

Running over to join Zeke, Raymond jumped inside the RV as UB40's *Red Red Wine* wafted from the stereo. The camper pulled away from the curb and onto the main street. Brian fell in behind the RV, beeped the horn once, and waved.

Off to the side, Michael waited for the vehicles to fade away. He then walked over to Peter and shook his hand.

"Good morning."

"Morning," Peter said. His lack of enthusiasm matched his father's.

Michael faced Mr. Crawford. "I came by to check on Makeda. How's she doing?"

"She's fine." Peter folded his arms over his chest.

"I talked to Neil," Michael said, ignoring Peter. "He wanted to thank you guys for cleaning out the refrigerators."

"No problem, son. We always clean up our messes."

Unfolding his arms, Peter asked, "What do the state authorities think?"

Michael decided to divulge a little information, maybe gain some trust—or at least decrease the hostility. "Bowling Green homicide detectives are still at both residences."

Scratching his scalp, Mr. Crawford asked, "Are they bothering you about what happened?"

"No, sir. When the police arrived at the Baptiste home Friday night, they located Jackie Baptiste in the upstairs hallway outside her bedroom. Right now, the assumption is bikers were involved. She was known to associate with a gang in the area. They're working off the theory she got mixed up in something, and it spilled over into their home."

With a quick glance down the street, Peter asked, "Umm. What's their explanation for the Senegal place?"

Concisely, Michael explained that after the authorities failed to locate Herman Baptiste's body at his residence, they tried to contact Mr. Senegal—knowing the two families were close. When calls to the Senegal home went unanswered, they dispatched a deputy to their residence. They located Herman Baptiste's body among the carnage. Along with the bodies of Gerard Senegal and both of their sons.

"So far, the detectives are working on the theory that a family dispute led to the homicides," he said. "Financial papers were scattered around the room and guns near their hands."

"Anything on the whereabouts of that physician lady?" Peter asked.

"Dr. Senegal? They tracked her to New York City. Nothing yet, but we alerted NYPD."

"Sounds like you've got your hands full," Peter said.

He shrugged. "What's next for you guys?"

Peter glanced at his father before letting his gaze wander over the neighborhood.

Clearing his throat, Mr. Crawford said, "We don't know yet."

"I see." Michael didn't believe them, but he understood. They weren't going to tell a stranger about their plans to go around the country killing monsters. His cell phone buzzed, but he ignored it. Again, he asked about Makeda.

Mr. Crawford ambled toward the front door. "She got hurt real bad the other night. She needs her rest."

Michael decided not to push his luck. Right now, his presence was not appreciated. Giving his best to Makeda, he left. He'd call her later.

CHAPTER 73

'TAMARA, HOW IS NADEGE doing?' Makeda asked, rolling over in bed, careful not to bump her left arm.

'She's fine,' Tamara said. 'I'm in Miami now, but my family speaks with her often.'

'Did she teach you sorcery, or did you figure it out on your own?'

'Let's get something straight. I'm a zauber—I know kasi kasi—but I'm not interested in the other stuff. I don't want to know what Nadege was warning you about, and I definitely don't want to be involved with the mwindaji. I did a simple favor for a family friend. Understand?'

Taking a deep breath, Makeda tried to sit up. Her arm ached. She moved slowly, not wanting to rip open her stitches.

'I understand. Thank you.'

No response. Tamara had shut her out.

Understandable. Being associated with the mwindaji came with risks, grave risks.

Glancing toward the window, Makeda heard murmurings outside. She thought her uncle and cousins left last night. By the time she managed to look out the window, the only people outside were Dad and Peter.

A bird flew by, and a squirrel scampered outside her window. The furry critter turned and glanced up at her. It froze.

Makeda smiled, until ... *Did that squirrel wink?*

A second later it scurried away into the foliage.

With her shoulder aching, Makeda collapsed back into bed. She needed to work things out, like how to contact Yewande, and how to control her new zauber skills. Who could teach her sorcery? Maybe Nadege, if she learned Creole.

Gazing through the window, she thought about Michael and her feelings for him. He was the last thing on her mind as she drifted off to sleep.

CHAPTER 74

THE STUDY'S WOODEN FLOORS creaked. This room was structured like the one in Kentucky, but less than half the size, nowhere near as opulent, and without a fireplace. Korlemo stormed around the room.

"I am not staying here. You need to make other arrangements for us. *Now.*"

Seated on the couch, Enu watched him pace back and forth. "What do you expect me to do, brother? You heard what happened in Ramsey. Herman and his family are dead."

Korlemo paused beside a small table in front of a window. Long, heavy drapes blocked sunlight that crept around its edges. He swung around. "Sylvia survived. Find her."

From her seat on the couch, Zainabu observed the brothers. If she didn't have her own priorities, she would watch them all night. However, Zorulo sent her to Korlemo with a purpose.

The demon wanted Korlemo by his side. It was time the ancient vampire paid his dues, and Zorulo was impatient. What she needed was a way to eliminate Korlemo at the same time she rid herself of Zorulo. It would be difficult. Reflecting on her own problems, she lost track of the conversation.

Slamming his hand down on a small table, Korlemo smashed it to bits. "Do it. I will not argue with you anymore."

"I must access the financial accounts."

Korlemo waved his hands dismissively and wandered into a chair. "Get them. I want to leave here immediately. Why would

Herman bring us to Michigan? He could have at least found a place in Grosse Pointe. We could have driven into Detroit for entertainment."

"He could not obtain a place in Grosse Pointe."

"Why not? I have enough money."

Enu sauntered toward the door. He glanced back as his hand cradled the knob. "But not the proper pedigree. You still act like the young man who dreamed of emulating King Kankan Musa. You possess neither the wealth nor importance, brother. Your own impatience brought us here."

A lamp struck the wall beside the opened door, where Korlemo hurled it.

Gazing first at the debris, then Korlemo, Enu said, "I will find someone to clean that up." He departed.

To Zainabu's amazement, Enu hadn't flinched. Though he catered to his older brother, she realized Enu didn't fear Korlemo. Perhaps she had underestimated him. Would she be able to bend him to her machinations?

Probably not. Enu already realized she had ulterior motives. He might be the more intelligent brother, though. Too bad he hadn't the strength or wealth of Korlemo.

Zainabu waited until her host was seated at the large desk in front of a bookshelf. She joined him, sitting in a chair before the desk. "This coincides with your dream."

Korlemo's pupils reddened. "What do you mean?"

She swallowed her anxiety. A vampire could smell fear. *You must control him.*

"The woman in your dream represents the mwindaji, and they are coming for you."

For a full minute, he glowered at her. She didn't move but allowed his gaze to search her.

"I thought you said Zorulo was the woman."

"No, I said Zorulo was *behind* the woman coming to get you. The woman is his tool, the mwindaji. He feeds them information to find you—to kill you. How else could they have located your whereabouts?"

Again, Korlemo stared.

Zainabu understood he was searching for some weakness. Zorulo had taught her a good interpretation was vague, because then the analysis could evolve as needed. *Good advice.*

He broke eye contact and looked over her shoulder toward the door. "What would you suggest?"

She leaned across the desk, lowering her voice. "You have spent your life running from the mwindaji. You need to take the offensive."

The look he gave her was one of pity. "There is not one mwindaji. There are splinter groups everywhere."

She settled back into the chair and grinned. "Yes, but only one group has unearthed your location. There is one group Zorulo uses. If you strike them first—eliminate them—Zorulo loses, you win. The other mwindaji will understand your power, and no one will dare challenge you again."

It took a moment for him to digest what she said. The color of his pupils turned black. He stood, came around the desk, and held out his hand for her. Accepting it, she rose.

Korlemo cupped her hand delicately as they ambled out of the study. He bent his head toward hers. Grinning, he asked in a false whisper, "And how do you propose we do this?"

She preened and allowed him to guide her from the room, glancing briefly at the dazzling, three-jeweled ring on his finger. If she maneuvered carefully, she could eliminate Korlemo, Zorulo, and that stupid zauber.

For some reason, that woman irritated her. *How could a demon like Zorulo have no knowledge of a zauber?* Maybe he wasn't as powerful as she thought. The idea thrilled her. Zainabu smiled up at the vampire, stepping over the broken lamp.

"I'll explain, but it will cost you—a lot."

CHAPTER 75

MICHAEL PICKED UP A newspaper from the diner countertop and left two quarters. He read while eating his breakfast. The story in the *Ramsey Gazette* suggested the medical staff at Lebanon Memorial sold illicit drugs. Authorities had discovered discrepancies in the hospital's finances. Law enforcement viewed Dr. Senegal as a perpetrator of a major financial fraud instead of a victim.

With a mouth full of potato hash and eggs, he reflected on the events of the past week. Folding the paper under his arm, he paid the bill and returned to his cruiser. He wanted nothing more to do with this whole sordid ordeal, but he still had to complete his reports. He checked in with dispatch.

"I'll be away from the radio. Call me on my cell if it's important."

Carlotta, the day shift dispatcher, said, "Let me know when you're done visiting your girlfriend."

Listening to laugher in the background, Michael signed off and drove to Lebanon Memorial hospital. He parked in the employee lot, entered the hospital, and proceeded to the morgue.

Friday flashbacks exploded in his mind as he approached the doors. Although the odors no longer bothered him, he still inspected the shadowed corners. He scrutinized the room, checking behind the door. On reflex, he touched his gun holster.

Now, he carried two guns—his service revolver and the gun Makeda had given him with the silver bullets. As usual, he found the doctor beside the stainless-steel sink cleaning equipment.

"Relax, Mike, and come on over."

"Hello, Neil."

Michael gave a furtive glance at the incinerators. Satisfied no more bodies were stacked over there like firewood, he brought his attention back to the doctor. "What are your plans?"

Drying his hands, Neil frowned. "What do you mean?"

"You serious? What do you mean, what do I mean?"

Neil removed his glasses and rubbed his eyes. "I'm going to keep doing what I've been doing: serving Ramsey as the medical examiner and staff pathologist—and now, interim medical director."

Michael's right eyebrow arched. "After everything that's happened?"

Neil flushed. "The people of Ramsey were not complicit in this."

Fearing he'd offended his friend, Michael didn't speak.

"We still need a hospital." Finished rubbing his eyes, the doctor reattached his glasses. "I was born here. My father was born here, and his father before that. I'm not abandoning Ramsey."

Michael watched the doctor return to the partially dissected corpse on the steel table, placed the hat on his head, and prepared to leave.

"Mike, why don't you stay? Be part of the solution."

Without answering, Michael departed. In the lobby he considered going upstairs to find Makeda but knew that would be unprofessional. Instead, he decided to stake out her car.

CHAPTER 76

AT THE CONCLUSION OF a difficult twelve-hour shift, Makeda joined the meager crowd of medical staff leaving the hospital. She couldn't wait to get home and rest.

A yellow-orange sun hovered above the treetops. Shielding her eyes from the glare with her left hand, she grimaced from the pain in her shoulder. Somehow, she had forgotten a vampire slashed open her arm. Cradling her wounded shoulder, she headed for her car.

The horizon lit up with a parade of dancing red-and-blue lights.

She smiled, deviated from her path, and headed for the police cruiser.

Leaning against the vehicle, Michael waited. His exhausted face mirrored her own—a testament to the recent catastrophes.

"What, no sirens?" she asked, grinning into his eyes.

His gaze met hers, then traveled down her arm.

Over the phone, she had explained what happened on the psychiatric floor. His handsome smile reached out to her now, and she welcomed it.

His muscular arms opened and pulled her in. "You look beautiful."

"Liar, but thank you."

Some strands of hair escaped from her ponytail. He reached up to tuck them behind her ear, tracing the outline of her face with his fingers.

Her skin burned with desire for him, but the hospital parking lot was the wrong place and wrong time.

"I forgot to thank you for saving my life," he said.

A frown crinkled her forehead as he moved closer. Placing her hand on his chest, she stopped him. "Michael, I'm leaving at the end of the month."

"Where will you go?"

"I don't know yet. We haven't decided."

A storm brewed behind his eyes. "We?"

Understanding his question, she allayed his fear. "My family. This is what we do, kill monsters. We did what we could in Ramsey. Now it's time to move on."

He threw back his shoulders and he retreated a step, still peering into her eyes.

She allowed him time to absorb the information. They remained silent, holding each other without touching.

He moved closer into her personal space. Again, he placed his arms around her waist. Inhaling deeply, she let her senses delight in him. She examined the firm line of his mouth, while he stroked her face.

He grinned. "What about your promise?"

Tender lips caressed her cheek before making their way to her lips. After the soft peck, he started to back away. She brought her hands up to his face and pulled him toward her, ignoring the pain in her shoulder. Their kiss became a passionate embrace. She allowed her hands to caress his body, unashamed of being observed.

After a few minutes, her lips broke away. "I didn't forget."

He escorted her to her car. Along the way, they discussed places where they could be alone.

"I don't believe I could ever relax in Ramsey," she said.

He paused, seeming to consider her statement. "How about we escape to the mountains?"

Gazing into his eyes, she explained if he booked two separate rooms, it was a deal.

He agreed.

After assisting her into the Honda, Michael followed behind in his police cruiser up to the rental home.

***

That night, Makeda lay in bed, staring up at the popcorn ceiling. From the living room, she heard Peter and Dad plotting an attack on the residence in New Jersey. Thomas's video games beeped in the background.

Makeda's thoughts flowed to Michael. She envisioned a romantic evening in a cabin with a fireplace surrounded by snowcapped mountains. Yawning, she drifted off to sleep. Faint sounds from her family filtered through her mind, then faded away. Her muscles slackened. She heard herself snoring.

'Makeda, can you hear me?'

She ignored the voice. Her brothers probably wanted her to cook dinner.

'Makeda!'

She sprang upright in the bed. Darkness had engulfed the room. Makeda strained to see. Her pupils dilated.

Video game noise oozed from under the closed door. If her brothers hadn't called her, then who did?

'Tamara?'

'It's me, baby girl.'

Makeda's body trembled. She tossed aside the blanket. '*Bajinu*?'

'Yes, it's me.'

She smiled, tasting tears as she bit her lip. 'Big Mama, I have so many questions.'

'I know, and I'll answer them all, but we must hurry. There's a lot to learn, and I'm not sure how much time we have.'

A slit of light leaked around the window shades. Makeda scanned the room.

'Why? What's wrong?'

'He's coming for you.'

At the edge of the bed, Makeda wiped away her tears. 'Korlemo?'

'Worse, a demon.'

Makeda frowned. Her fingers crawled along the bed, and she gripped the machete.

I hope you enjoyed *Dark Blood Awakens*, the first in
my mwindajis paranormal urban fantasy series.
Please leave a book review and share your experience
with other readers.